Jill Mansell worked for many years at the Burden Neurological Hospital, Bristol, and now writes full time. Her novels PERFECT TIMING, MIXED DOUBLES, HEAD OVER HEELS, MIRANDA'S BIG MISTAKE, KISS, GOOD AT GAMES, SHEER MISCHIEF and MILLIE'S FLING are also available from Headline.

Fast Friends

Jill Mansell

headline

First published in 1991
by Bantam Books, a division of Transworld Publishers Ltd

This edition published in 2002
by HEADLINE BOOK PUBLISHING

20 19 18 17 16 15 14

ISBN 0 7472 6742 1

Typeset by Avon Dataset Ltd, Bidford-on-Avon, Warks

Printed and bound in Great Britain by
Mackays of Chatham plc, Chatham, Kent

HEADLINE BOOK PUBLISHING
A division of Hodder Headline
338 Euston Road
London NW1 3BH

www.headline.co.uk
www.hodderheadline.com

For my mum,
who typed my manuscript and
correctid my speling

Prologue

Camilla stared at the girl sitting cross-legged on the bed opposite her. 'But what is subversive behaviour?' she asked, curiosity mingling with excitement. With those dark eyes, heavy, slanting eyebrows and incredible cheekbones, Roz Vallender exuded an aura of exotic mystery which transcended her sixteen years. Camilla's mother, no doubt, would have taken one look and pronounced her 'dangerous to know'. Camilla, however, was instantly enthralled. 'And why did they expel you?' she continued breathlessly. 'What exactly did you *do*?'

Roz, having in turn studied the plump, eager blonde with whom she would be sharing this large but slightly shabby room, decided that Camilla Avery-Jones would be a push-over. All she had to do in order to maintain the position of superiority she had held at her last school was to start as she meant to go on.

'Gambling, smoking, drinking,' she began, ticking them off on her fingers with studied casualness. 'Organizing a sit-down protest, seducing the history teacher, class non-attendance – that was because I was seducing the history teacher of course . . .'

The other girl gasped, audibly impressed. 'What was he like?'

Roz smiled. 'He was a she, actually. No, I'm joking. Strictly men only. But it all added up to subversive behaviour so my mother sent me here instead. Cigarette?' She tossed the packet of Sobranies towards her new room-mate, who first shook her head then cautiously removed one.

1

'So who else shares this room?' she said, proffering a cigarette lighter and watching the girl's inexpert attempt at inhalation. She had achieved the upper hand already, she realized with some pride. Easy. So easy when you knew how.

Glancing across at the third bed, Camilla replied with enthusiasm, 'Oh, you'll like Loulou, Loulou Marks. Everybody does – she's terribly funny and nice. Last Friday she ate thirteen Mars bars for a bet and when she complained of stomachache Matron told her that it served her jolly well right. It wasn't until Saturday morning that they realized she had appendicitis and rushed her to hospital!'

Roz, who was in the process of blowing a string of perfect smoke rings, shuddered momentarily at the mention of the word 'hospital'. Then she pulled herself together, dismissing the memory and visualizing instead the absent Loulou, whom everybody liked so much. It wasn't too hard to envisage the kind of person who would eat thirteen Mars bars – she undoubtedly weighed 13 stone, made fun of her size in order to court popularity and earned great favour with the hockey team by using her incredible bulk to defend their goal and flatten anyone who dared approach her.

'She sounds great fun,' she remarked dutifully, whilst inwardly reflecting that a female Billy Bunter would be just as easily manipulated as Camilla. Those kind always were. And there was an added bonus too: at least these two tanks wouldn't be able to borrow her clothes.

Glancing at her watch Roz ground out her cigarette in the upturned biscuit-tin lid beside her, rose from the bed and unsnapped the locks on her trunk. 'Better unpack, I suppose. Who else is here whom I should know? I'm only the new girl so you'll have to tell me who's who at Elm House.' With an air of complicity she added, 'I don't want to waste time meeting no-hopers, after all.'

Just the right balance, she decided as she stuffed piles of expensive, fastidiously ironed underwear into drawers which were pathetically small. Arrogant, but willing to acknowledge the need for help when necessary. Camilla could provide her with what she needed to know until she formed her own élite circle of friends. Maybe, if this girl was very lucky, she'd be allowed to join it.

By the time they reached the echoing dining hall two hours later Camilla was firmly entrenched in her role as party hostess and took great personal pride in introducing Roz to only the right people. Roz, in turn, watched and listened and said not very much at all as each of the girls was introduced. When she did speak, she was careful to either shock or flatter only as far as it was possible to get away with it.

At midnight, Camilla lay awake gazing restlessly into the darkness. The room smelled different since Roz's arrival: a mingling of expensive scent, foreign – and distinctly forbidden – cigarettes, Pernod and pot-pourri. And she *felt* different too, although she couldn't quite understand in which way. Roz was mysterious, beguiling and had bags of charm, but Camilla couldn't help feeling vaguely uneasy at the same time because the girl was so incredibly self-possessed it was unnerving. She had, decided Camilla, a take-it-or-leave-it attitude that surrounded her like an aura and so far it had captivated everyone. But although she had told Roz practically her entire life story this evening, she had learnt scarcely anything in return. Except that her full name was Rosemary – which she hated – and that she had been expelled from her last school, and had seduced her history teacher, if it were true.

And she was *so* good looking. Camilla, whose own fair colouring and tendency to plumpness were the bane of her life, wished fervently that she could have looked like Roz, that she could have had even a tenth of her self-assurance. But she knew herself well enough to recognize that that would never happen in a million years. Turning over on to her side and settling down to sleep she contented herself instead with the thought that she and the tantalizingly enigmatic Roz would become friends. Maybe even best friends.

Over the course of the next couple of days Camilla could only watch and admire as Roz established herself with mesmerizing thoroughness in her role as leader, managing to make almost every girl feel that she alone was the one with whom Roz most wanted to be.

Camilla, despite having succumbed herself, still harboured suspicions that Roz's endless stories weren't always true. They were so bizarre that at least *some* of them had to have been made up, surely.

'But I thought you said you'd spent last summer in Milan?' she queried one evening when they were alone together in their room. 'That was when you met Claudio.'

'Three *weeks* in Milan,' corrected Roz in her calm voice as she refilled their mugs with wine so dry that Camilla had to struggle not to pull a face with every mouthful. 'Geneva was afterwards – much more exciting. My mother was having an affair with a Swiss financier, which meant that I could do whatever I liked. I met Sebastian in a restaurant beside Lake Geneva and by the end of the afternoon he'd taught me to water ski. By the end of the night,' she added with a faint, conspiratorial smile, 'he'd taught me a lot more.'

I don't believe you, thought Camilla. At fifteen?

'What happened?' she asked aloud, a note of challenge in her voice. Roz, hugging her knees, nodded casually towards the cluttered desk between their beds.

'I came home, of course, and Sebastian went back to university. He writes to me every week. His letters are in there somewhere – if you promise not to breathe a word to anyone I'll let you read them.'

And naturally, as if to prove that Roz didn't need to lie, there *were* letters, sixteen in all, and photographs of Roz and Sebastian laughing together at the lakeside. Sebastian, *naturally*, was blond, tanned and handsome. How could he possibly have been anything less?

The following afternoon, Roz returned to their room between classes to find an intruder rummaging energetically through her chest of drawers.

'And just what the bloody hell,' she demanded icily, 'do you think you're doing?'

The girl looked up, apparently unconcerned. 'Me?' she said with mock surprise. 'Oh, I'm just a knicker fetishist. These are nice . . . Janet Reger no less!' Holding up the jade green silk panties, she let out an appreciative whistle. 'My favourite kind.'

Stalking across the room, Roz snatched the knickers from the girl's grasp and would have slapped her face if she hadn't danced rapidly out of the way. Her black eyes glittered as she surveyed her adversary with contempt. The girl was small, slender and undeniably pretty, with rippling silver-blonde hair, huge grey eyes and very white teeth.

'Now, now,' she scolded cheerfully. 'No need to get your Janet Regers in a twist – you'll only snap the elastic.'

'Get out,' said Roz, advancing towards her once more, her jaw rigid with anger. 'How *dare* you come in here and go through my things. And let me tell you right now that *nobody* speaks to me like—'

'Forgot my geometry set!' panted Camilla, bursting pink-faced through the door and cannoning into Roz's back. Then she let out a squeal of delight and rushed across the room, flinging her arms around the grinning blonde.

'Lou, I had no idea you were coming back today! This is fantastic!'

Loulou, submitting to Camilla's enthusiastic embrace, cast a derisive half-smile in Roz's direction. 'Well, I'm glad you think so, at least,' she drawled.

Roz, stunned by the revelation that this beautiful, fragile-looking, sharp-as-glass girl was the missing Loulou Marks, could think of absolutely nothing to say.

Loulou, however, simply laughed.

'So you're Rosemary,' she said, making no effort to move towards her. Turning to Camilla, she went on: 'Is she always this bloody bad-tempered or is it just that time of the month?'

'Oh no,' retaliated Roz coolly, recognizing at once that in Loulou she had found a true adversary. 'I'm always this bloody bad-tempered, particularly when I find a complete stranger going through my underwear drawer.'

Loulou shrugged, then winked at Camilla who was watching the exchange with unconcealed dismay. Camilla always wanted everyone to be friends; Loulou found it far more entertaining to discover for herself whether the friends were worth having before she made any kind of commitment.

'I was looking for that copy of *Playgirl* I bought last month,' she explained. 'I thought I'd left it in that drawer.'

'You could always apologize,' said Roz tightly.

Tilting her blond head to one side as if giving the matter some consideration, Loulou said, 'Could I?'

'Oh go on, Lou.' Camilla, clenching and unclenching her fingers in agitation, was appalled at the prospect of needless animosity. She hated scenes. 'Just say "sorry" and then everything will be all right.'

'OK,' said Loulou, finally. Holding out her hand, she took a single step in Roz's direction. 'I'm sorry I rifled through your knicker drawer. But I'm even more sorry,' she added with a wicked smile, 'that I couldn't find my copy of *Playgirl*.'

This girl was a real threat. Roz knew that if she didn't pull out all the stops this time she ran the risk of finding herself flat on her back, unceremoniously kicked off her throne.

'In that case,' she replied, her tone softening as she clasped Loulou's slender hand, 'I'm sorry too. Everyone calls me Roz, by the way. And I really do hope we can be friends.'

Loulou, straightfaced, said, 'Oh, I'm quite sure we will be. Rosemary.'

Chapter 1

'I just want to know. How many lovers do you have?'

Roz turned her head away and gazed across at the amethyst hills beyond the window. Outside the air was white and cold; inside the bed was warm and Nico's brown body warmer still. His question, whispered with a touch of despair, bothered her slightly for she couldn't decide whether or not to lie and lying was something she didn't particularly relish.

'Wistfulness really doesn't suit you,' she told him affectionately and he flung out a tanned arm in exasperation.

'But I *feel* wistful, dammit! And I can't stand it when you won't answer my questions.'

'Oh, seventeen then,' murmured Roz, running light fingers along his spine and sensing their effect. If he persisted now, she would have to tell him the truth and, hopefully, three would sound perfectly sedate by comparison.

'Tell me,' he urged, his slanting green eyes reflecting love, only half wanting to know. Roz's mouth curved into a slow smile.

'If I didn't *have* them, they wouldn't be lovers,' she reminded him. 'And do they really matter, anyway? I'm here with you now, after all. What could be nicer?'

Nico sighed, realizing that the answer to the question he had dreaded asking was slipping away. Roz, as unreachable as ever, was his only as long as he held her in his arms. He just wasn't used to being treated like this.

'I want to marry you, you know that,' he said helplessly.

Roz laughed. 'Of course you do.'

'I'm wealthy, I'm so damned good looking that hundreds of girls send me their phone numbers every week, I have a great future and I'm brilliant in bed. Even you have to admit that I'm brilliant in bed.'

Solemnly, Roz nodded. She couldn't argue with that, and any minute now Nico was about to prove it to her all over again.

'So why, *why* won't you marry me?' he exclaimed, throwing himself on to his back and staring hopelessly up at the midnight-blue ceiling.

Outside, she glimpsed the mist rolling in like thunder, encircling the hills and the house in which they were cocooned. God, this was hard work. Not that she wanted to hurt Nico, of course, but sometimes she simply couldn't help it.

'I just can't, darling. It wouldn't be fair.'

'To me?' Nico, the superstar, looked shocked and ready to persuade her otherwise.

Roz reached for him, pulling him against her slender body and burying her face against his neck to hide the uncontrollable, affectionate laughter threatening to escape.

'No, sweetheart. I meant it wouldn't be fair to me. Make love to me now, Nico. It's getting foggy outside and you have a long drive home tonight. You mustn't leave it too late.'

'Bitch. Why on earth can't I love a nice girl?'

'Probably,' said Roz between kisses, 'because they're all so extraordinarily dull.'

An hour later, Nico left. When she had watched the sleek black BMW accelerate away from the house until it was swallowed into the mists, Roz ran a hot bath and wandered back into the bedroom to choose what she would wear to dinner tonight with Jack.

Jack, Nico and Sebastian. Did having three lovers, wondered Roz idly, make her a tramp? But then they were all so nice and in a way she loved each of them, albeit an unpossessive, distracted form of love.

But it works, she reminded herself. The more distracted I am, the more they think of me. Every time Nico appeared on television he captured the undivided attention of literally millions of women, yet he came to Roz knowing that her own attention was divided.

Jack, married to a woman about whom she knew nothing except that she clung to her husband like a burr, adored Roz because she was uncomplicated and undemanding. She didn't make things difficult for him and she enjoyed sex.

And Sebastian . . . Well, he was quite different, but the same principle still applied; except that in his case it wasn't always easy. She had loved him for so many years now, knowing all the time that if she dropped her guard even once he would disappear from her life for ever. Sebastian admired her because she was a career woman, because she worked as hard as he did. He had neither the time nor the patience for a clinging woman and Roz had learnt to accept that. She adored their occasional meetings. To lose them would be to lose a small but vital part of her life. Some of Sebastian was better than none, she reminded herself. And during those long gaps between Sebastian's visits there were always the others to occupy and amuse her.

In a way she was controlling all their lives and she adored every moment of it. Almost every moment, anyway.

* * *

'One more sound out of either of you and I swear to God I'll boil you both in oil,' whispered Camilla under her breath as the beginnings of another argument filtered through to the kitchen from the sitting-room. Out loud she yelled, 'Shut up!'

'Didn't say a word,' remonstrated Jack, appearing in the kitchen behind her and irritating her beyond belief by dumping a pair of black brogues on the table she had just finished setting for dinner. 'Can you give these a polish when you've got a moment, Mill? I need them tonight and I'm running late already.'

Deeply aware that Jack, in his grey city suit was looking sleek and handsome, and feeling hideous in comparison, Camilla pushed her fingers through hair that badly needed a wash.

'Clean your own bloody shoes,' she murmured through her teeth. A bad move; she saw the look of irritation in his eyes. 'And don't ever call me Mill again,' she added, only managing to sound sulky. 'I'm going to have a bath.'

'Oh no,' Jack grabbed her arm as she attempted to slide past him. 'There's only enough water for one bath and I'm having it. You can have yours later.'

Tears welled up in Camilla's eyes and for a moment she remembered when she had always fought them back, purely in order to save her make-up. It had been months now since she'd even worn any so she let them fall – and instantly hated herself for it.

'You had a shower this morning,' she argued.

'And now I'm having a bath,' insisted Jack, knowing that since he didn't feel sorry for his wife, he would win. God, she'd been so pretty when he'd married her.

'For your mistress?' gasped Camilla recklessly, then held her breath. There, she'd said it. For weeks it had stuck in her throat like a golf ball and suddenly it had been said, popping out almost of its own accord. All she needed now was the courage to hear Jack's reply.

'No, for the window cleaner,' he said coldly, without a trace of guilt. Damn him, he was an insurance broker, she thought as he released his grip on her arm. He was used to looking people in the eye and lying to them.

'And I'll be late for the meeting if I don't get washed and changed now, so be a good girl and stop behaving like a neurotic housewife. We need this contract if we're going to have a decent holiday this year.'

Camilla blinked and turned away from his clever, lying eyes, picking up a saucepan of boiled potatoes and tipping them into a colander. But if he really did have a mistress, why would he keep talking about a month in the States, dangling it like a carrot in front of her?

'Whatever happened to shared baths?' she said wistfully, and felt Jack's irritated sigh like a slap in the face – a reaction either to the suggestion or to the nauseating little-girl voice with which it had been made. He hated it when she spoke like that, but she really couldn't help it.

Awkwardly, he patted her shoulder. 'Not such a good idea when I'm in a hurry, old thing.' The lame excuse was a peace offering so that she could pretend their marriage was happy, and Camilla felt the tears burning at the back of her eyelids once more. What was the point of having a beautiful house and a beautiful husband, when all she ever did was feel ugly and cry? She sniffed, and turned away.

'And don't call me old thing, either.'

* * *

Lying back amidst the silk cushions of the *chaise-longue* – which sounded romantic but was incredibly uncomfortable unless there *were* piles of cushions – Roz twisted on to her side and flipped channels on the TV with the remote control. It was pretty uncool, she knew, to watch oneself on television – 'Oh my dear, I can't *bear* to!' – but she loved it. It was no worse than looking in the mirror and talking to yourself, after all – and it wasn't as if the interviewer had made mincemeat out of her. She hadn't had any trouble with him at all.

Roz ran her hand absent-mindedly along the slim curve of her thigh, naked beneath the silk wrap, and watched a commercial for cat food that sent shivers of revulsion along her spine. Cats were fine, but the advert was so appalling that if she'd owned a cat she would be forced to buy some other brand of food, purely on principle.

And she was feeling rather cat-like herself now, she realized, stretching lazily and admiring the smooth brown lines of her arms. Jack, married Jack, would have told his wife by now that he had a business meeting tonight and that she shouldn't expect him home before midnight. It was only thanks to Roz that he ever returned when he said he would; Jack was always ready to spend the night with her.

Going to bed with a man, she thought, was one thing. Sleeping with him was another matter entirely. Besides, she didn't want Jack to stop feeling unsure of himself and to start taking his good fortune for granted.

The chat show was starting and Roz put Jack instantly from her mind, a convenient habit she had learnt as a child. The television host showed a lot of teeth and launched into his introductory monologue, pitted with excruciating *bons mots* which made Roz shiver out of sympathy. Though why she should feel sympathetic towards a man who earnt so much, so undeservedly, she couldn't for the life of her understand.

'And tonight we have with us the beautiful and talented Roz Vallender,' he lied, for the programme had been made two days ago. Roz watched herself and smiled with satisfaction.

Camilla, immersed in the programme, watched intently with almost vicarious pride as Roz dealt with the interviewer's clumsy attempts at flirtation. Roz answered his questions with that famous razor-sharp wit yet at the same time managed to convey the impression that he was clever too, a trick which Camilla remembered she could just as easily reverse.

Fifteen years, she realized. It was almost exactly fifteen years since she had last seen Roz when, at seventeen, they had both left Elm House and had vowed fervently to keep in touch. She had written to Roz once, the letter returning unopened, with 'Gone away' scrawled across it and she had never received a single letter or even a postcard. So much for keeping in touch. Roz was my best friend, she thought with a trace of bitterness. And I was Roz's . . . room-mate.

Well, they'd certainly both changed in fifteen years. Camilla even managed a wry smile at the thought. Here she was in her velour dressing-gown and matching slippers, hugging a mug of tea, glasses perched precariously on her nose, and remembering that she hadn't plucked her eyebrows for weeks.

And there was Roz, gypsy-eyed and glossy mouthed, in scarlet silk which shimmered each time she spoke. She was as clever and beguiling as ever, of course, and it was a sure bet that she was wearing silk stockings. The memories were coming back now, old jealousies resurfacing as the initial burst of pride faded and sank.

15

I ought to contact her, thought Camilla. It would amuse her to see me now, how I am. Roz had grown into her looks; always striking, she was now almost breathtakingly beautiful. And her old room-mate? I was pretty, Camilla told herself fiercely. Now I'm simply . . . faded. Almost as if Roz had drawn my looks from me like a vampire and added them to her own.

'And how's your love life, Roz?' the interviewer was saying with what he hoped was an impudent grin.

'Fine, thanks. How's yours?' said Roz, examining her polished fingernails and smiling as the audience erupted with raucous laughter. Camilla glanced at her own nails around the mug, short and unvarnished and flecked with white. A house-wife's hands. Roz had lovers, whilst she was stuck with two children and a husband who said he had a headache whenever she kissed him in bed.

'And you're living in Gloucestershire now, I understand.' The interviewer decided to move on to safer ground and Roz, from the *chaise-longue*, nodded her approval before listening carefully to her reply. As her television self described the house she glanced around the sitting-room for confirmation. Cotswold stone walls, tapestry curtains, exotic rugs strewn over polished parquet, 'architectural foliage' and miraculous concealed light-ing. Next week, *Homes & Gardens* would feature it; the ultimate in country chic and effortless stylishness, and women – it was almost always women – would sigh over the photographs and storm down to John Lewis in search of tapestry curtains of their own. According to the features editor, anyway.

'. . . so you don't miss the bright lights of London?' asked the interviewer with an enormous wink, and Roz saw out of the corner of her eye the headlights of a car drawing nearer, along the narrow lane leading to her house. Plenty of bright lights to keep me amused on these long winter nights, she thought with a momentary twinge of annoyance because Jack was here earlier than she'd expected him.

'I'm never bored,' she told the interviewer smoothly. 'There's always something to do, even in the country. Plenty of people have learnt that over the years.' It was exactly the kind of *double entendre* the audience loved and they erupted once more, laughing and applauding idiotically as if she had said something original.

The car stopped outside and Roz flipped the remote control once more, switching herself off. As she rose to her feet the doorbell rang twice, as it always did when Jack had his finger on it. This habit of his, she reflected, was just beginning to irritate her; maybe the affair was on the wane, after all.

Dear Roz, Camilla wrote for the third time that evening. It was extraordinarily difficult to know what to say to someone whom you hadn't seen for fifteen years. The first attempt had sounded like a cross between a fan letter and a very dull diary, but now that the idea had taken root she was determined to re-establish contact. Anything that might liven up her life was worth a try, and she didn't have the nerve to parachute out of a plane.

Guess who – a voice from the past! This is Camilla (no longer Avery-Jones, I'm now Mrs Stewart) and having just watched you on TV, I thought how nice it would be if we could get together sometime and catch up on all the gossip. What a lot has happened since we left Elm House! (Camilla didn't mention that most of it had happened to Roz – let her think that she wasn't the only one with the thrill-a-minute lifestyle.) I'm living in London, so next time you're in town, why don't you give me a ring and perhaps we could meet for lunch. Do get in touch. It would be so nice to see you again.

Camilla hesitated, then signed it 'Love from Camilla' and hoped it didn't sound odd, although 'Yours sincerely' would have sounded even odder. And then before she could have second thoughts she stuffed the letter into an envelope and addressed it to Roz c/o 'The Johnnie Mason Show' at the BBC. There, she had done it. From now on – as always, thought Camilla with a rueful smile – the ball was in Roz's court.

Chapter 2

'Why on earth should Roz Vallender want to get in touch with *you*?' sneered Jack. Camilla fixed her gaze on the television and felt her stomach lurch. She wished now that she hadn't mentioned it, that she had waited until she had received a reply. It would have been far better if she could have casually announced that she had a lunch date with Roz.

'We were best friends at school,' she muttered, and Jack waved away her words with an impatient gesture.

'Don't I know it. You've told me enough times, for Christ's sake. And if she'd wanted to stay friends she could have contacted you years ago. You're only making a fool of yourself.'

Apprehension mingled with annoyance, but for a moment he experienced a rising spiral of excitement, too. Unsure whether he was actually in love with Roz, but definitely infatuated with her nevertheless, the thought of his wife and mistress renewing their old friendship added an irresistible *frisson* of danger to the situation. Which was, after all, partly the reason for most extra-marital affairs, he acknowledged without guilt. And his affair with Roz was undoubtedly exciting.

'She was interviewed on "The Johnnie Mason Show" last night,' Camilla tried to explain. 'It was a spur of the moment decision. It doesn't matter, anyway, if I don't hear from her,' she added defensively. 'I just thought it was a good idea at the time.'

What would you say, wondered Jack as he watched his plump

JILL MANSELL

wife take another biscuit from the tin in front of her, if I told
you that whilst you were watching Roz on TV last night I was
making love to her on her living-room floor?

'It's ridiculous,' he said flatly. 'You won't hear from her. Roz
Vallender's wealthy and famous. Why on earth should she want
to see you again, now?'

Nico spotted the letter lying beneath Roz's glass coffee table
and read it whilst he waited for her to finish dressing upstairs.

'Are you going to phone her?' he said when she appeared in
the doorway, shimmering in silk the colour of old gold, a long
jacket and short skirt that showed off her slender legs.

'We went to school together.' Roz smiled. 'I ought to reply to
her letter really, but . . .'

She gestured helplessly with her hand and Nico frowned.
Close to his own family and friends, he was never able to
understand why Roz chose to remain so remote from her own.
She had mentioned in passing the other week that she hadn't
seen her mother for three years and the knowledge had upset
him.

'Why don't you want to see her?' he persisted, risking her
annoyance. 'It would be nice. She only wants to meet you so
that you can catch up on each other's news.'

Roz looked doubtful but not, thankfully, irritated by his
insistence.

'I suppose,' she said slowly, 'I'm just not terribly interested
in hearing about other people's lives. If they are more exciting
than mine, I'm envious. If they are dull and unhappy, then I'm
bored. So there really doesn't seem to be much point, darling,
do you see?'

'No,' Nico shrugged. 'But it's your affair.'

Roz grinned, picked up her bag and slipped her arm through his. Their table at the restaurant was booked for nine and although she and Nico would be seated immediately whatever time they arrived, she was starving.

Harrods was revving up for Christmas even if no-one else was, thought Camilla, shifting her carrier bag from one hand to the other and surreptitiously rocking back on her heels in order to ease the weight from the balls of her feet. She always felt like this in Harrods. The customers were generally so chic, so flawlessly dressed and made-up that she felt compelled to make an effort herself.

And now, after three hours, she thought unhappily, my high heels are killing me, my face is red and shiny because my coat is too hot and my hair is falling down.

To add insult to injury, the impossibly elegant girl standing a few feet away was looking effortlessly cool and comfortable in black lace trousers and black leather boots. People like that, Camilla decided, people with all-year-round tans, expensive blond hair and twenty-two-inch waists, were always around when you didn't need them.

Coffee. If she made her way to the coffee bar on the next floor, removed her stifling coat and rested her feet, she would be good for another hour at least. Harrods – or rather its customers – might be intimidating but she so adored spending money there that she couldn't bear to leave yet, and the pre-Christmas buzz had lifted her spirits immeasurably. It was more fun here, anyway, than staying at home watching Jennifer, the new nanny, amuse her own children more efficiently than she herself ever could.

Everyone who had passed through the perfume hall on the ground floor and had been sprayed had evidently now congregated in the coffee bar on the third floor as Camilla wrenched off her coat and slid into a chair. DKNY mingled with Eternity and she held her breath, regretting being caught in the crossfire but feeling too tired to search for another free seat. She would enjoy her coffee, demolish the fat slice of chocolate cheesecake on the plate before her (cheerio diet, see you tomorrow), and decide whether to splash out on a set of ludicrously expensive violet silk underwear with which to fascinate Jack, or to spend the money on sensible shoes for the children.

'. . . and you'll never guess who I've just seen in the lingerie department,' announced a fat woman proudly to her friend with whom she had just met up. They were crammed into seats opposite Camilla's and had strong Birmingham accents.

'I think I saw Michael Caine in the food hall,' the other woman retaliated, and Camilla tried not to smile.

'Well, I *know* who I saw,' said the first with increasing importance. 'Recognized her straight away, of course, after seeing "The Johnnie Mason Show" last week. You know who I mean, Marion. That dark girl who's got her own programme on Wednesday nights. Whatever's she called now? The name's on the tip of my—'

'Roz Vallender?' said Camilla, so astonished that she spoke without thinking, and the fat woman slapped the table with relief.

'That's it, of course it is. Couldn't think of it for the life of me, dear. I just saw her as large as life in the lingerie department,' she confided. As Camilla blurted out, 'But I know her . . . We were at school together,' she felt a sudden surge of adrenalin, excitement mingled with fear, clutch at her stomach.

'Well, that settles it,' announced the fat woman, addressing Camilla as if she were a schoolgirl once more. 'If she's your friend you must go and see her, say hello. It wasn't two minutes ago, after all. Jessie and I'll wait here for you and if you could just ask her for a couple of autographs whilst you're there, for our grandchildren, of course . . .'

If Roz was there, Camilla decided, she would bump into her accidentally whilst in the process of choosing the violet silk underwear set she had yearned for earlier. She wished now, as she entered the lingerie department and glanced anxiously around, that she hadn't sent what Jack had so scathingly termed the fan letter. It put her at something of a disadvantage and a chance meeting would have been a much nicer way of re-acquainting herself.

And there – less than ten feet away – was Roz.

Experiencing another jolt almost akin to an electric shock, Camilla stopped and stared for a second at the slight, dark figure she remembered so well from fifteen years ago, even more slender in the flesh than she appeared on television and unfairly elegant in a white T-shirt, tight flared jeans and a scarlet fedora. Then, every hastily laid plan rushing from her head as the sheer pleasure of meeting her old friend again took over, she flung her arms wide and called out: 'Roz! I can't believe it . . . how *are* you?'

In the noisy, chaotic atmosphere of Vampires, Loulou reigned supreme. She often felt that in her business life at least, she had hit the jackpot. The restaurant, which had started life as a wine bar and become almost of its own accord a hugely popular meeting and eating place, was her own. In the kitchen and behind the bars her staff worked like navvies, watched over by her manager; all she had to do was be there, the decoration on the top of the cake, doing what came naturally. Simply, the more appallingly she treated her customers, the more they loved it.

A beautiful, witty and extremely feminine version of the late Peter Langan. One journalist had described her thus in an upmarket national newspaper some years ago, and trade had doubled practically overnight. Visitors to Vampires were insulted if they weren't insulted and Loulou, who had been sacked from thirteen office jobs before she was twenty, usually for saying what everyone else longed to but did not dare say, never failed her customers. It was all so easy, so enjoyable and so amazingly profitable that she couldn't understand why everyone didn't do it. It hadn't even been too arduous sleeping for a fortnight with the sleepy-eyed journalist before persuading him to run the feature in his newspaper.

'Take those terrible things off this instant,' she said sweetly to a man in his thirties, fixing her gaze upon his green-and-white checked trousers, and amidst the noise at the bar the customers who had heard her command abruptly halted their conversation and turned to stare at the offending item of clothing.

'Dammit, Lou. Why do you always pick on me?' protested the man, lighting up a cigarette and preparing to argue. Loulou pulled her 'What can you do with an idiot' face and turned to address her other customers.

'OK, we'll put it to the vote. You lot don't look as if you've got an ounce of sartorial elegance between you, so I'll vote. Trousers off. And Tommy, as long as you continue to wear hideous clothes, I'll tell you to remove them or get out. It's that simple.'

Having dressed in anticipation of the event, Tommy disposed of his trousers to reveal tanned legs and scarlet boxer shorts with 'Long Vehicle' printed across the front. Laughter erupted, several flash guns exploded (for Tommy, son of a viscount, was always newsworthy) and Loulou took the opportunity to announce that if Tommy walked into a wall with an erection he would most certainly break his nose. It wasn't true, of course, as she herself could testify, but neither Tommy's wife nor her own present boyfriend would be thrilled to hear it. Besides, no-one came to Vampires for compliments.

'Don't do it, darling,' she called across to a woman entering the bar with a too-trendily dressed younger man. 'He's only after you for your money. Never be *that* desperate . . .'

Busy abusing the woman – pink and white and turning pinker by the second because she knew only too well that the loud accusations were perfectly accurate – Loulou failed to spot the entry of the two women until a long fingernail prodded her spine and she swivelled round on her chair with a shriek of outrage. Then she flung her arms around Roz's neck and yelled even more loudly, 'You old tart, what on earth are you doing here? Hallowe'en isn't until next week, for God's sake. Ah, and I see you decided to bring your mother along.' With perfect solemnity she clasped Camilla's unsuspecting hand and said, 'So you're the raddled old trout I've heard so much about. Well, we don't do special prices for pensioners, but since Roz is an old pal I'll stand you both a drink.'

'Lou,' said Roz evenly, enjoying Camilla's shell-shocked expression, 'you must remember Camilla Avery-Jones. From Elm House. We met quite by chance in Harrod's knicker department this afternoon . . .'

And if I've had to put up with her I don't see why you

shouldn't suffer too, signalled her expression.

'Of course!' exclaimed Loulou, gazing with astonishment at Camilla's flushed face. 'I do remember you now. But my God,' she added with deliberate slowness, 'how you've *changed.*'

But despite the pained look she had given Loulou, Roz was intrigued. Camilla Stewart had mentioned in passing that her husband's name was Jack, and Roz, whilst acknowledging that his name was a relatively common one, was wondering whether Camilla's Jack could possibly also be hers.

'And you haven't changed at all,' Camilla was gushing, oblivious to Loulou's implied insult, as she hoisted herself on to a bar stool. 'I can scarcely believe it, bumping into Roz like that and now coming to Vampires and seeing you. This is just incredible, you couldn't possibly understand. I haven't had such a marvellous day for years!'

And it really had been a marvellous day, she told herself dreamily as she sipped a second glass of the rich, warm Beaujolais and gazed at the two of them, now deep in conversation together. Roz, with her striking dark looks, was simply too glamorous for words and Loulou, with her waist-length rippling blonde hair and innocent eyes, looked like an angel. Between them they were capable of intimidating even the most self-possessed person and Camilla experienced a flush of pride, unselfishly admiring them. She wasn't in their league – she knew that – but at least she was here, *with* them.

And she, at least, had a husband.

That was it, she realized with excitement. All through their schooldays together, Roz and Loulou had collected and carelessly discarded members of the opposite sex and the only experience more embarrassing than being excluded had been the times when they had offered her their cast-offs. Now at least she was the one with a man of her very own, a handsome one at that, and she longed quite suddenly and fiercely to show him off to her two old schoolfriends.

'My husband and I are having a dinner party next week,' she said, reaching over and touching Roz's arm. 'Will you come? Both of you? We can't simply lose touch again after meeting up like this.'

Please, please say 'yes' she begged silently, as Roz frowned. It would show Jack too, that she hadn't made a fool of herself by writing to Roz. He would be impressed, both with his wife and her glamorous schoolfriends, and she would regain some of the self-respect which had been eroding steadily away for years.

'When?' asked Roz, stalling for time, and Camilla thought quickly.

'Monday.' She guessed it to be the night when they were most likely to be free, and Roz nodded slowly, glancing across at Loulou to gauge her own response. Loulou shrugged, indicating that she was easy.

'We'd be able to meet your family,' said Roz, her expression thoughtful. 'What does your husband do, by the way?'

Camilla smiled happily. 'He's a broker, working in the City. Yes, of course he'll be there. You'll like him, I'm sure.'

Incredible, thought Roz. It *had* to be the same Jack Stewart.

'I'm sure I will,' she replied, sipping her wine. To herself she added: It rather seems as if I already do.

Jack had phoned thirteen times so far, but Roz had left her answerphone running even when she was at home, only picking up calls once she had established that they weren't from him. She was still intrigued, but also a little angry with Jack. Always priding herself upon her honesty, it irritated her to realize that he must have known that she and his wife had been to school together. Why else would he have never even mentioned Camilla's name? And why did he feel he had to keep it a secret . . . surely he knew Roz well enough to realize that it would hardly make any difference to her? Yes, Jack's motives were definitely questionable, Roz decided. She might be amoral, but she was never purposely deceitful and she was determined now to find out why Jack had chosen to be so.

At six o'clock Camilla slumped down at the kitchen table. She was exhausted and Jack wasn't being any help. All day she had been working in the kitchen, preparing an elaborate four-course meal for ten guests, and half an hour ago he had arrived home from work in a foul temper and had promptly disappeared into his study.

So much for thinking that he would be proud of her for arranging tonight's dinner party and for inviting two such illustrious guests, she thought sadly. Instead he had reacted almost angrily when she had told him and all her happiness had seeped away, leaving her wishing she had never even suggested the bloody party in the first place. If Jack was going to spend the entire evening in a sulk he was hardly likely to impress either Roz or Loulou.

But the food did smell magnificent. In the steamy warmth of the kitchen the scent of the *boeuf bourgignon* mingled with the comforting aroma of baking potatoes. And the seafood cocktails, lined up on the kitchen table looked so pretty on their lettuce beds that surely no-one would be able to resist them. In the fridge the creamy syllabub was all prepared. On the shelf above it sat the white marble cheeseboard, carefully wrapped in clingfilm so that the ripe Stilton and Brie wouldn't taint the delicate flavour of the dessert.

Everything's ready, thought Camilla. Except me.

Jack, stabbing at the phone for the tenth time that day, realized that he was furious not only with Camilla but also with Roz. She simply had to be playing one of her irritating games with him, having guessed that Camilla was his wife. He had meant no harm by the small deception and now she was clearly angry with him for not letting her in on the secret. By refusing to answer the phone she was making sure, as always, that she had the upper hand. What a bitch she was, leaving him to guess how she would handle the situation.

'Jack, can I come in? I need a hand with this zip.' Camilla's voice followed the tentative tap on the door and he suppressed a fresh surge of irritation, remembering that it was he, after all, who had instructed her always to knock before entering his study. Dropping the phone back on to the hook, he rose to his feet and opened the door, coming face to face with Camilla's effort to look less like herself, more like Roz. It was, he thought with a jolt of unexpected sympathy, like dressing a puppy up as a lizard. Camilla's voluptuous figure was naturally suited to pastel colours and lace, but, in her efforts to streamline herself, she had chosen a sharp, ruthlessly tailored dress. Her dark blond hair, which so suited her when it curled loosely to her shoulders, had been scraped back into a chignon which cruelly emphasized the beginnings of a double chin, and the soft blue eye make-up she usually wore – on special occasions only – had been replaced by less flattering shades of poison-ivy green and rust brown.

For a fraction of a second as Camilla turned her back to him to reveal smooth creamy flesh and the unfastened zip, Jack wondered whether he should tell her that the outfit was a disaster, that she still had time to change into the pale pink wool dress which made her look like a rose. For heaven's sake, she was even wearing a new, cloying perfume instead of the usual flowery scent he had always associated with her. Roz would know that Camilla was emulating her and would be inwardly laughing all evening. Suddenly Jack didn't want his wife to be the object of his mistress's amusement. It was unfair and he felt sickened by the prospect of it. The sense of clandestine excitement had vanished and all he felt now was shame.

'I much prefer you in your pink dress.' The words came out more brutally than he had intended and he regretted them instantly, for at least until that moment Camilla had *felt* attractive. When he had closed the zip and she turned slowly round to face him there were tears in her eyes.

'Thank you, Jack,' she said in a low, trembling voice. 'You certainly know how to boost a woman's ego.'

By eight forty-five all the other guests had arrived apart from Roz and Loulou, and Camilla was struggling not to appear concerned. Surely they wouldn't fail to turn up, without even phoning to let her know? Was the evening that unimportant to them? Oh God, she prayed as she held out a plate of hors-d'oeuvres and watched Margaret Jameson choose the biscuit with the largest prawn on it, please just make them turn up and I promise I'll never complain about anything else again.

The cow, thought Jack, not knowing whether to be relieved or angry again. She isn't going to come. She's chosen to humiliate us and make us look ridiculous in front of our friends. I'll bloody kill her if she doesn't turn up, I swear I will . . .

When the doorbell rang Camilla thought for a moment that it was an hallucination. Then she realized that the other guests had stopped talking and that Jack had turned pale, pausing in the act of pouring a drink as if someone had pulled his plug out.

'Super, just in time,' she heard herself saying. The incredible confidence with which the words came out both amazed and impressed her. Stuff you, Margaret Jameson, she thought happily, for looking at your watch every three minutes and whispering to your husband out of the corner of your nasty, narrow mouth. My friends are here and they're going to impress the hell out of you.

Chapter 3

'Oh well, here we go,' murmured Roz as Camilla's silhouette advanced towards them and the front door was flung open.

'Cami, you look wonderful!' she said with a quick hug and a smile. 'I'm so sorry we're late but I was held up at the television studios and then when I went to meet Lou she was in the middle of a slanging match with a photographer from the *Express* and I simply had to wait and see who won. Have we held everything up?'

'Of course not!' Camilla looked so happy to see them both that Roz almost felt guilty. She hadn't lied, but neither had she mentioned the fact that they and the photographer had sunk two bottles of champagne in order to celebrate his defeat. 'Come in and meet everyone – we've got time for another drink before we eat. Lou, shall I take your coat?'

Loulou slid out of her studded leather jacket and adjusted the wide neckline of her gold lamé top. In a tight black leather mini skirt, seamed stockings and stiletto heels she looked both incongruous – angel turned tart – and stunningly beautiful. Camilla felt a thrill of triumph just wondering what Margaret Jameson would make of her.

Roz, too, was spectacular in suede jeans and a man's white dress-shirt, her dark hair slicked back from her face so that her wayward features were enhanced to feline proportions. As Camilla led the way back into the sitting room – the expectant hush told her that their every word had been overheard and rapaciously stored for retelling at future parties – she felt the sudden crazy urge to fling open the door and announce proudly that the prodigal daughters had returned.

It was going to be all right, Jack decided with considerable relief. Roz, the bitch, was behaving perfectly and had met his eyes without even a flicker of recognition when Camilla had proudly introduced them to each other. And Christ, she looked beautiful tonight. Roz and Loulou were like night and day, one so mysterious and dark and the other so ethereally fair. He couldn't tell whether Loulou had been briefed on the situation; she, too, greeted him with absolute decorum. He watched for a second as Loulou sucked an ice cube with an unconsciously provocative gesture, then hastily looked away once more as a prickle of sweat caught against his shirt collar. God, if he wasn't already sleeping with Roz, he could quite easily have been tempted to make a serious play for this gorgeous friend of hers.

'So you three girls were at school together,' said Margaret Jameson, who loved to dominate dinner party conversations and who was in her element here, with the famous Roz Vallender at one end of the table and the gossip columnists' darling, Loulou Marks, at the other. She could hardly wait to name-drop at the next bridge club meeting on Thursday and fully intended to squeeze every last drop of newsworthiness from tonight's dinner.

Roz smiled bleakly, toying with a mushroom on her fork and Camilla, realizing that Roz wasn't intending to answer Margaret's rhetorical question, rushed blindly in.

'I look so much older than Roz and Lou, I expect,' she said hurriedly. 'And they're both so wonderfully slim, of course, whereas I put on *stones* when I had the children, although even when we were at school I was much bigger than they were. I must look ten years older by comparison now . . .'

You're kidding, thought Jack, and risked the briefest of smiles in Roz's direction. Roz, to her amazement, felt her stomach curl with disgust at his complicity and dropped her fork to her plate with a crash.

'Don't put yourself down, Cami,' she said in a firm voice. 'You've got a perfectly good figure, and most men prefer a few curves anyway. Don't you agree, Jack?' she concluded, fixing him with a distinctly cool gaze.

The super-bitch, he thought to himself, inwardly furious. Well, two could play at that bloody game.

'Absolutely,' he replied, smiling at Camilla more persuasively than he had for years. 'I love my wife just as she is, don't I darling?'

Flushing with pleasure and embarrassment, Camilla grabbed her wine glass and swallowed the contents. Jack *never* complimented her on anything any more and to have done so in front of all their guests – even if Roz, bless her, had rather forced the issue – made her feel quite exhilarated.

'Thank you, darling,' she said, attempting to sound as casual as if he paid her at least a dozen such compliments every day. 'More courgettes, anyone?'

As the dinner progressed, Roz and Loulou became more animated, sensing the reason for their invitation and obligingly forming a double-act in order to entertain the other guests and retain Camilla's credibility among them. Roz was still angry with Jack for some reason she couldn't clearly define and Loulou had decided quite simply that she didn't like him. If he thought he was being clever, entertaining both his wife and mistress at the same table and being seen to get away with it, she thought he was merely fatuous – and entirely resistible.

Twice he had turned his smooth seducer's gaze upon her, confident that she would respond, and twice she had longed to hurl her plate at his handsome head. She was also slightly ashamed of herself. At first when Roz had explained the situation, Loulou had thought it amusing. Now that she was here, however, and able to see how desperately hard Camilla was trying, she was sickened by the deception and her heart went out to Camilla, the most innocent of innocent parties. It was clear that Jack had sapped whatever confidence she had once had, and now he was playing on it with brutal, self-centred satisfaction, entirely for his own amusement. She wouldn't have minded betting, either, that he was just as selfish in bed.

Oh, no charmer this one, thought Loulou with compassion for Camilla who so obviously worshipped him.

At the same time Camilla wondered if she had ever been happier in her life. Looking around her subtly lit sitting-room, at her guests talking and laughing and so obviously enjoying themselves, she wanted to burst with joy and pride. Her house looked lovely – she was thankful she had rushed out and bought those bronze and cream chrysanthemums at the last minute – and dinner had been a huge success. And since I cooked it, I have been a success too, Camilla realized almost with amazement. Roz had praised her home and admired her ludicrously expensive dress and Loulou had noticed the photographs of the children and had complimented her extravagantly.

'They're beautiful, Cami. A pair of absolute stunners – and they look so much like you.'

Really, she thought happily, it had been *the* most perfect evening.

'Well, I'm afraid I have a hideously early start tomorrow morning,' Roz announced at eleven o'clock, and was gratified to sense the disappointment of the rest of the party. She was the main attraction, after all. As soon as she left, their sparkling moods would begin to disintegrate and they, too, would make guilty excuses to leave.

Rising to her feet and smoothing her hands over her narrow suede-clad hips, she gave Camilla a perfect smile. 'I'm afraid I've had far too much to drink so I'll abandon the car, but it's too cold to walk. I have a small apartment in the Barbican,' she added, catching the look of astonishment on Camilla's face. Presumably she imagined that Roz was planning a midnight hike down to the Cotswolds. 'Could I possibly phone for a cab from here?'

'Oh, that's silly,' protested Camilla, 'Jack can drive you. The Barbican's only a couple of miles away. It wouldn't be any trouble, would it darling?'

'Of course it would be trouble,' Roz replied evenly, so that only Jack would read the underlying meaning into her words. She smiled at Camilla once more, without even glancing in his direction. 'He really shouldn't risk it. Please, I'd be much happier taking a cab.'

Feeling guiltily relieved, because she didn't feel confident enough to maintain the party unaided, Camilla jumped to her feet.

'In that case I'll phone one now. Jack, could you refill some glasses while I'm gone?'

The fern-like study was cool and quiet as she reached for the phone and leant against the edge of Jack's desk before dialling. More alcohol than she was used to had blurred her senses slightly, but it wasn't an unpleasant feeling. She struggled for a few seconds to recall the taxi-cab number before remembering that she had phoned them this afternoon in order to catch the florist. Ordinarily she would have walked, but thanks to her earlier extravagance she now had the number on memory.

Press M, thought Camilla with a giggle, for motor car. M, for marvellous, miraculous dinner party. M for magnificent evening.

'Hello,' said a female voice as the telephone was finally answered.

'Oh, hello, would it be possible to book . . .' began Camilla, but the female voice on the other end of the line continued without pausing.

'This is Roz Vallender. I'm not at home at the moment but if you'd like me to call you back,' said Roz's silkily persuasive recorded voice, 'do please leave your name and number after the tone. Thank you.'

Standing silent and unnoticed in the shadowy doorway, Roz saw Camilla's expression freeze and guessed instantly what had happened. Obscurely, she had almost known that it would and now she experienced a shuddering jolt of remorse.

Chapter 4

Camilla never knew afterwards what made her do it. At the time, however, it had seemed there was simply no other choice. Some part of her mind was telling her: Your life is changing . . . in a couple of minutes you'll go completely to pieces . . . but in the meantime, just before that starts, do something that will hurt him back.

And although she had always been uncritically adoring of her husband, Camilla knew that humiliation would do the trick far more effectively than tears or recriminations.

As if still frozen in a dream she moved past Roz, murmuring 'Excuse me' as if she were a stranger in a lift. Back into the sitting-room and to the dinner guests so unsuspecting. Smiling absently at Loulou who was curled up like a leather-clad kitten on the settee, Camilla crossed to the low coffee table and picked up her wine glass. As she sipped the ice-cold Sancerre she heard the sitting-room door click shut and from the corner of her eye glimpsed Roz's slender outline.

So she's wondering what I'm going to do, thought Camilla with a smile. It was rather exciting, in a weird kind of way. She felt detached, as if she were just another onlooker or a member of an audience.

There was Jack, laughing too loudly at one of his own jokes and surreptitiously eyeing Loulou's stocking-clad legs. He looked so handsome and successful and so very sure of himself that Camilla wondered for a brief moment whether what she planned to do was fair. Then she remembered afresh that in just a few moments, when this dreamlike numbness wore off, she would have to face up to the worst event of her life.

Replacing her wine glass carefully on the table she clasped her hands around the large, fat white bowl of bronze and cream chrysanthemums and lifted it into her arms. Jack shot her an impatient glance, clearly thinking that she was starting to clear up in the hope that their guests might take the hint and leave.

Put them down, he mouthed at her and Camilla smiled at him for the last time.

'No,' she said in a clear, carrying voice. 'You have them, darling.' And the contents of the bowl, a sudden bright tidal wave of chrysanthemum petals and feathery leaves and at least three pints of water, flew straight into Jack's handsome face.

It was the most outrageous gesture she had ever made in her life and it gave her the most gloriously satisfying sensation she had ever known. The stunned expressions on the faces of their guests and the incredibly sudden silence – broken only by the sound of water dripping steadily on to the floor – was sheer perfection. She wanted to laugh aloud at the absurdity of it all.

But at the same time she realized that she was just as likely to burst into tears and that now was the moment to escape.

'Thank you all for a most memorable evening,' she announced in a voice that was amazingly calm. 'And now if you would excuse me, I think I shall leave.'

The frosty pavement glittered beneath the street lamps and to keep her mind occupied Camilla counted each pool of light as she walked. Seven street lamps. No sound other than the rhythmic click of her own high heels as she headed down Marson Road towards the common. There would be no lights there, only trees, but it seemed as good a place as any to be aiming for.

'You were terrific, by the way.' The voice scarcely startled Camilla at all, despite the fact that she hadn't realized she was being followed. It was Loulou, barefoot and silent, who had chased after her and now she felt tears of gratitude welling up at the thought that someone had cared enough to do so.

'You'll freeze,' said Camilla uncertainly, eyeing the blonde girl's paper-thin gold top, and Loulou grinned.

'Well, you certainly won't. Margaret Jameson's doing her nut back there because you walked off with her bit of rabbit.' She touched Camilla's arm, feeling the softness of the mink fur beneath her hand.

'Is that why you came after me?' said Camilla, saddened. 'To take her coat back?'

Loulou gripped her arm tightly, pulling her to a halt and then impulsively flinging her arms around her. It was like hugging a large, unhappy animal. Camilla's eyes reminded her of next door's spaniel and now that she had stopped walking her entire body was beginning to droop with defeat.

'You idiot, of course not,' she said gently, trying not to shiver as the freezing night air shot down the back of her shirt. 'I spoke to Roz. She told me all about it. Your husband got what he deserved and if you hadn't got there first, Roz probably would have done the same thing herself. She didn't know, you see.'

Amazed that she was still able to speak so calmly, despite the hot tears trickling down her cheeks, Camilla said, 'It's odd. It never occurred to me to take it out on her. Whatever else Jack's done to me, I'd always thought that at least he was faithful. And now that I know he hasn't even been that ... I can't

cope . . . everything's spoilt.' Her voice cracking, rising as she
fought for control, she said, 'Oh, Lou, what on earth am I going
to *do*?'

Loulou considered the problem as rapidly as only a bare-
footed, scantily clad female on the verge of hypothermia could.
Her shoes she had abandoned in the hallway of Camilla's house,
but she had her handbag with her. Camilla had nothing but a
stolen fur coat.

'Do you want to go back, sweetie?'

'I can't. I really, really can't.'

'Then that's settled,' said Loulou briskly, though her eyes
were kind. 'You must come and stay with me.'

Chapter 5

In the weeks that followed, Camilla came to realize how lucky she was to have been taken in by Loulou, whose irreverent humour and down-to-earth attitudes did far more good than the quiet sympathy and exaggerated concern she might have received from anyone else.

'I'm giving you a week to be really, really upset in,' Loulou had cheerfully informed her the morning after the fateful dinner party. 'And that's pretty generous because I only ever allow myself four days. So, for the next week you can be as miserable as you like, drink as much as you like and cry buckets. But after that you have to be cheerful again – why waste your precious time grieving over a man who isn't worth it, after all?'

And while Camilla had obediently taken her old-new friend's advice, Loulou discovered for the first time what it was like to look after someone else, to be in the position to help them, and she adored every minute of it. Like a well-meaning but hopelessly incompetent nanny, she attempted to cook appetizing meals for Camilla, working on the assumption that since Camilla was overweight, food would bring her the most comfort. And since she refused to order food from her excellent restaurant, feeling that it was mainly the thought that counted and that Camilla would appreciate it more if Loulou did it herself, the meals were so appalling that they were almost funny. Loulou, whose restaurant featured in all the good food guides, was incapable of cooking even a potato.

'Lovely,' said Camilla, struggling manfully with burnt cauliflower and a cheese soufflé the consistency of a place mat.

'If you're going to get on in life,' Loulou told her sternly, 'you really must stop being so polite. This food is hideous, and you know it and I know it, so why don't we just chuck it in the bin and open an enormous bottle of Chablis instead?'

In that first week, Camilla appreciated afterwards, she had consumed more alcohol than she usually drank in a year. It helped to blur the edges of her grief, to make the future seem not quite so black and best of all it put her to sleep faster than Pentothal. As yet, she had made no plans for the future, concentrating solely instead on the realization that her marriage was over. Other women, she knew, were able to accept their husband's flings and infidelities but never for a moment did it cross her mind to do the same. Maybe, if it hadn't been Roz, if Jack had had an affair with some unknown secretary, it might just have been bearable. But it *had* been Roz, and as a result their marriage was obliterated. Her children, their children . . . she couldn't even think about them just yet, beyond wondering how Jack would have explained her sudden disappearance from their lives. Though it horrified her to feel so little, she was simply too numb, too wounded at present to do otherwise.

But she had plenty of time in which to allow her tears and jumbled thoughts to come to the surface. For all Loulou's air of fragility, she worked punishing hours in the wine bar, sometimes fourteen or fifteen hours a day, and although she would pop up to her flat above the premises every couple of hours or so to check on Camilla, fry her an inedible snack or regale her with snippets of the wickedest gossip, Camilla was alone for the vast majority of the time.

'Come down and join us whenever you want,' Loulou urged on the fifth day, but Camilla backed off in alarm.

'I'd be the spectre at the feast,' she protested. 'Just listen to them.' From the flat they could hear a regular hum of music and voices punctuated with screams of laughter. Just the thought of joining them made her shudder.

Loulou pulled a face at her customers, through the living-room floor, then leapt up from her position on the leather sofa and ran over to give Camilla a hug that enveloped her in a cloud of Chanel.

'I know, I know. *Bloody* people – how dare they have fun whilst you're going through hell? But just remember, Cami. At a rough guess I'd estimate that eighty per cent of that crowd downstairs have been through something similar once in their lives. Most of them are divorced, at *least* once, and even those who are married aren't necessarily happy. I know it's no comfort to you at the moment but *no-one* goes, through life without getting hurt. And those that do,' she added paradoxically, with a dismissive gesture of her slender hands, 'are such God awful shits that the rest of us wouldn't want to be like them anyway.'

'Like Jack,' said Camilla, shredding an amber rosebud which had unaccountably found its way out of its silver vase and into her restless fingers. Loulou vigorously shook her head.

'No! OK, he's a shit, but I'll bet you he's as miserable as sin right now. The difference between the two of you is that he deserves it and you don't, but what you have to do is to come out on top. You've got two more days of feeling sorry for yourself, Cami, then it's time to get going with the old rehab. In a year's time I *guarantee*,' she thumped the coffee table now for emphasis, making their wine glasses shudder, 'that you'll be able to face Jack and feel sorry for the bastard. You're going to win this one and I'm going to help you do it.'

Loulou had far more faith in her than she did herself, Camilla thought wearily when she was alone once more. Sinking back into the soft leather of the settee she closed her eyes and pictured Jack, imagining what he might be doing at this moment. Saturday afternoon. On the one hand he could be in bed with Roz – her mind instinctively recoiled from the thought – but alternatively he could be sitting alone, as she was, in their living-room regretting his behaviour and wishing he had never met Roz in the first place. Funny, until Loulou had mentioned it just now it had never occurred to her that Jack might be unhappy, as well. She felt her self-esteem rise by a single, hesitant notch and realized to her amazement that she was smiling.

'You caused it. You do something to help,' said Loulou, her expression rigid. Roz, unused to criticism from anyone, particularly the woman she regarded as her closest friend, stared back at her in astonishment. A small knot of unease formed in the pit of her stomach.

'Lou, you know damn well I had no idea that Jack was Camilla's husband until a couple of weeks ago. It's not as if I did it on purpose . . . that would have been *really* tacky. And now I've told you I have no intention of seeing him any more. Isn't that enough? Do I really have to help her, as well?'

'Of course you really have to help her as well, you selfish bitch,' yelled Loulou, causing her bar staff to smile and the customers at adjoining tables to nudge each other in anticipation of one of her famous outbursts. 'She's lost her husband, her kids and her home. Right now she's upstairs wearing my last ex-husband's dressing-gown because none of my clothes fit her and she doesn't even have any of her own. Camilla has nothing left in the *world* at this moment. All I'm asking you to do is go to her house, pick up some things and get some money from her old man so that she can start getting herself straightened out. I've offered to lend her some cash, but she's too proud.'

'You could go yourself,' Roz pointed out, relieved that Loulou had at least stopped shouting.

'We've got people off sick and this place is a madhouse. I simply can't take the time off at the moment. It's your turn to do something decent for a change.'

Loulou was looking grimmer by the second and Roz understood that she was cornered. By Loulou and . . . of all people . . . Camilla.

'OK, I'll go this afternoon,' she conceded, her tone deliberately casual. 'But I think you should know that I'm not exactly Jack's favourite mistress at the moment. He called me yesterday and asked me to live with him.'

'And?' said Loulou, equally casually.

Roz shrugged and smiled. 'I told him to go play with the traffic.'

Chapter 6

The moment Loulou emptied the four suitcases of clothes into a heap in the centre of her living-room floor, she realized she'd made a big mistake.

Practically everything Camilla owned was beige with elasticated waists and miles of room for growth. It was all perfectly hideous, she thought faintly; just seeing it in the middle of her precious scarlet and gold living-room made her feel slightly ill.

Camilla, evidently thinking otherwise, gave Loulou an awkward hug. 'It's so kind of you to have gone to all this trouble. Having my own clothes ... it makes everything seem less strange ...'

I can't say it, thought Loulou, I mustn't say a word, I simply *mustn't*, but – oh dear – I can't help it.

'I'm sorry, darling, but you can't possibly wear these clothes,' she burst out helplessly, her blonde hair flying as she shook her head in despair. 'They're too awful ... depressing ... most of them, anyway,' she amended hastily, glimpsing the stricken expression on Camilla's face. 'Cami, they really aren't *you*.'

'Of course they're me,' protested Camilla. 'I chose them!'

'Well, maybe they *were* you,' Loulou explained, edging towards the heap which reminded her so much of a dead elephant and pulling from it a grey knitted dress with a high frilly collar and fluted sleeves. 'But they aren't any more. Just look at this, Cami. It's hideous. It won't do anything for anyone, least of all the person wearing it.'

Camilla looked at it, drooping sadly from Loulou's fingers, then transferred her attention to Loulou's pencil-slim figure tightly encased from neck to knees in crimson velvet.

'If I had a figure like you I might be able to get away with it,' she struggled to explain. 'If I wore an outfit like yours I'd look like a haemorrhage.'

Loulou laughed and tossed the dress behind the settee. 'So you try and camouflage yourself instead. Don't worry, darling, after a couple more weeks living on the food I cook for you, you *will* have a figure like mine. But in the meantime we'll go shopping and buy you a few replacements for all this. It all has to go, Cami. I'm going to get you noticed in future. And,' she added sternly, seeing the woebegone expression on Camilla's face, 'I'm going to make sure you *enjoy* being noticed!'

Roz's conscience was bothering her. And the mere fact that it was bothering her only served to alarm her all the more, since much of her life and almost her entire career had flourished simply because she didn't allow her conscience to get in the way of anything at all.

Since leaving the traumatic years of her adolescence behind her, she had managed to build herself an entirely satisfactory life. Her dazzling career in television had almost been too easily achieved. It had begun as a bet by a friend who had challenged Roz to sleep with a producer they had met at a particularly drunken party. The producer, proud of his reputation as a stud, had been so humiliated by his disastrous performance – blighted by at least a dozen tumblers of rum punch – and so grateful for Roz's patient understanding that he had promptly offered her a job as his assistant. And from the moment that Roz had first stepped into the TV studios with their aura of chaotic glamour and barely controlled tension, she had known that this was exactly what she wanted to do with her life.

From then on her natural drive asserted itself. Friendships were forged and lost, useful lovers came and went, and she quickly learnt that clever ideas could be borrowed, adapted and relaunched as her own. It wasn't dishonest because everyone else was doing it too; Roz simply ensured that she was heard and taken notice of with greater efficiency than anyone else. And it had culminated, in just six years, with the glittering prize of her very own chat show, 'Memories'.

Her personal life had been equally ruthlessly planned, and she had always taken care to ensure that her career remained entirely separate from her private social life. The lovers from those two worlds were strictly segregated, her diaries a miracle of modern planning.

The idea of marriage was anathema to Roz, a silly game she neither wanted nor needed to play. Other women's husbands were fair game, but the thought of getting one of her own quite simply chilled her. Before you knew it he'd be demanding to know where you'd been the night before and searching your pockets for clues.

No, lovers were far more sensible and understanding, and until now she'd always been lucky.

Nico, it went without saying, was divine. Her horoscope had warned her that she was in for a spectacular weekend and it had been even better than that. Meeting him at one of Loulou's famously debauched parties and spending the next three days in bed with him had been a coup by anybody's standards.

After that her very lack of interest had bound him to her and now, over a year later, the affair was still going strong. As long as Nico continued to propose marriage to her and as long as she refused to accept, there was no reason why anything should happen to spoil it . . .

Darling Sebastian on the other hand . . . Roz's lips curved into a smile at the thought of him. Sebastian would never dream of asking her to marry him, yet their long-standing affair meant more to her than almost anything else in her life. What could be more romantic, after all, than a relationship forged over fifteen years ago and maintained between two countries for such an amazing length of time. Sebastian took pride in her career successes, whilst spiralling equally dramatically up the banking ladder in Zurich. They were a couple of achievers, he was fond of telling her, who had their lives under perfect control and knew how to keep them that way. The brevity of her flying visits to Zurich and his own occasional weekends in England when he could manage to juggle his schedule were exactly what they both needed to keep their relationship exciting and alive. And if Roz ever felt that maybe their time together needn't be quite so ruthlessly rationed she made sure she kept those thoughts to herself. She and Sebastian were two of a very particular kind and she wasn't going to do *anything* which might risk frightening him off.

No, Sebastian and Nico were perfect, just as they were. Jack had been fairly perfect, too. Until he had gone and spoilt everything, of course, by reminding her that somewhere, deep down, she did still possess the tattered remains of a conscience.

'Talk to me, Nico,' said Roz with a hint of impatience. 'I don't always just want sex, you know.'

'You surprise me,' Nico grinned, sliding his hand slowly up her thigh and experiencing the usual thrill when he reached the top of her sheer silk stocking and the even silkier texture of warm, bare skin. Stockings and suspenders never failed to turn him on, even if his hand seemed to be having quite the opposite effect upon Roz this evening.

'Sometimes,' she continued crossly, removing the offending hand as if it were a dead animal, 'I'd prefer it if you treated me as a friend instead of a lover.'

Nico responded with a wink. 'Can't we be both?'

Glaring at him, Roz snapped back: 'Can't you be serious?' God, he was purposely trying to irritate her and tonight of all nights she could do without it, she thought with rising frustration. Sebastian would have taken her seriously, would have realized that she wasn't in the mood for jokes – if he weren't in bloody Zurich. Jack was out of the window now, so Nico was all she had left. She really needed another man, she decided, closing her eyes and falling back against the *chaise-longue*.

Nico rose to his feet, crossed to the drinks cabinet and poured himself a large Scotch.

'So tell me what's on your mind,' he said eventually, still with his back to Roz. 'It is man trouble, I take it?' It cheered him somewhat to discover that the thought of Roz with another man no longer lacerated him with jealousy. After thirteen months, maybe he was beginning to grow out of the obsession which had at first gripped him so fiercely that he hadn't been able to control his feelings towards her. Falling in love – or lust – with a bitch wasn't exactly conducive to happiness. He'd already realized that, to his great cost. But as Loulou had said when he'd last met her at Vampires, nice people were so unutterably boring the only way to last an evening in their company was to either get drunk or fall asleep. And no-one had ever fallen asleep when they were talking to Roz.

'It's woman trouble, actually,' she said now, kicking off her high heels and swinging her legs up on to the *chaise*. 'Makes a change, I suppose. And no, I'm not turning into a dyke,' she added, displaying the first flicker of humour since his arrival at the cottage that evening. 'You remember that letter I received from someone I was at school with? She wanted to meet me for a drink.'

Nico nodded, returning to sit beside her and carefully not registering any surprise when Roz curled up against him, kittenlike and seeking comfort. Her dark head nestled against his shoulder and he placed his free arm around her, enjoying the unexpected, friendly intimacy and breathing in the clean scent of her freshly washed hair.

'You didn't want to see her,' he remembered, 'and I couldn't understand why. Presumably you did, though.'

'We bumped into each other quite by accident in Harrods and she invited me to a dinner party. Loulou as well. I still didn't really want to go – I suppose you'd made me feel vaguely guilty.'

Roz, he reflected, was a man's woman, instinctively mistrusting her own sex because she expected them to behave as she herself did. It was odd, Nico felt, that in fact the only female friend she did have was Loulou, who was so very attractive and who by any standards could be regarded as a threat or a rival. Women like Roz, in his experience, almost invariably had plain or unattractive friends who could never hope to compete with them.

'What was she like?' He was beginning to enjoy playing the role of amateur psychiatrist. 'Gorgeous?' Had she somehow managed to make Roz feel inadequate, he wondered, amusement mingling with disbelief.

'God, no!' she almost laughed aloud at the idea. 'Camilla's

turned into every teenager's nightmare of what it could be like to hit thirty. She looks like the before pictures in those before-and-after-I-lost-a-hundredweight adverts. She's got two children, no dress sense and she looks so pathetically eager to please all the time – like an optimistic rabbit – that I just want to throw something heavy at her . . .' Roz's voice trailed off as she remembered how Camilla had thrown that enormous bowl of chrysanthemums over Jack. She had been amazed at the time that Camilla had had the imagination to pull off such a magnificent stunt. Privately, she had been betting on a torrent of tears and a rapid retreat to a locked room.

'So why is she woman-trouble?' persisted Nico, offering her his glass of Scotch and noticing as Roz reached out to take it that several fingernails showed distinct signs of having been bitten. That worried him more than anything else – Boadicea was more likely to bite her nails than ice-cool, perfectly groomed Roz.

'Because I've been . . . seeing,' she chose her words carefully, 'her husband.'

The ormolu clock above the fireplace carried on ticking as if nothing had happened and Nico stared at it, willing himself to feel similarly unconcerned. He was an Italian, but he had been trying for months to overcome – or at least hide – his innate Italian jealousy. And it wasn't as if he hadn't realized, he told himself carefully, that Roz was seeing other men beside himself. It just wasn't particularly pleasing to be told about them, even if he had practically dragged the truth out of her tonight.

'You mean you've been having an affair with him,' he said, needing to hear it confirmed absolutely. Christ, he thought, I must be a bloody masochist.

'Yes.'

'Do you love him?'

Roz shook her head, then raised herself away from him to meet his gaze. Nico's slanting green eyes were filled with pain and such desolate sadness that she wished she hadn't told him. He was the last person in the world she wanted to hurt, but the need to talk – her own selfish need to share her problems – had overwhelmed her like a great tidal wave, and she had been unable to stop herself. Now she wished she hadn't said it. It was just one more piece of evidence proving that she was a total bitch.

'So you've been having an affair with this married guy, but you don't love him,' continued Nico, his voice an expressionless drawl. Do you love me, he longed to say, but you could only take masochism so far in one evening. Roz didn't lie and he couldn't cope with her devastating truthfulness at this moment.

Please, please don't ask me, prayed Roz silently at the same time, her fingers tightening on his arm. She knew Nico well enough to know exactly what was going through his mind.

'So what's the problem – he doesn't want to see you any more? I can understand that, of course,' said Nico, attempting to inject some humour into the conversation. 'An ugly, dried-up old spinster like you.'

Roz smiled bleakly, grateful for the feeble joke but realizing at the same time that she was in danger of bursting into tears. Kindness was a far more effective method of making her cry than arguments and recriminations.

'He wants to marry me.'

I want to marry you, thought Nico. Aloud he said: 'Doesn't he have a minor obstacle in his path at the moment – like his wife?'

'Would you be an angel and pour us both another drink?' said Roz resignedly. 'I think I'd better tell you exactly what happened at Camilla's disastrous dinner party.'

Chapter 7

'Right, your week of mourning is up. Today is the first day of the rest of your life,' announced Loulou cheerfully, jerking Camilla into wakefulness. It was the first decent night's sleep she'd had since leaving Jack.

'What's this?' she asked lazily, as a tray was thrust into her lap, and Loulou had to lift it for a few seconds whilst she struggled into a sitting position. The Georgian silver tray was covered with an exquisite cloth of creamy Brussels lace; upon it was a cereal bowl, a crystal vase containing a single white rose, and a narrow crystal glass.

'The cereal bowl is empty,' she ventured, and Loulou shook a finger as she collapsed on the side of the bed.

'Your eyesight is worse than you realize, my girl. That bowl contains your breakfast. Here,' she thrust a soup spoon into Camilla's hand. 'Enjoy.'

Once Camilla had finished her bowl of breakfast Bollinger with Loulou watching over her like a nanny, they drank a toast with more of the same to 'The new Camilla.'

'But I'm thirty-two,' she protested.

'You can be new at any age, darling. Personally I plan to be new at seventy, when I shall dye my hair burgundy and take a marvellous lover young enough to be my grandson. Now hurry up and drink your drink – it's time to give your poor battered ego a boost. On second thoughts, I'll drink your drink and deprive you of a few more calories. You go and jump on the scales.'

Lightheaded with champagne Camilla did as she was told, tottering giddily towards the bathroom and shedding her nightdress as she went. It was amazing, she thought hazily, how quickly her inhibitions had fallen away since she had been staying here with Loulou. Until last week she would never have dreamt that she could walk around naked in front of another person – she had been far too self-conscious to do so in Jack's presence – but when Loulou took her bath each evening she demanded that Camilla sit on the loo seat and hear her gossip, and it had made her own inhibitions seem ludicrous.

'I think I've lost weight,' she called out uncertainly, wishing she had her glasses and peering fuzzily down at the scales.

'You daft, drunk, half-cut cow,' said Loulou affectionately, appearing beside her and scrutinizing the scales with the eye of a connoisseur. 'Last week you told me you weighed nearly eleven stone. You're down to ten stone and half a pound. Between your lousy husband and my even lousier cooking you've managed to lose almost a stone. Didn't you even realize?' she exclaimed and Camilla shook her head, scarcely able to believe it herself. Loulou had given her a week in which to get over Jack and since she was used to obeying his orders, she had accepted it without question. Jack was almost all she had thought about – there had been no time to consider the fact that her bulk was disappearing almost of its own accord.

'You'll be a respectable size fourteen,' said Loulou with satisfaction. 'Now get some clothes on, you brazen hussy, and we'll go and stun Knightsbridge with it.'

It wasn't until four o'clock that afternoon that Camilla realized exactly how well planned Loulou's campaign had been, and she was deeply touched by the enormous effort her friend had made. Incredibly she was being transformed before her very eyes – and it was her eyes which had been the first to be transformed. When the optician had fitted her with tinted soft contact lenses her grey-blue eyes had instantly become a thing of the past. Now they were of a sapphire blue shade so deep they bordered on violet, and the effect of the colour was almost magical.

Still blinking, she had next been whisked into 'Faces First', run by Suki, a friend of Loulou's, for the first professional make-up of her life. By shading and highlighting her face with squashy, feather-soft brushes Suki had given her a bone structure she had never known existed.

Stunned, Camilla watched her reflection in the stagelit mirror as Suki deftly altered her appearance. She wasn't just a changed person; she was a completely different one. Now she looked like one of those women whom she had always envied. She looked elegant, immaculate . . . and far, far more self-assured than she felt. But at the same time Camilla realized that she was also beginning to *feel* more self-assured than she had for many years. It was as if a small, new leaf was slowly unfurling within her, preparing to grow and take root, and suddenly Jack began to seem less important. Guiltily catching herself wondering for a moment what he would think if he could see her now, she firmly thrust the thought out of her mind. A far more worthwhile exercise was wondering what an unattached, non-philandering, thoroughly *decent* man would think if he saw her now, for although the question was purely academic at this stage – it was still nice to think that other people might find her attractive.

'I've finished, love,' said Suki, standing back at last and

surveying her work with approval. 'And if I say so myself, you look smashing. Special occasion is it, tonight? Got a hot date?'

'It's a very special occasion,' interjected Loulou firmly before Camilla could reply. 'And yes, she's got a hot date. With me.'

'Explosion', with its aggressively trendy black and gold decor and loud, finger-snapping stylists, was the kind of hairdressing salon Camilla would have run a mile from but with Loulou gripping her arm and dragging her up the front steps, she didn't have a lot of choice in the matter.

'Don't go green on me now,' she said briskly. 'Rocco's the best scissor-merchant in town and heaven knows, he's what you need with your hair.' Which was more or less what Rocco, a blond Italian Cockney with flashing green eyes and a bewitching smile, had to say when he ran disparaging fingers through Camilla's lank, dark blonde hair.

' 'Orrible, 'orrible,' he murmured, surveying the disaster area. 'Still, never mind. The worse it is when they come in,' he said cheerfully to Loulou who had pulled up a stool beside them, 'the better they look when you finish with 'em. Now don't even ask me what I'm going to do,' he added sternly, turning to face Camilla once more. 'Just keep quiet and trust me. And if you don't like the result, you can take the scissors to me own 'air. Deal?'

Two hours later Camilla stared into the mirror, her new eyes reflecting anguish.

'I hate it,' she said flatly. 'It's a disaster. It doesn't suit me, it's a terrible colour . . .'

Unable to go on, she bit her lower lip and gritted her teeth hard, but the smile she was trying so hard to suppress was proving uncontrollable. Her mouth twitched and the smile began to spread, becoming wider and wider until it dissolved into laughter and her whole body shook with it. 'It's sensational,' she cried, shaking her head and watching as the tumbling, silver and gold waves bounced miraculously back into place. 'I can't believe it, I don't know how to thank you both . . .'

'You could start by promising never to pull a stunt like that again,' said Rocco, leaning back against the wall and clutching his heart. 'For just a second there I thought you was serious, sweetie. 'Ad the old ticker going a bit I can tell you, to think that you was goin' to set about me own 'air with a vengeance.'

'Ah, Camilla, you shouldn't tease poor Rocco,' scolded Loulou with a smile. 'She has a wicked sense of humour, I'm afraid,' she confided to him and Camilla felt the shy green leaf within her unfold a fraction further, as she realized with a surge of joy and amazement that it was the first joke she'd played in years. And she had done it without even thinking about it.

'The last time I was in Harrods was when I bumped into Roz,' she murmured, shivering slightly at the memory as they entered the hallowed green portals.

'You've come a long way since then, baby,' said Loulou dismissively, winking at her favourite doorman and making a beeline for the perfume hall. 'Nothing boosts a woman's ego like her favourite scent, so we'll just treat ourselves in here and then it's upstairs to spend the real money.' She sighed, closing her eyes in ecstasy. 'And you have the even greater pleasure of knowing that it's Jack's money you're spending.'

'I won't spend too much of it,' argued Camilla, feeling suddenly guilty. 'I should really be using it sensibly, looking for somewhere to live. There's enough money for a deposit on a flat . . .'

'The clothes you'll be buying will be an *investment*, dummy. By the time we've finished you'll look so great you won't *need* a deposit for a flat. At least a dozen love-struck men will be queuing up to buy one for you and you can say, "Only Belgravia would do, I'm afraid. Well, maybe Mayfair at a pinch . . ." '

'Loulou!' exclaimed Camilla in dismay.

'Ah, you see you aren't the only one who can make wicked little jokes,' replied Loulou with a grin.

'Now what we need is colour,' she explained, managing to collar a salesgirl. 'My friend here has just returned from the great Australian outback – haven't you, Sheila? – and she needs a complete new wardrobe. She's allowed one little black dress, a Donna Karan of course, but apart from that we want colour and lots of it. And no office clothes, if you catch my drift.'

'No office clothes, madam,' repeated the salesgirl solemnly. 'If you'd like to follow me . . .'

Chapter 8

It was like the Christmas mornings she remembered from childhood, thought Camilla, as she surveyed her new personality, strewn around her in shimmering piles like some incredibly upmarket jumble sale. Sensitive with wonder, her fingertips stroked the ivory satin shirt, experiencing the texture as if it were a new and marvellous food, whilst her eyes feasted upon the fuchsia pink Nicole Farhi strapless evening dress, the impeccably cut white wool loose jacket and matching trousers, the striped silk jacket in ice-cream shades of pink and lilac, the plain, wide shouldered taffeta dress by Jasper Conran which was of exactly the same lapis-lazuli shade as her eyes . . .

'Now I need another cash injection to pay the dry-cleaning bills,' murmured Camilla, who had been devoted to polyester for the last ten years. She tried to feel ashamed of her extravagance but it wouldn't happen. Her mouth kept stretching into a wide smile of pure satisfaction and the Christmas-morning sensation simply refused to go away.

'I'll go and see Jack tomorrow, see what I can do,' Loulou assured her, keeping a straight face. 'I'll just say: Hi, Jack. Your poor cheated-on little wife blew the cash you gave her and now she'd like the same amount again. This time she might even get around to buying some knickers. On second thoughts, why bother? Who needs knickers anyway?'

'You wouldn't dare!' exclaimed Camilla, appalled. Then she

thought, why not? There really was no reason why Jack shouldn't be shocked. He no longer mattered to her. The children, however, were another matter. 'How did he seem when you went to see him?' she asked for the first time, unable to hide the anxiety in her voice. It was no good, she couldn't cut him out of her life so quickly and completely. A husband wasn't a bad appendix. She still cared about him. And about Charlotte and Toby, desperately.

'He was OK,' said Loulou casually, having felt it unwise to mention at the time that it had been Roz who had made the visit. And judging by the look on Camilla's face it wasn't quite the moment to admit to it now. 'He doesn't deserve it, but he's just about OK. Hey, let's not spoil a good day talking about that lower-than-dirt little creep. I've got to get downstairs and hurl a few insults in the direction of my beloved customers. You,' she concluded, circling her index finger in Camilla's direction, 'have fifteen minutes to change into that divine little Jasper Conran creation and admire yourself in the mirror. Then you come down and join me, and we'll watch how far Dirty Dicky O'Neill's eyes pop out of his head when he clocks you.'

'I'm a fraud,' Loulou told Christo, her favourite barman, as she watched him expertly uncork four bottles of Beaujolais. 'A bullshitter and a fraud. *How*,' she demanded, tearing a glossy leaf from a potted palm with unnecessary ferocity, 'do I have the nerve to stand there and tell Camilla not to pine over her God-awful husband, when for the last three days all I've been doing is pining for one of mine – and he's even more of a bastard than hers.'

'Which one?' said Christo calmly, taking the spiky-edged

frond of greenery from Loulou's agitated fingers and dropping it into the bin behind the bar.

'Mackenzie,' she admitted, her face the picture of gloom. 'The very worst one, of course. You'd think I'd have the sense to find some better way of spending my time – like sitting on a bed of nails or playing Russian roulette – but no, I have to keep thinking about him, all day and all night, and at the same time put on a brave face for Camilla. It's too much.'

'What about Julian?'

'Gone to Sweden for a fortnight. Do you think that's why I've started thinking about Mac again?' Loulou gave him a wry smile. 'You're absolutely right, of course. Celibacy doesn't agree with me – it's just that I don't think Camilla could cope with it if I had a man in my bed while she was staying with me. Seems a bit heartless, somehow.'

'Careful, Lou. If people could hear you now your reputation would be in tatters. This crowd,' he indicated with a nod of his head the party of Sloanes who regularly inhabited Vampires, 'would die laughing if they thought you had a conscience.'

'Oh, sure,' said Loulou disdainfully. 'They'd wet their knickers all right. But they aren't going to find out, are they? Because if you so much as breathed one single word, my darling, I would garotte you with your own cheese wire. And don't think I'm talking about your neck.'

Loulou Marks always maintained that her earliest memory was of pointing to a stranger on a train and shouting, 'Mummy, *look* at that ugly man.' Her mother, smacking her so hard that she hadn't been able to sit down for days, had uttered for the first –

but by no means the last – time those immortal words: 'Loulou, don't be so *rude*.'

It was ironic, she felt, that her hugely successful living was now made from being as rude as she liked, to as many people as possible. Insulting them came as naturally to Loulou as breathing, and they cherished her for her ability to come out with what everyone else longed to say but did not dare. By a stroke of marvellous good fortune what could have been a handicap had turned instead into a wonderful way of making a living and still having enough left over to satisfy her ludicrously expensive tastes in cars, clothes . . . and men.

Loulou married Jerry Nash on her nineteenth birthday. The wedding, held in church, was the whitest her guests had ever seen, thanks in part to Celestine Marks's fond belief that her daughter was still a virgin. She was also practical enough to realize, however, that the marriage was unlikely to last and insisted upon at least one church wedding, 'Because in future you might only be able to do eet in Registry offices, *ma petite*, and they are too 'orrible for words.'

Equally firmly convinced that this was the Love Affair of all time, and that she and Jerry would live for ever in the most spectacular married bliss imaginable – what did mothers know, after all? – Loulou happily went along with Celestine's plans. There were a few anxious moments when Jerry announced that no way was he going to wear a morning suit, or any suit at all for that matter; he was a singer in a band and he was going to wear his best pink lurex jacket with the silver lapels and matching drainpipe trousers – or nothing.

The anxiety and arguments lasted precisely thirty-five min-utes, until Richard Marks drew his prospective son-in-law into the less heated atmosphere of the kitchen and spoke to him as persuasively as he knew how. When they emerged, Jerry announced with a casual shrug that OK, he'd wear the penguin suit after all, no big deal, and Celestine heaved a sigh of relief that could almost have been heard in Paris. Richard, thinking that £500 was a small price to pay for his beloved wife's happiness, reflected at the same time with deep sadness that now he knew precisely what kind of person his daughter was marrying.

The wedding, amazingly, went off without a hitch. The marriage itself, however, to no-one's real surprise, was a ghastly tangle of hitches from start to finish and lasted exactly seven months and three days. When Loulou returned home from work one day and discovered her handsome husband making love on the staircase to a wanton looking redhead clutching a 'Save the Seals' collecting tin, she wrenched the heavy tin from her hand and brought it down on Jerry's head so fiercely that he slid out of the woman and down the stairs with a series of jolts which crippled his ardour for weeks. The scalp wound, requiring seventeen stitches, was almost negligible in comparison.

The divorce, on the other hand, had been the most painful experience of Loulou's life, so painful that she had dealt with it in the only way she knew how – by pretending that the marriage had never happened. In the space of a fortnight she had found herself and her five large suitcases a new life in Glasgow.

'Have you done much bar work before?' asked the bar manager, and Loulou fell instantly in love all over again. With his deep voice and brown eyes and black tangled curls; with that heavenly Scottish accent, those clinging ultra-faded button-fly Levis and thrillingly taut brown forearms; with the sheer *height* of him . . .

and oh, when he smiled he revealed the most bewitching dimple she had ever seen . . .

'Speak to me,' he commanded humorously, passing a strong, beautifully shaped hand in front of her eyes. 'I said, have you ever done . . .'

'Oh sure, tons,' lied Loulou absently, struggling to regain her senses in the face of such heavenly perfection. Her stomach was down by her knees somewhere and she wasn't at all sure that she wasn't about to keel off the bar stool, her sense of balance appearing to have left her completely in this moment of revelation. It absolutely had to be love.

'You're supposed to tell me about it,' the bar manager reminded her gently. He had introduced himself as Mac, she remembered. Such a wonderful, romantic, kissable name . . .

'Yes. Sorry. Um, well . . .' With a suitably vague gesture she almost succeeded in knocking over a soda syphon and three glasses.

'God, sorry! Yes, I've worked a lot in clubs and pubs . . . down south. London, Bristol, Bath. Can I have the job?' she blurted out helplessly, her silver-grey eyes wide and appealing. She would die if he turned her down now, just when she had fallen so desperately in love with him.

Meanwhile Mac was wrestling equally as desperately with his conscience. He made and lived by his own unbreakable rules and the one that was causing him trouble at this moment was the one which stated firmly that he would never get involved with a fellow member of staff. He'd seen the unhappy results of other such relationships too often to hope that they might not happen to him. It was always, but *always*, a fatal mistake.

Yet here was this gorgeous girl, lying her head off – she certainly wasn't twenty-three for a start and he seriously doubted whether she had ever been on the working side of a bar – and gazing at him with such an angelic, hopeful expression that all he wanted to do was take her to bed. But if he refused her the job there was a chance that he might never see her again and that was every bit as unthinkable as becoming involved with a member of staff.

Well, he decided suddenly, he'd just have to make damn sure that he would see her again. But really, it was asking too much of his hormones to expect him to be able to work alongside this beautiful blonde angel and to keep his hands to himself.

'I think, perhaps, that giving you the job here might not be a terribly good idea,' he began to explain slowly, but his words were cut off by a shriek of agonized dismay that could have shattered every glass in the house.

'No!' Loulou gasped, unable to bear the thought of losing him or to tolerate the fact that he was rejecting her. Couldn't he *feel* the chemistry between them, for God's sake? Was he *completely* unaware of the way things were? 'Oh, please don't turn me down,' she begged frantically. 'I've got to have a job – I've no money and nowhere to live and I'll have to sleep in a doorway and I'd work so hard you wouldn't believe it. I *love* this place,' declared Loulou with another sweeping gesture to indicate the smoky, tatty public bar with its nicotine-stained windows and battered wooden furniture. 'And I swear to you that I'll be the best barmaid you ever had. Please, please give me a chance to prove it. Please, Mac? Will you? Please?'

I don't *have* barmaids, thought Mac with unhappy resignation. Clearly the hormones would have to wait. In the face of such tumultuous persuasion, how on earth could he refuse her this chance when she was so desperately in need of work?

'OK,' he said with a reluctant grin that sent Loulou's heart plummeting once more 'You win. When do you want to start?'

Chapter 9

Mac broke his unbreakable rule within forty-eight hours. He had probably broken it within forty-eight seconds, since his involvement with Loulou was forged almost instantly, but he gamely managed to hold out for almost two whole days before being inveigled into her narrow bed in the tiny room above the pub.

It had been hopeless, pretending to himself that it wouldn't happen. Loulou was so adoringly besotted with him, and so determined that he should in turn be besotted with her, that he simply had no choice in the matter. When she had called downstairs as he was preparing to leave after the lunchtime opening, asking him to please come up and kill a monstrous spider which was taking up most of the bath, he had semi-suspected that her intentions weren't entirely honourable.

When she opened the door, wearing only high heels and an utterly bewitching smile, he knew for certain. Only later did he learn that Loulou had never possessed an honourable intention in her life.

At first, however, the relationship worked perfectly. Mac's heart wasn't in his job, it was merely a means of saving money. He was a photographer, and one day he intended to be a *known* photographer, right up there along with Lichfield and Bailey. Every penny he earnt went towards either a better camera, a newer lens, or more film. Being a bar manager was only work, whereas photography was life itself.

Loulou, on the other hand, after a series of mistakes so awful they rapidly turned into mini-legends, took to her new-found career like a hippo to mud. The dour, working-class Glaswegian men who frequented the pub in order to escape their shrill, endlessly complaining wives gave the new barmaid a particularly hard time at first. She wasna even a Scot, for heaven's sake. But they found themselves reluctantly enchanted by her merciless barrage of repartee, her ability to out-swear even dirty Murdo McLean, and the way she habitually undercharged them for their drinks. Before long, the sons of these uncompromising, not easily impressed, men got to hear about the bonnie wee lassie from down South who had tipped the contents of an ice bucket down Jimmy McKendrick's trousers in order to cool off his 'nasty wee willy, the very, *very* smallest one I've ever had the misfortune to see.'

Full of admiration for the slip of a girl who had publicly humiliated Glasgow's most persistent flasher and had finally persuaded him to keep his parts private, the sons took to popping in for a quick drink with their fathers, then staying on to feast their eyes and ears upon Loulou Marks. She was unique in their experience, and so obviously *enjoyed* herself that her passion for life became infectious. The Ramsay Arms, previously a grimy, old men's pub of few words and no laughter, was totally rejuvenated within the space of two months, with Loulou buying the teller of the best joke each night an enormous drink, leading the singing which became a new nightly ritual, and organizing a never to be forgotten drag evening when even the most determinedly dour old Scotsman turned up in an ill-fitting dress and high heels.

'If I hadn't seen it with my own eyes, I would never have believed that this was possible,' said Mac, finishing his third roll of film. Loulou was planning a rogues' gallery of incriminating photographs above the bar. 'I never even knew that old Joey Blair *could* laugh.'

'I've just managed to bring the old devils out of themselves a little,' Loulou said modestly, trailing her fingers along the smooth curve of his hip in a deliberately provocative manner. She was so in love with this man, he really could have no idea. *He* was the only reason she had worked so hard to make the pub into a success. Happy punters were more likely to say 'and have one for yourself,' and every time they said it the jar beside the till gained another 80p. In two months the happy punters, unbeknown to themselves, had bought Mac a superb Nikon.

'You're a miracle,' he said now, reloading the camera and dropping a kiss on the very tip of Loulou's perfect nose.

'Then why don't you marry me?'

Only Mac's lightning reflexes saved the camera as it slipped from his hands. Catching it, and realizing that he was shaking, he placed it with care on the bar.

'Oh Lou, you don't mean it.'

'I do,' she said fearfully, watching his expression and finding that he was giving nothing away. 'I do, I do.'

'Sweetheart, you said that less than a year ago to Jerry, if you remember. You're not even twenty-one yet and already you're a divorcee. You can't just dive in all over again.'

'I can, I can,' insisted Loulou stubbornly. 'It's so different this time, you've got to believe me. More than anything in the world I want to be married to you.'

Around them, men in Crimplene dresses, the hairs on their legs poking through their American tan tights, sang 'Knees up, Mother Brown' and hurled their handbags into the air. Frozen in

Fast Friends

time, Loulou and Mac gazed into each other's eyes, oblivious to the noise and laughter.

'I'm poor,' said Mac eventually. 'It wouldn't be fair to you. You deserve so much more than anything I can give you.'

'I only *want* what you can give me. What *only* you can give me,' she said with mounting urgency. God, it was hard, proposing to a man with a conscience. 'Besides, I like being poor.'

Mac, struggling to do the right thing and slowly beginning to realize that yet again Loulou was willing him to do the opposite, was running out of excuses. He wanted to marry her, dammit – who wouldn't want to marry this gorgeous, gutsy girl, after all? – but he had plans for his life, real plans and marriage had long ago been ruthlessly edited out of them. Just as sleeping with a fellow member of staff had been. Oh shit, he thought, battling with his conscience. What the hell was he going to do?

'The novelty would soon wear off.' He attempted to sound adult and reasonable. 'Poverty's only ever fun for six months at the very most. You'd absolutely hate it, darling.'

Sensing that she was at last beginning to wear him down, Loulou shook her head so violently that the rippling silver blonde hair swung out in an arc, brushing Mac's face – just the way he liked it.

'I can work, we can make enough money not to be disgustingly poor, and you can concentrate on your photography. Stop giving me these bullshit reasons, Mac! Do you love me?'

Weakened, and hoping to God that this highly incriminating conversation wasn't being overheard – he would never live this down – he bent his dark head.

'You know I do. But that isn't . . .'

'Oh yes, it is!' intercepted Loulou forcefully, closing in now for the kill. 'That's *all* that matters. It's the very best reason in

73

the world for getting married and don't you dare argue with me any more. Now, I fully intend to marry you. So, will you marry me? It would make matters a great deal easier if you could just say yes.'

Those silver-grey eyes. That incredible hair. That delicious body. The incomprehensible female logic of the woman. And how could he possibly resist her unique personality?

'I do,' said Mac, smiling. 'I do.'

Loulou, replaying the memory of that evening in her mind, was appalled to find that her eyes had filled with hot, frustrated tears. Tears were quite out of the question, particularly at this moment. Camilla, the new Camilla, was making her entrance and it was a sure bet that she was feeling a lot worse than she was herself. Her marriage to Mac had lasted just ten months and Camilla had been married to Jack for ten years. Was the grief magnified twelvefold, she wondered, quite unable to assimilate how that must feel.

Swiftly, abandoning her own gloomy thoughts, Loulou slid down from her bar stool and moved quickly towards her friend. Apart from today's shopping excursion, this was Camilla's first venture into the outside world as a separated woman. And it was glaringly obvious.

'You look amazing,' Loulou told her, not quite truthfully. The make-up, hair and clothes were there, but Camilla still projected her ugly duckling mentality, her expression absolutely rigid with fear at the thought that any minute now she might be accused of masquerading as a swan. It was clear that she was still desperately in need of self-confidence, and Loulou knew exactly who could give it to her. Help was at hand in the form of Miles Cooper-Clarke and there he was, standing not 20 feet away at the opposite end of the bar. Now if Camilla would just stop looking like a terrified gerbil the evening stood a chance of being a success – the first small step along her long road to recovery.

Camilla, every bit as panic stricken as Loulou suspected, avoided looking at anyone at all by concentrating on the decor of Vampires instead. The first time she had been here she had been so overwhelmed at finding herself in the exhilarating company of both Roz and Loulou that the wine bar itself had quite escaped her notice. On this, her second sortie, she turned her attention entirely to the way Loulou had decorated her renowned bar.

From the black ceiling hung a single Victorian chandelier flinging facets of light like diamonds around the central area of the room. Gilt-framed oil-paintings were hung above the tables bordering the room, their haunting Gothic scenes cunningly lit from below in order to heighten their mystery. The only other source of light was from the many candles, grouped together on black plates so that the dripping crimson wax formed interlacing patterns, amid the stalagmite candles of all shapes and sizes.

The walls, too, were crimson, what Loulou called Vampire red, and the black marble floor was flecked here and there with droplets of the same crimson paint, so bloodlike – as Loulou had told Camilla with relish – that a murder could quite easily go unnoticed so long as the body was disposed of without a fuss.

All the tables and chairs were black, apart from two red velvet chesterfields which lined the entirely mirrored far wall, and these favoured seating positions were so zealously fought over that Loulou was frequently called upon to arbitrate and make the critical decision as to whom should be allowed to occupy them.

Camilla's attention was diverted now by Loulou's hand upon her arm as with the other she hailed a customer lounging at the other end of the gleaming black bar.

'Hey, Miles! I wanted to introduce my friend here to a good-looking man, but it looks as if I'll have to make do with you instead. Come over here and meet Camilla.'

Gulping down her entire glass of much needed white wine, Camilla wished at that moment that – much as she liked her friend – she could gag her. Only her trust in Loulou, who seemed convinced that this was the perfect way to get over Jack, prevented her from running out of the wine bar and back upstairs to the sanctuary of her bed. Maybe, just maybe, she thought helplessly, Loulou was right.

Miles Cooper-Clarke flashed his famous white-capped smile, smoothed his Clark Gable moustache with a practised gesture, and was only slightly put out by the realization that the attractive, well-rounded blonde whom Loulou wished him to meet was looking not at him, but determinedly down at her feet. A shy one, was she? No problem there, he decided, relishing the challenge! The quiet women were always the wildest once he succeeded in persuading them to drop their guard.

Oh God no, thought Camilla as Miles and his liberally applied cologne arrived before her. Eau Sauvage was what she had bought Jack for years, although he wasn't much of a cologne man and had only worn it under protest. Still, she must have unscrewed the bottle on his dresser a hundred times to inhale the clean-smelling scent and since he had never worn any other kind, she couldn't help but associate it with him.

'*Enchantée, mademoiselle,*' said Miles, who had been born and brought up in Kent. He bowed and extended an alarmingly well-manicured hand towards Camilla, who felt sick.

'Oh, cut the crap, Miles,' Loulou intervened, glimpsing the panicked expression in her friend's eyes. 'No need to push the boat out, she isn't that rich. Just be nice, for God's sake. *Normal* nice.'

'Who's normal and nice in Knightsbridge?' riposted Miles, but he toned down the megawatt smile for Camilla's benefit and shook her hand in a purely businesslike fashion. Miles Cooper-Clarke wasn't a gigolo, he just happened to find wealthy women more interesting and somehow more attractive than poor ones. And if it gave these dear wealthy women pleasure to buy him gifts, or to pay for their more extravagant outings together, how could it be wrong to refuse them? Loulou's friend was well dressed, but she didn't possess the vibes that told him she was wealthy, and judging by the look of thinly disguised terror in her rather pretty eyes he guessed that she was either newly separated from her husband or just out of a long-term affair. He'd seen that look of vulnerability too often before not to recognize it.

'Camilla. Why don't we just ignore Loulou and get to know each other? What would you like to drink?'

This isn't working, Camilla told herself, trying hard not to panic. I can't sit here and pretend I'm enjoying myself. Oh, how could Loulou do this to me?

'On the house,' said Loulou firmly, plonking a carafe of white wine on the bar between them. 'And I'm going to have to leave you now because apparently some joker has just emptied his dinner plate over his boyfriend's head in the restaurant. See you later.'

She disappeared through the door to the restaurant and Camilla felt as if her oxygen line had been cut. Her knuckles turned white as she watched Miles refill her glass. Just pretend he's a business colleague of Jack's and you've got to make polite conversation with him, she instructed herself fiercely. You've done it often enough before, after all. Ask him about his family, his home, his career and look *interested*. It'll be all over soon, like the dentist . . .

'Do you want to talk about it?' asked Miles, interrupting her disorganized thoughts, and Camilla turned white.

'Talk about what?'

'Whatever it is that's making you look as if you're sitting in the electric chair waiting for the switch to be pulled.' He had spotted the wedding ring by now, and past experience had taught him that women liked to talk about their problems. He listened, let them realize that he was on their side, and gradually they began to treat him like a friend. Then, once they had learnt to trust him it was easy to get them into bed. And this one, even if she didn't have money, looked as if she might be worth it anyway.

'Your husband,' prompted Miles. 'My guess is that he ran off with another woman. Am I right?'

Chapter 10

'This is becoming a bit of a habit,' said Loulou severely, eyeing Camilla like a schoolmistress although the effect was somewhat spoilt by the fact that she was naked. 'Now I'm not saying that it's necessarily a bad habit, but when I buy a carafe of wine I'd rather it was drunk than poured over a customer. Next time try and hang on until *they've* bought one.'

'I'm sorry, Lou.'

'Don't be sorry, darling. It was all quite in keeping with the atmosphere of Vampires, after all. But what on earth did poor old Miles do to deserve it?'

Camilla, who had been crying for four hours, wiped her bloodshot eyes with the edge of the duvet and shook her head.

'Nothing, really. I'm just not ready for men like him yet. He asked me if my husband had run off with another woman and made it sound so . . . commonplace . . . that I couldn't stand it. It was just as if he was guessing what I'd eaten for breakfast!'

'Oh, baby,' said Loulou sympathetically, patting Camilla's heaving shoulder. 'I suppose to Miles, it is commonplace. Like he said, who's nice and normal in Knightsbridge? Probably only you.'

'Will he complain about his suit being ruined?' sniffed Camilla, her conscience beginning to prick her, and Loulou laughed.

'It was clever of you to have thrown white wine over him, not red. If it makes you feel better you can pay for it to be dry cleaned, but I wouldn't. It'll teach him to be less insensitive next time.'

Camilla shivered beneath the bedclothes. 'There won't be a next time if I can help it.'

'Not you, dopey. I meant the next woman he meets. Every forty-five seconds,' she lied, improvising rapidly, 'another marriage in London bites the dust. That means an awful lot of grieving women falling prey to the so-called charms of men like Miles. You have to realize that you aren't the only one, Cami. It helps, truly it does.'

'Why is it always the women who have to suffer?' said Camilla resentfully. 'Don't the men ever go through it too?'

Loulou thought for a moment about her own ex-husbands. 'I think so,' she mused. 'A lot don't. But a few of them . . . I think they suffer as much as women. In a different way, somehow. But I promise you, Cami. Some men *do* go through it too.'

The Christmas spirit was beginning to get through to her at last, Camilla realized with relief, although at the same time she still felt vaguely guilty, as if she didn't deserve to feel this cheerful. Yesterday she had seen her children for the first time since leaving home two weeks ago and tomorrow she would see them again to give them their Christmas presents before Jack drove them to Yorkshire to spend the holiday with his parents and their noisy, cheerful family. Toby and Charlotte adored their grandparents and innumerable relations and were so excited by the prospect of seeing them that they had scarcely seemed to register the fact that Camilla would not be going with them.

The realization had both hurt and reassured her. Her own children, whom she was now missing terribly, didn't seem to mind at all that their mother had 'gone away for a holiday', greeting her as casually as if she had just returned from a visit to the supermarket, yet at the same time Camilla knew that it was far better for all of them that it should be like that. If Toby and Charlotte had clung to her, weeping and pleading with her not to leave, she would have been distraught, not knowing what to do.

As it was, she had been able to cope. Jack, knowing that she was coming back to the house to see the children, had left for the office early. Everything was clean and tidy. And Jennifer, the most competent nanny Camilla had ever known, had assured her that she was coping perfectly well and that Jack had increased her salary in order to cover the extra work entailed by Camilla's absence.

'Two children or three, it doesn't make much difference to me,' she assured Camilla with a wry smile. 'I give Jack the same food as the kids and tell him off if he leaves his shoes in the sitting-room.'

'Is he . . . home much?' asked Camilla hesitantly, unsure how to phrase the question uppermost in her mind. She didn't even know if Jennifer was aware of the circumstances surrounding her abrupt departure. Had Jack told her about Roz? Had Roz perhaps been there with him? She didn't really want to know, but some inner compulsion drove her to find out. Bravely, she met Jennifer's sympathetic gaze and tensed herself in preparation for her answer.

'Every night he comes home at six o'clock,' Jennifer replied straightforwardly. 'He doesn't go out, just watches television until it closes down, then he goes to bed.'

There, that wasn't so bad after all, thought Camilla. She had dared to ask, and had got the answer she wanted. Curiosity overcame her and she asked again.

'And how does he ... er ... seem, to you?'

Jennifer tried not to smile at the suitably vague terms Camilla was employing.

'I think he's seen the error of his ways, if that's what you mean,' she said simply, then reached across and squeezed Camilla's hand. 'Of *course* I know what happened at that party. I made him tell me. And you did the very best thing, Camilla, honestly. My father had an affair, but when Mum found out she didn't do anything about it because she was afraid to. When that affair ended he found another woman ... and then another ... and didn't even bother to pretend it wasn't happening. I hated him for it, and I'm afraid I despised my mother for her weakness, but she always said she couldn't manage without him, even though she was desperately unhappy with him.'

Recalling Loulou's words: 'There's a lot of it about,' Camilla swallowed and said, 'What happened?'

'Mum died,' said Jennifer simply, 'of cancer. My father remarried a year later and now he's having an affair with his secretary. You see, no-one's ever done anything to try and stop him. And that's why I'm glad *you've* had the guts to make a stand. The short, sharp, shock treatment, I suppose. Leave, give Jack a few weeks to realize what he's lost and what a bastard he's been, then come back and start again on equal terms. I'm all for it, Camilla. I'm completely on your side. When you decide to come home again he'll be as good as gold.'

In silence, Camilla gazed around at the well-loved objects in the living-room which were so familiar. Everything in the room was a reminder of some part of their lives together and she felt the dull ache of gathering tears as she turned to face Jennifer once more.

'But I'm not coming back,' she explained slowly. 'Not in a few weeks, not ever. I want to be with Toby and Charlotte, but I can't live with Jack again. That's all over. I can't forgive him, I'd never trust him, and I'd be just as unhappy as your mother was, wondering when he was going to do the same thing again. I've got a right to be happy, Jennifer, and it's *my* life to do what I want with. I'm sorry if this places an extra burden on you, but if you feel it's too much then we'll just have to find another nanny and of course you needn't worry about your references. We'd all hate to see you go, but I'd understand. I can't pretend, though, that this separation is temporary. I'm going to divorce Jack and it's only fair that you should know that now.'

As she spoke aloud the thoughts which until that moment she had only hesitantly considered, Camilla felt the tears recede and a sense of swelling pride take their place. She felt more convinced of the rightness of her actions than at any time before. She was making her own decisions, deciding the future of her own life, and at last realizing that she did, indeed, *have* a future without Jack.

It was a powerful, almost exhilarating sensation and in her triumph she was unable to suppress a new, confident smile that almost spilled into laughter.

Jennifer smiled back, recognizing the change in her employer and privately applauding it. If only her mother could have been as brave in the same circumstances, she thought, how different things might have been. Having had neither the strength nor the will to fight the battle with cancer, she had died. Maybe, just maybe, if her frame of mind had been more positive she might still be alive today.

'Don't worry about me,' she assured Camilla, her voice faintly husky now as her own emotions asserted themselves. 'There's no reason at all for me to leave. I'm very happy here and as I said before, the extra money Jack's paying me more than makes up for the extra work involved. I'll miss you not being here as well, of course, but I certainly won't leave.'

'Oh Jennifer, I'm so glad,' said Camilla with heartfelt relief.

For a few seconds both women were silent, listening to the muted screams and laughter of Charlotte and Toby as they played boisterously upstairs.

'There's just one other thing I'd like to say,' Jennifer ventured, almost diffidently.

'Go ahead,' said Camilla with concern, thinking Oh God, what now?

She waited whilst Jennifer scrutinized her.

'I have to tell you,' she began slowly, teasingly, then broke into a broad smile, 'you look absolutely . . . fantastic!'

Remembering Jennifer's words now as she held brightly patterned wrapping paper around one of the presents she had bought this morning for Charlotte and tearing a strip of Sellotape off with her teeth, Camilla experienced once again the flood of almost indecent pride which had swept over her in response to the compliment. She had promised herself that from now on she would always make the effort to look good. This morning, shopping for the children's Christmas gifts, she had swept into Harrods feeling wonderfully confident, not at all as she had felt that day when she had bumped into Roz.

Looking good, feeling good, she thought happily, and best of all . . . still losing weight!

'Spaghetti bolognese. With tons of garlic and mushrooms

and lots of red wine in the sauce,' Loulou had replied dreamily when Camilla had asked her last night what she would most like for Christmas.

'Difficult to gift-wrap,' she had remarked, dead-pan. 'And it might leak a bit, but if you're sure that's what you want . . .'

'Oh darling, I'm positive. All my *boring* old chef ever cooks is fillet steak and chicken and *boring* old lamb, and you know only too well what my own cooking's like. What my stomach yearns for is spaghetti. So *that's* what I most want for Christmas.'

Halfway through the seemingly endless task of wrapping presents, Camilla had suddenly decided that she would dash over to Fortnums, buy all the ingredients and make Loulou her longed-for spaghetti bolognese. They could share it before the wine bar reopened in the evening, and it would go a tiny way towards repaying her friend for her wonderful generosity over the last fortnight.

Now she hummed happily to herself as she moved about the kitchen, chopping mushrooms, crushing the garlic and stirring the simmering pan of minced beef in its thick tomato and basil sauce. Loulou had phoned through an hour earlier to let her know that she would be out for the afternoon, but that she would definitely be back by five and could she ask the chef to grill her a rare steak. Camilla had cheerfully agreed, and done no such thing. As she tipped half a bottle of rather good red wine into the heavy pan of sauce she told herself with determination that this would be the best spaghetti Loulou had ever eaten.

Nico parked the muddy white Ferrari on the double yellow lines outside Vampires and slid out of the driver's seat, shivering as the icy December wind penetrated his thin black sweatshirt.

After a day in the recording studios arguing with his sound engineer and accomplishing precisely nothing, he felt in need of Loulou's effervescent company. Ever since Roz's sudden withdrawal into herself she had been most unstimulating company and Nico found himself now beginning to run out of patience. How sympathetic could a man be, after all, when the woman he loved complained to him about the problems caused by one of her other lovers? She was a selfish bitch, he told himself not for the first time, and although he was sure that what he felt for her was love, he wasn't at all convinced that he actually *liked* Roz. It had been time, therefore, for a tactical withdrawal, and Loulou's was the ideal place to withdraw to. Also, less selfishly, he had some news for her concerning Mac, although whether she would regard it as good news or bad he wasn't sure.

Shivering violently, he pushed open the glossy black door bearing the discreet brass plate engraved with Loulou's initials and entered Vampires. The lunchtime session was almost over now; time had been called and only three or four parties of pre-Christmas revellers in varying degrees of drunkenness were left, attempting to gear themselves up for a return to their offices. Loulou, however, was nowhere in sight and Nico claimed the attention of one of the barmen while at the same time taking care not to catch the eye of any of the office girls. He wasn't in the mood for drunken propositions and an extended round of autograph signing, and alcohol-sodden females were the worst pain of all.

'Is Loulou upstairs?' he asked, and Christo shook his head.

Shit, thought Nico.

'She went out a little while ago, but she did say she wouldn't be that long,' Christo explained. 'If you come back in a couple of hours . . .' he hesitated, observing Nico's weary expression. He *was* a friend of Loulou's after all. 'Or maybe you'd prefer to wait upstairs for her. She wouldn't mind, would she?'

'If she did, I'd shoot her,' said Nico with a wry smile. 'Thanks, I'll go straight up. She'll probably come home and find me asleep . . .'

Damn, thought Christo a few seconds after Nico had disappeared up the stairs leading to Loulou's flat. I forgot to tell him that there was someone else there as well. Ah well, let's just hope that Camilla isn't a frenzied Nico Coletto fan – the poor fellow looks as if that's just what he doesn't need at this moment.

Since there was no point in knocking, Nico simply opened the door and marched straight into the flat. Abruptly he was plunged right back to his childhood as his senses were assailed by the most evocative, marvellous aroma of Italian cooking. It wasn't the first time it had happened, of course; whenever he entered an Italian restaurant the heady wafts of garlic and herbs instantly had the same effect, but this was *Loulou's* flat, and it had to be quite simply the last place on earth where he would have expected to encounter such sensational smells.

Chapter 11

Camilla, sandwiched inside Loulou's sunbed, heard the front door open and close and quickly switched off the power. Leaping to her feet and wrenching off the protective goggles, she hurried towards the bedroom door, wanting to enjoy Loulou's surprise when she saw the spaghetti bolognese.

'Merry Christmas!' she shouted happily, bursting into the living-room.

'And a very merry Christmas to you, too,' said Nico with a grin as he eyed her naked body with undisguised pleasure. Obviously one of Loulou's crazy friends. 'I'm beginning to feel better already. Are you really my Christmas present? Last year all I got was socks and handkerchiefs, but this is much more . . .'

'Aaaargh!' wailed Camilla, wishing she could die, and Nico watched in fascination as she blushed. All over.

Then she was gone.

Laughing to himself, he wandered into the kitchen and tasted the bolognese sauce. Then he poured himself a glass of red wine from the half-empty bottle beside the oven. Wonderful. Finally, settling himself lengthways on the red velvet sofa and nursing his wine glass against his chest he waited patiently for the blushing nude to reappear.

Ten minutes later he stood up and knocked on the bedroom door, which had remained firmly closed.

'Hey. You haven't committed suicide, have you?' he said softly.

'Yes.' The reply was a muffled one.

'Oh. Well, in that case would you care to come out and wait in the sitting-room while I call the ambulance?'

'Can't.'

'Why not?'

'Too embarrassed,' said Camilla, feeling herself beginning to blush all over again.

'What if I told you that I was a doctor, and that I see naked women every day of my life?'

'Are you?' she whispered, a flickering note of hope audible in her voice.

'No,' confessed Nico, 'but what if I *told* you that I was? Couldn't we just pretend?'

'Please go away,' Camilla implored him. 'I really *am* embarrassed, you know.'

'I know,' said Nico gently. 'Are you still . . . unclothed?'

After a long silence, he heard her say: 'No.'

'Well, in that case,' he opened the door and entered the room, 'why don't we just forget what's happened and introduce ourselves. I'm Nico.'

Having begun to see the funny side of this utterly ridiculous situation a few minutes earlier whilst she was buried beneath her duvet, Camilla now emerged from its snowy depths and took Nico's solemnly proffered hand.

'Delighted to meet you,' she said, her eyes sparkling with suppressed laughter. 'Jane Smith.'

'The truth,' demanded Nico severely. 'After all, you no longer have anything to hide from me.'

Camilla nodded. When their first initial encounter had been that revealing, what *could* she have to hide? It just amazed her that in the presence of such a stunning looking man –

presumably one of Loulou's many boyfriends – she could actually retain her sense of humour. Slowly, she pushed back the duvet and emerged from the bed, fully clothed.

'I have to say,' murmured Nico conspiratorially, 'that I preferred you as you were earlier, but either way you make a terrific spaghetti bolognese.'

'You're welcome to have some. I cooked it for Loulou but there's way too much for her to finish. Shall I heat it up now?'

'What about you?'

'Diet,' said Camilla firmly, patting her stomach. Nico pulled a face. Having inherited more than his share of Italian genes he appreciated sensuous, beautifully rounded figures like the one this mysterious female possessed. As far as he was concerned most women these days were far too thin.

'I'll eat if you'll eat,' he told her, pulling her to her feet. 'And we'll save some for Lou when she gets back. Agreed?'

'Agreed.'

Nico was totally captivated by Camilla's reluctant smile, dragged from her quite against her will. A man surrounded wherever he went by women offering him anything he desired, he felt as ridiculously triumphant now as if he had succeeded in singlehandedly taming a wild tiger cub. For this woman, quite obviously, had no idea at all who he was.

'Are you a friend of Loulou's?' she was asking him now as she padded barefoot into the kitchen and filled a heavy saucepan with water. Then she pulled a wry face. 'How stupid of me. Of course you're a friend, otherwise you wouldn't be here. Have you known her long?'

'A few years,' said Nico, salting the water whilst she ripped open a new packet of spaghetti. Camilla watched him and smiled again. How odd, she thought, that she could chat so freely to this complete stranger and feel so completely at ease with him. And how very different it was from her disastrous encounter last week with Miles Cooper-Clarke. Tall, rangy in his black sweatshirt and drastically faded Levis, with his streaky blond hair falling across his tanned forehead and his thickly lashed green eyes narrowed with concentration, he was stirring the sauce like an expert.

'Are you in the restaurant business as well?' she asked with interest. He certainly didn't look like a chef, but then neither did Robert, who worked for Lou.

'I was, years ago,' said Nico, who had once worked in McDonald's for extra cash when he was still at school. She really didn't have any idea who he was, he thought, feeling more cheerful than he had for days. 'Right. Spaghetti's on, sauce is simmering, so we have a few minutes to ourselves. What are all these?'

Turning away from the kitchen he was pointing towards the pile of still unwrapped presents in the centre of the floor. 'Scrabble! I haven't played Scrabble since I was a kid. My sisters used to hit me if I spelled a word wrong.'

'I bought it for my son, he's eight,' Camilla told him and Nico thought: Married. Of course. He almost said jokingly: 'I should have guessed; wonderful child-bearing hips,' but realized in time that a woman who was capable of blushing all over probably wouldn't appreciate the observation. Not that it was intended as a criticism by any means; he thought well-rounded hips were amazingly sexy. From what he had seen, this woman had a superb body. Wisely, however, he forbore to state his opinion aloud, since she was quite capable, he sensed, of closeting herself in the bedroom once more.

'Would your son mind, do you think, if we were to have

just one game before you wrapped it up for him?' he said longingly.

'You really are the most appalling cheat,' exclaimed Camilla, trying not to laugh. Since Loulou didn't possess a dictionary she could only listen in disbelief to Nico's long, involved explanations of words which he insisted were real, half of which sounded suspiciously Italian anyway.

'I swear on my life!' declared Nico, his green eyes innocent. 'A zuka is a wonderful vegetable, rather like an aubergine, but slightly smaller and more rounded.'

'And fitting perfectly on to a triple-word score,' she observed. 'Incredible.'

'You don't believe me?' he protested, clutching his heart. 'Shall I phone my dear old mother so that you can ask her yourself? Why, at this very moment she is probably sitting at her kitchen table peeling delicious zuka in preparation for the evening meal . . .'

'We'll phone her,' intercepted Camilla firmly, calling his bluff and reaching for the phone. 'Where is she?'

'At home, in northern Italy.'

He grinned as she dropped the phone back on to the floor. 'Why, how good of you, deciding to believe me after all. That's another fifty-four points to me, I think.'

When Loulou returned home at almost five o'clock, Nico and Camilla were still sprawled on the living-room floor, so engrossed in their game that they didn't even notice her arrival.

Loulou gazed in astonishment at the cosy scene, registering the empty wine bottle and glasses beside them, the totally relaxed atmosphere and the laughter in Camilla's eyes as she accused Nico of stealing her Q. She guessed instantly that

Camilla had no idea whom she was lying next to; if she had known that Nico Coletto was one of Britain's most successful rock stars and a huge sex-symbol to boot, she would be paralysed with shyness. And if she knew that he was another of Roz's lovers Loulou doubted whether she would even remain in the same room as him.

Her heart softened and she felt a small surge of personal triumph as she realized how lovely Camilla was looking. The other night, when she had dragged her down into Vampires and placed her at the mercy of Miles Cooper-Clarke, all the make-up and finery in the world had been unable to disguise her inner anxieties. But now, bathed in the intimate glow of the twin brass lamps on either side of the sofa, her exquisite new hair-style endearingly tousled, and her lipstick scarcely visible, she exuded confidence and joy.

With Miles, an ordinary man, she had been cripplingly ill at ease, Loulou recalled wryly, yet here with Nico – who was by any standards extraordinary – she was at peace.

From her position in the doorway, Loulou smiled. There couldn't be that many people in Britain who wouldn't recognize Nico when they saw him. Trust Camilla to be one of that tiny minority.

'Zuka!' she exclaimed, having crept up behind them, and Camilla jumped. Nico, who could detect the click of a photo-grapher's camera at fifty paces and who had known all along that Loulou had returned, reached out and grabbed her slender ankle, pulling her down in an untidy heap beside him.

'Rinti?' howled Loulou, transfixed by the outrageous words he had been allowed to get away with. Camilla, she knew instinctively, would never cheat like that.

'Keribel!'

'Sshh, Lou,' Nico chastised her, pulling a lock of her rippling blonde hair for emphasis, 'you know perfectly well that a keribel is a child's rocking-chair. Look, I'm winning by seventy-two points. Isn't that incredible?'

'It's a miracle of modern cheating,' she observed drily.

'Oh, come on. Jane knows I'm not cheating. Merely because I have a more extensive knowledge of the English language . . .'

'Jane doesn't know you aren't cheating,' interjected Camilla, 'she just doesn't have a dictionary to prove that you are, that's all.'

Loulou stared at them, wondering exactly how much they had had to drink. 'And who the bloody hell,' she demanded of Camilla, 'is Jane?'

Grinning broadly, Nico said: 'Jane is the woman who greeted me, stark naked, when I arrived here a couple of hours ago. But you don't want to hear about that, it really wouldn't interest you. Your go, Jane.'

'Tell me, tell me, tell me!' yelled Loulou in a fever of anticipation. 'It's my *business* to know all the gossip and scandal that's going around. I *have* to know, for the good of my health.'

'Gossip and scandal?' said Nico, pretending to concentrate on the letters Camilla was putting down. 'OK, I'll give you gossip. 'I'm doing an interview for *Cosmopolitan* tomorrow morning.'

Ah, he must be a journalist, thought Camilla. That would explain his ability to lie so convincingly.

'Who gives a damn about your lousy interview,' declared Loulou ferociously, punching him on the shoulder.

'Such gratitude,' murmured Nico. 'I simply thought you might be interested to know who they'd got in to take the photos, but obviously . . .'

94

'Mac!'

'. . . you aren't interested in knowing that either, so it's a waste of time even telling you that it's at my place, at twelve thirty . . .'

'Mac? Is it *really*? Oh, I just *knew* something was going to happen, I was only thinking about him this week. Mac!'

Rolling on to his side, Nico studied the expression on her face, faking astonishment.

'So you're glad I told you?'

'Ah, you're an angel,' exclaimed Loulou, launching herself at him and covering his face with kisses. Camilla watched in amusement, trying to remember which of Loulou's husbands Mac was. Either the second or the third, she thought, but Loulou had listened so unselfishly to Camilla's depressing litany of problems that she had scarcely had time to do more than briefly mention in passing her own tangled love-life. And Mac, it appeared, was still an important part of it.

'I'm afraid I did something very wicked this afternoon,' confessed Nico but Loulou, still clinging to him like a puppy, shook her head.

'I don't care, I forgive you.'

'Jane made you the best spaghetti bolognese in the world, and I ate it.'

'You're a bastard,' she said affectionately, 'but I still forgive you. Was it wonderful?'

'*Bellissimo*.'

'That's all right then. Only the very best for my darling Nico.'

At that moment, disentangling himself from her clutches, he spotted the word Camilla was setting out along the bottom of the board, managing to encompass *two* triple-word scores.

'*Quiglioni*? What in heaven's name is *quiglioni*, for God's sake?'

Camilla smiled innocently at him. 'It's derived from the Italian language,' she explained. 'It means "man of huge appetite who eats all the spaghetti." You surprise me, Nico. I really thought you would have been familiar with that one.'

Chapter 12

Shrinking further into the depths of her velvet-lined coat, Roz set her glossy red lips into a determined line and braved the freezing December morning air. Her brown, high-heeled boots tapped out a rhythmic staccato as she crossed the icy road and headed for Hyde Park.

She needed to think. In less than an hour, she had to be at the television studios for a meeting to discuss the first programme in her new series of 'Memories'. In an hour she would have to deal tactfully with a frenetic producer, his ever-flappable assistant, and a whole team of equally excitable people, none of whom spoke when they could shout, nor discussed when they could argue. And she would have no time whatsoever to think.

As she entered Hyde Park with its acres of crisp, heavily frosted grass and silver-filigreed trees, her spirits lifted slightly. It didn't compare with the Cotswolds, of course, but it had a citified beauty of its own and at least it was relatively quiet at this early hour.

Confiding in Nico had been a big mistake; she realized that now. Almost every man she had ever met had been possessive, but Italians appeared to be even more so. Maybe the time had come to move on, leaving Nico behind, but then . . .

Roz sighed, breathing out a white cloud of mist which vanished in an instant. It *would* be a damn shame if he had to go. Lovers as skilful and generous as Nico were hard to come by. Or rather, not hard to come by, she thought with a tiny smile as she recognized her own unintentional pun. And Nico was definitely a sensational lover; she had had enough experience with men to know that.

But was the relationship spoilt anyway, now that Nico knew rather than merely suspected that she had taken other lovers?

Roz gave up thinking for a moment and watched a silky haired Afghan hound launch itself in pursuit of a stick. Long ears flying, honey blond coat rippling like the sea, it pounced on the stick and returned it, wagging its tail and gazing up in devotion at its balding, portly master.

Such uncompromising adoration, thought Roz with a trace of jealousy. Would the Afghan mind for more than five minutes if its owner brought home another dog? Why couldn't men be more like dogs, uncritical and loving, and unhampered by the need to be the only one?

Gazing across at the Afghan, Roz remembered with a painful jolt that Camilla had been almost dog-like in her devotion; loyal, unquestioning, seeking no more reward than friendship. And in return she had treated her so badly that had she *been* a dog, she would have been taken away by the RSPCA and given a better, far nicer owner.

Roz smiled wryly to herself once more, at the ridiculous turn her thoughts had taken. This was worse than Orwell's *Animal Farm*, for heaven's sake! Camilla was a human being, after all . . . it just irritated her that her conscience wouldn't let the situation rest. What had happened had happened, she told herself decisively.

'Roz.'

Having vaguely heard the footsteps behind her a few seconds earlier, she swung round as a hand touched her arm. Jack, his handsome face reddened by the icy air and his eyes watering slightly, looked both apprehensive and determined.

'You followed me,' said Roz flatly, and he nodded.

'I've been waiting outside the TV studios all week, but the commissionaire wouldn't allow me in, and since you won't return my calls . . .'

'Quite,' she cut in, her voice crisp and impersonal. 'I told you when I came to the house to pick up Camilla's things that there was no point in discussing the situation. It's over, Jack. You disgust me.'

With an expression of bewilderment, he gestured with his gloveless hand. 'How can I disgust you, for Christ's sake? You knew I was married, so don't try and give me the morality bit. I didn't disgust you a few weeks ago when . . .'

'I didn't know you were married to *Camilla*,' retaliated Roz fiercely, her dark eyes glittering with disdain. 'Because you purposely didn't *tell* me. Did it give you a thrill, Jack, to be the only one in on the secret? To play your clever little game?'

His eyes shifted away from her, then darted back as his mouth twisted into a derisory smile. 'You don't like it,' he accused her, 'because you think I made a fool of *you*.'

Roz longed to hit him, but instead kept her hands deep in the pockets of her coat. What he said was partly true, after all.

'Oh no.' She shook her head. 'I don't like it because you *chose* – for your own amusement – to make a fool of your wife, who didn't deserve it. If you had any sense at all, you'd apologize to her, spoil her to death and beg her to come back. Not that she doesn't deserve better, of course, but because you and the children are all she has. Go back to Camilla, Jack, and for God's sake, leave me alone.'

'She won't come back,' he replied slowly, after a few seconds of icy silence. 'She told Jennifer, so there's no point in my even asking her. She's left me for good, Roz, but it's you I love anyway. Darling,' he said, reaching towards her, his voice suddenly husky, 'we have to talk. Properly. I only want to be with you. *Please*.'

'But I don't want you,' snapped Roz, almost overcome with revulsion. Her eyes blazed as she glared at him and he almost flinched at the hatred in them. 'I don't want *you*, Jack. Can't you understand that? And now, for God's sake, just leave me alone.'

Chapter 13

'We came down to London just after we got married,' said Loulou, fiddling with the wildly unsuitable gold lamé scarf around her neck and driving Camilla to distraction with her hyperactivity. She would never have imagined that Loulou could be so nervous, yet here she was in the fourth outfit she had tried on in an hour, acting like a teenager on her first date. It was oddly comforting, in a way, Camilla thought, to discover that men – or rather one man in particular – could reduce the invincible Loulou to the consistency of overcooked spaghetti.

'I managed to get a job straight away as the manageress of a brasserie in Clapham, but we'd decided that Mac had to keep his time free to concentrate on his career, so we lived – in considerable squalor, of course – on my salary. I thought it was wonderfully romantic.' She sighed again, breathing smoke all over Camilla. 'But after a couple of months Mac began to get frustrated. Typical Scottish male, of course; he simply couldn't handle the idea that he was being supported by a woman. Then I met darling Omar one night at the wine bar. Omar Khalid. He'd just bought this place and he needed someone to run it for him, so I agreed to come here if he doubled my salary. I didn't have any idea then, of course, how wealthy he was. He didn't even flinch and I started here two days later. It meant longer hours but I thought Mac would be pleased because of the extra cash.' She pulled an exaggerated face. 'But of course I hadn't reckoned on that fearsomely macho Scottish pride of his. He

101

did his damnedest to persuade me not to take the job, so it became a battle of wills and you know what I'm like when I make up *my* mind. Mac was an absolute pig, refusing to take a penny more than necessary of my money. He gave up smoking, wouldn't touch alcohol, and practically starved himself. I wasn't even allowed to buy him a Chinese takeaway on a Saturday night,' she exclaimed in remembered horror. 'So, of course, we fought like cat and dog whenever I was at home – such a shame, because we still loved each other madly – and the only way to stop the fighting was to not *be* at home. He was . . . oh God, is that the time? We'll be late!'

Leaping to her feet, fanning her wet nails furiously and visibly vibrating with agitation, she twirled in front of Camilla. 'I'll have to tell you the rest later. Am I OK?'

Loulou, Camilla thought, looked absolutely stunning . . . but maybe just a little over the top for a cold Tuesday morning in December.

'You look great,' she said warmly, then hesitated. 'But I can't help wondering . . .'

'Say it,' commanded Loulou, biting her lower lip. 'I know what it is, but say it anyway.'

'Well, wouldn't it have been better to play it cool and turn up in jeans?' Camilla suggested reluctantly. 'Not that I've got much experience in these matters, but . . .'

'Oh, I know, I know,' said Loulou, sounding forlorn but at the same time brushing the suggestion determinedly aside. 'And you're absolutely right, of course, but if there's one thing I've never been able to do it's play it cool. Besides, Mac knows me too well to fall for it. He expects me to wear the wrong clothes. If I wore something *appropriate*,' she made it sound worse than AIDS, 'he probably wouldn't even recognize me. But thanks for being honest enough to say it,' she concluded gratefully, bending to kiss Camilla's cheek. 'Now, are you ready? We simply must leave so that we're there before Mac. I don't want him to think that we've only turned up to see him!'

Camilla gave her a doubtful smile. Mac couldn't possibly think that the presence of Loulou – looking like a Dallas Christmas tree – was a coincidence, yet Loulou herself believed implicitly that he would. How easy it was, she thought sadly, to see the mistakes made by others, while remaining so utterly blind to one's own.

'I'm ready.' She stood up, and glimpsed her reflection in Loulou's stagelit mirror. It still shocked her to see her new self, for a brief moment to catch herself unawares. The difference gave her a thrill each time. 'I feel like a chaperone.'

'Happily,' grinned Loulou as they headed for the door, 'you don't look like one.'

Nico's house, overlooking Wimbledon Common, captivated Camilla instantly. Huge, rambling and Victorian, its walls hung with Virginia creeper and almost every window ablaze with light, it epitomized a truly English home. Twin Christmas trees strung with what seemed like miles of white lights flanked the heavy oak front door, and the glittering lights of another could be seen through the hall window. Only the electrically operated gates and the notices reading 'Beware – Guard Dogs' struck a discordant note.

'Tell me the truth,' she demanded as Loulou's navy blue MG screeched noisily to a halt at the head of the gravelled driveway. 'Just how famous *is* Nico?'

Loulou tried to suppress a grin, her own anxieties forgotten for a moment. She had felt it only fair to warn Camilla that

Nico was not, as she had first imagined, a journalist, but in order to break her in gently had somewhat skated over the truth.

'Well, I suppose he's a *bit* famous,' she conceded, privately amazed that the almost inevitable clutch of school girls who hung around the front gates hoping for a glimpse of their idol were not in evidence this morning. Nico, apparently, wasn't worth freezing for in temperatures of four below zero. 'He's sold a few records in his time, but you mustn't let it bother you. You've met him now, so you know how lovely he is – not a bit intimidating.'

'How many records?' persisted Camilla slowly. Not having known who Nico was was beginning to make her feel as gauche as failing to recognize the Queen at one of her own garden parties, but since marrying Jack, who was a Radio 4 person himself, she had become hopelessly out of touch with what was popular.

'About six million, I think,' said Loulou over her shoulder as she jumped out of the car. 'That's here in the UK, of course. He's sold a lot more than that in Europe. Italy's crazy about him.'

Camilla swallowed hard, wishing she could sink down in her seat and hide in the car until it was time to leave, but even as the thought formed in her panicking mind, the front door was opening and Nico appeared.

'Christ, it's cold,' he shouted, holding out his arms as Loulou ran across the gravel towards him. 'Jane! I hardly recognized you with your clothes on. Now come inside at once and help me with this mulled wine I've been concocting.'

He grinned as she came reluctantly towards him, and gestured apologetically with his free arm. 'I'm sorry, I know I should have come clean yesterday, but I couldn't resist it. Are you cross with me?'

'Very,' said Camilla, straightfaced, then added: 'Embarrassed.'

Loulou, almost bursting with impatience, said: 'He isn't here yet, is he? Are we in time?'

'If we hurry,' replied Nico solemnly, 'you may even be able to sink a few drinks before they arrive. That should calm your jangling nerves ... will you stop *juddering*, Lou? And get inside this damn house?'

He certainly looked more like a rock star today, thought Camilla, as he led them inside. In close-fitting dark green leather trousers and a darker green T-shirt upon which, in scarlet, were the words 'Italians do it *bella*', he presented an altogether more dangerous image than that of yesterday. Yet the easy, unaffected smile and good humour were unchanged and she clung to that fact with gratitude. She had felt at ease with Nico before; knowing now how well known and how wealthy he clearly was shouldn't make her react any differently towards him. If only she could just stop thinking about it ...

The interior of the house was spectacularly decorated and incredibly untidy. In the centre of the wood-panelled hall stood a twenty-feet-long carved oak table covered with pieces of drum kit, empty beer cans and dust. Silver candlesticks, tarnished and spotted with green wax, stood sentinel at either end of a vast fireplace. The parquet floor was dull and splattered with mud.

'Like it?' said Nico, turning to Camilla.

'It's a beautiful house,' she said carefully, glancing up at the cobwebs.

'But a bloody mess,' he admitted with a rueful expression.

'My housekeeper's a darling, but she was inconsiderate enough to fall in love a few weeks ago with the milkman. Couldn't get a stroke of work out of her, and then last week she announced that she was going away on holiday with him to Spain. What could I say? I just hope that if and when she comes back she'll remember how to work the Hoover. First love,' he shook his blond head and sighed. 'It's an alarming thing.'

'How old is she?' asked Camilla, thinking that to hire such a young and obviously vulnerable housekeeper was asking for trouble.

Nico grinned. 'Fifty-three.'

The kitchen was even worse and Camilla's hands itched when she saw the mountains of washing-up. By the look of it, Nico was working his way through his fourth dinner-service in an attempt to avoid getting his hands wet.

'You could always hire someone temporary.' Even Loulou sounded faintly shocked. Nico looked vague.

'Keep forgetting to get around to it. Marian should be back in a few days or so. She'll sort it all out then, I expect.'

They took it in turns to taste the mulled wine, before pouring it into an enormous silver jug and retiring with it to Nico's chaotic sitting-room. Scarlet and grey silk-lined walls were hung with gold discs and framed photographs which only made Camilla feel more ashamed. Even she could recognize Paul McCartney, the Princess of Wales and Elton John, with whom Nico had been photographed. Hastily, she swallowed half a glass of the hot, spicy drink, and felt it course through her bloodstream like a drug. Loulou, by now visibly apprehensive, was already well into her second and when the doorbell rang moments later she automatically reached for a refill.

'Why am I here?' she wailed loudly, pulling a carefully pinned ringlet of gold ribbon from her hair in violent agitation.

'Because you bloody well insisted upon it,' Nico told her, rising to his feet. Camilla breathed in the scent of warm leather as he passed.

'No, no! I mean what's my *excuse*?' clamoured Loulou, shredding the ribbon and looking aghast. 'I can't remember why I'm supposed to be here and Mac will guess that . . .'

'Stage fright,' he said with a shrug in Camilla's direction, and left the room.

'You've brought me here because I'm going to be his new cleaning woman,' said Camilla quickly, without even stopping to think.

'Oh, that's brilliant!' exclaimed Loulou, still pale, but smiling with relief. 'Cami, you're an angel. What would I do without you?'

No, thought Camilla with a rush of affection and sympathy – for their ex-husbands were the source of both their problems – what would *I* do without *you*?

Having had Mac described to her by Loulou, Camilla had known to expect a tall, lean man with black gypsyish curls, dark eyes and an exquisite dimple, but there was far, far more to him than that. He was attractive, certainly, but he possessed an arresting quality which would automatically draw the attention of even the most indifferent onlooker. Unconscious sex appeal mingled with lazy grace and a sureness of his actions which was almost hypnotic. It was easy to see why Loulou had fallen in love with him, and equally impossible to know what Mac was thinking behind that proud, handsome exterior.

Loulou might have been suffering from stage fright, Camilla thought several uncomfortable minutes later, but she didn't deserve to, for surely only actresses suffered from that.

And Loulou was no actress. Every pent-up emotion was etched with dazzling clarity upon her mobile features in perfect contrast with Mac's quite unreadable expression when he saw his ex-wife sitting cross-legged in the centre of the sofa. Camilla still couldn't quite believe that Loulou had actually said, with a bright, false smile, 'Well, hello, fancy meeting you here!' Equally toe-curling had been the entirely unconvincing way in which she had immediately launched into a breathless explanation of her presence there.

'... so I suggested that Camilla would be *just* the person to take over as Nico's new housekeeper and Nico was thrilled. He insisted that we dash straight over ... so here we are!'

'Amazing,' murmured Mac, with that dark, Scottish-accented voice which made spaghetti of Loulou's knees.

Amazing isn't the word for it, thought Nico, glancing across at the girl who had introduced herself to him as Jane Smith, after having been caught by him with rather more than just her trousers down. He had guessed that it wasn't her name, but he certainly hadn't realized that this was the old schoolfriend who had left her husband after discovering that he was having an affair with Roz. How could he have guessed, after all? Roz had dismissed her as 'a great white whale, all knitting patterns and co-ordinated bathroom fittings'.

Nico recalled that first memorable meeting, when he had admired for too few seconds Camilla's voluptuous, lightly tanned body, and later devoured the exquisite meal she had cooked. Camilla was a little shy, certainly, but in his experience that was an all-too-rare quality in a woman. He could easily imagine how she would be overawed by someone like Roz, but she was undoubtedly easier company, and considering what she must have gone through in the last few weeks she was coping incredibly well.

Don't judge people by your own standards, darling, he thought, mentally addressing Roz and experiencing a wave of emotion dangerously close to dislike for the woman who was his mistress. And don't dismiss her as easily as you have, because if you do, you're sadly underestimating Camilla.

The interview, as pre-arranged by Nico's agent, lasted exactly one and a half hours. *Cosmopolitan*'s features writer was determined not to be captivated by Nico's famous charm and asked dozens of questions about politics upon which he patiently declined to comment.

'We want to know about your serious side,' she persisted, whilst Mac sorted out the lighting behind them in preparation for the photographic session. Camilla saw him smile as Nico, straightfaced, said, 'That would be my left side.'

'And what do you like to do when you aren't working?'

'Screw,' replied Nico, then he winked at Camilla. 'And look at naked women.'

Camilla blushed.

'Anyone in particular?' said the woman from *Cosmpolitan*, determinedly unshockable.

'I don't know,' he tilted his head to one side and gazed steadily at her through half-closed eyes. 'What are you doing tonight?'

'The bastard,' sobbed Loulou, streaking her face with mascara as she rubbed her eyes with balled-up fists like a child. 'He did his bloody best to act as if I wasn't even there. All that worrying and I would have been better off not going anyway – how can *he* be like that when *I'm* like this?'

Camilla, unfamiliar with the MG which Loulou was far too drunk to drive, struggled to manipulate the ferocious clutch.

'He knew you were there, Lou. He's just . . . better at hiding his feelings, I suppose,' she said lamely, wishing that she could say something more positive.

'Do you think he guessed that I was only there to see him?' asked Loulou, then kicked the dashboard with her booted foot and swore colourfully. 'Of course he did! And I bet he loved it. He makes me so mad I feel like going off and getting married again, just to spite him.'

The declaration sounded so absurd that Camilla laughed.

'You could always have Jack.'

Loulou sniffed loudly then managed a watery, reluctant smile. 'I know it sounds daft, Cami. But the only reason I married Hugh was to teach Mac a lesson. You don't know what I'm like with bloody men, you really don't.'

Chapter 14

Christmas Day, as far as Roz was concerned, was the absolute pits.

Particularly when it was spent alone. Carelessly forcing the cork out of the bottle of Lanson with her fingernails so that it ricocheted off the ceiling and champagne foamed over her hands on to the lilac silk bedcover, she tipped the bottle to overfill her solitary glass and mentally ticked off all the people with whom she had not been invited to spend Christmas Day.

Roz's thoughts turned to Nico as she relived yesterday's difficult conversation with him. To her eternal shame, out of a mixture of loneliness and desperation, she had buried her pride and phoned him.

'Just thought I'd ring and wish you a merry Christmas. Where will you be?' she had said, despising the tell-tale note of weakness in her voice.

'Oh hi, Roz. We're going to see my sisters.'

'We?'

'I'm taking Loulou with me,' Nico had added, answering the question she refused to allow herself to ask. 'Poor kid, she's had a bit of a rough time recently. She ran into Mac again and the reunion didn't go quite as she'd hoped, so I thought she needed cheering up. If Lucia and Bianca and their brood of banshees can't take her mind off Mac, nothing can.'

There was no mention of Camilla, and Roz had no intention of asking him if Loulou still had a house guest. It had hardly

111

been the most relaxed of phone calls and Nico, though polite, had sounded quite unlike his usual, warmer self.

Almost as an afterthought, it seemed, he had said: 'What are you doing for Christmas, then?'

'Oh, the usual,' replied Roz, her pride by this time biting like shoes three sizes too small. 'Loads of parties, lots of people to see.'

And it was true, she reflected. It was simply that none of the parties were on Christmas Day itself, when they were most needed.

'That's great,' Nico had said absently. 'Well, have a good time. Bye.'

The day stretched endlessly ahead of her, threatening to last at least five times as long as a normal one. Roz sipped her champagne moodily, flicking through the TV channels with the remote control to be greeted by cartoons, children in hospital, the morning service and more children in hospital. Terrific. Heaving a long drawn-out sigh she gazed around in dissatisfaction at the midnight blue, lilac and gold bedroom. What on earth was the point, she thought, of wearing a négligé and lying in a king-sized canopied four-poster bed in one of the most seductively styled bedrooms imaginable when there was no-one there with her to seduce? The only thing to do, clearly, was to drink her way through the solitude until sleep returned and this hideous day came to its silent, interminable end.

If Camilla had known that Roz was spending Christmas day alone and lonely, she might have felt a little better herself.

As it was, though, the black depression had descended and since just before six o'clock – years of motherhood had conditioned her to wake up particularly early on this of all mornings

– she had wept non-stop into her coffee. All the suppressed tears of the past few weeks now poured down her cheeks and the aching hollowness in the pit of her stomach clutched at her like a knuckle-dustered fist. Resentment and hatred towards Roz, who had everything any woman could possibly want but who had, nevertheless, wanted more, burnt within her and for the first time she experienced a yearning for revenge.

The sensation was so alien to her nature that it quite shocked her. Rising quickly, she crossed to the ornately gilded mirror, framed by Loulou with holly and gold feathers, and surveyed her tear-stained reflection with dislike. At this lowest of ebbs, without both make-up and confidence, she had reverted to the unattractive, insipid woman who allowed life to beat her. So much, she thought with self-hatred, for her insistence that she wanted to – and *would* – spend Christmas on her own.

It had seemed so important at the time, when Nico had invited her to stay with him and Loulou at his sister's house in Bath. It had been a statement of self-confidence, an assurance to both them and herself that she was able to cope without the moral crutch of their company, and she *had* meant it, *had* been confident that she could achieve this small but important goal set by herself. The more they had urged her not to stay in London, registering their doubts that she was strong enough to do so, the more strongly Camilla had reacted. In the end she had had to insist that they leave her behind and they had only reluctantly agreed after making sure that the flat was filled with festive food, bottles of champagne, their phone number in Bath and a pile of lavishly wrapped presents which put the small gifts she had bought them to shame.

And they had only left last night.

It's only another day, exactly the same as all the rest, she told herself savagely as she turned away from the mirror and felt the burning of incipient tears once more. So why did it have to be so bloody *different*?

Switching on the television, she realized almost immediately that she had made another mistake. Having worked so hard to suppress the memories of Toby and Charlotte, she found herself with a relentlessly cheerful disc jockey visiting children unfortunate enough to be in hospital on Christmas Day. Their little faces and heart-breaking smiles were more than she could bear. She could remember *every* detail of her children's faces, the sound of their voices when they laughed – and when they cried. The newly washed scent of their bodies as she hugged them at bedtime. What *had* she done? Was this really the best thing for them all – or should she go back? Sinking to her knees before the television set, tears pouring unheeded down her cheeks, Camilla wished for the first time in her life that she was dead.

Cautiously pushing open the swing door, its chocolate brown paint scuffed and scratched with years of careless use, her knees were instantly attacked by a pair of chubby arms, enfolding her legs as if she were a box of groceries. Brown eyes and a huge, gappy grin greeted Camilla when she looked down and before she could even steady herself against the door jamb the child yelled 'Pick up' and released its grip on her knees in order to fling its arms wide before her. She wasn't sure whether it was a boy or a girl, but that didn't matter. Bending down, she scooped the plump child, who was wriggling with delight, into her arms.

'What's your name?' she said carefully, disentangling a strong fist from her hooped earring.

'Pretty,' announced the child unhelpfully, and shrieked with laughter.

'Happy Kissmas.'

At the far end of the ward, which had been decorated for Christmas with more enthusiasm than taste, several nurses were supervising lunch, pulling wheelchairs up to a cluster of pushed-together tables and hauling other children into normal chairs, or on to their laps. Still carrying the squirming child, who was now twisting handfuls of her hair around its arms, Camilla made her way towards them. Unlike the television programme she had watched earlier, there were no families with the children on this ward. The smell of turkey mingled with disinfectant and urine and the tiny fake Christmas tree was placed on top of a cupboard, well out of reach from inquisitive hands.

'Hello, I'm Camilla. I phoned earlier and was told by one of the sisters that it would be all right to come along.' It was impossible, she realized, to be shy when a small child had its fingers in your ears and its legs wrapped around your waist.

'The more the merrier,' said one of the nurses, smiling at her and expertly twisting a wheelchair into place before the table. The occupant, a boy of about ten, gazed ahead with sightless eyes and repetitively banged the side of his chair with a twisted hand.

'I'm Carol, this is Tina, Marie, Jeannie and Tom,' she nodded to each of the other nurses in turn. 'And it rather looks as if you're stuck with that baby gorilla there,' she added with an infectious grin. 'His name's Martin. We call him Marty. If you'd like to sit down, I'll give you his plate and you can feed him.'

'Pretty,' announced Marty, his dark shiny hair swinging as he turned and kissed Camilla wetly on the nose.

'Yes, darling,' said the girl whose name was Marie, and who

115

had noticed Camilla's puffy eyes beneath the carefully applied make-up, 'she's a very pretty lady, and she's going to make sure your lunch goes into your mouth instead of all over the floor.'

'How old is he?' said Camilla.

'Six. He's a bugger for earrings. I'd take yours out if you want to keep your ears intact. Want to pull a cracker, Marty?'

'Happy Kissmas,' said Marty, ripping the cracker to shreds all by himself and screaming with delight when Camilla manoeuvred the yellow paper hat on to his darting head.

'His nappy's wet,' said Camilla, as a dark stain spread over her elegant shirt.

'I'll see to him' said Carol, reaching across to take him from her.

Camilla's arms tightened around his plump little waist. 'It's OK, I know how to change a nappy,' she said happily. 'I'll do it when he's finished his food.'

'You did *what*?' yelled Loulou down the phone, at midnight.

'I went to St Stephen's,' repeated Camilla patiently. 'I've been there since lunchtime. I loved it.'

'But that's the loony bin!'

'It's a hospital for the mentally handicapped. I went along to help out on the children's ward. Most go home for Christmas but some can't. They've either been abandoned, or the families simply can't cope with them. Do you know, Lou, that the nurses there draw lots to see who can work on Christmas Day? Three nurses came in, even though it was their day off. I couldn't see Toby and Charlotte this year, but I suddenly realized that I *could* be with children who weren't able to see their own parents. It was wonderful, there's a little boy there called Marty who has Down's Syndrome and he . . .'

'She's flipped,' whispered Loulou to Nico, her hand over the mouthpiece. Then she grinned at him, because it was difficult not to grin at a rock star wearing a blue plastic necklace out of a cracker and a pair of false Dracula teeth. 'But she sounds more cheerful now than she has since she moved in, so who am I to say anything if a visit to a loony bin makes her happy?'

Chapter 15

Meeting and instantly flooring Omar Khalid with one of her more reckless insults had been one of the most important events in Loulou's life. Possibly *the* most important, she sometimes felt, since Vampires had stayed with her for far longer than any of her three husbands or numerous lovers.

It had been fate – she had never for a second doubted that – which had caused his pale blue Silver Shadow Rolls-Royce to break down directly outside the shabby Clapham wine bar where she was working at the time. Men like Omar travelled between Heathrow, Mayfair, Knightsbridge and maybe Surrey, but they never intentionally *went* to places like Clapham. Which explained why it had to be fate that had quite deliberately snapped the accelerator cable and worsened Omar's mood to the extent that he had stormed into the wine bar and demanded irritably: 'Give me an orange juice and a cigar.'

Loulou, who had spent most of the night fighting with Mac because he categorically refused to keep the expensive lambs-wool sweater she had bought him, was in no mood for further displays of male arrogance.

'What are we, a goddamn charity?' she had snapped back through tightly clenched teeth. 'You probably earn more in a day than I do in a year. And you want me to *give* you an orange juice and a cigar? Would you give *me* that car of yours? Mind your manners and pay for what you want or take a hike.'

Omar Khalid, accustomed as he was to the ultimate in

deference and humility, actually felt himself turn a shade paler. Through his quick mind ran a series of conflicting emotions jostling for position: shock, amazement at the audacity of this stunning looking young girl, a faint sense of outrage, a stronger one of admiration . . . and amusement, because he had never in his life been addressed in such a manner and it really made rather a refreshing change.

The wine bar, since it was not yet midday, was entirely empty. Late morning sunlight streamed through the stained-glass windows behind the girl, surrounding her with colours which only enhanced his image of her. She was an angel.

Without moving a muscle or opening his mouth to speak, Omar gazed at her, drinking in her shimmering blonde beauty and defiant eyes. Incongruous amidst the leafy foliage and brass fittings, she looked so ferocious that he didn't want to do or say anything to spoil the exquisite moment.

And then she smiled a dazzling smile, and he was utterly, *infinitely* lost. It was the smile of the century; melting, beguiling and at the same time so *knowing* that it gripped the very centre of his soul. This is it, thought Omar. This is the girl I want.

'The car is yours, of course,' he said, inclining his head and permitting himself the smallest of smiles in return. 'And I do most humbly apologize for my rudeness, which was unpardonable. May I now have my orange juice please, and the honour of knowing that you might forgive me, madame?'

Loulou, enjoying her victory enormously, leant across and tickled the seventh richest man in the world beneath his smooth brown chin. 'For a Rolls-Royce, sweetie,' she said in cheerful tones, 'I can forgive *anybody* practically *anything*.'

Omar was even further enchanted, though perplexed, when

he later learnt that Loulou had been joking and that she steadfastly refused to take seriously his perfectly serious offer of the Rolls-Royce.

'I'm used to driving a Mini, for Christ's sake,' she giggled. 'How the hell do you suppose I'd ever manage to squeeze a Roller into a parking space?'

'That is not a problem,' replied Omar with a shrug. 'Naturally, the chauffeur will park it . . .'

Bestowing gifts upon Loulou proved difficult, if not impossible. She either howled with laughter at the idea of accepting the more extravagant ones – and Omar Khalid was not at all used to being laughed at – or very touchingly attempted to return in kind the smaller ones.

Each time he bought her a drink during his now daily visits to her wine bar, she would invariably buy him one in return. By the end of the week he had proposed to her.

'I wish to propose to you,' he said, his brown eyes solemn, and Loulou burst out laughing.

'I'm already married, dipstick! Hey, that's pretty appropriate for you, being in oil, wouldn't you say? I'm wittier than I thought.'

'I propose,' continued Omar, leaning across the polished bar, 'that you leave this place and become the manageress of a new wine bar, which I happen to own.' He felt it unnecessary to mention that he had owned it for less than twelve hours.

Loulou stared at him, and his stomach muscles tautened in admiration.

'I didn't know you had one.'

'There are many things about me of which you are unaware. It is in Knightsbridge, and very much larger than this,' he gestured with a sweep of his hand around the small, now crowded bar. 'There is a restaurant also, attached to it, and a large flat above which would, of course, be yours.'

'Why are you offering it to me?' Loulou challenged him, and he shrugged.

'It needs you, my dear. It very badly needs you.'

Exactly a month later, redesigned and renamed, Vampires opened amidst a whirl of expertly planned publicity, although it was not that alone which made it such an instant – and then lasting – success. Loulou did that herself, simply by being there in the right place and at the perfect time. People with plenty of money to spend, tired – like Omar – of being pandered to, welcomed Loulou's irreverent attitude with open arms, a joyful explosion of champagne corks and a tireless compulsion to return.

'He wants your body,' Mac told Loulou, his Scottish pride by this time severely dented by the manner in which the oil-rich Omar had so effortlessly altered their lives. Loulou was fast becoming a celebrity, and he was still struggling to make even the poorest of livings. 'That's if he hasn't had it already,' he added unfairly, yet unable to stop himself.

'Darling, you *know* that isn't true,' said Loulou absently, as she rearranged a line of bottles above the sleek new black marble bar. 'Omar simply thought I was the right man for the job.'

Mac watched her, so happy and so totally involved in her work that she was oblivious to his own jealousy. 'That's exactly it,' he said, his voice dangerously quiet. 'You're the right man for the job, and I'm the housewife who gets her allowance every week. I won't be your wife, Loulou. Don't expect me to be.'

121

She turned, exasperated by his stubbornness. 'You're so bloody *Scottish*, Mac. What does it matter who's earning the most money at the moment? I've had my lucky break, that's all. You'll have yours, sooner or later. Why can't you just be grateful to Omar for giving me mine now?'

Mac's eyes glittered. 'I don't *want* to be grateful to Omar,' he said bitterly. 'Do you think I don't notice the way he looks at you, dammit? Why the bloody hell should I be grateful to a man who only wants to sleep with my wife?'

Exactly four weeks later he moved out.

'Now I know why it's called the monthly curse,' Loulou had joked feebly to her friends, while inside she disintegrated and died. 'I realized that we women had to expect period problems but this is ridiculous.'

And when, just three months after Mac's departure, Omar Khalid was killed in a freak air accident over the Persian Gulf, the curse was compounded. Grieving for both her lost husband and the man who had been both friend and benefactor to her for such a short period, she turned to Roz.

'He never laid a finger on me,' she sobbed, 'but Mac wouldn't believe me. Poor, poor Omar. And now that they're both gone, poor me.'

'Perhaps Mac will come back,' said Roz, 'now that Omar's . . . gone.'

'Why should he?' Loulou sniffed inconsolably. 'He still thinks I was unfaithful to him and how the hell can I prove that I wasn't? They can hardly test to see if my hymen is still intact.'

Loulou was right, and at the same time Mac felt that his assumptions had been proved correct when she was contacted by Omar Khalid's high-powered lawyers and informed that Vampires was hers.

'You're telling me that he didn't even go near you, yet he left you a property worth almost one and a half million pounds? I wasna born yesterday, you know,' he shouted, his Scottish accent increasing in direct proportion with his jealousy.

Loulou, longing to hurl something at his head, jammed her fists into her trouser pockets and faced him with unconcealed fury.

'You nasty, vicious bastard!' she yelled back, unable to stand the torture of being innocent but proven guilty. 'Sex isn't the be-all and end-all for everyone, you know. You might not be able to think further than your dick, but some people can manage without it. *I* certainly can. In fact since you walked out, sweetheart,' she went on heedlessly, wanting only to wound him now in return for the pain he had caused her, 'it's been a positive pleasure not having to sleep with you. You never did a bloody thing for me anyway!'

It was odd, thought Roz as she lay back and submitted to the ineffective foreplay of the man kneeling over her, that sex – the sexual act – could be the ultimate pleasurable pastime with one man, yet so unutterably dull with another. How could one affect her so deeply, whilst another left her ice-cold.

Lost in her own thoughts, she stifled a laugh, which David Shearing interpreted as a sigh and plunged into her so vigorously that she winced. Any moment now she would have to begin faking her orgasm, and she didn't really know whether she could be bothered. Men like this didn't deserve even a fake, she thought, but then if she didn't pretend he might carry on longer and the only thing worse than boring sex was a boring sexual marathon.

It was best to get it over with as quickly as possible, Roz

decided, and raked her fingernails along his spine. 'Oh, David, yes, yes . . .'

Chapter 16

Outside, pale green buds unfurled along the slender branches of the young elm trees surrounding the house and clumps of daffodils dotted the lawns on either side of the gravelled drive. Camilla crossed the kitchen to turn down the central heating a notch, because Nico liked the temperature inside the house to be at least tropical and after an hour and a half of vacuuming she was beginning to feel pretty tropical herself.

Bending down to wind the flex back on to the vacuum cleaner she paused for a second and smiled to herself. Who would have thought a few months ago that she could wear a pair of size twelve 501s and actually *bend down* in them?

But then, who would have imagined that she would be here, housekeeping for one of Britain's most popular and successful rock stars, let alone looking after him, who certainly required a great deal of looking after, and who didn't help matters by constantly urging her to 'sit down and relax, Cami. We can both do the washing-up later.'?

Throughout his upbringing in an extremely Italian household, Nico had watched his father issuing commands and his mother obeying them, assuming every imaginable duty without complaint. It had made his stomach churn, yet to protest was hopeless for his mother invariably, and infuriatingly, sided with his father. So Nico had suffered in silence, vowing to himself that never would he treat a woman in such a chauvinistic manner, and now Camilla was learning to suffer – not always silently – as a result. It was undoubtedly an admirable quality in a man, but it drove her insane. She was his housekeeper, yet he was too honour-bound to let her housekeep without interruption, and since he was as eager to learn as he was to help, simple tasks like preparing a meal took three times as long as they should have done.

Only last night he had removed three quarters of the leaves from the Brussels sprouts and painstakingly carved crosses in the *tops* of the acorn-sized remains. And after their dinner the ridiculously expensive washing-up machine had remained redundant whilst Nico had splashed around in the sink, washing saucepans first and glasses last, and losing three solid silver knives down the waste disposal. It had taken Camilla two hours to retrieve them this morning.

Yet she loved her new, unexpected life and knew that it suited her. Her work was endlessly appreciated, the nightmare of her separation from Jack and the children was at last beginning to fade, and she was regaining confidence so long buried that she had almost forgotten it ever existed. Nico's enthusiasm for music, food, parties and fun was infectious and their easy relationship, though Camilla still couldn't understand it, was infinitely precious. The almost instantaneous camaraderie hadn't needed to be worked at; she had never had to try *less* hard in her life, yet it worked, effortlessly and of its own free will. With Nico, and to almost the same extent with Loulou, she could simply be herself.

And here I am, she thought, reaching for the phone as it started to ring for the tenth time and catching a glimpse of her reflection in the kitchen window as she moved. If I'd passed myself in the street six months ago I wouldn't have recognized me. Someone had once remarked that death was nature's way of telling you to take it easy. Well, maybe divorce was nature's way of telling you it was time to go on a diet.

She picked up the phone, hoping that it wasn't the BBC again. Nico was supposed to have rung them this morning and had sloped off instead to look at a helicopter he'd taken a fancy to.

'Hello.'

'Ah, yes. May I speak to Nico please?' said the voice at the other end and Camilla almost dropped the phone. Horror flooded through her. There were some voices which one could never forget and Roz's was indelibly stamped in her memory. Roz. Jack. That fateful dinner party. Involuntarily, Camilla turned towards the doorway, almost expecting the nightmare scene that had taken place in Jack's study to be repeated. Stupid, stupid, she told herself fiercely. This was no recorded message, this was Roz on the other end of the phone. And she was asking to speak to Nico.

'I'm afraid he isn't here,' said Camilla, thinking wildly that she should be disguising her own voice, but unable to conjure up an accent in time. Why was Roz phoning Nico, anyway? For her TV programme? Did they know each other? But if that were the case surely either he or Loulou would have mentioned it before now. He couldn't know Roz, she thought possessively. It wouldn't be fair.

'I see. Well, are you expecting him home today?'

'Who's speaking, please?' prevaricated Camilla, her voice stiff and businesslike, and Roz's soft laugh made her skin crawl.

'Oh, don't worry, I'm a very close friend of Nico's. My name's Roz Vallender. Are you writing this down?'

It was an effort to speak; all the oxygen seemed to have been sucked from her lungs. 'Yes.'

'Well, would you let him know that I'd like to see him tonight. I'm at my London flat. If he can't make it, could he ring me. Got that?'

Hesitating for a suitable length of time, Camilla said, 'What number shall he ring?'

Again, the smooth, confident, overtly sexual laugh which knew no rejection. 'Don't worry about that, dear. Nico knows my number well enough. Goodbye.'

So there it was, thought Camilla numbly as the line went dead. The casually dropped bomb, wounding and maiming indiscriminately, but always seeming to land on her. There could be no mistake; Nico and Roz either had been – or still were – lovers, and once again she was the last to know about it. Greedy Roz, taking whomever she pleased to her bed, had most probably been seeing both Nico and Jack at the same time since the tone of her voice hadn't suggested that she and Nico had been out of touch for any serious length of time. She hadn't even had the *decency*, Camilla realized with a mixture of burning jealousy and hatred, to be faithful to the man whose mistress she was. Well maybe, just maybe, it was time to let Roz discover what it felt like to be on the losing side for once.

Not daring to analyse her muddled motives, knowing simply that she had to do it, Camilla set to work with a bottle of white Chardonnay and great attention to detail. Lunchtime slipped into afternoon and by seven in the evening, everything was done. Nico, invariably an hour late anywhere, had left that morning saying that he would be home by six thirty at the latest. Camilla, falling into an armchair and pouring herself another small glass of wine, reckoned that she had another half-hour in which to plan the finer details of the campaign. Several minutes later, when none whatsoever had come to mind, she gave up and had another drink instead. How, after all, could she be expected to plan a seduction? She had never in her life tried it.

Chapter 17

'You look exhausted.'

'I'm not exhausted, I'm just windswept,' said Nico with a grin, running his fingers through his blond hair and trying to look guilty. 'I bought the helicopter.'

'Then you're exhausted and broke,' Camilla told him, pushing an enormous glass of Scotch into his hand and marvelling that she could still talk to him naturally. 'Let's hope the cheque doesn't bounce.'

'Let's hope the helicopter doesn't either. Cheers.' He took a gulp of his drink and almost choked. 'Christ, there isn't any water in it. Are you trying to get me drunk, Cami?'

'Of course,' she replied lightly, allowing her gaze to drop the length of his body. 'When I've done that I shall take compromising photographs of you and send them off to the *News of the World*. I hope you're hungry, by the way.'

'Ah.' He regarded her gravely. 'You've drugged the food as well, to make doubly sure. Have I time for a shower before it's ready?'

'I should hope so,' admonished Camilla as she disappeared in the direction of the kitchen. 'You want to be nice and clean, don't you, for the *News of the World*?'

She was just putting the finishing touches to the steak *au poivre* when Nico returned wearing only a pair of white Fiorucci jeans and a loose, cotton shirt. She had turned up the central heating quite deliberately two hours earlier.

He tweaked a strand of her hair as she poured the cream and brandy sauce over the tender fillet steaks. 'That looks great, Cami. And you're looking pretty good yourself tonight. Going out somewhere special?'

Camilla shook her head and hoped that she hadn't overdone it. She had taken great care to ensure that she looked 'pretty good' rather than done up to the eyeballs, which was why she was wearing just a plain white silk shirt and a clean pair of ultra-faded jeans rather than anything deliberately glamorous. And Nico would have to be very close indeed before he could smell the subtle fragrance of the perfume she was wearing.

Nico carried the plates through to the sitting-room, where Camilla had laid a small table and lighted fat beeswax candles. She followed him with the bowls of buttered courgettes, incredibly garlicky mushrooms and golden sautéed potatoes. Two bottles of good Beaujolais, opened earlier in order to have time to breathe, stood at opposite ends of the table glowing ruby red in the candlelight. Not too obvious, she told herself reassuringly; Nico liked candles and often lighted them himself. Music, though, was a different matter. She had rummaged through his vast CD collection earlier and unearthed an Eva Cassidy CD, then had chickened out and hurriedly returned it to its case.

The choice must be left to Nico, and she'd just have to pray that he wouldn't choose something too earsplitting.

'Now, what goes well with steak *au poivre* and Beaujolais?' mused Nico, surveying the stacks of records and CDs as he always did before sitting down to eat, and Camilla held her breath. If he played Eminem now she wouldn't be able to go through with it.

She almost sagged with relief when Ella Fitzgerald at her most laid-back flooded the room with her sexy voice and the accompaniment of a slow, mellow tenor saxophone.

'Good old Ella,' murmured Nico, sliding on to his chair and winking at Camilla. 'Every time I hear her she just makes me want to take all my clothes off.'

The thought made Camilla's skin tingle. She looked pointedly down at his bare brown feet. As Nico's housekeeper she knew only too well that he didn't possess a single pair of underpants.

'It wouldn't take you long,' she observed drily. 'Do you realize that you're in the very worst position in the world to play strip poker?'

'Or the very best,' he replied with a wicked smile as he heaped mushrooms on to his plate. 'And you don't have too much of an advantage yourself, Camilla. I may be young and innocent' – she pulled a face – 'but even I can tell that you aren't wearing a bra.'

'Eat your steak,' instructed Camilla, wondering what Roz was doing at this moment and whether Nico would realize soon that she had disconnected the phone. How clever she was, she told herself, to have thought of absolutely everything. 'Eat,' she repeated, 'and tell me all about your new helicopter.'

Now what do I do, she wondered two hours later, praying that her courage wasn't about to fail her.

Here were the soft lights, the slow music and the man and woman who were supposed to fall into bed together, but somehow she couldn't quite find either the words or the way to get them there. Should she just say it? Just do it? And what if Nico howled with laughter at the craziness of the idea or – even more humiliating – rejected her with a polite smile and an awkward pat on the head?

Don't even think about it, she told herself fiercely, scarcely listening to Nico's scurrilous account of the reasons for the break-up of one of the film world's most famous marriages. She had to go ahead, carry out her plan, because she was jealous and somehow revenge would shrink that jealousy.

An eye for an eye, a man for a man, she thought, boosted by the smooth, warm Beaujolais.

Nico had brought girls home for bed and breakfast before now and it hadn't bothered her. Just because she no longer had a sex life herself, she didn't begrudge the rest of the world carrying on as if nothing had happened.

But Camilla seriously wondered whether she could ever completely forgive Nico for sleeping with Roz. It was a form of betrayal, and although in her heart she realized that the reason he hadn't told her about his relationship with Roz was because he didn't want to upset her any more, she was still furious with him. She felt foolish, uninformed, a child from whom grown-ups kept secrets. She could imagine Nico and Loulou discussing it together, deciding that it would be better if Camilla didn't know. Well, this time it would be Roz who wouldn't know.

But first she had to make it happen.

'You aren't listening to a word I've been saying,' protested Nico, jerking her back to the present. He stretched, catlike, and tilted the half-empty wine bottle towards Camilla's glass. 'And I *shall* be asking questions later,' he warned her, straightfaced.

It occurred to him that there might be something on her mind. Cami wasn't normally this quiet, and she seemed different tonight somehow, an air of recklessness when she did speak combining with her usual measured wit. And there were brief moments when she appeared almost awkward, as if she had something to tell him, but couldn't quite pluck up the courage to come out with it.

'Have you broken something?' he said suddenly, and Camilla frowned.

'No. Why, do you think I should?'

'Only if you really want to. You look a bit strange, that's all.'

She smiled, pretending to take offence. 'How very debonair of you to say so. I cook you a brilliant steak, share your cheap wine, listen to your appalling gossip and all you can tell me is that I look strange.'

'You look very nice,' he teased her.

But she looked better than that; gorgeous was the rather old-fashioned word which sprang into his mind as he lay back against the grey silk cushions and surveyed Camilla through half-closed eyes. The silk shirt, shimmering in the firelight, was just transparent enough to reveal the darker shadows of her nipples. As Betty Grable and Marilyn Monroe had in their day been gorgeous, so was Camilla, thought Nico with typically Italian appreciation. Her body had real curves and her lightly tanned skin glowed, exuding warmth. Whenever Camilla threw back her head and laughed, revealing white teeth and a slender brown neck, Nico longed to take her in his arms, to run his fingers over that adorable body, to kiss her soft, smiling mouth.

But Camilla, unfortunately, was off-limits. Her bruised innocence, her trust in him, and the recent drastic end to her marriage had forced him into a moral corner; they had a platonic relationship in which he took enormous pride and pleasure, since apart from Loulou he had never had a truly platonic friendship with a woman. Now he had two and he didn't want to lose either of them, but, Christ, it was frustrating to want someone like crazy and to feel impelled not to do anything about it.

Besides, whereas it was perfectly OK to screw the au pair

girl, somehow sleeping with the housekeeper didn't have quite the same ring to it.

'What are you thinking?' he asked idly, to change the subject, and Camilla regarded him for several seconds, her long-lashed turquoise eyes thoughtful, before replying.

'There is someone,' she said, breathing very shallowly, 'whom I very much want to go to bed with. But I don't know how to get them there. What if they turned me down?'

Nico felt his heart thudding slowly and heavily. It hadn't behaved like this since he was a teenager. What did she mean, *someone*? Was she referring to him? Was she telepathic?

Perhaps she meant someone else, he thought wildly, but the way she was looking at him all of a sudden made him doubt it ... Christ, what could he *say*?

'Anyone who turned you down, Cami, would have to be crazy,' he replied, choosing every word with care. If she meant someone else, he would die. If she meant him, he would have to face the dilemma of choosing between the moral decision at which he had arrived months ago, and the burning need he had to make love to her right now.

The silence deepened, broken only by the intermittent crackling of the fire. Nico could hear his own breathing.

'So you think,' said Camilla at last, her voice catching slightly, 'that if I just ... went ahead and let him know what I wanted, he wouldn't mind too much?'

'I'm sure he wouldn't.' It was a struggle getting the words out. Desire flooded through him as he caught the expression in her narrowed eyes and he had to force himself not to move towards her. Instead, Nico waited while Camilla apparently thought his words over, taking great care to digest each one. 'You could just reach across and touch him,' he continued slowly, 'and see how he reacts. Then you'd know for sure that he wasn't going to reject you.'

Camilla nodded, her hair gleaming in the half-light, her mouth still pensive. Then, just as he was beginning to think that she would never move, her hand stretched out, coming to rest upon his brown forearm.

'Like this?' she murmured tentatively, and Nico swallowed hard before inclining his head in agreement.

'Like that.'

'And then, should I move a little closer?'

Silently, holding his breath now, he nodded once more.

'Like this?'

'Just like that. Exactly like that . . .'

Chapter 18

The situation was so erotic, so slow and hesitant and desirable that Nico didn't know if he could stand it. He felt like a virgin now, both helpless and enthralled by the prospect of what lay ahead. He who was so experienced was the innocent one and Camilla, whom he guessed must be light years behind him as far as sexual experiences were concerned, was completely in charge.

When the butterfly touch of her warm fingers insinuated slowly up his arm and she edged closer still, so that he caught the first faint breath of her perfume, Nico could no longer help himself. Gently, he caught her other hand in his and pulled her towards him until his mouth was inches from her own.

'Would it be right to kiss him?' she whispered, searching his face with an intensity that almost melted his soul.

'I think that might be the very best thing you could do,' agreed Nico, hearing the unsteadiness in his own voice and aching with need for her.

'Like this?'

Careful, thought Camilla, pulling away at last. I'm on my way, but it does have to be *my* way. Keep control. Don't even think about how wonderful it feels. I mustn't lose the upper hand.

Nico had a beguiling mouth and a clever tongue. It was almost impossible not to compare his kisses with Jack's, and there really *was* no comparison at all, but then maybe Jack kissed differently when he was making love to Roz, as he had kissed differently when he had first made love to Camilla.

But back to the present. Here she was with Nico, who was allowing her to make all the moves and who showed absolutely no sign at all of wanting to hurry the proceedings along. It was up to her to do something, and clearly the decision to be made next was whether she should lead him up to his bedroom or hers, or make love to him right here.

Until tonight, she had never done it anywhere but in bed.

That was it then, she decided with a small smile. She was a changed woman, wasn't she? So the floor it had to be.

'Stand up,' she instructed, and when Nico obeyed, her fingers went surely to the front of his jeans, unzipping them with one long, slow movement. Their bodies touching now, she could feel the hard warmth of his desire for her against her stomach, the equally unyielding muscles of his chest and abdomen through the gossamer silk of her shirt.

So, thought Camilla with relief, she was, after all, still capable of making a man want her.

Moments later her clothes slid to the floor to join Nico's and all that existed in the world were their warm, naked bodies and that magical desire.

She had succeeded in bringing him this far; now it was time for Nico to take the lead.

'Your turn,' she murmured, and he smiled, running his index finger lightly along the sensitive line of her collar-bone and gazing with frank appreciation at the splendid swell of her breasts.

'You're beautiful, Cami. You should go without clothes more often.'

The tiny joke was ostensibly to put her at ease, she realized, yet she wasn't in the least nervous. Bizarrely, it seemed that

Nico was the one more in need of reassurance now.

'Remember the first time we met?' she said, bringing her arms up to rest lightly upon his own shoulders. 'I was naked then, and I thought I'd die of embarrassment.'

'You aren't embarrassed now, though?'

'How could I be?'

And then his arms closed around her, properly, and she felt the unclothed heat of their bodies as they met fully for the first time. Shyly at first his tongue probed her mouth, then his hands were upon her hips pulling her gently against him in time with the rhythmic deepening of the kiss. Minutes later he sank almost in slow motion to his knees, his mouth caressing her breasts, her taut stomach and her thighs. The feel of him was almost too much for Camilla. She closed her eyes, willing herself to remain unmoved. It was vital that Nico didn't realize how deeply he affected her. He had, after all, done these same things with Roz.

Then he drew her down on to the rug beside him and with one graceful movement rolled into position, taking his weight with his arms. She could feel him, ready for her, resting exactly over the most sensitive part of her body.

She waited, holding her breath and unable now to look at him as he began to move back and forth over her, rocking himself gently against her until she bit her lip in order to stop herself crying out. She was so *ready* for him that the waiting was almost intolerable.

'Camilla,' he sighed, and her fingers, digging into his smooth brown back, silently answered him. She lifted her hips a fraction and Nico entered her, filling her until helplessly she heard herself sighing too.

And as soon as he began to move, slowly and deliberately and with perfect control, she knew without doubt that she would reach a climax. It would be impossible not to . . .

It was the ultimate irony, she thought, that *this* time – when all she wanted to do was show Nico that he *wasn't* perfect – it was actually going to happen.

It never had while she was with Jack.

Remember Roz, Roz with Jack and Roz with Nico, she told herself desperately. Think of anything, *anything* but this . . .

But the spiralling sensations were increasing of their own accord, as if her body recognized a sensational lover even if her mind was determined to deny it. In desperation Camilla stopped moving, but the exquisite pleasure of Nico's body merely increased and she realized that her climax was inescapable.

Closing her eyes and gritting her teeth, forcing herself to remain immobile, Camilla gave herself up to the escalating pleasure flooding her like a drug. The need to cling to him, to move against him and cry out was unbelievable, but she forced herself not to admit by a single movement what he had made happen. Her breath was held, her body quite still. Please God, he mustn't realize what he had done.

Only when at last the ebbing circles of rapture had died away and she trusted herself to continue, did she reach for him once more and pull him deeper still inside her.

'Don't stop, Nico,' she murmured, and buried her face against his neck with great care in order to ensure that he would neither see nor feel the hot tears upon her cheeks.

Despite the mounting, almost unbearable excitement within him, Nico controlled himself, taking pride in the fact that he was able to do so in order to give Camilla the time she needed. Women, he knew, weren't like men in that respect; they required more time in which to allow the sensations to build, and plenty of careful stimulation to the different erogenous areas of their bodies. Their own pleasure was as important to him as his own. But not having realized until now quite how badly he had wanted to make love to Camilla and how very much he did want to please her, he began to be concerned when he realized that he was failing her.

He had tried everything, and still she gave no sign of achieving that pleasure which he so desperately wanted to give her. Knowing that he couldn't last much longer, he tried to think. What else could he possibly do . . .?

'Tell me what you want,' he murmured, slowing down and brushing her neck with his lips, but Camilla ran her fingernails along the curve of his spine, pulling him closer and whispering 'I only want you,' and Nico was lost. His breathing quickened, his back arched. The self-control, too long sustained, disintegrated as he cried out Camilla's name . . .

'You didn't enjoy it, did you?' he said with a trace of sadness, later.

Camilla, sunk deep inside the midnight blue silk robe he had brought for her, gave him a forgiving look and for a brief moment despised herself for her treachery.

'I never do anything I don't enjoy,' she said reassuringly, stroking his arm, but Nico just looked even more upset.

'But nothing happened. It can't have been much fun for you.'

When most women faked it, they pretended they had when they hadn't, she thought with a faint twitch of her lips. How many did it the other way around?

'At least I didn't pretend, like lots of women,' she argued reasonably. 'You wouldn't have wanted that, would you?'

'No. Are you disappointed with me, Cami?'

'I'm only disappointed with me,' she said in a low voice. 'You mustn't blame yourself, Nico. It wasn't your fault, after all. I'm sorry,' she continued wearily, 'maybe I should have pretended, like other women do. So *many* women fake it, Nico, but I just couldn't. It wouldn't have been fair, to either of us.'

'Better luck next time, maybe,' he said, brightening and kissing her fingers.

I'm a bitch, such a bitch, thought Camilla, but I've got to do it.

Slowly she drew her hand away. 'There won't be a next time, Nico,' she told him calmly, while inside her soul wept for what she was doing. 'I really don't think that would be a very good idea.'

The tears which she had earlier concealed from Nico now rolled unheeded down Camilla's face and neck as she lay alone and lonely in the centre of her too-large double bed.

So she had done it and where had it got her? Her easy, friendly relationship with Nico was lost for ever and she had carried out the cruellest of deceptions, all because she no longer wanted to be the odd one out. She had yearned to be in there, with all the rest of them, doing the things they did and playing the same sexual games.

And too late she had learnt that playing these games was just as likely to bring unhappiness as pleasure. She had abused and hurt Nico, and shamed herself.

Wiping her face with the edge of the duvet, she stared up at the ceiling and recalled the final moments of his own joyful climax. She had breathed in the soft, honeyed scent of his chest as his body had stiffened, and exalted in her power over him whilst his breathing had deepened and he had called her name in wonder.

Sex with Jack had been silent, almost mechanical, and quite without the melting tenderness which Nico had shown towards her. Once, during a furious argument, Jack had told her that she was hopeless in bed and from then on, Camilla had concentrated grimly on trying to improve, but the harder she worked the more elusive her own climaxes had become, obstinately refusing to happen.

It had never occurred to her for an instant, she realized now, that maybe it was Jack who was the rotten lover.

'Are you asleep?'

'Yes,' replied Nico, and his subdued tones brought a fresh lump to her throat. Hesitantly, she approached the bed, grateful for the fact that he hadn't switched on a light. Apologizing for and explaining her awful behaviour was going to be difficult enough, even with the darkness to shield her shame.

'I'm so sorry, about . . . earlier.'

'I told you, you aren't the one who should be sorry. It was entirely my fault.'

As she had known it would, his Italian male pride wouldn't allow him to forgive himself, because in his eyes he had badly failed her. Her heart clamouring in her chest, Camilla took another step forward and reached out towards the dark shadowy figure in the bed.

'But it wasn't your fault,' she spoke abruptly into the darkness, 'because I was lying earlier. I did enjoy it, every second of it. You were amazing. And when it . . . happened . . . I just didn't let you know, because for some stupid reason I didn't want you to know how much you affected me. So I *am* sorry . . .'

'Don't,' commanded Nico sharply. 'Please don't say that. I don't want you to have to make excuses to me, *for* me. I don't want you to feel *sorry* for me. I can stand your disappointment, Camilla,' he continued, his voice bitter. 'I can just about cope with that. But the one thing I certainly *cannot* stand is your pity.'

As the extent of the damage she had done sank axe-like into Camilla's mind, she felt something within her die. Nothing she could say now would succeed in convincing Nico that he was blameless. He was Italian, extremely well known, and famously irresistible to women. Having never known rejection before, he was now quite unable to cope with it.

Realizing that he really hadn't deserved this, Camilla hadn't any choice other than to say what she did, after that.

'Don't worry. I realize that I can't stay here. I'll leave tomorrow.'

And when he hadn't replied, she felt as if she'd been kicked in the stomach. So this was what it was like to hurt people.

No fun at all.

Chapter 19

Nico was out and Camilla was packing, hating herself, when the doorbell rang. Probably someone from the domestic agency she had phoned earlier, requesting a housekeeper who could take over immediately. Someone safe and middle-aged, who wouldn't cause Nico any problems.

But it wasn't, quite.

Camilla drew back, feeling sick, as for the first time since *that* night she came face to face with Roz.

Even more astounded, Roz said: 'Good Lord! What on earth are *you* doing here?' And when Camilla didn't reply, she continued, 'Maybe we should talk.'

Once inside the kitchen, Camilla prepared coffee and avoided looking at Roz, while Roz found her gaze almost irresistibly drawn towards Camilla, unable to believe how amazing she looked. Loulou had very casually mentioned that Camilla had 'got her act together', but she hadn't hinted to what extent. Shaken as she obviously was by this unexpected confrontation, the difference in the woman was astounding. Previously mousy and plump, Camilla now generated colour, from her artfully styled tawny blond hair to her fuchsia pink Charles Jourdan high heels.

Roz experienced that momentary uncomfortable sensation of insecurity which only ever made itself felt when she was in the company of a female attractive enough to present a threat.

The coffee-making ritual over, Camilla seated herself at the opposite end of the kitchen table and forced herself to return the gaze of the woman who had changed her life. For several moments no-one spoke. Camilla concentrated upon examining Roz's white Ellesse track suit. She would have bet money that beneath it Roz was naked. Hadn't she come to see Nico, after all?

'You've lost a lot of weight,' said Roz eventually, and Camilla threw her an icy stare.

'It's been known to happen when a marriage breaks up,' she replied tonelessly. What did Roz really want to talk about? The Cambridge diet?

'You're looking well, anyway,' said Roz defensively and for a split second Camilla almost felt sorry for her. She looked small, and hunted, like a wild animal. Her famous poise was slipping, it seemed. *At last*.

'I'm feeling well, considering. What else would you like to say, now that you're here?'

Roz considered the woman sitting opposite her, appreciating that it wasn't only her appearance which had undergone a drastic change. Until today, she would have doubted that Camilla even fully understood the word 'cool', yet here she was now playing the Snow Queen to the hilt.

Since it wasn't in her own nature to apologize, the words didn't come easily.

'I suppose . . . I'm sorry about what happened. To you . . . and Jack.'

Again the disconcertingly direct gaze. Despite the heat, Roz shivered.

'You suppose,' Camilla spoke the words slowly, as if they were a new and foreign language to her. 'Shouldn't you be sorry about what happened between *you* and Jack?'

'All right. That too. I'm sorry for all of it.' Roz shifted uncomfortably in her seat, pushing away her untouched coffee cup and wishing now that she had simply turned and left when Camilla had answered the door. 'I presume that Nico isn't here?'

'No, he isn't. You weren't really expecting me to forgive you, were you?' Dismissing the subject of Nico, Camilla leant forwards, her turquoise eyes glittering with intent.

'I suppose not. It just seemed the right thing to say, under the circumstances. I wasn't *expecting* you to be here, for Christ's sake.' Roz shook her dark hair away from her face in an unconsciously defiant gesture. Throughout their time together at school, *she* had controlled Camilla quite effortlessly. Watching her now, in perfect control, was far less entertaining. It was like Laurel slapping Hardy – until it happened, unthinkable.

'It was me, of course, whom you spoke to on the phone yesterday,' said Camilla, glancing out of the window as if the weather were more important than their conversation.

'I realize that now,' Roz began to lose her temper. 'And it was you, *of course*, who didn't pass on my message to Nico.'

Camilla's smile was triumphant. 'I disconnected the telephone, too.'

'And you really thought you had the right to do all that?'

'Why not? I can do anything I want. You certainly do.'

Itching to slap Camilla, and realizing that this was something she most definitely must *not* do, no matter how gratifying it would be, Roz rose from her chair. She had to get out of here.

'I have a letter here for Nico,' she said evenly, placing the sealed envelope on the table between them. 'This time, I think you should make sure he receives it.'

Camilla didn't even glance at the envelope. Picking up

the coffee cups and crossing to the sink, she emptied their untouched contents down the drain.

'What a waste,' she said briskly. 'Don't worry, I'll see that he gets it. You can find your own way out, I presume?'

Knowing that she was being ridiculous, she sprayed air-freshener around the kitchen as soon as Roz had left so that no trace remained of the heady, sensual perfume she had been wearing.

It was a shame, she thought idly, that she couldn't obliterate Roz herself at the touch of a button.

Then, as she snatched up the envelope, the tears began to flow unbidden down her cheeks once more. Too much had happened in the last twenty-four hours and now she was compounding her own wickedness by reading another person's private correspondence. This was what Roz had reduced her to.

But at the same time she felt entirely justified in doing so. It would make her feel better for a start, as if in some small way she was getting back at Roz. And what could it be after all, besides an 'I'd like to see you' note? Camilla ripped the envelope open.

Darling, Wonderful news – I'm pregnant.
You're going to be a genuine Italian papa. And with our looks and our brains, how can our baby fail? Phone me.
All love. Roz.

Dropping the letter on to the table, Camilla wondered whether Roz had left it in her care knowing beyond a shadow of a doubt that she *would* read it.

Chapter 20

When Loulou opened the door wearing an enormous violet T-shirt and nothing else Camilla stepped back, embarrassed.

'Lou, I should have called first. Am I interrupting something?'

'Only a CIA meeting,' replied Loulou, reaching out and deftly removing Camilla's dark glasses before she could protest. 'What's with the shades, sweetie? Ah ... say no more.'

The eyes were red, but not too red, and Camilla sounded cheerful enough, which was a relief.

'I cried, but not for long,' Camilla explained matter-of-factly. 'But look, if you've got company I can come back later.'

'No need.' Loulou stepped aside and waved her past. 'I was just being a lazy toad. Come in and tell me all the gossip. How's Nico?'

When Camilla had removed her coat and curled up in the overstuffed armchair with a glass of Sauvignon and Loulou had resumed her sprawling position on the sofa opposite, Loulou repeated her question.

'Nico's fine, but I'm afraid we've had a bust-up,' she said lightly, although her fingers were tightening their grip around her glass.

Loulou almost bounced off the settee in dismay. 'But why!'

she wailed. 'I thought you two got along brilliantly. Whatever happened?'

Camilla forced an uncomfortable smile. 'We got on a bit too brilliantly, I'm afraid.'

'Nico seduced you!'

'Actually, I suppose you could say I seduced Nico. It was a big mistake. I moved out this morning, as soon as I'd hired my replacement. It was all my fault,' she added with a shrug, knowing that Loulou would be relaying their conversation back to Nico, 'but what's done is done. *C'est la vie*, and all that. I've taken a room at the Arundel Hotel until I manage to find myself a flat.'

Loulou leant across to refill Camilla's glass which, to her surprise, was empty. 'What a bloody shame,' she said sympathetically, then with a wicked grin said: 'I've never been to bed with Nico. What's he like?'

'Lovely,' said Camilla, her eyes sad. 'The best. And I wish to God that I'd never done it.'

'You could always move back here with me,' Loulou suggested hesitantly, and Camilla burst out laughing.

'Of course I can't.'

'Why the hell not?'

'Simply because, dear Lou,' she explained slowly, 'I'm not blind. I can't help noticing, for instance, that that crumpled little heap of material over there by the door to your bedroom is in fact a pair of boxer shorts.'

'You're jumping to conclusions,' said Loulou, going pink. 'They could be mine.'

'There's a bottle of Armani aftershave on the top of the stereo,' suggested Camilla, and watched the shade of pink deepen from sugared almond to rose.

'I *like* Armani aftershave.'

'Particularly when it's worn by a good-looking male,' teased Camilla. 'So, who is he?'

'Oh, he's gorgeous!' sighed Loulou, abandoning all pretence and collapsing back against the cushions with a look of ecstasy on her face. 'I'm really, really in love this time.'

'Two reallys,' observed Camilla with admiration. 'He must *really* be special.'

'He is, he is.' Loulou sighed gustily once more, raising her glass in a salute and managing to splash red wine into her shimmering silver hair. 'And you'll be able to meet him later, he's coming over at four.'

'From the boxer shorts, I had the impression that he was living here.'

'He will be, before long.' The first shadow touched Loulou's face. 'It's just that at the minute he's sharing a flat with this girl, but as soon as he's sorted that out he'll move in with me.'

Camilla was silent for a moment. The last time Loulou had been this excited about a man it had been Mac, and her high hopes had been shattered. Now some inner instinct was telling her that events weren't going to run their course quite as smoothly as Loulou was predicting.

'He's living with this girl, then?' she said warily, and Loulou gestured with her free hand, dismissing the question.

'She's nothing to worry about. They were on their last legs before I even met Josh. You don't think I'm doing a Roz, do you?' she said suddenly, gazing at Camilla with a wounded expression in her eyes. 'They aren't *married* or anything, after all.'

'Of course you aren't doing a Roz,' Camilla responded. 'She's in a class of her own, isn't she? I just meant that I don't want you to get hurt. I hope everything works out for you both. Really I do.'

'When you meet him, you'll *know* that it will,' Loulou reassured her. 'I promise.'

Thoughtfully skirting the subject of Nico, Loulou steered the conversation around to Camilla's children. Camilla's eyes promptly filled with tears.

'I feel so guilty. I love them so much and I miss them terribly, but I simply can't cope with the idea of fighting with Jack to get them back. He says that I left *them*, so I can take a running jump. We've agreed on joint custody but Jack's using every excuse to stop me seeing them.'

'But Toby and Charlotte are happy,' said Loulou gently. 'It isn't as if they're suffering, is it? They're away at school most of the time, and Jack has Jennifer to help him with them when they're home. You told me yourself that you're getting on better with both of them now than you did when you were there all the time.'

'I know,' Camilla nodded awkwardly. 'But that only makes me feel more guilty. Maybe I wasn't a good enough mother. If I'd been better, they might miss me more.'

'Bullshit. Just thank your lucky stars that they're as well adjusted as they are and make use of the breathing space. You *need* some time on your own. In a year or two you'll be on your feet again, running some wildly successful business, and then you'll be able to buy a house big enough for the three of you and sort everything out with Jack.'

'Run a wildly successful business?' Camilla had to smile. 'Me?'

'If you set your mind to it, you could. Look how far you've come in just a few months. But if you really don't feel up to running one,' said Loulou with a naughty smile, 'marry one instead. Who cares who earns the money, so long as you have the right to spend it.'

Camilla hadn't any idea what to expect when she met the new love of Loulou's life, but she definitely hadn't expected him to be black.

Or that big. She could understand why Loulou leapt off the settee and slid her feet hastily into a pair of stilettos before running to fling her arms around Josh's waist. The man had to be six foot five at least.

And black.

Camilla felt guilty all over again, this time for being so surprised. She recalled how one day Toby had come home from nursery school and raved about his new friend, Leroy. Jack had said, 'Is he black?' and Toby had replied thoughtfully, 'No, he's brown. The same as Mummy's coat.'

Of course, Josh was brown too, his skin the colour of peanut butter, tawny against the whiteness of his baggy cotton shirt and loose-fitting beige trousers. And he was very handsome; his face looked as if it had been carved by a skilful craftsman. A small gold ring pierced his left earlobe and a gold Rolex gleamed upon his right wrist. When Loulou had finished hugging him he came towards Camilla, Rolex arm outstretched. She caught the scent of Armani aftershave and smiled, taking his hand.

'Cami, this is Josh,' said Loulou proudly, sliding her arm back around his waist. 'And this, darling, is my friend Camilla whom you've heard me talking about.'

'I remember,' he said cheerfully, and Camilla realized that he spoke with a slight Scottish accent. 'You were at school with

Lou and Roz Vallender. Well, I love Lou, but I can't stand the sight of that bitch Roz, so what do you think I'll make of you?'

It was the kind of blunt, verging-on-rude comment that Nico would have made and Camilla relaxed instantly.

'I bet I can't stand Roz more than you can't stand her,' she said, and Josh threw back his perfect head and laughed.

'Hey, I like you already. Lou, get us a beer, will you? We have to drink to this.'

'I found out today that Roz is pregnant by the way,' Camilla told Loulou as she was handed an ice-cold can of beer. She felt no shame nor guilt at passing on such private news.

'Poor baby,' remarked Joshua, but Loulou was fascinated.

'How did that happen?'

'In the usual manner, I suppose.'

'But *who*?' persisted Loulou, her eyes alight with intrigue. 'And how on earth did you get to hear about it first?'

Then it clicked and she threw up her hands in an agonized, helpless gesture. 'Oh Christ! Nico. Poor you, finding out like that. He told you last night and *that's* why you left.'

'Wrong,' said Camilla, amused by the way Loulou's mind had raced wildly ahead and feeling relieved because that really would have been an awful way to have found out. Roz may have been the catalyst, but at least her pregnancy hadn't. 'I decided to leave last night. It wasn't until this morning that I saw Roz and learned about the baby.'

She could tell that Loulou was biting her tongue, simply longing to ask how that meeting had gone but feeling that just for the moment she should keep quiet.

Joshua filled the moment of silence. Having drained his can of beer and handed it back to Loulou, he said, 'Got another one for me, angel?' then turned his eyes to the ceiling. 'That Roz, she isn't exactly a one-man woman, is she?' he remarked thoughtfully. 'I wonder if Nico Coletto really is the father of her child?'

Chapter 21

Marbled sunlight filtered through the pale green leaves of the beech trees, bringing much needed warmth to Roz's cheeks. The recent rain had left the long grass bright and springy which she noticed as she strode back towards the house.

Walking into the village to pick up a newspaper had seemed such a rural, *healthy* thing to do, but choosing to do it the morning after her announcement to the Press had been a big mistake. The inhabitants of Littleton Grey, having overcome their initial self-consciousness at having a media celebrity in their midst, were showing signs of becoming distressingly over-familiar with her. And gossip concerning Roz Vallender was so much more fascinating than that about widowed Mrs Everton and John Davies, the sub-postmaster.

'Says in the paper that that pop star chappie's the father,' said Maudie Thompson doubtfully, as she counted out the change with maddening slowness amidst the cluttered, haphazard interior of the village shop. 'But he don't drive a blue car does he? Isn't his the black one?'

Bitch, thought Roz, smiling so that Mrs Thompson wouldn't guess what she was thinking. She lived here; she couldn't make life difficult for herself in Littleton Grey.

'My brother drives a blue car, as a matter of fact. Maybe you were thinking of him?' she suggested sweetly. From the corner of her eye she could see a group of four teenagers dawdling in the High Street outside. 'Thank you, Mrs Thompson.'

'Oh well, don't forget that we sell all that baby stuff here,' said the woman, gesturing aimlessly towards the back of the shop. 'Everything you need, *Miss* Vallender.'

Roz didn't doubt it. She left the shop hurriedly, wishing now that she could jump into her car. Being recognized was something she was accustomed to, but glimpsing the sly looks on the faces of the teenage girls as she passed them made her uneasy. Here in this small village, pregnancy outside wedlock was still something of which to be ashamed. In their eyes she had been caught out; 'in the club' and without a husband to show for it.

'Hey, miss,' one of them yelled after her, while the others burst into giggles. 'If you ever want a babysitter, I'll do it. An' I got all Nico's records. He's the business. I'll do the babysittin' for free if he drops me home after.'

'That ain't all you'll do for free an' all, Shirley Birkett,' spluttered one of the other girls, and they all collapsed with laughter against the front of the shop.

Village idiots, thought Roz viciously, burrowing into her fur coat and ignoring them totally. *Damn*, she wished she'd brought her car.

And now, as she rounded the corner and the front of the cottage came into view, Roz swore again. A pearl-grey Bentley was parked outside on the drive. Her first thought – reporters – faded with the realization that not many of them drove Bentleys. Someone from the TV company? A big boss, who had driven down to deepest Gloucestershire in order to castigate her for daring to become pregnant without asking first if it were allowed? She briefly considered slinking back into the cover of the bushes and waiting until whoever it was disappeared, but at that moment the driver's door was thrown open and the mystery solved.

Roz swore for the third time. For Christ's sake, what was her *mother* doing here?

'You naughty girl, I've been waiting here for hours!' declared Marguerite Martineau, her black kid-gloved hands upon her narrow, leather-clad hips. Then she opened her arms wide, in the manner that reminded Roz so strongly of school open days that she could almost smell chalk.

'I've only been out for half an hour, mother,' Roz told her, as she kissed Marguerite's amber-shaded cheek, 'and if you'd used your mobile you wouldn't have needed to wait at all.'

'Then it's a shame you didn't use yours, darling,' reprimanded her mother triumphantly.

'I'm sorry. Come inside and have a drink. It's lovely to see you again.'

Marguerite slipped her arm through her daughter's as they walked together across the gravelled driveway to the front door.

'Of course it is, darling. In times like these a girl needs her mother. As you well know, Roz,' she added, catching the expression in her daughter's dark eyes. For a brief moment, Roz's face reflected the painful memories her mother had evoked. Recovering quickly she turned to her and said: 'Oh, come inside and let's have a drink.'

Marguerite Martineau, born with the somewhat less enticing name of Margaret Trott, was looking good.

She's fifty-five, Roz thought, mentally counting on her fingers. She must have had a face lift – when she had last seen her two years ago she had had bags under her eyes, hadn't she? Now there were none, just fine tanned skin and those arresting topaz eyes. As immaculately co-ordinated as ever, Roz was mildly surprised that she hadn't come down in a car that matched her outfit.

'So, darling,' remarked her mother brightly, leaning back in her chair and lighting a cigarette with a black and gold Dunhill lighter which *did* match, 'you're pregnant. Any idea who the father might be? And any plans to marry him?'

Roz was too accustomed to her mother's ways to be shocked. And to be fair, although she did know who the father of her baby was, it was more by luck than judgement that she had been able to narrow it down with such accuracy.

'Since you obviously read about my news in the paper,' she said evenly, 'you must also know who it is.'

'And are you going to make an honest man of him?'

'Now there's a question.'

Roz's poor opinion of marriage had been founded early on in her life having watched her parents plough five into the ground between them. The very idea had horrified her. What was the point, after all, of tying oneself to a single person and pretending that you were going to be faithful to them? At least, that was what she had always thought, until now.

'Tell me everything, darling,' said Marguerite, trying hard to sound cosy. 'After all, I am your mother. And you know that nothing you say will shock me.'

'All right,' Roz said cautiously, realizing that although it was quite out of character for her, she did need to talk about it. My hormones must be up the creek, she thought, feeling suddenly alone and out of control. 'Nico's the father. I didn't exactly say so to the Press, but when one of them hazarded a guess, I didn't deny it. I hope he doesn't think I've done it deliberately.'

Her mother smiled and stubbed out her cigarette. 'If that young man doesn't know by now what the Press are like, no one does. He isn't exactly unused to their attentions now, is he? But how does he *feel* about the news, sweetheart? Why isn't he here with you? He is rather gorgeous, I must say. You'll have a splendid looking baby, at least.'

Roz felt sick. As she leant across to pour coffee from the jug into two wide cups, she noticed that her hands were shaking. Admitting defeat was something she very seldom did.

'That side of things isn't working out too well,' she whispered with reluctance. 'It seems I've finally met a man who isn't interested in me.'

'But, for heaven's sake, why not?' exclaimed her mother indignantly. Roz was her only child, after all. 'He was interested enough a few months ago. And he's Italian, too! I thought his kind were supposed to adore children.'

'Only their own, apparently. And this one *is* Nico's,' said Roz, feeling hot tears behind her eyelids because her mother was taking her side. 'I wrote him a note and he didn't reply to it so I phoned him up and all he said was: "It's not very likely to be mine, is it?" And then he hung up. I haven't heard from him since.'

'The ungrateful little shit!' exploded Marguerite, topaz eyes blazing as she snatched up the telephone from the coffee table. 'Give me his number this minute, Roz, and let me speak to him.'

'Mother, really!' Despite everything, Roz started to laugh. 'What a very working-class line to take.'

Marguerite stared at the phone as if it were a kitten that had just peed all over her hands, and dropped it back on to the table. Then she had the grace to smile at her actions.

'It would sound a bit silly, I suppose. But I still don't understand why he doesn't want *you*, darling, regardless of the child. You've always had any man you cared to choose.'

'It's complicated,' said Roz, fidgeting with the silk fringe of the cushion beneath her arm. 'You see, I was seeing a man at around the same time as I was . . . seeing . . . Nico, and by a bit of bad luck he turned out to be the husband of someone I was at school with. Do you remember Camilla Avery-Jones?'

'Oh sweetheart, you know how I am with names. All school-girls sound alike to me. Which school are you talking about for a start?'

'Elm House.'

Marguerite's eyes narrowed in concentration, then fixed their gaze upon Roz. 'I think I *do* remember. Wasn't she the plump, fair-haired one? Rather too eager to please?'

'Yes, that's the one,' said Roz drily.

'And she wrote to you afterwards. I had to open the letter in order to find out the address so that I could return it.'

'Mmm,' replied Roz, her expression thoughtful. 'So it was pretty ironic, discovering that she was this man's wife. She also discovered that I was his mistress, of course, and she left him. They're filing for a divorce now.'

'If it hadn't been you, it would have been someone else,' declared her mother with the fatalistic air of someone who had, in her time, been in all these situations.

'Yes. Anyway, Camilla then met Nico through Loulou and it appears that he took her under his wing, so to speak. She became his housekeeper,' Roz explained, relating the news which she had only herself learnt last week after telephoning Loulou. 'And I think she must have developed some sort of crush on Nico because as soon as she found out that I was expecting his child, she walked out of the job. I get the impression that Nico's blaming me for lousing up Camilla's life and that this is his way of paying me back. He has ... scruples, Mother. And I'm just not used to men with those.'

Camilla stared at her fourth, slightly grimy-looking living-room, turned away from the sight of an even grimier kitchen glimpsed through the open doorway, and felt her toes curling with distaste inside her shoes. For such an astronomic rent, she had at least expected something clean.

'You innarrested?' asked the skinny man who was letting out the flat, and Camilla forced a regretful smile, while in her jacket pocket she fingered the slip of paper bearing the fifth and final address she had to see.

'It's lovely, but I'm afraid I was really looking for somewhere with a larger kitchen.'

'You no innarrested then?' he said in a monotone. 'Never mind. Plenny more to see it. No bother me, lady.'

Outside in the fresh air again, Camilla turned over the slip of paper and prayed silently that the address in Ealing would have windows you could see through. She had saved it until last because it was a house-share, something she had wanted to avoid. Living with Loulou had worked out, but she was aware that she had been very lucky. Sharing with a stranger would be a lot more difficult, all sorts of problems could arise. She recalled a scene in her mind from *The Goodbye Girl*, when Marsha Mason was woken up at four in the morning by Richard Dreyfuss humming his mantra whilst practising yoga in the nude. Who knew what horrors might lie in store for her at 43 Edgerton Avenue, Ealing?

When she reached the house twenty minutes later, however, she began to feel fractionally better. The sun had come out, which always helped, and the slightly overgrown garden at the front and side of the Victorian terraced house looked peaceful and reassuringly normal. Two grey cats stalked through the dewy undergrowth and from an open upstairs window she heard the halting, childish strains of a Souza march being practised on an out-of-tune piano.

Camilla knocked on the blue front door and held her breath. Inside, the piano stopped playing, a child yelled out, 'Door', and Camilla heard the sound of high heels clattering down a wooden staircase at speed.

'Hi! You're either from the Electricity Board or Home-finders,' declared a redhead with huge conker-brown eyes and a wide grin. As she stuck out one hand in greeting she pushed the other through her haphazard top knot of corkscrew curls and glanced over her shoulder at the small red-haired girl who had followed her to the door.

'I'm not from the Electricity Board,' said Camilla, shaking the woman's hand and smiling at the girl who looked to be about five.

'Thank God, because I've fixed the meter. Do come in, you don't look a bit like the agency made you sound. I was rather expecting a female bank manager.'

'That's nothing,' said Camilla, straightfaced. 'I was expecting Richard Dreyfuss.'

'How disappointing for you – you've found old Mother Hubbard instead! I usually try and hide the children somewhere inconspicuous when I'm showing people around. It puts them off, you see, they simply don't want to share a house teeming with brats, but they really are quite well-behaved brats. And it's too late to lock them in a dark cupboard now,' she added sadly as another small girl appeared on the staircase, 'because you've already seen them.'

'I heard one playing the piano,' said Camilla, to be friendly and show that it hadn't put her off. Turning to the five year old, who was unsuccessfully attempting to hide behind her mother's slender, jean-clad legs, she said: 'Was that you?'

'No,' replied the girl, brown eyes wide with innocence. 'That was Mummy.'

'I only bought the bloody thing last week,' said the woman, laughing delightedly at Camilla's *faux pas* and waving aside her attempts at apology. 'Don't panic, I know I'm awful at the moment, but I've always wanted to be able to play a piano. Every year I challenge myself to learn something new. Follow me,' she went on, leading the way through to a large, comfortably cluttered kitchen smelling deliciously of cinnamon and hung with copper pans, upside-down bunches of dried flowers and several very amateurish paintings. Camilla forbore to ask whether the children had executed these – one foot at a time was enough for any mouth – and besides, in her eyes the house was perfect. She already knew with absolute certainty that this was where she wanted to live.

The redhead clapped her hand over her mouth in dismay. 'How *rude* of me! I'm Zoë Sheridan, and this is Augusta, my eldest. We call her Gussie. The one on the stairs is Finola, Fee for short. No doubt we'll trip over her in just a minute when I show you the bedroom, but they really are good children, very quiet and their manners are far nicer than mine . . .'

'I like children,' said Camilla firmly. 'Truly, I'm not put off. I'm Camilla Stewart.'

They shook hands again with mutual relief, and Zoë showed her the rest of the house, apologizing all the time for the mess and explaining that as soon as she got organized she would be hiring a cleaning woman. The sunny sitting-room was dotted with children's toys and discarded clothes, but Camilla saw only the appealing warmth of it; this was a real home, as she had once had, and she felt at home here already.

Her bedroom, very small but decorated with bowls of scarlet and white silk flowers to match the wallpaper, was perfect. Whilst Zoë was fussing over a loose flake of paint on the windowsill, Camilla said carefully, 'I expect you have lots of other people to see before you decide. May I just say that I'm very interested in moving in here, and leave you my number so that you can contact me . . .?'

'You're *really* interested?' cried Zoë, amazed and delighted. 'Well, in that case, I don't need to see anyone else, do I? You can move in as soon as you like. Are you *sure* you don't mind about Gussie and Fee?'

'I'm sure,' said Camilla happily. 'And I've been staying in a terrible hotel for the last few days, so I'd like to move in tonight, if that's possible.'

'Done!' said Zoë. 'Thank God!'

Chapter 22

'Buy a bottle of champagne, Lou,' Joshua ran his hand absent-mindedly over her bare back, sending shivers down it as he always managed to do. Loulou breathed in, inhaling the crisp scent of his aftershave and looked fondly up at him. Josh looked spectacular in a dinner jacket, even though he had spent most of the evening complaining that the wing-collared shirt irritated his neck. The gold silk bow-tie and matching handkerchief in his top pocket were the only splashes of colour; apart from their vividness, darling Josh was as pure black and white as a Charlie Chaplin film. So long as he didn't open his mouth to reveal that wicked pink tongue of his, she thought smugly as she searched her evening bag for her purse.

She giggled as his fingers moved and the wide *diamanté* strap of her dress slipped off her pale shoulder. She had chosen the extravagant Zandra Rhodes creation specially, in order to match Joshua. The tight-bodiced, full-skirted black taffeta was saved from indecency only by the single strap which snaked up from her left breast, over her right shoulder and all the way down her back until it reached her left hip. The black taffeta, strewn with black-and-silver net butterflies, was slit to the thigh and lined with silver satin. Loulou had happily made sure that she looked spectacular, and her current favourite press photographers, particularly excited by the sight of her new 'close friend', had used up several rolls of film on the pair of them.

'This is crap, man,' Joshua had murmured out of the corner

166

of his mouth, quelling his Scottish upbringing and adopting a heavier-than-usual Jamaican accent.

'I know, I know,' hissed Loulou, clutching his arm and tossing back her wildly disorganized hair. They had fallen into bed earlier in the evening, overcome with lust, and there had been precious little time afterwards in which to get ready for the ball. 'But it's publicity. For *both* of us.'

'It's still crap.'

She watched him now as he headed towards the champagne bar, and shivered involuntarily, although the 2,000 guests ensured by means of body heat alone that she couldn't possibly be cold. The champagne bar was situated in the old library and had been strung with what seemed like miles of fairy lights for the occasion. It was weird, mused Loulou, to think that she was finally back here, in stuffy old Elm House, for a decidedly debauched all-night charity ball. She scarcely recognized the oak-panelled library, but then, that wasn't really surprising since she had always made a point of avoiding anything to do with books. The dining-room, where ranks of knackered refectory tables usually stood, was occupied now by a band too loud even for her practised ears. The massive hall where morning assembly had been held was pounding with the music of a rock group and heavy with the scent of cannabis. The washrooms, where she and Roz had smoked innumerable cigarettes, was now crammed with bright young things repainting their lips and snorting cocaine.

Plus ça change, thought Loulou with a wry smile. At least this night would be making tens of thousands of pounds for charity. The more the guests drank, smoked and snorted, the higher they got and the more they spent. Would the Renal Transplant Unit really be bothered if it knew that it had gained

167

its donation largely by virtue of illegal substances?

Like hell they would, she thought, draining the glass and wishing that Josh would return. And at least she wasn't getting through the night on coke or speed. No way. She was doing it purely on champagne. The champagne that she was buying at £40 a bottle. Christ, the amount she'd spent so far would surely buy a new dialysis machine. And – the thought crept unbidden into her slightly muddled brain – Josh had paid for none of it. Not a single drink. And quite abruptly, after several weeks spent resolutely denying that any such doubts ever existed, Loulou realized that all those hidden qualms were finally, unwillingly, becoming a reality.

She found herself in that most difficult situation: being wildly in love, but at the same time chillingly aware that it was all going to end in tears. Something was wrong and if *she* didn't have the experience to recognize the dawning symptoms, she told herself sadly, then no-one did.

Joshua was with her for neither her mind nor her body. And finally acknowledging the true reason for his apparent devotion didn't give her any happiness at all.

I must be mad, Mac told himself as he elbowed his way past a crowd of dickie-bowed stockbrokers and their Sloaney girl-friends. One of the men had his trousers round his ankles and everyone was shrieking with laughter. If it's that small I'm not surprised, thought Mac dismissively.

But he was still convinced that he was mad, coming all the way down to a charity ball in Gloucestershire in the very faint hope of seeing Loulou.

He didn't even know why he had done it. Impulse, presumably. But it was quite alien to his deliberately laid-back character. The idea of her had simply overwhelmed him earlier this evening, and he had driven almost against his will to Vampires. How would she react when she saw him there, after their last non-eventful meeting? Mac had been hollow with anticipation when he had walked into the packed wine bar – and quite disgusted with himself when he realized how disappointed he was to discover that she wasn't there.

Finally, he had asked Christo Moran where she was.

'The Easter Ball, at Elm House,' Christo had responded with a typically Irish shrug, at the same time pouring Chardonnay at lightning speed into six glasses. 'Some charity do at her old school.'

Shit, thought Mac, taking the glass which Christo had poured for him. All that anticipation and now this. What a waste. And this was his fifth drink in an hour.

'Call me a taxi,' he had demanded, and Christo had nodded sympathetically, only too aware of the power Loulou was capable of wielding even when she wasn't aware of doing so.

'Where to, Mac?' They both knew already what the reply would be.

'Elm bloody House,' said Mac, draining his glass in one. 'Gloucester-bloody-shire. I must be bloody mad.'

And now he was here, the only male in the entire place dressed in faded Levis and a baggy white linen shirt without a tie, only reluctantly allowed inside because he had employed every last ounce of his charm upon a very gay-looking doorman.

'My wife thinks I'm still in Egypt,' he had told him with a totally disarming smile. 'She's here with her sister and it's her birthday. I've flown back specially. I promise you, this will make her night.'

The doorman had pouted upon hearing the word 'wife' but an encouraging wink from Mac and a handful of tenners had finally done the trick. He was in.

Now all he had to do was locate Loulou among the frantic, heaving noisy masses. It shouldn't be too difficult, he thought sardonically; there were only about two thousand of them crammed inside the place. If he could make his way up the main staircase upon which a jazz band was playing 'Sweet Georgia Brown', and jostle for position at the carved-stone balustrade overlooking the main hall, he might have a chance of spotting her. Damn the woman, he cursed. And damn himself for succumbing to his own sudden desperate urge to see her.

Noise, noise, noise, thought Loulou miserably, realizing that she had been hiding in the loo now for over twenty minutes. Searching the bottom of her bag for stray aspirin to numb her headache, she stared at her reflection in the age-spotted mirror above the basin. The unglamorous fluorescent lighting wasn't doing anybody any favours, but it wasn't only that.

I'm not happy, she thought, reaching automatically for the fuchsia-pink lipstick which would show off her mouth to its best advantage, but which couldn't make her smile. Half of her wanted to run away, to disappear into the night and escape the problems which were becoming more menacing with every glass of champagne she drank. The other half wanted to stay, either to fight it out or simply pretend it wasn't happening. That, of course, would be the easiest thing to do for the moment, but it wouldn't solve anything.

Pathetic, she told her reflection, mouthing the single word with perfect clarity. The girl standing next to her dropped a pot of shimmering eye shadow into the basin and said, 'Shit.'

'Absolutely,' said Loulou, from the heart.

'You think you've got problems,' said the girl, abandoning the glass pot and zipping her make-up bag with a decisive gesture which made her look like an efficient secretary. Loulou noticed her eyelids were wet with recent tears. 'My fiancé disappeared upstairs with some little tart over an hour ago. They're in one of seven locked rooms on the second floor and I've shouted through the keyhole of every one.'

Despite her own unhappiness, Loulou was fascinated. 'What did you shout?'

'I said, "That's my husband you're bonking, and for your information, darling, I've got a gun," ' explained the girl gloomily.

'And do you?'

'I wish I did.' She managed a weak smile. 'You've cheered me up a bit. Can I buy you a drink? My name's Poppy.'

'I'd love a drink,' said Loulou, her own spirits lifting, 'but could we possibly have it in here? I rather need the privacy at the moment.'

'No problem,' said Poppy briskly. 'I'll go and get a bottle of bubbly, and you can tell me why you're having such a shitty evening.'

She turned to leave, clutching her purse, but Loulou deftly removed it from her grasp. 'Just outside the champagne bar you'll see a man holding a bottle of Moët. Tell him you're a friend of Loulou's and that she'd like her drink. Bring back the Moët and two clean glasses.'

Poppy looked doubtful. 'There are going to be a couple of hundred men holding a bottle of champagne.'

'Ah,' said Loulou, carefully gathering up her glittering skirt and sliding down the wall into a sitting position, 'but this one, you see, is black.'

Chapter 23

Where the hell *was* she? Mac leant against the balustrade, searching the crowds below for the instantly recognizable, rippling hair of his ex-wife. For almost an hour now he had been leaning and looking, and so far three women whom he had never seen before in his life had waved and smiled back at him, and climbed the curving staircase in order to introduce themselves. But there had been no sign of Loulou.

Was she actually here, after all? He was beginning to doubt it now, recalling the ricocheting decisions she had always been capable of. It was quite possible now that Lou was sitting in some seedy pub in North Wales playing dominoes with the locals, but at the same time some sixth sense told Mac that she was here. It was just a question of discovering exactly *where*.

Damn her, he thought with a trace of irritation. Loulou's spur-of-the-moment decisions always seemed to work out for her. Yet here he was, as out of place as a nun in a nudist colony, making his first truly spontaneous action in years . . . and it was proving to be a total disaster.

'It's not the fact that he's Jamaican,' explained Loulou, balancing her champagne glass precariously on her bent knees and examining a tiny hole which had appeared in one of her sheer black stockings. 'It's just that he bullies me. He does it very nicely, which is why I've only just realized that that's what it really is.

Do this, do that, buy this . . . but at the same time he's calling me angel and running his hand down my back. I guess I'm just a girl who can't say piss off,' she concluded with a sigh, leaning her head back against the cool white tiles and realizing that she was beginning to feel slightly drunk. What a relief, though, to finally voice the thoughts which had been subconsciously troubling her for days.

'Well, darling,' said Poppy, her cut-crystal accent becoming more pronounced with every glass of champagne, 'with your looks, you don't have to put up with gigolos, so if you know what's good for you, you *will* learn to say it. I suppose he's sensational in bed,' she added with a directness which Loulou found reassuring. She nodded, and Poppy said, 'I thought as much. He looked as if he would be when I introduced myself. Those kind always are, though, aren't they?'

'You mean good-looking men?'

Poppy laughed and shook her head. 'I mean bastards. Which is why, of course, they so often manage to get away with it.' Then she looked serious again, remembering why she was spending the evening in the ladies' lavatory instead of dancing out in the main hall. 'And speaking of bastards, I wonder how mine is getting on. What are we going to do, Loulou? Your man's been waiting out there for you for quite some time and he wasn't exactly thrilled when I told him you'd be back in five minutes.'

'Perhaps he's given up and gone home,' said Loulou wistfully, then gave herself a mental shake. Bloody hell, she hated being wistful. It simply wasn't necessary. She should be grateful to Poppy for helping her sort out her muddled ideas. Briskly she rose to her feet. 'But I don't care *what* he's doing,' she announced with a new determination, her silver-grey eyes flashing and her fingers snapping as she gestured Poppy to follow her lead. 'Let's see what we can do about your bastard. Do you think he'll still be in one of those rooms upstairs?'

'Oh, bound to be,' said Poppy gloomily. 'Yours isn't the only one who's good in bed, you know. Jamie always takes his time.' Then she brightened and winked at Loulou. 'Particularly when there's a madwoman shrieking through the keyhole that when he comes out she's going to shoot him.'

'Well, let's go then,' Loulou urged, helping her to her feet and tucking the almost empty bottle of Moët under her free arm. 'I think it's time we practised a little coitus interruptus.'

Mac was on the verge of giving up and going back to London when he heard Loulou, her voice echoing from the far end of the darkened corridor on the first floor. To his utter disgust he felt his heartbeat quickening and experienced a diving sensation in his stomach.

Without even daring to think, or to wonder how she would react when she saw him, he headed away from the gallery encircling the hall and made his way along the wide corridor, which was unlit. His eyes, accustomed to the glittering bright lights from the chandeliers, strained in the blackness to detect shapes or movements, but were unable to make such rapid adjustments. There were no sounds now, either, and for a second he wondered whether he had been hallucinating, conjuring up the sound of Loulou's voice because it was what he so badly wanted to hear.

Then he caught the rustling sound of taffeta skirts and realized that someone was standing just a few yards away from him. Narrowing his dark eyes, he glimpsed a flash of silver amidst the darkness and drew to a silent halt, his heart thumping wildly. If this was Loulou, what was she *doing*? And with whom? Dear God, this was all a terrible, humiliating mistake! If she's with a man, thought Mac, his stomach churning with jealousy, what on earth can I do? As only the second of Loulou's three ex-husbands, he hardly had any rights, after all, and none which permitted punching the other guy's lights out, which was what sprang most immediately to mind.

I'll go, he decided, praying that he could make his escape undetected. It had been wrong to come here. Now all he could do was have the grace to admit that to himself and leave.

Slowly and with extreme caution, Mac took first one step backwards, then another. Just as he was about to take his third step towards retreat, he heard Loulou's voice again. And this time he heard with astounding clarity exactly what it was that she was saying as she hammered her fist against a heavy wood-panelled door.

'You lousy son of a bitch, have you told her you've got herpes? I'd get out of there fast, sweetheart, if I were you – he'll only give to you what he gave to me. And I may not have a gun this time, but I'm still deadly serious.'

For several seconds there was total silence, whilst both Mac and the occupants of the room digested this thought-provoking statement. Then Mac heard angry male voices inside the room, and footsteps heading purposefully towards the door. Glimpsing another flash of silver as Loulou moved backwards, he ran unthinkingly towards her, reaching out into the blackness until his fingers encountered bare flesh. A shoulder. As Loulou squealed with fright and the door began to rattle he located her arm and yanked her towards him so fiercely that she stumbled on her high heels.

'Get *off*! Who is it? Let *go* of me . . .' she protested, wriggling like an eel, but Mac knew from long practice how to deal with that. Hoisting her expertly over his shoulder, and without saying a word, he started down the corridor just as the door began to open, heading back towards the noise and bright lights of the ball. It wasn't, he thought ironically, quite how he had envisaged his reunion with Loulou. But then when had anything ever gone according to plan where she was concerned?

Loulou was thinking as fast as she knew how, and she was thoroughly confused as a result. Was she being rescued or kidnapped? And whilst it would seem logical to assume that the man over whose shoulder she was unceremoniously dangling was Joshua, he didn't *feel* like Joshua. Cautiously raising her arm, she touched his hair. This definitely wasn't Joshua, she thought, realizing at the same time that the champagne she had consumed was battling against gravity in her stomach.

'Stop!' she hissed, pounding his shoulder. 'I feel sick, for Christ's sake. Put me down . . .'

But even as she spoke it became apparent that what her subconscious had already realized was becoming an inescapable, unbelievable reality. The silky texture of the hair she had touched, the grip of those hands around her thighs, that graceful, catlike stride . . .

But how was it possible that Mac was here, rescuing her from the clutches of two infuriated gay boys without even uttering a single word? What was he *doing* here? Was it really him?

They reached the end of the corridor, and as they rounded the corner to emerge upon the balustraded gallery, Loulou realized that she was being put down. But she kept her eyes resolutely shut, as she put out her hands until they rested against broad male shoulders. Adrenalin was hurtling through her body as if it were Brands Hatch and she was trembling slightly, sick now with anticipation and the thundering rush of love which she was quite unable to suppress.

'Lou, open your eyes and look at me.'

That voice. That melting, softly Scottish-accented voice was what got to her most of all, and she felt the rush quicken, electrifying every nerve-ending in her body. Finally convinced at last that he was real, she dared to meet his gaze.

Oh, that dear face! Those beautiful brown eyes with their thick, dark lashes and the fine tracery of laughter lines fanning out at the corners even though he wasn't laughing. And that irresistible mouth . . . how could one mouth be so exquisite, yet as cruel as Mac's had been when he had left her?

'What are you doing here?' she murmured, still mesmerized by his face and fighting the urge to kiss him.

'No, me first. Do you really have a gun?'

'Of course I don't have a gun!'

'Do you really have herpes?'

'Mac!' It was a wail of protest, and his mouth betrayed the glimmer of a smile.

'Well, I had to ask, didn't I? Who were you shouting at, back there . . . or who did you *think* you were shouting at?'

'Someone I've never even met,' dismissed Loulou with impatience. 'It's not important. Oh Mac, can I give you a hug?'

She had said it a thousand times before, and on most of those occasions it had irritated him. He had loved her, but her constant need for affection, for *proof* of that love, had somehow cheapened it for him. What did a hug or a kiss prove, after all? Nothing.

Now, however, things were very different.

'Only if I can hug you as well,' he said hesitantly, and Loulou's grey eyes promptly filled with tears. Reaching for him, sliding her arms around him, she gave herself up to the embrace she had been missing so badly, for so long.

Nobody could hug like Mac.

'*Now* tell me what you're doing here?' she pleaded when he finally released her. 'In particular, what are you doing here in those clothes?'

Not that he didn't look adorable, of course, but it was rather noticeable apparel amidst the formal black and white worn by every other man present at the ball.

'I came to see you,' he said simply, and this time the tears spilled over, trickling unheeded down Loulou's cheeks. Touching each tear in turn, he added: 'This wasn't supposed to happen.'

'I'm happy. You know I always cry when I'm happy,' she said, sniffing inelegantly. 'You *should* know that.'

'I do. I remember you watching the Olympics on TV.' Taking a clean linen handkerchief from his shirt pocket, he wiped her wet cheeks, taking care not to smudge her eye make-up. 'You burst into tears every time somebody won a medal. By the end of the Games you'd almost completely dissolved.'

Loulou smiled. 'And you used to tell me that—'

'Well hel-lo!' said Poppy loudly, appearing behind them with a huge and knowing smile all over her face. 'Not interrupting anything, am I?'

'This is Poppy,' explained Loulou, disentangling herself with reluctance from Mac's arms. 'Poppy, meet Mac, my ex-husband. It was Poppy's boyfriend I was shouting at – or who I *thought* I was shouting at – when you found me,' she added rapidly, hoping that the girl would have enough presence of mind not to mention Joshua. 'We came down together as a threesome, but he decided to make up a fourth, the sod.'

'Loulou decided to pay him back,' Poppy continued, her wink scarcely visible to the naked eye. 'But sadly she was wasting her time. I've just found Jamie fast asleep on a pile of fur coats in the downstairs cloakroom. He's been there all the time. Are you two quite sure you are divorced?' she added suspiciously, observing the rapturous expression upon Loulou's face.

'If we aren't, it means our solicitors ripped us off,' said Loulou, disguising the pain with flippancy.

Poppy shrugged. 'Oh, well, anyone can make a mistake. Anyway, we're going to abandon you, Loulou. Jamie and I are leaving.' Delicately she added, 'Will you be all right with Mac?' and Loulou beamed.

'I'll be very all right. Thanks for everything, Poppy, and come and see me soon at Vampires. We mustn't lose touch.'

Another infinitesimal wink from Poppy, and she was gone. Mac reached for Loulou once more. Somehow he just couldn't hug her enough now.

'I can't believe you came here without a partner,' he said, edging her towards the balcony as a singing crowd of men and girls careered past them. Loulou swallowed and shrugged, wondering where Josh was at that moment.

'I'm a gay *divorcée*,' she told him lightly. 'I'm not afraid to venture out on my own.' Which was a big lie, but what else could she say? She didn't even dare risk a glance over the balcony, in case she spotted Joshua. For both her sake and Mac's she had to persuade him to leave with her now.

It occurred briefly to Loulou that she should feel guilty, abandoning Joshua so far from home, in a situation alien to him, but somehow he no longer mattered. Mac had come all this way to see her and she had never stopped adoring him for a moment. Joshua, on the other hand, had never stopped adoring himself. And so what if he was good in bed? Mac was better.

'You look wonderful,' he told her now, amazed at the ease with which he could say it since endearments and flattery didn't come easily to him.

Loulou's heart turned over; Mac was paying her a compliment and she hadn't had to prise it out of him with a crowbar – it was purely voluntary! It made her want to cry all over again.

'I'm a bit tipsy,' she admitted, swaying slightly and using the excuse to steady herself against him. 'Do you think we could go outside for a while? I could do with some air.'

The gravel crunched beneath their feet as they walked past the rows of gleaming cars parked closest to the house. To their left, like great prehistoric birds, two helicopters stood in silence upon the grass, their rotor blades wreathed in mist. A girl in a pale pink ball gown and a man with his white tuxedo slung carelessly over his shoulder walked ahead of Loulou and Mac, then melted into the darkness beyond the towering elm trees.

Loulou envied them; their arms had been around each other's waists and it had looked so easy and comfortable that she couldn't understand why she and Mac weren't similarly entwined.

But they were walking two feet apart and suddenly she was overwhelmed with shyness. If she hadn't known him better, she could have sworn that Mac was feeling exactly the same way. Since blurting out that unexpected compliment, he hadn't uttered a single word.

'I've missed you,' she ventured finally, because what the hell, *someone* had to say *something*.

He turned to look at her, but the pearly light was behind him and she couldn't see his expression at all.

'I haven't missed you,' he replied in a low voice. 'I haven't allowed myself to miss you. But tonight,' he paused and shrugged helplessly, 'I couldn't stop myself.'

'I'm glad.'

'Are you . . . seeing anyone else at the moment, Lou? I want to know the truth.'

Damn, she thought, anxiety mingling with guilt. That he had asked was a good sign, maybe indicating jealousy, but it reminded her of how moral Mac was. He demanded both truth and faithfulness, and whilst Loulou had always remained faithful to him, she hadn't always been able to resist telling the occasional, very *small*, white lie.

And now here she was, practically being forced to tell another one. Already.

'No, I'm not,' she said firmly, wondering whether the denial sounded as false to his ears as it did to her own. Which was doubly ironic when you considered that she really wasn't seeing anyone else, not since two hours ago. It was just that the person she wasn't seeing didn't know it yet.

'I'm *really* not,' she repeated anxiously, and saw Mac nod, believing her.

'That's all right, then.'

'And I'd like to go, now. I'd like *us* to go now.' Shyness wasn't going to get her where she wanted to be, as quickly as she wanted to be there. It was time to be brave, she realized.

'Your place or mine?'

Mac laughed quietly. 'You haven't changed, Lou.'

'Yes, I have,' she promised him. 'I've changed for the better.'

'In that case, let's go inside and phone for a taxi.'

Her gaze slipped beyond him to the great black silhouettes standing motionless on the grass. 'Why don't we take a helicopter?'

'Lou, you're quite mad,' he told her affectionately. 'You don't even know how to fly one.'

She laughed out loud and took his arm, steering him back towards the main entrance of Elm House. 'You have no sense of adventure, darling. But OK, if you're going to be stuffy about it, we'll just have to take the pilot along too.'

It was exactly like falling in love, she thought, as the rotor blades whipped round at full speed, flattening the grass that surrounded them and scattering frozen leaves like confetti. Everything happened so *quickly*; one second they were on the ground and then the next, with a tremendous surge of power and noise, they were airborne.

Loulou, strapped into her seat with the pilot on her left and Mac on her right, peered out through the bubble of perspex as the ground tilted sharply beneath them and the helicopter wheeled round and suddenly upwards, soaring into the black sky. The sensation really was *just* like falling in love; exhilarating and alarming and quite, quite irresistible.

'We could have taken a taxi,' shouted Mac, above the tremendous noise. Turning, she kissed his smooth brown cheek. 'Too slow, darling. And besides, I've always wanted to sweep you off your feet.'

Chapter 24

The moment Loulou awoke the following morning she slid carefully out of bed, reached for her bag and slunk into the bathroom. She had to be looking good when Mac woke up – the fact that he had seen her naked face hundreds of times when they were married counted for nothing now. This was starting over and she needed the security of freshly brushed teeth, blusher, mascara and a comb through her tangled curls to bolster her fragile ego.

But it wasn't easy, applying rosy blusher to maximum effect when her mouth kept breaking into a smile she couldn't control. Last night. What a truly incredible, brilliant, unforgettable night it had been.

And Mac, her very own darling Mac had been so . . . vulnerable. Yes, that was the word, decided Loulou as she studied her reflection in the mirror above the marbled basin and saw the unstoppable smile widen once more like a flower in the sun.

He had been *vulnerable*, and she found it unbelievably touching. It was as if he had realized too late how severely he had incriminated himself, how wide open he had left himself to scornful rejection, and when Loulou had responded instead with warmth and joy he had almost melted with relief into her arms.

It had been an expert seduction, she recalled now, almost giddy with happiness as she applied just a slick of petal-pink lipstick. Every caress, every kiss, every sinuous movement of her body had been geared to giving him pleasure, and to showing him how much pleasure he gave her in return.

They had made love three times and her body ached exquisitely this morning, to remind her of that fact. Dreamily, Loulou unstoppered the bottle of Christian Dior aftershave and inhaled the scent which always reminded her of him. How many times in the last few years had she paused beside the Dior stand in Harrods or Selfridges and doused herself with Eau Sauvage because it brought back memories of Mac? What a masochist she had been.

But now he was back in her life and she really didn't need to stand naked in the bathroom with her nose in a bottle. The real thing was lying in bed just a few yards away.

And everything was going to be all right. Everything from now on would be absolutely 150 per cent perfect.

It wasn't until they had finished breakfast in bed – strong French coffee, fresh orange juice and the still-effervescent remains of last night's celebratory champagne – and made love for the fourth time, that Loulou began to experience her first doubts.

Typically, she had removed the problem of Joshua from her mind as easily as if he were no more awkward than an overdue phone bill. Last night, following Mac's astonishing appearance, Joshua had simply ceased to exist in her thoughts.

But Loulou had to be back at Vampires by twelve thirty in order to host a birthday party for a well-known Fleet Street journalist and Mac was showing every sign of wanting to accompany her. And now, far too late as usual, she realized that Joshua would be back at her flat ready for a confrontation that would make the shoot-out in High Noon look like a chimps' tea party. He simply wasn't the type to sit back and accept the fact that she had abandoned him in Gloucestershire and run away with another man, even if the other man was one of her ex-husbands.

Joshua was going to be incredibly, unbelievably angry.

Mac, if he learnt that she had lied to him, would be angrier still. And while the prospect of Josh's unleashed fury was bearable, the idea that she might lose Mac so soon after finding him again was impossible to even contemplate.

This, then, was where her problem now lay.

'But you must have work to do, baby,' she said hopefully, snuggling against his chest. 'And this birthday bash is going to be the most awful bore. Why don't I just shoot back in a cab, get it over with, tidy up the flat and meet you back here at about six. We can have dinner at Ma Maison – is it still your favourite? – and then maybe go on to Annabel's for . . .'

'You aren't getting rid of me that easily,' Mac interrupted her, tracing the curve of her left breast with a slow, tantalizing finger. 'I'm coming back with you now. Unless there's a problem?' he added jokingly. 'You're not hiding some new husband away in that flat, are you? I warn you, I shall look in every wardrobe when I get there –'

'No new husband,' said Loulou unhappily. There was no-one, absolutely no-one as determined as Mac when he wanted to be. If Joshua was there she was doomed, but maybe by some miracle he wouldn't be. 'Come on then, darling, we'd better get dressed if we're going. Let's hope this afternoon won't be too boring, hmm?'

Boring wasn't the word for it. Loulou's hopes soared when, having entered her flat as cautiously as a burglar, she saw that every trace of Joshua had vanished. He had been back and removed every incriminating item. Even his toothbrush and razor were gone, she discovered when she crept into the bathroom. And her own possessions, to her surprise and relief, were intact.

The tight knot of anxiety in her stomach relaxed with a great whoosh of relief as she realized that there was not going to be a problem, after all. Joshua had behaved in a decent, honourable fashion and, realizing that he was no longer needed, had quietly removed his possessions and himself from her life.

Loulou was both amazed and overwhelmingly grateful. There was no longer any need to worry. Everything was going to be *all right*.

'The flat looks just the same,' said Mac, standing with his hands on his hips in the centre of the sitting-room and surveying the home he had shared with Loulou for only four short weeks. He sounded vaguely surprised and she smiled. She knew what he meant. Her very own personalized brand of clutter was unchanged; her messiness was still what dominated the highly desirable residence, and it was particularly noticeable to Mac because his own penthouse apartment overlooking the Thames was one of those stark monstrosities so beloved of men and so bereft of clutter that it made Loulou cringe. In Mac's sterile, immaculate flat practically the only sign of life had been the photographs lining most of the walls, photographs which he had taken and which portrayed the different, spiralling stages of his now hugely successful career. And even they were all black and white.

'It looks nice.' He nodded his approval, his dark eyebrows still signalling faint surprise. 'Friendly.'

'I'm a very friendly person,' said Loulou lightly. 'Stick around, and you'll find out just how friendly . . .'

She hesitated and realized to her astonishment that she was blushing. It was the first reference either of them had made to 'the future'. So far, by unspoken mutual consent, they had avoided the subject entirely, Loulou because she was far too worried about the problem of Joshua to dare consider such an enthralling prospect. And Mac had done likewise, she presumed, because he was naturally far more cautious where relationships and futures were concerned.

Disconcertingly, he watched with interest as the colour suffused Loulou's cheeks. Even more disconcertingly, he said, 'Hmm,' in a thoughtful manner, and didn't elaborate further. Another annoying trait of Mac's, she remembered, was his way of keeping his private thoughts private. She had never quite mastered the art of reading his mind.

It was bizarre, thought Loulou, that they had once been married to each other and that they had just made love four times in indecently rapid succession, yet there still existed an almost palpable constraint between them that prevented any discussion about what was surely the most important subject of all.

'Do sit down . . . help yourself to a drink . . .' she urged, still flustered. Christ, she had almost said: Make yourself at home! 'I'll just take a quick shower and change. Can't very well wear this, can I?' And plucking futilely at her ball gown, she turned and fled to the safety of the bathroom before Mac's watchful silence unnerved her completely.

The party downstairs was in full swing by the time Loulou and Mac finally made their entrance; Loulou in an electric blue creation and Mac in a black jacket worn over a crisp white shirt and yet another pair of his beloved and authentically faded

501s. 'I'm a photographer,' he had explained with a shrug when Loulou had reminded him that everyone else would be wearing a suit – at least to begin with. 'I can get away with it.'

And why should she mind? Loulou asked herself with a naughty smile. She adored 501s. Those tantalizingly slow-to-undo button flies only served to heighten the anticipation . . .

'Lou, my angel!' roared Terry Howard, spotting her from his position at the bar where a great deal of money was changing hands at a frenzied rate. 'Come over here and let me give you a massive birthday kiss.'

'It's *your* birthday,' Loulou yelled back above the considerable noise of the bar crowd. 'I'm supposed to give *you* one!'

Terry rolled his eyes. 'Promises, promises.'

'I'm not at all sure I want to kiss you, anyway,' she complained when she finally reached him. 'You're far too old, ugly and lecherous.'

'Ah,' he replied affectionately, enfolding her in his burly arms, 'but I shall spend enough money here this afternoon to keep you in younger men for the next year, and that can't be bad, can it?'

'You might have to pay your young men, Terry,' countered Loulou as he gave her a slobbery, whisky-sodden kiss on the cheek, 'but I certainly don't have to pay mine. Mac, come over here,' she shouted, twisting around to catch his eye. It was stupid, she knew, but Mac had never fully understood how necessary to a successful business these hugs and kisses were. That slight degree of mistrust which he had never been able to overcome had caused countless arguments during their marriage.

This time, she vowed to herself, she was going to make him see how needless such jealousy was.

She was going to make damn sure that nothing went wrong. He wasn't going to get away from her again.

'Mac, you must meet Terry Howard,' she said, praying that Terry wouldn't choose this moment to make one of his bad-taste jokes about her love life. 'Terry, this is Mac, my ex-husband.'

'I've heard of you. You do excellent work,' said Terry, shaking Mac's hand. 'And you have one hell of an ex-wife, if I may say so. As for you, Lou,' he went on, turning to her, 'I had no idea that you were ever hitched to *the* Mac. Whatever went wrong between the two of you? Doesn't anyone ever bother to work at staying married these days?'

Terry's outspoken manner and journalistic style was legendary. Loulou, her toes curling up in embarrassment, glanced at Mac from beneath her lashes and couldn't make up her mind whether she should knee Terry in the balls or give him another kiss. Talk about coming straight to the point, she thought faintly.

But when Mac's arm slipped around her waist, her insides contracted with love. His warm hand found hers and she felt his fingers interlace with her own, then gently squeeze them. How, she marvelled, could such a simple gesture make her *melt* like that? And what did Mac mean by it?

Having apparently considered Terry's words – the whole world knew that Terry was devoted to his wife of twenty-six years – Mac took a sip of his drink and nodded thoughtfully.

'Maybe you're right,' he said, and Loulou held her breath. 'We were pretty young then, and perhaps we didn't try as hard as we might have done. But sometimes people can learn by their mistakes. I think I have, and I hope Lou has too. Who knows, we might have better luck if we try again.'

Unable to stop herself, and with tears of happiness glistening in her eyes, Loulou launched herself into Mac's arms, scarcely daring to believe that he had really said those words, but at the same time not giving him a moment to reconsider. Showering him with tiny, frenzied kisses and clinging to him as tightly as was humanly possible, she murmured, 'Oh Mac, oh darling, I love you,' in between kisses, and was only dimly aware of the raucous roar of approval from the rest of the party.

'I have to warn you that anything you might say or do,' said Terry, placing his arms around both of them like a boxing referee, 'will definitely be taken down and used in tomorrow's gossip column.'

'Oh, yes, please,' cried Loulou effusively, so grateful to him for saying the words which had prompted Mac's reply that she simply had to give him another kiss. 'You're one hell of an ugly fairy godmother, Terry, but you're an absolute darling, anyway.'

'Drinks on the house?' yelled one of the younger journalists hopefully, and drunk with love and sheer ecstasy, Loulou raised her hand at Christo behind the bar.

'Why not? Drinks on the house for everyone!'

Then a voice behind her said with silky iciness: 'Does that also include me?' and she froze. Shit, no. Please, please no, oh God, *no* . . .

'What the fuck did you think you were doing with me – playing some fancy white woman's game?' demanded Joshua loudly, and Loulou closed her eyes, dying inside, too stricken to even think of a reply. She had thought she was safe; the possibility that Joshua would decide to confront her in public hadn't even crossed her mind.

But he had, and he was here. And so . . . oh shit, please no, no . . . was Mac.

'I asked you a question,' Joshua persisted, his Scottish-

Caribbean voice horribly clear above the abruptly hushed conversation around the bar. Half of Fleet Street was listening, determined not to miss a single word, Loulou realized numbly. But they didn't matter, and under any other circumstances she could easily have handled Joshua.

If only Mac wasn't here . . .

'What's the problem?' said Mac, his own tone measured and deliberately calm, his arm remaining protectively around Loulou's quivering shoulder.

'Ah, another Scot!' exclaimed Joshua, his words rife with sarcasm. 'And a white one, this time.'

'Now look here . . .' began Terry, moving between Loulou and Joshua, but Mac interrupted him. Narrow-eyed, he stared at the towering figure of Joshua and repeated slowly: 'What's your problem?'

'The bitch is the problem,' said Joshua, and Loulou began to shake violently. 'You're welcome to her – I don't need her kind of trouble – but maybe you should know what you're taking on, because she'll probably do the same to you, man. When you're living with a girl you don't expect her to run off in the middle of the night leaving you in Gloucestershire at some fucking ball without a word of explanation. Got it?'

'Got it,' said Mac quietly. 'And now that you've said what you came here to say, perhaps you'd leave. This is a private party.'

'Yeah, but think about it,' said Joshua coldly. 'She might be a good lay, but she's a cheating bitch as well. Here's your key, bitch,' he added, tossing the narrow brass key at her feet. The tiny, tinkling sound broke the stunned silence and Loulou took a step backwards, casting a stricken glance in Mac's direction.

'Leave now,' he instructed Joshua evenly, and to Loulou's

relief Joshua turned. Without uttering another word, he left.

'Oh, thank God,' she whispered, clinging on to Mac's arm for support. 'Darling, I'm so sorry about that . . . it was all the most horrible mistake . . .'

'It certainly was,' he said slowly, removing her hand from his arm with a finality that chilled her to the bone. 'Let go of me, Loulou. I'm sorry too, but it was my fault for even thinking that you'd changed.'

'You don't understand! Mac, you have to listen to me,' she babbled frantically. 'It's not what you think, I swear it isn't.'

'But it is,' he contradicted her brutally, his dark eyes cold, reflecting his disgust. 'It's *exactly* what I think. I just should have thought of it earlier. Goodbye.'

'No!' she screamed, as he turned and made his way through the enthralled crowd of journalists towards the door. 'Mac, wait. Please! You can't leave me now! You can't!'

Chapter 25

Bloody typical; a decent British summer, thought Roz irritably, mopping a trickle of perspiration from the valley between her breasts. Just when she didn't bloody need it.

Even in the shade she was still uncomfortably hot, but it was equally stifling inside the house. Whatever she did she felt perfectly vile and it seemed that there was nothing she could do to escape it.

With a sigh of irritation she hauled herself into a better position on the sun lounger and crossed her ankles, then remembered that crossing your ankles caused thrombosis and almost certain death and threw down her book in disgust.

I look like a whale, she thought, and not for the first time, remembering feeling bloated and uncomfortable years previously. She hated the sight of her smooth, brown belly glistening with Ambre Solaire and swollen beyond belief. It couldn't be normal to look this abnormal, surely. It was God's way, she presumed, of making sure that pregnant women didn't get any sex. By transforming them into totally undesirable creatures He ensured that no man in his right mind would want to go anywhere near them.

And no men, in their right minds or otherwise, had been near her for so long now that she probably wouldn't be able to remember what to do anyway, she thought, wincing as the baby kicked out beneath her ribs. Bloody baby. Bloody men. Bloody *bloody* weather.

The only thing that cheered her even slightly was the prospect of Loulou's visit, partly because Lou had sounded even more fed up on the phone than Roz.

'We'll be miserable together,' Roz had said consolingly.

'No, we won't. I can be far more miserable than you,' Loulou had promised her.

'You can try, sweetie. But I warn you, I'm a hard act to follow at the moment.'

'Bloody hell,' exclaimed Loulou with characteristic frankness. 'I see what you mean. No wonder you're miserable. Are those tits *real*?'

'It's all real,' said Roz, gazing dispiritedly down at her hugely swollen breasts and vast stomach, spilling over the sunflower yellow bikini. Then she looked up and saw from the expression on Loulou's face that she was joking.

'You ass, does getting knocked up take away your sense of humour? You look fine, Roz. Sort of ... maternal.' Loulou burst out laughing and took off her dark glasses, stepping forward to give Roz a kiss. In a brilliant violet off-the-shoulder number, Loulou exuded wealth and health. She was even looking happy, thought Roz with a stab of envy.

Having weathered the shock of discovering that she was pregnant, she had planned on being happy herself, of course. She had day-dreamed for hours, envisaging the surprise of her friends when they witnessed the transformation of bright, snappy, single-girl-about-town Roz Vallender into glowing, serene mother-to-be Roz Coletto. She had been convinced that Nico would be utterly captivated by the idea of becoming a father, and that he would insist they married. Maybe it was something to do with the hormones, but the idea of being married was no longer repellent to her; she wanted to be cosseted, spoiled and loved. Nico's flat refusal to even see her had been the biggest shock of all.

The amount of press interest hadn't helped either. Nico hadn't exactly denied that he was the father, but his brusque 'No comments' had aroused much public speculation as to the reasons for his non-involvement. Roz, in turn, had been forced to adopt an aloof, 'we-have-our-reasons' attitude in order to salvage the small amount of pride she had left. Her visions of herself and Nico as the next Ma and Pa Walton, idyllically happy with both their children and each other, were looking less likely to happen. Instead she was faced with the far less exciting prospect of single parenthood and a rapidly nose-diving career.

'I don't want to be maternal,' she said, when Loulou had flopped down on to the thickly padded white sun lounger opposite and poured herself a tall glass of iced orange juice. 'Nico clearly doesn't want me to be maternal and Eric Daniels doesn't want me to be maternal so badly that he offered to pay for the abortion himself.'

Eric Daniels was Roz's producer on 'Memories', the chat show which she had presented for the last two and a half years. Nudging fifty and trendy to the extreme, he had thrown up his hands in horror upon hearing Roz's news. He couldn't have been more appalled if she had told him she was a mass murderer.

'But it's none of his business!' declared Loulou indignantly. 'Unless he was the father, of course.'

Roz pulled a face. 'What a revolting thought. No, apparently chat show presenters mustn't get pregnant unless they have husbands. The public doesn't allow it. And, of course, the fact that Nico refuses to acknowledge the baby makes mine the worst crime of all. If I even dared to venture on to a TV screen millions of outraged viewers would switch over to the other side. According to Eric my viewing figures would be approximately twenty-seven. I'm a corrupt, depraved woman who makes Lucrezia Borgia look like a nun. The next series starts in October and unless I get married before then, they'll be using someone else.'

'Oh Roz. I'm sorry. Christ, can you believe it? It's supposed to be the age of equality but women still get this hassle. You've made me feel quite guilty. I'm as miserable as sin but at least I'm not going to lose my job.'

'Tell me about your sins,' urged Roz, wanting to change the subject. 'What's been happening? I feel like a recluse, stuck out here in the sticks. Tell me everything – you never know, I might be able to help.'

Loulou took another sip of her orange juice, stalling for time while she considered her choice of words. If it wasn't all such a sad and sorry mess it would almost be funny.

'You *can* help, actually,' she said slowly. 'You can give me all those baby clothes when yours has grown out of them.'

'No!' Roz sat bolt upright, and the baby kicked protestingly beneath her ribs. 'You're not serious, Lou!'

'It's like when you buy a really expensive outfit and then your best friend goes out and gets another one exactly like it,' prattled Loulou. 'I hope you don't think I'm copying you so that we can both look the same, God forbid.'

'Are you *really* pregnant?'

'Yeah. Only I call it in pig. A pig that's been well and truly poked. You don't seriously think I'd be drinking neat orange juice otherwise, do you?'

'Whose is it?' said Roz, curiosity vying with astonishment.

She still couldn't quite believe that Loulou had made the same catastrophic mistake as herself.

Loulou removed her dark glasses and swung them from her fingers as she surveyed Roz's expression. 'Let's put it this way,' she said evenly. 'There's only one thing I'm absolutely sure about, and it's that this baby is definitely going to be black. Or white.'

'*What?*'

'You heard me,' said Loulou, replacing her glasses so that her face became a mask once more. Idly, she surveyed the perfect Cotswold scene, all so damned pretty and normal-looking that the sight brought tears of exasperation to her eyes. For the last hundred years or so, families had lived here; *normal* families with parents who were married, children who were truly wanted, and maybe the odd puppy here and there just to complete the revoltingly picturesque scenario.

What would those families think if they could hear the conversation taking place in this sleepy, sunny garden today? Two women with supposedly successful lives in the tumultuous fast lane of central London, both caught in the same sad old trap because no matter how wealthy they were, they couldn't buy themselves a settled, traditional existence.

'So who are they, and are they still around?' persisted Roz, realizing that she *was* feeling better, having learnt of Loulou's predicament. It was always comforting to hear other people's bad news, after all.

'Well, they're still *alive*, I suppose,' said Loulou gloomily, stirring the ice cubes in her drink with her finger, 'but they certainly aren't around me. It was the classic girl meets boy, girl meets another boy, girl gets found out situation. I haven't seen either of them since. Oh Roz,' she burst out, aching with the unfairness of it all, 'I didn't do it on purpose! The second one was Mac and we'd just got properly back together again when the other guy turned up and blew the whistle on me. I was truly, ecstatically happy for about fifteen seconds and then . . . bang! All over. Mac stormed out. And now here I am,' she concluded with a mournful look, 'in the bloody pudding club.'

'Are you going to keep it?' asked Roz, eyeing Loulou's flat stomach. It was likely that there was still time to choose.

'Oh, I've thought and thought, but I can't get rid of it,' Loulou shook her silver-blonde mane decisively. 'I know I'm mad, but I can't. You see, it still might be Mac's.'

Chapter 26

Nico surfaced from sleep and lay with his eyes closed, one arm above his head and the other outstretched as he tried to remember where he was. The texture of the sheets was unfamiliar, but then they always were these days. By stretching the fingers of one hand he discovered that the headboard was wooden, varnished and ornately carved. The bedside table, by contrast, was plain and sharp edged. The lamp resting upon it was . . . a lamp.

It was no good; he still couldn't figure it out. Knowing that he was making a mistake, Nico opened his eyes. Oh, look at that – a hotel room. What a surprise.

He surveyed the Spanish style room with boredom and loathing. The heavy black wood carving was everywhere, adorning the door frames, the TV table, even the air vents. The rest of the huge room, walls, thick carpet and bedlinen, were all white. A single colossal picture on the far wall was also black and white.

Rolling over in the king-sized bed and realizing that he was the only thing in the whole damn room that wasn't monochrome, Nico reached for the brochure lying next to the lamp. So this was where he was; the Hotel Balfour, Las Vegas.

He studied the Rolex on his wrist. Wednesday 3 July. 2.30 p.m. And just to make matters even worse he had the niggly remains of a hangover as well. Just what he needed. Fantastic.

Stepping into the shower – tiled in black-and-white marble,

naturally – Nico considered his situation. Why, he wondered as the hot needles of water bombarded his body, was he here, doing something that was so little fun? It had been his record company's idea that he should make this promotional tour in order that he might well and truly 'break' in the States. More publicity equalled greater recognition which in turn sold more records and so made more money. More money for both the record company and himself. But was it really worth all this monotony, boredom and unutterable *dullness*?

Of course not.

Pouring shampoo on to his head and lathering it with such vigour that his hangover intensified in protest, Nico concentrated his thoughts. The real reason why he had allowed himself to be persuaded across the Atlantic was simple. He was just as bored at home.

In the last few months he had written scarcely any songs at all, and those few he had managed to complete were so pitifully below standard that he had destroyed them himself, before anyone else could hear them and do the same. Officially, he had been taking a well-earnt rest. Unofficially, he was totally disinterested.

And what was there at home, anyway? On that disastrous day when Camilla had removed herself from his home she had hired Hazel Hampton to replace her and he still hadn't been able to figure out whether she had done it deliberately out of spite, or whether it had been a genuine mistake. But how, he wondered with renewed exasperation, could he possibly be expected to *enjoy* the company of a housekeeper who, at forty-one, gazed at him with such open and helpless adoration that he felt permanently ill at ease, and who insisted on calling him, 'sir'?

He couldn't fault her work; Camilla had kept the house clean and relatively organized, but Hazel, her pale, eager eyes able to spot a dust particle at fifty paces, had turned the place into a laboratory. She was an excellent cook, but he had never seen her eat. Whenever Nico spoke to her she blushed violently and took so long to stammer out her replies that he lost all track of the conversation.

And it was purely because she was so shy, and so desperately eager to please that he didn't have the heart to replace her. Also, he had a nagging fear that if he tried to, she would throw herself off the top of the BT Tower. Making no mess when she landed, naturally.

So work was no fun. Home was no fun.

Somehow, Camilla had managed to remove all the fun from his life as efficiently as she had cleared her room on the day she'd left.

Nico sighed; he'd finally – after far too many hours of soul-searching – come to the conclusion that Camilla was simply too terrifyingly honest.

He still winced at the memory of her quiet disappointment, her attempts to tell him that his failure to please her really hadn't mattered. He would *never* be able to forget the saddened, pitying look in her eyes . . .

And although he hadn't even wanted to take anyone to bed since that night, his ego had taken such a colossal battering that if he had, some dreadful inner warning bell made him wonder if he'd actually be able to perform at all.

So much for Camilla, whom he wanted to hate but could only succeed in missing terribly.

And finally, of course, there was Roz. He could hardly leave her out of it, could he? That messy situation was perhaps the least fun of all, what with his own muddled sense of guilt and morality vying with doubt and at times plain disbelief.

Should he have accepted the facts as they had been presented to him, without once even asking himself whether they were accurate? Didn't he owe the child that much, at least?

But then, did he owe Roz herself anything, after the way she had behaved? Christ, it was difficult. Even his manager, Monty Barton, hadn't been able to decide what he should do, although that opinion was less to do with morals than plain cash. Would it harm Nico Coletto's glittering career if he failed to publicly acknowledge his child, or would it be worse still if he did the Right Thing and married Roz? His image was not, after all, one which lent itself to family life and fatherhood.

Stepping out of the shower and shaking his blond head so that a spiral of water droplets fanned out around him, Nico picked up a white bath towel and half-heartedly rubbed himself dry, thinking dark thoughts about capricious women, the havoc they wrought, and blackmail.

He refused to allow himself to be threatened by any of them. And he would start by putting a call through to Monty Barton's room and telling him that the appearance he was scheduled to make on 'The Susie Sellars Show' this afternoon was cancelled. Due to an incredible lack of interest on the part of the invited guest.

Shooing away a persistent fly and kicking off her espadrilles, Loulou leant back and wondered what she could possibly talk about that would effectively change the subject, but at the same time avoid those sensitive areas concerning Camilla and Nico. Her way of dealing with unpleasant events was by simply putting them out of her mind, and she had quite successfully ignored the fact of her pregnancy for hours whenever thinking of it had become too confusing.

Roz, however, was obviously so delighted to learn that they were both on the same sinking ship that she couldn't stop talking about it, speculating and giving advice – most of it in the form of dire predictions. She was, in fact, being more boring than Loulou had believed possible.

'. . . and then you have to go along to these revolting ante-natal classes where everyone else looks even more cowlike than you do and the sadistic old bitch who runs it shows video nasties about giving birth. It's all perfectly disgusting,' concluded Roz languidly, although Loulou detected a flash of triumph in her narrowed, dark eyes.

'I don't want to know,' she said, her voice firm.

'But you *should* know,' Roz insisted, pointing at her swollen brown stomach, 'I *know* you, Lou. You're just pretending that it isn't happening, but you can't, not this time. It isn't going to go away of its own accord. Well,' she amended with a faint smile, 'there's always a slim chance that it might, I suppose, but as far as I can make out miscarriages only happen to women who are desperate for children. So you and I have to be prepared for the whole bit.'

'Hey, you really know how to cheer a girl up,' said Loulou draining her glass. 'Ever thought of joining the Samaritans?'

'I've thought of phoning them.'

She was really enjoying this, Loulou realized. 'Well, I told Camilla yesterday,' she retaliated crossly, 'and *she* said having babies was a fantastic experience. She really enjoyed being pregnant.'

'All fourteen stones of her,' remarked Roz cuttingly. So

Loulou had told Camilla first, she thought with a stab of jealousy.

'She weighs less than nine now, and looks great,' Loulou countered, realizing that Roz was beginning to irritate her. 'And that new business she set up is really taking off.'

'I did her a favour then, having a fling with her husband.'

'Don't be such a bitch.' God, it was so tempting . . . the urge to tell Roz about Camilla and Nico . . .

'I am a bitch,' said Roz sadly. 'I know I am, but I can't help it. Blame it on my upbringing.'

'That's no excuse.'

'It's the best one I've got. And if it makes you feel any better,' she added with a burst of honesty, 'being a bitch isn't that much fun. I'm not particularly happy, you know.'

Loulou, hiding the surprise she felt at hearing what practically amounted to a confession, pulled a face. 'Who is, at the moment?'

'Camilla, by the sound of it,' Roz twisted the halter-neck tie of her bikini around her index finger. 'Do you know, I'm almost jealous of her. Whoever would have thought it? *Me*, jealous of *Camilla*.'

Still not quite able to take in the fact that working could be so absorbing and enjoyable, Camilla was doing as much as possible as fast as possible, as if afraid that there was some kind of unwritten time-limit upon the enjoyment.

Not that working for Nico had been awful, of course; it was just that that had been housekeeping, much the same as she had done when she had been married to Jack – but with better company. This was entirely different, a *proper* job, whose success depended upon her own abilities and capacity for hard work. And Zoë's too, of course, for where would she have been without Zoë, her knowledge and her contacts?

Camilla could still recall in absolute detail the sunny morning in April shortly after she had moved in with Zoë, when she had admired her new landlady's grace and perfect posture, as she finished washing Fee, her three-year-old daughter. Dressed in daffodil yellow leggings and an ancient yellow and white sweatshirt, with her bright russet corkscrew curls piled on top of her head with the aid of three clothes-pegs, she wore not a scrap of make-up and yet her beauty was irrefutable.

'You could be a model,' observed Camilla, and Zoë promptly dissolved into fits of laughter.

'I'm afraid you're ten years too late, Cami, but thanks all the same,' she giggled, picking Fee out of the bath.

'But you *could*,' persisted Camilla. Scooping Fee up into her arms, she breathed in the delicious scent of just-bathed toddler.

'Ten years ago,' said Zoë, crossing her arms and leaning against the sink, 'I couldn't leave the house without being recognized. I dreamt of the day when people would no longer know who I was. You've just made me realize that that day has well and truly arrived.'

Seeing the confused expression on Camilla's face, she continued: 'I *was* a model, darling. Catwalk, photographic, *Vogue* . . . the lot. It was hard work, but lots of fun. I even met the Queen once . . .'

Camilla groaned. 'I've put all my feet in it again. The first time I ever met Nico I didn't recognize him. And now you, too. But why on earth did you give it up if you enjoyed it so much?'

Zoë threw a pointed glance in the direction of her youngest child. 'Why does any model give up when the going's good? Babies. There isn't much call for a catwalk girl with a forty-two-inch waistline. And my husband wasn't thrilled with the idea of me carrying on working afterwards. And then . . . and then . . . I realized that I was simply too far out of touch and too bloody old. So there you are,' she concluded with a self-mocking smile. 'Tragic, isn't it? The rise and fall of Zoë Sheridan, all in the space of three and a half years. Chuck over my walking sticks, Cami – I'm going to hobble into the sitting-room and have another bash at that knitting.'

'But that's crazy!' exclaimed Camilla, outraged by Zoë's flip comments. 'You're only twenty-nine, for heaven's sake. And you haven't got a husband to contend with now. Why on earth don't you go back to it if you enjoyed it so much?'

Zoë shrugged and helped herself to a chocolate biscuit. 'It just seems a bit daunting, I suppose, the whole idea of starting again from scratch. I've kept in touch with quite a few of the girls from the old days and they all feel much the same. The hassle of getting everything sorted out is simply too much, what with the kids and those snooty agencies. It's a tough business, Cami, and we're just not tough enough any more to compete.'

'Aren't there any friendly agencies who will help you get back on your feet?' asked Camilla and Zoë laughed at the naïvety of her question.

'Why should they bother, when they have more than enough models who don't need help? People like us – out of touch and tied down with children – are more trouble than they're worth as far as they're concerned. If I were an *organized* person, with a nanny and an understanding agency, I'd do it like a shot. But here I am,' she popped the rest of the chocolate biscuit into her mouth and paused while she swallowed it, 'thoroughly disorganized and quite unemployable. Now why are you looking at me like that? Are you scheming, Camilla, or have you gone into some kind of trance?'

Sheridan's had been born that night, when the children had been put to bed. Sitting Zoë down with a bottle of Rioja, Camilla had outlined the plan which had materialized almost of its own accord in her mind, and Zoë had listened with rapt attention, her conker-brown eyes registering at first astonishment, then growing interest and finally undiluted excitement. She was the one with the know-how, and Camilla the one with the time and energy to put the plan into action. The agency should be called Sheridan's because, although Camilla in her ignorance had not recognized Zoë, people in the industry would still remember the name. Zoë's friends, all those with young children, would leave them at Zoë's house while they worked. No model ever threw away her old portfolio so it needed only to be updated. Camilla would organize the advertising, the bookings – all the time-consuming work which the girls found so daunting. She would be able to manage all this because the agency would be small, with maybe just a dozen clients on its books . . .

And now here she was just three short months later, working twelve-hour days in order to co-ordinate the assignments of fifty-six models, all of whom had been introduced to Sheridan's by word of mouth, and who between them possessed eighty-seven children.

As the agency had expanded the idea that either Zoë or Camilla would look after the offspring of working models had rapidly become impractical. Instead, she had scouted around and finally managed to discover a barely used church hall less than a quarter of a mile from the house. Having organized a lease for a more than reasonable rent, the crèche was now run by two qualified child-minders and a flexible rota of model-mums. As a result, those mothers were able – for a modest sum – to leave their children at the crèche whenever they were required to work, safe in the knowledge that they were both happy and expertly cared for.

The existence of Sheridan's itself had become known to advertising agencies, department stores and magazines, largely by word of mouth as well – their own advertising campaign had been cleverly chosen and pared down to the absolute minimum; any more had proven quite unnecessary, since fifty-six ex-models had their own extended network of contacts and news of this new, cleverly co-ordinated agency which employed utterly trustworthy, wonderfully experienced girls had spread like wildfire throughout the circles which mattered most. Sheridan's girls, professional and all thrilled to be working once more, were still undeniably beautiful, but they also had an extra, hard-to-define quality which was solely due to the fact that they were women rather than girls. They had more personality, somehow, and this showed through in their work. Happy to be working, doing what they had always known how to do best, happy to be earning once more, and secure in the knowledge that while they worked their children were being well looked after at the boisterous Sheridan crèche, their true personalities shone, unhampered. They had *élan*, charisma and character.

Sheridan's girls, the clients all agreed, were a delight, an absolute joy to work with.

'Oh shit,' said Camilla aloud. Pen in one hand, she had been flipping through the *Daily Mail* with the other, because Zoë was featured on the fashion pages modelling city suits. And there on page eleven, hitting her like a body blow, was a photograph of Nico.

It wasn't the first time, of course, but the reminder of him still affected her, and it still hurt like hell.

How to make a complete idiot of yourself in one easy lesson, she thought bitterly, scanning the piece which accompanied the picture. Nico was in the States on a promotional tour and was rumoured to be about to start work on a single with Stevie Wonder. The report also stated that while his erstwhile 'friend' Roz Vallender remained at home in the Cotswolds to await the birth of her child, Nico had been spotted dining out with a young American actress, star of the latest Jackie Collins mini-series.

That hurt, too, despite everything Camilla had learnt about press reports while she was living with Nico. For some time now she had been nursing the tentative idea that she might see him again, explain her terrible behaviour and beg him to forgive her for it. In her wildest dreams, he did. In real life, however, she knew deep down that she had wounded Nico's pride, betrayed his kindness and killed his trust in her too thoroughly to allow him to forgive.

'We were such good *friends*,' she had said helplessly, attempting to explain to Zoë what had happened. 'And out of pure spite, I wrecked everything.'

'Well, it's a shame,' said Zoë, attempting to console her. 'But it isn't the end of the world, is it? He'll get over it. Cheer up, Cami – worse things have happened at sea.'

And Camilla's own sense of pride had prevented her from going on to explain why else she found the situation so upsetting. It would sound simply too juvenile for words to say that she had discovered – too late – that she had fallen in love with Nico.

She could just imagine the expression on Zoë's face. 'I see. So you slept with him once, made him think he was completely useless in bed, left him – and *then* decided, *weeks* later, that you loved him? Isn't that rather an odd way to go about things, darling?'

So Camilla had suffered in silence, trying to tell herself that she didn't really love Nico, that it was all part of the guilt-pattern, and that she should simply chalk it up to experience. Her relationship with him had been a freak of nature anyway – why on earth should someone like him wish to be involved with her? They were on entirely different planets. That night would only ever have been a one-off anyway . . .

Leaving the claustrophobic confines of the Hotel Balfour – although heaven knew how such a vast monstrosity could possibly make him feel claustrophobic – Nico sauntered lazily along the dusty sidewalk, relieved to be out in the fresh air even if it was at least 100° C in the shade, with practically no humidity whatsoever. The sun blazed down, scorching the sand-blasted streets, and it was only now that he fully appreciated the efficiency of the air-conditioning system in the hotel.

But he wasn't going to let the fierce desert heat drive him back into that Spanish-styled monument to bad taste, nor into one of the endless lines of gambling establishments for which Las Vegas was famed. Gaudily lit, brash and noisy with the clatter of money and the electronic machines which paid out a precisely calculated percentage of that which went in, he felt only discontent and derision for those who mindlessly played for hours, sometimes days, on end.

Adjusting his dark glasses and pushing his hands into the pockets of his black cotton Levis, Nico ignored the heat and turned off the main street in search of normality. Somewhere, *somewhere* in this brash, unreal town there had to be some small signs that it was real; a supermarket, a hairdressers, a dry-cleaning store, a normal shop that sold Marmite, and Branston pickle and proper sausages . . .

For twenty minutes, during which time his beige shirt grew darker with perspiration and he grew increasingly homesick, Nico strode grimly on. Eventually he found a narrow street not entirely populated with casinos and amusement arcades.

Stopping first at a slightly tatty supermarket, he emerged with a sturdy brown-paper carrier containing crusty bread rolls, smoked ham, ripe Camembert and several cans of beer. Plain, normal food, if not exactly English. When he had asked the bored assistant if she had any Marmite she had responded with a blank stare compatible with brain-death.

In this blistering heat he wasn't even hungry, but just clutching the bag of food was reassuring. Nico paused on the sidewalk, wondering which way to turn. To his left stood a hairdressing salon from which a vast middle-aged woman with bouffant hair was emerging. Across the road was a McDonald's, next to it a clothing store with its windows full of screamingly loud Hawaiian shirts and over-embellished cowboy boots.

He turned right, simply because there seemed no other choice.

'Oh shit, shit, bugger and shit!' wailed a voice and his heart leapt. The despairing tones, and the particular choice of words, reminded him acutely of Loulou. It wasn't, of course. But it was an English voice, and the first he had heard for days – since even his manager adopted a sliding mid-Atlantic drawl the moment he stepped on to foreign soil. Slowly, praying that the voice wouldn't turn out to belong to something horrific, Nico made his way towards it.

He ducked just in time as a carton of soap powder hurtled towards his head, spraying blue-white powder like artificial snow in all directions. But if the box missed him, bouncing on the sidewalk and landing in the dusty road, the powder did not. He halted dramatically, his spirits rising. She might not be Loulou, he thought triumphantly, but she was giving a damn good impersonation of her. Whoever would have guessed that there could be two of them?

'I'm so sorry!' exclaimed the girl, clutching his arm and attempting to brush away the soap powder which had settled on it. Nico's skin was so warm that it actually seemed to be melting.

'Can you forgive me?' she continued frenziedly. 'I couldn't help it – I'm English. We have no control over our actions, you see.'

'Oh, I don't know,' replied Nico, shaking his head and watching the powder fly like dandruff. 'I thought it was an extremely controlled action. Out of interest, was it kicked or thrown?'

She looked remorseful. 'I kicked it. Are you dreadfully angry with me?'

'Dreadfully,' he told her, straightfaced, and she looked even more appalled.

'You could take off your shirt and throw it into one of the machines . . . oh, you're joking! You naughty thing! As if I didn't feel bad enough.'

'And I'm from England, too,' he observed with a faint smile, holding out his hand. 'My name's Nico. How do you do?'

As she smiled and shook his hand, he waited for recognition to dawn.

And in that same split-second she both recognized him . . . and realized with absolute certainty that recognition was exactly what he didn't need right now.

Maybe it was female intuition, maybe the expression in Nico Coletto's fabulous eyes . . . that scarcely discernible hesitation before he had spoken his name . . . that wary smile . . . but somehow she just knew that this was her chance of a lifetime and that recognizing him now would not be the smart thing to do.

Nico, awaiting her reaction, realized that he was holding his breath.

It didn't happen.

'Caroline Marriott,' she said, her tones pure Kensington, her grip surprisingly firm. 'How lovely to meet a fellow foreigner. But I really do feel you ought to let me wash your shirt. I promise not to do with it what I did with my own.'

Stripped to the waist and feeling like a Levi's advert, Nico watched Caroline set the washing-machine in motion and attempted to analyse his feelings.

Was it simply his acute homesickness that was bringing back so many memories today? First of all, this girl's fluid cursing had reminded him of Loulou. Now, the smell of the Supawash Laundromat was taking him home; it was almost as if he were sitting in his own kitchen once more, gossiping with Camilla while she sorted through mountains of washing and cleaning all in one efficient go. He had *loved* being there, keeping her company while she worked and teasing her.

So the clean, soapy atmosphere of this Las Vegas laundromat reminded him – almost painfully – of Camilla, the girl who was now washing his shirt reminded him of Loulou, and her very Englishness reminded him of . . . England. But was the attraction he felt for her simply a result, a natural progression, of those memories – or did it exist in its own right?

While Caroline was engrossed in the business of sorting through her own pink-streaked washing, searching for anything which might possibly have escaped the ravages of the crimson silk shirt, he leant back against a dryer and covertly studied her, searching for clues.

She was beautiful, with her dark blue eyes, pert nose and wide mouth. Tawny brown hair, sleek and shiny, swung to her shoulders and perfectly complemented her deep tan. Small in stature, maybe five foot two or three, she possessed voluptuously curving breasts and hips, but her waist, clinched by a wide tan-leather belt, was tiny. Also, he concluded thoughtfully, Caroline Marriott had an extremely good pair of legs.

But were all these attributes really enough to explain this rising attraction he felt for her, he wondered – or did it have more to do with the fact that her eyes reminded him slightly of Camilla's? That her curving hips reminded him of Camilla's curvy hips? And that at this moment she was sorting through her laundered clothes with precisely the same expression of concentration that Camilla had always adopted?

'How about some lunch?' he suggested. After all, if he got to know her better he might be able to sort this strange situation out. Instant attractions weren't his line of business, at all.

'It's gone four o'clock,' Caroline reminded him, straightening up and tossing a marbled pink and white skirt into the bin. 'And you,' she added with a lop-sided grin, 'are practically naked.'

'Come and sit down,' said Nico, patting the wooden bench beside him. 'I have a picnic. And dress is purely optional.'

She really was from Kensington, he learnt during the course of the impromptu picnic. Having fled from London following the break-up of a tortuous relationship with a Lloyds underwriter, she had taken up a post as nanny to a New York family who were 'friends of Mummy's'. Six months later, realizing that six-nights-a-week babysitting was not conducive to the formation of a new and exciting social life – and by now emotionally recovered enough to want one – Caroline had moved to Las Vegas and obtained work as a croupier at the Happy Larry Casino. Here, the hours were punishing, but at least they were varied. She learnt to work from two in the afternoon until midnight, and go night-clubbing afterwards until dawn. Another week she would dance until dawn, go home to shower and change, and then work on the blackjack tables from eight in the morning to six in the evening.

'I'm impressed,' said Nico, finishing his third can of beer and tossing it in the direction of the bin. 'When do you sleep?'

'Oh, we Marriotts are a hardy breed,' Caroline confided, tucking her slender brown legs beneath her and breaking open another roll with capable hands. 'We don't need much sleep. Waste of time. I don't like wasting time.'

As she leant forward he caught her scent, warm, spicy and alluring. She was hypnotizing him with her low, English voice. Her skin, smooth and velvety, intrigued him; she was like a soft fruit, rounded and ripe. And what did she *mean*, saying that she didn't like to waste time? Nico wasn't normally slow on the uptake but today was different – he felt different. He wanted another drink; maybe it would sharpen his senses.

'Tell me about you,' said Caroline. Her dark blue eyes softened and for a second looked astonishingly like Camilla's. Nico watched, mesmerized.

'I can't stand it here in Vegas,' he said, 'but there are problems back in London so being over here for a few weeks is a smart move.'

'Woman trouble?'

'You could call it that,' he shrugged, thinking of Camilla, and Roz, and his old harridan of a housekeeper. 'It's slightly complicated.'

It was certainly intriguing, thought Caroline, studying him intently and noting the edge of desperation in his voice. Having been away from England for a year and a half she was out of touch, with absolutely no idea of what could be troubling him. She hadn't worked in a casino for the past year without learning to recognize a gambler when she saw one. Nico wore that same air of impulsiveness borne of despair. He was in the mood, she sensed, to take a risk because a risk was a challenge and accepting a challenge was better than dwelling uselessly on the past.

'Are you married?' she asked casually, her heart pounding against her ribcage.

Nico shook his head. 'No.'

'Would you like to be?'

He laughed. 'Married? To whom?'

With outward calm she took a small sip of her beer and balanced the half-eaten roll on her knee.

'Me. If it would help. I'm willing if you are.'

'Nico? It's me.'

He blinked slowly, struggling to properly awake. The phone

slipped from his grasp and fell on to the pillow beside him. Cursing softly, not wanting to wake Caroline, he picked it up and held it to the ear furthest from her. He'd forgotten his mobile in the rush to escape the UK.

'Nico?'

'Who's me?' he murmured. As if anyone could fail to recognize Roz's voice even with the Atlantic separating them.

'Roz.' She sounded impatient. 'I called your record company and they told me where to reach you.'

'Why?'

'Don't be *dense*, Nico. We're having a baby, aren't we? I rang to let you know how everything's going.'

He didn't have the energy to argue with her. Lying back against the pillows, he glanced across at Caroline, still sound asleep. Sunlight streamed through the window, turning her golden skin to warm silk. Her sleeping form seemed suddenly even more desirable compared with the unwelcome sound of Roz's low, sly voice on the phone.

'So, how's it going?'

'Fine. Very well indeed.'

'Terrific.'

She sighed, across thousands of miles. 'Such enthusiasm. I also wanted to find out how *you* are. How's the conquering hero getting on in the States?'

Despite himself, Nico smiled at the unwitting Americanism. 'I'm getting on just fine,' he replied evenly.

Several dollars' worth of silence followed. Then: 'I miss you, Nico. We should be together.'

Ah, this was more like it. Roz at her most persuasive, sincerity oozing down the phone. Next to him, Caroline shifted, her warm, bare thigh brushing against his. Recalling last night, he began to feel better and returned the pressure.

'This is a waste of time,' he said quietly. 'Even if that baby is mine, I still don't trust you. I don't love you.'

'You did!'

'That was when I didn't really know you. That was *then*, Roz.'

'But can't you understand how I feel?' she urged, and he heard desperation in her voice. 'At least think of the baby, Nico. We should be married.'

Perhaps we should, he thought. Maybe that was the best idea yet. He and Roz really *should* get married.

But definitely not to each other.

Five hours later, Caroline kissed him on the mouth and said: 'Well, this will be one in the eye for Roz, won't it?' and Nico realized that she had not been asleep during that fateful phone call earlier.

'You were listening,' he said, his green eyes surveying hers for her reaction and finding only fun. Maybe it was just as well that she already understood the situation; it saved any awkward explanations later. 'I don't want you to think she was the reason for all this.'

Which wasn't strictly true, he told himself with a trace of guilt, but Roz hadn't been the entire reason, after all. She was part of it, just as Camilla was part of it. And of course, there was Caroline herself – she had to be included as well. He might grow to love her, he was *definitely* sure that he fancied her like hell . . . and she had told him continuously last night how fantastic he was in bed. Wasn't it supposed to be true that if two people had a successful sexual relationship, nothing too terrible could go wrong between them?

Only, he recalled wryly, if the woman was Roz Vallender.

He gazed down at Caroline, beautiful in a beige silk dress, her tawny hair artfully pinned up to reveal the slender curves of her neck and smoothly tanned shoulders. Feeling his eyes upon her she looked up, her smile bewitching, her eyes mischievous and lustful.

'It doesn't bother me,' she said, lightly touching the tip of his nose with her finger. 'I'm not afraid of competition. And I've always enjoyed a challenge.'

'But it wasn't because of Roz,' he repeated with determination, almost managing to convince himself, if not her.

'$5 a photograph, mistah,' yelled an under-sized Mexican boy as they emerged from the coolness of the building and were blasted by heat and dazzling white sunlight. He waved an ancient camera, his dark eyes alight with hope.

'Do you have $5, mistah?' said Caroline, squeezing his arm.

Nico reached for his wallet. 'I think we can afford to splash out, just this once,' he confided and extracted two $10 bills. 'Four photos for the family album, please. And make them snappy.'

'OK, mistah. I take great pictah,' the boy assured them, gesturing with a skinny brown arm that they should move closer together. 'OK, now very happy . . . kiss the bride, mistah. Hey, OK! OK!'

Chapter 27

The day really couldn't get much worse, thought Roz wildly, wrenching the parking ticket from her windscreen and attempting to rip it to shreds. The plastic bag enclosing it resisted the assault, to her fury, and she threw it to the ground, grinding it beneath her heel.

Morning sickness which had continued into the eighth month of her pregnancy, a sodding parking ticket, and no job.

She had been sacked because she was having a baby, and because she wasn't married. How bloody provincial could you get?

Right, kiddo, she told her unborn child as she grimly dragged open the car door and started up the engine. We're going to Vampires. It's time you had your first drink.

Loulou was leaning against the bar, exchanging gossip with Christo and secretly yearning for a ham and banana sandwich, when Roz appeared in the doorway looking tragic.

Loulou expertly tipped a young tell-it-to-the-tabloids actor off his stool.

'How charming of you to offer the lady a seat,' she said smoothly, steering Roz on to it. Her glossy dark hair looked limp and the pallor of her skin was almost startling. Even her long-lashed eyes seemed less bright than usual as she glanced almost furtively around her and adjusted the folds of her charcoal grey Calvin Klein dress with agitated fingers.

'Something bad?' said Loulou in a low voice, as Christo

moved diplomatically away. 'Do you want to go upstairs?'

'I want,' replied Roz in a low, controlled voice, 'a drink. Give me a spritzer.'

Despite herself, Loulou hadn't been able to help reading baby books. Her own baby had not been planned, but now that it was clearly going to arrive anyway, she had found it easy, almost exciting, to take good care of it. No cigarettes, no alcohol, hardly any late nights and plenty of real food . . . She hadn't known she possessed such self-control before.

'How about an orange juice?' she offered casually, and Roz fixed her with a glare that would have stripped paint.

'Don't get *maternal* with me, for Christ's sake – one glass of wine won't hurt it. I've just been sacked.'

'Oh Roz, no. The bastards.'

'Oh Loulou, yes,' said Roz, signalling to Christo. Her eyebrows, those slanting black lines which so clearly relayed every emotion, lifted as she gestured impatience with the TV company.

'It's hardly the end of the world, I suppose, and it isn't as if I wasn't half expecting it. There's trendy old Channel 4, of course. I could always go over to them.'

She sipped her drink, then took a larger swallow, licking her lips appreciatively while Loulou watched her, attempting to gauge the true extent of her despair.

'So you were pissed off anyway and losing your job was the final straw?'

Roz shrugged and nodded. 'Pregnancy is the pits, Lou, it really is. *And* I got a parking ticket. My father sent me a postcard this morning, from Peru. It said "How's the most desired woman in England?" You should have seen the postman's face when he handed it over – Littleton Grey is *burning* with gossip about me at the moment and that card was just the icing on the cake for them.' She paused, lacing her fingers around the sides of her glass. 'They're laughing at me because Nico doesn't want to know. That's what I really can't handle.'

'You should get away,' Loulou told her firmly. My God, she thought with a rush of surprise, I sound like a mother already.

'I should stay and fight,' declared Roz, the light of battle at last reappearing in her dark eyes. 'What happened this morning has made up my mind, Lou. I've lost my job. I'm not going to lose Nico as well.'

Beyond Roz, Loulou became aware that Christo was frantically waving to catch her attention.

'Telephone for you,' he called across, and she frowned, puzzled by his expression.

'Bring it over here, Christo.'

'The connection is faint and there's too much noise over there,' he replied with determination, and Loulou sighed, sliding down from her seat and patting Roz's hand.

'I won't be a minute.'

When she reached Christo, she said crossly, 'What the hell's the matter with you?'

'Nothing at all.' He gave her a bland look. 'I just thought it might be easier to talk over here. It's Nico, calling from Las Vegas.'

'Hey!' cried Loulou, grabbing the receiver from him with both hands and blowing Christo a kiss. Whatever Nico's shortcomings as far as Roz was concerned, he was still *her* friend and hearing from him always cheered her up. Turning her back on the bar and glimpsing Roz's dark reflection in the mirrors lining the wall, she blew more enthusiastic kisses into the phone.

'And how's my favourite all-American boy! What's happening, Nico?'

'Loulou, is that you? Is it the middle of the night over there – did I wake you up?'

There was music playing in the background, and the babble of voices. Nico sounded excited and a little drunk.

'It's lunchtime, you fool. How's everything going? Are you having fun – did you win me a casino yet?'

'Oh, I'm having fun. It's five o'clock in the morning and I'm on my second bottle of Tequila. Guess what I did today . . . no, yesterday now? Come on Lou, guess.'

He was very drunk indeed. 'I can't guess. Tell me before your dime runs out. What did you do yesterday that brought all this on?'

The line grew fainter and the music louder; jamming the phone against her ear she glanced guiltily over her shoulder at Roz and saw that she was ordering herself another drink.

'. . . went and got married, Lou.'

'Who?' she exclaimed in disbelief, and the transatlantic line miraculously became clear.

'I did. Me and this girl. I met her yesterday . . . no, the day before, in a launderette, and we married each other. No-one else knows yet – you're the first. My mother's going to kill me when she finds out.'

His mother wasn't the only one, thought Loulou, her heart turning somersaults. How the hell was Roz going to react to this? And what did Nico think he was doing, marrying someone he'd met only the day before – in a launderette of all places?

'Are you truly happy?' she demanded ruthlessly, and heard Nico hesitate for a second.

'What sort of question is that?' he protested. 'Weren't you happy on all your wedding days?'

'Hmm. Well, as long as you *are* happy, then congratulations. I'm sorry if I don't sound terribly enthusiastic, but you don't need me to tell you what a pile of shit you're landing me in. I'll have to let Roz know about this before it hits the Press.'

'Yes.' He sounded more sober now, and defiant. 'But I *am* happy, Lou. I had to do it. You understand that, don't you?'

'Of course,' she said, praying that what he had done was more than simply a means of escape. Few people had managed to waste as many marriages as she herself had, but that didn't mean she didn't take the idea of them seriously. 'I'll look forward to meeting her when you get back. She must be a terrific lady.'

'Of course she's a terrific lay,' said Nico laughing. 'We both are. I'll see you soon, Lou. Take care of yourself.'

'And you,' she said, feeling helpless, but the line had already gone dead.

'Come upstairs,' she urged Roz, wondering how she was going to tell her.

'No. I like it here.' Roz clung obstinately to her drink, then viewed Loulou with almost telepathic suspicion. 'What's up?'

Seeing that she had no intention of moving, Loulou retrieved her stool and planted herself firmly upon it.

'That was Nico.'

'I guessed it might be.' Eyes bright, Roz clasped her hand and said rapidly, 'I was about to tell you just now . . . yesterday I phoned him in Las Vegas and told him that we ought to get married. Lou, he said maybe we should. Don't you think that means he's prepared to –'

'He did,' blurted out Loulou, realizing that, like dead soldiers, it didn't matter how she said it. 'Got married. Yesterday.'

* * *

Bastard, son of a bitch, bastard.

Staring ahead, her fingers seemingly glued to the steering-wheel, Roz accelerated hard and tried to make sense of it all. As the dark blue Mercedes sped along the M4 she struggled to organize the jumbled thoughts in her mind. Without realizing it, she had pinned all her hopes, her entire future, on Nico and this searing, slashing betrayal was almost more than she could bear. She wasn't Camilla, or even Loulou, both of whom seemed to expect, almost to invite, disasters – she was Roz Vallender and until now she had always been in control, getting whatever and whomever she wanted without even having to work at it.

It angered her still more to discover that she couldn't overcome the problems which faced her now. Other women coped in the same situation, so why was *she* finding it so desperately difficult to accept?

Shaking her dark head and tightening her grip on the steering-wheel as the speedometer touched ninety and she passed a car transporter loaded with Sierras, all identical, she wondered if it was that which troubled her. The fact that from now on she was going to be more ordinary, more vulnerable . . . like so many other women.

Nico had done it on purpose, she could see that clearly enough. She had been *chasing* him, pursuing him like one of his despised groupies, and he had drawn back in horror and disgust, retaliating by showing her in the plainest way possible that she no longer interested him. How many more obvious ways were there of letting her know than by marrying someone else?

The way she had behaved was deplorable. Blackly, bitterly,

Roz wished she could cut it out of herself. It was a malignancy and she wanted above all else to be rid of it.

At that exact moment an eight-year-old Mini doing seventy in the fast lane had moved over in order to allow Roz to overtake, then unaccountably swerved back again, just enough for its front bumper to touch her rear one. Shocked by the contact and over-compensating for the momentary loss of control, Roz's Mercedes careered along the edge of the crash barrier, finally ricocheting off it and smashing back into the side of the purple Mini.

The impact of that second collision seemed like an explosion. When both cars had finally come to a halt after what seemed like hours but which had in fact been less than twenty-five seconds, Roz fumbled with the door handle, stumbled awkwardly from her car and crawled across the inside lane, finally collapsing on the hard shoulder beside the crumpled front wings of the Mini. Deathly pale and icy with shock she lay there like a stunned rabbit, her dark eyes wide and staring, her breath coming in short, quickening gasps. Her dress was patched with blood and her fingers clawed the road as waves of pain gripped her, dulling both her vision and her mind as they slowly grew in intensity.

Shaken but miraculously unhurt, the driver of the Mini got himself out through the passenger door and made his way round to Roz. He turned away, sickened, and covered his eyes with a trembling hand when he saw the swollen bulge of her belly and the ominous dark blood staining her dress.

It was all a blur to Roz. Dazed, she realized that the police and an ambulance had arrived and from then on she allowed herself to think no further, sinking into the oblivion of a painkilling injection and the soothingly matter-of-fact voices of the ambulance men as they lifted her with smooth efficiency on to a stretcher.

'Is anyone hurt? Have I hurt someone?' she murmured, her pale forehead creasing as she struggled to speak.

'No-one else was injured,' the burly ambulance man assured her, monitoring her pulse with one big hand and briefly lifting the hem of her dress in order to reassure himself that the flow of blood was lessening. 'We'll have you into hospital in no time at all, Mrs Vallender, so don't you worry.'

'But I am worried,' she said through clenched teeth. 'It's my fault, all of it. I'm pregnant. What am I going to do now?'

Having smelt alcohol on Roz's breath, the police waited in the casualty department of Gloucester Royal Hospital until Roz had been examined by the doctors, and then breathalysed her. Although she had only had two spritzers, they had been generously poured and consumed on an extremely empty stomach. The level of alcohol in her blood proved to be just over the legal limit and the charges were drunk and reckless driving. She had been travelling at something in the region of ninety miles an hour according to eyewitness accounts, and had also told the police officers, amidst tears and confusion, that the accident had been entirely her own fault.

Before you could say BUPA, Roz found herself bang in the middle of Gloucester Royal's busy obstetrics ward. Having recovered from the initial acute shock of the accident, and after being strongly reassured that the baby was alive and apparently suffering no ill effects, she was feeling much better, physically at least. The spectacular laceration on her left thigh, which had been sustained as she stumbled from the car on to broken glass and which had bled so copiously at first, had been cleaned and stitched, the pain reduced now to a dull ache. As the shock subsided however, her anger at this new trauma – just when she least needed it – inflamed and grew. Her mood blackened. Niggling irritability vied with plain bad temper. Together they rose within her like a swelling, slow-motion wave.

To her disgust she was surrounded on all sides by openly curious women whose stomachs were all at least as large as her own. Their stares infuriated her, as did the manner of the ward sister, who was brisk in her actions to the point of roughness and was obviously a raving Socialist to boot, determined that Roz Vallender wasn't to get any preferential treatment just because she was well known.

'I'm a member of a private health scheme,' pointed out Roz irritably, examining with distaste the stiffly starched hospital gown she was forced to wear. It hadn't been like this last time round. 'I don't want to be in a public ward. Don't you at least have side wards?'

'We have one side ward,' the woman informed her tartly, 'and it is occupied, *Miss* Vallender, by someone much sicker than yourself. You may make arrangements to be transferred to a privately run hospital as soon as the doctors here are satisfied that you are stable enough to be moved, but I'm afraid that until then you'll just have to put up with us.'

Roz stared at her with dislike. 'Then could I at least have the curtains drawn around my bed? Ow, that hurts . . .'

'We need to be able to keep an eye on you,' replied the sister, continuing to pump air into the thick cuff around Roz's upper arm until it felt as if her hand would explode. Abruptly the tautness was released and she wrote the blood pressure reading on to a chart at the foot of the bed.

'You'll have to learn to withstand more pain than that, dear.' Her tone was deliberately condescending now. 'And you should be grateful that that wee baby of yours is still all right. You might easily have lost it in that accident, y'know.'

Roz's eyes narrowed; her fists clenched at her sides. 'I didn't crash the car on purpose. It *was* an accident, so don't try and make me feel any worse than I do already.'

Evenly, the nursing sister replied, 'I wouldn't dream of it, dear. But even I can smell alcohol on your breath – maybe if you hadn't been drinking the accident wouldn't have happened in the first place.'

'Oh, go away,' shouted Roz, fighting back tears of frustration and anger. 'Just get out of here and leave me alone. You're a bitch and I'm reporting you to the consultant. Women like you shouldn't be allowed to look after people who are ill.'

Over the next twenty-four hours Roz dug herself deeper into a hole of her own construction. The doctors insisted that she stay on the ward under observation, the nursing staff treated her with the barest minimum of courtesy and the other patients, having heard her call their beloved Sister Mason a bitch, all decided that she was a jumped-up ill-mannered hussy. Roz hated them all back in return, with a vengeance.

Within hours of her arrival the news was relayed to the Press and they had an absolute field day, telephoning and turning up in droves. If the hospital staff were too professional to voice their personal opinions of Roz Vallender, the women patients had no such scruples, taking enormous delight in informing the avid-for-news reporters about her foul mouth and vile temper. After a sleepless night, Roz was forced to endure the humiliation of lying in bed while twenty-seven pregnant women sat up in theirs, avidly reading twenty-seven copies of the only tabloid newspaper which had chosen to feature her on the front page, right next to a piece on Nico and his mysterious new bride.

'He's gorgeous,' declared a red-head called Sharon, glancing across at Roz and addressing her neighbours in an over-loud voice. 'I'm dead glad he's married that Caroline Whatsername, mind you I can see now why he didn't want nothing to do with her over there. Bet he's glad he got away from her, too, stuck-up cow.'

Keeping her eyes closed and lying perfectly still, Roz said in a clear voice, 'Get stuffed.'

'I already have, thanks,' replied Sharon, amidst much muffled laughter. 'But at least I had a husband to do the job for me.'

Christ, thought Roz, I can't stand any more of this. I'm going home, right now.

Opening her eyes she hauled herself into a sitting position and began sliding her legs towards the edge of the bed. At precisely that moment a strange tugging sensation gripped her lower back. She paused, drawing in breath, then stared in horror and disbelief at the damp patch on the sheet beneath her.

As she watched, the patch grew, seemingly of its own accord.

'Oh shit,' said Roz, feeling the wet warmth between her legs and tensing as another wave of pain began low down in her stomach. That was it then – the great escape plan well and truly thwarted. She was being prevented from leaving by her very own baby, who quite clearly had no taste at all and wanted to be born in this hell-hole of a hospital. Mistake Number One, sweetie, thought Roz with a wry smile. But never mind; we all make them. You're just starting earlier than most.

Chapter 28

'Mummy, I hate Gus. Tell her to give me back my hat,' yelled Charlotte, hurling herself at Zoë's five-year-old daughter and wrenching the floppy pink sunhat from her head.

'Five minutes ago you told me you hated the hat,' said Camilla, raising her eyebrows at Zoë and signalling despair.

'I do hate it,' Charlotte informed her triumphantly, hurling it on to the bleached grass and stamping on it with her bare foot. 'But it's still mine and Gussie can't have it.'

Zoë groaned and covered her eyes. 'You've got a Bolshevik on your hands, Cami. Charlotte, are you *sure* you want to be a nun when you grow up?'

Charlotte glared at her, quite immune to Zoë's sense of humour. She didn't care for her mother's new friend. Accustomed now to the endless spoiling of her father and grandparents, it came as quite a shock to her that her mother no longer gave in to her as she had in the past. Now, her mother was a lot more fun when all was going well between them, but if Charlotte stepped out of line she was rapidly reminded of it and punished accordingly. She didn't quite know what to make of her new mother, with her make-up and perfume and butterfly-bright clothes.

'Give me some cake,' she declared now, her tone challenging, her lower lip sticking out.

'May I have some cake, please,' Camilla corrected her. 'Yes,

232

you may, just as soon as you've apologized to Gussie and given her your hat.'

'I won't.'

Her mother shrugged, unconcerned. 'Fine. In that case, no cake. Gussie darling, would you like some?'

'She can't have any!' squealed Charlotte, outraged. 'I hate her – and she *can't* bloody have any.'

The squeal increased in volume and rose an octave when Camilla smacked her bottom. It was the first time in Charlotte's life that she had been struck.

'And I hate you,' she wailed furiously, her grey eyes swimming with tears.

'Yes,' said Camilla firmly, her own gaze steely with determination, her newfound assertiveness coming to the fore. 'And you're being pretty horrible yourself at the moment. You have to grow up, Charlotte – your father might put up with your nasty little tantrums, but I certainly won't. Now go inside and wash your face and hands. When your manners have improved, maybe you can have something to eat.'

'Well, well, look at you!' said Zoë with an admiring whistle while Charlotte, kicking her feet in the dusty gravel of the path, made her way slowly towards the house. 'Executive superwoman no less, with her mobile on her lap and her business under control, making deals in the garden and teaching her kids a thing or two at the same time. *Cosmopolitan* will be queuing up to interview you before you know it, my sweet.'

Camilla's smile was self-deprecating. 'You should have known me when I was still married. The children ran rings around me and even trying out a new recipe made me twitchy. I was the original doormat.'

'In that case I'm glad I didn't know you,' Zoë declared. 'And for God's sake, don't tell all that to *Cosmopolitan* when they arrive.'

Camilla fell silent, remembering the day Loulou had dragged her along for moral support to Nico's house when the girl from *Cosmopolitan* had been due to interview him and Mac had been commissioned to take the photographs. That day's events had proved traumatic for all concerned; Loulou had been devastated by Mac's disinterest in her, and – months later – she herself had single-handedly destroyed her own relationship with Nico.

If she ever day-dreamed, even for a second, that maybe one day she and Nico could somehow put the disastrous events of the past behind them and renew their relationship, she buried the thought almost instantly. For now, the flourishing business was her life; that, her friendships with Loulou and Zoë and the budding, still tentative new relationship she was building with her children. Now that she was seeing them three times a week she felt confident that it would grow and improve, and that once they learnt to accept the change in their mother, it would become better than it had ever been before.

So for the moment . . . no men. Problems like them she could quite easily do without.

She turned as something tugged timidly at the sleeve of her shirt. Charlotte stood before her, looking distinctly ill at ease but remorseful.

'I washed my face and hands, Mummy,' she said, her eyes searching Camilla's for forgiveness. 'And I'll play with Gussie too.' It was the nearest her daughter had ever come to an apology, thought Camilla, bursting with pride both for Charlotte and herself.

'I'm glad to hear it, darling,' she said fondly, brushing a strand of light brown hair from her daughter's smooth forehead.

'You and Gus could be such good friends. When you're hungry I'll make you both some lunch, OK?'

Charlotte assumed an expression of great importance. Reaching behind Camilla's chair, she picked up a tray and carefully handed it across to her. 'I've made *you* some,' she announced, pointing to the glass of raspberryade, a mangled peanut butter sandwich and a plate piled high with flapjack and fruit cake. 'And the paper was on the front door mat so I brought it for you to read,' she added anxiously. 'You like reading the paper, don't you, Mummy?'

Camilla, wanting to laugh and cry at the same time, bit her lip and said, 'I *love* reading the paper. Thank you, sweetheart – this is very thoughtful of you. Mmmm . . .' she took a sip of the disgustingly sweet drink and rolled her eyes in appreciation, 'just what I wanted.'

Charlotte beamed, hopping from one leg to the other. 'I'm good at making lunch, aren't I, Mummy?'

'You certainly are.' Catching sight of Zoë, silently applauding behind Charlotte's back, Camilla said, 'And I'm going to share this lovely sandwich with Zoë, because she's *my* friend. Here you are, Zoë . . .' Carefully dividing the sandwich, which had evidently started off being spread with blackcurrant jam before Charlotte had finally decided that it should be peanut butter instead, she handed it across to Zoë.

'How heavenly,' remarked Zoë, pulling a face that only Camilla could see. 'And how nice to have *friends*, Charlotte, don't you think?'

'Gussie's my friend,' said Charlotte complacently, basking in the warmth of her mother's approval. 'I'm going to go and be nice to her right now.'

When she was out of earshot, Zoë said in a low voice,

'Congratulations on the rebirth of your daughter, even if this is all rather too *Sound of Musicky* for me.'

'Shut up,' replied Camilla, grinning as she quietly tipped her drink into the grass beneath her chair, 'and eat your lovely sandwich.'

'Don't tell me to shut up; I'm your *friend*,' retaliated Zoë, expertly tossing her half of the sandwich over the fence into next door's garden. 'And instead of sitting there looking smug, why don't you read your paper?'

Camilla stared in horror at the front page, willing herself to have read it wrongly. Her fingers, she noticed irrationally, were gripping the paper like frozen claws. It had to be a mistake . . . it *had* to be.

But the headline screamed 'Nico – Married!' and as she continued to gaze at it, and at the picture below of Nico embracing a small, curvaceous girl, she realized that there could be no mistake whatsoever, no doubt at all that the one event which had never even crossed her mind had actually happened.

Those brief doubts which she had taken such pains to bury; that faintest of faint hope that somehow one day, miraculously, they would be reconciled, was now obliterated. While she had been wasting time, mourning the loss of their fragile relationship, Nico had been busy falling in love with someone else . . . and marrying her.

Chapter 29

'I need a woman,' repeated the male voice on the phone and Camilla, acknowledging that it was an extremely sexy voice, deep and American accented, reached for the appointment book.

'What kind of assignment is it, and when is it planned for?' she asked, tapping her pen against her cheek and wondering why it was that men with impossibly sensual telephone voices always turned out to be fat, pink and sluglike.

'I shall need her tomorrow, from about nine in the morning until midnight,' said the American voice caressing her ear like silk. Despite herself, Camilla smiled and softened. He really did sound gorgeous.

'Is it a photographic assignment, Mr . . .?'

'Lewis. I daresay she'll have her photograph taken, yes.' He paused, then added casually, 'But all I really want is a companion, an escort if you like, for the day.'

Correction, thought Camilla, her sense of humour fading fast: why was it that men with sensual telephone voices always turned out to be sex-obsessed creeps?

'Mr Lewis, Sheridan's is not that kind of agency,' she told him coldly. 'Please do not call this number again.'

When the doorbell rang forty minutes later she cursed Zoë for always losing her keys – how had she ever managed before Camilla had moved in? – and made her way gingerly towards the front door, splaying her bare toes and praying that the wet nail polish she had so painstakingly just applied wouldn't smudge.

Sunlight streamed through the door's crimson and green stained glass, its fruit-gum shades reflecting upon the polished wooden floorboards of the hall. Beyond the coloured glass, however, she was able to make out the outline of a figure which definitely wasn't Zoë. There appeared to be some kind of giant out there, the fact that she was barefoot only accentuating his great height.

'Good morning,' said Camilla, her no-thank-you-we-already-have-double-glazing expression firmly in place, her eyes on a level with the centre button of a Mediterranean blue Paul Smith shirt. Her gaze shifted sharply upwards, registering dark curly chest hair, a strong brown neck and an even more deeply tanned face with so many quirky, intriguing features that she couldn't take them all in at once. Very dark, untidily curly hair, amused dark blue eyes and a wry, lop-sided smile were most immediately noticeable, but as he stood there, towering in the doorway and saying nothing for a second or two, she observed too that he had one crooked incisor, laughter lines so deep they were almost bags, and an indentation which could have been a scar or a dimple high up on his left cheek.

'I'm really not a pervert,' he said at last, 'but when you told me not to phone again, I had no way of letting you know that. So I thought I'd call round in person, seeing that I was more or less in the neighbourhood.'

'Oh,' said Camilla, stunned.

'Do you think you might allow me a second chance to explain?'

Still stunned, she nodded. Leaning towards her, his left hand propping up the stonework beside the front door, he reached with the other for Camilla's right hand – which was hanging limply at her side – and solemnly shook it.

'Delighted to make your acquaintance. Matt Lewis.'

'The golfer,' said Camilla, who hadn't been married to Jack and his sixteen handicap for ten years without picking up some knowledge of the game.

He nodded. 'And I do still need a woman. May I come in?'

'Of course,' said Camilla hastily, pulling herself together and wondering where on earth she should put him. The living-room carpet was awash with Zoë's dress patterns and half-cut-out material, as far as she could remember the kitchen was also a mess, and the spare bedroom which she and Zoë had converted into an office still looked far too much like a bedroom to consider inviting a stranger inside it. Particularly a stranger as obviously virile and attractive as Matt Lewis.

'You'll have to watch out for pins,' she told him with a shrug, leading the way towards the living-room. 'Almost all our business is conducted over the phone so we don't have a proper office, I'm afraid. Would you like a cup of tea, Mr Lewis? Or coffee?'

'Tea's fine.' He stood back, admiring the smooth twin curves of Camilla's shoulder blades as she bent to retrieve the crackling tissue-paper patterns and bright scarlet satiny material strewn over the floor. As she moved, one of the thin straps of her amethyst silk top slipped from her beautifully rounded shoulder and he glimpsed the even more tantalizing curve of her breast. He smiled at the speed with which she pulled the strap up again, rosy colour touching her cheeks. Throwing the heap of paper and material behind a chair, she came towards him and this time held out her hand.

'I'm Camilla Stewart, Zoë Sheridan's business partner. Sorry

239

I was a bit abrupt on the phone, but—'

'I have a way with words,' he supplied, his blue eyes betraying hidden laughter. 'Well, I can tell you, Miss Stewart, it isn't that often I get the phone slammed down on me. I daresay it taught me a lesson. But I asked one of the receptionists at the hotel to give me the name of a modelling agency and she told me that Sheridan's was the very best in London, so I thought you were probably worth pursuing.'

'It's Mrs Stewart,' said Camilla automatically. Surprise and delight shone in her eyes. 'The hotel receptionist really said that?'

'Well,' admitted Matt, 'it did just happen to turn out that her sister's boyfriend's cousin's wife is one of your models, so maybe she was biased.'

'Oh.' She looked momentarily downcast, then: 'But we're the best *new* agency, anyway. Why don't you sit down and I'll make some tea.'

Matt glanced at his watch. 'It's almost lunchtime; why don't we go and have something to eat instead? We golfers have to keep our strength up, and maybe by buying you lunch I can make up for my earlier *faux pas*.'

'Oh, that would have been lovely,' said Camilla with genuine regret, biting her lower lip and looking so adorable that Matt felt a sudden desperate longing to put his arms around her. 'But I really can't – I have a thousand things to do and Zoë won't be back for hours. I'm sorry,' she said, her smile only increasing his determination. 'But if you're absolutely starving I could make you some peanut butter sandwiches. Sit down,' she urged again, turning away and heading towards the kitchen.

The sight of those irresistible shoulder blades was simply

too much for Matt Lewis. 'No,' he said, dead-pan. 'I certainly will not.'

The Red Rose in Covent Garden was dark, dramatic and decadent, and Matt almost died. To her amazement Camilla realized that he was genuinely embarrassed by the provocative mirrored ceiling, crimson damask drapes and walls hung with distinctly erotic paintings.

'We can't stay here,' he protested, 'it looks like a whore-house!'

Camilla smiled and stood her ground, resisting Matt's attempts to move her out, amused and touched by his obvious discomfort. She still didn't have the faintest idea what she was doing, dropping everything and dashing out to have lunch with a tall, persistent stranger, but now that she was here she wasn't going to leave.

'They have a very pretty walled garden behind the restaurant – we can sit outside and eat. They do wonderful food here.'

'Strange place,' murmured Matt, his dark eyebrows still fixed with doubt. 'I had the idea that a restaurant called The Red Rose would be kind of cosy and Shakespearian, you know?'

'Well, you were right the first time when you said it looked like a whorehouse. It was going to be called The Brothel, but there were complaints from outraged residents, so they changed it before the police closed them down and arrested all the waitresses for soliciting.' Explaining all this to Matt, and realizing that he had been more taken aback by the restaurant's interior than she had on her first visit here two months ago made Camilla feel terrifically worldly – something she was still unfamiliar with. And to feel worldly in the company of Matt Lewis, this overwhelming American with the curly dark hair and big shoulders, was surely even more incredible. Whoever would think, looking at her now, that this impromptu lunch date – forced upon her against her better judgement – was the first social occasion she had experienced for almost three months?

Although it was mid-September the weather was still incredibly good; the Indian summer predicted by the weathermen had actually materialized and in the sheltered high-walled garden of The Brothel – for it was still known by its original name – the temperature was up in the high seventies, golden sunlight bathing the terracotta and bleached cream flagstones and the tubs of bright flowers dotted between the tables.

Reminded of al fresco lunches in Greece with Jack, when she had sweltered in voluminous blouses and long skirts, afraid to reveal her pale bulk to the world, Camilla slipped off her pink and white blazer and welcomed the sun's warmth upon her bare, lightly tanned shoulders.

'A year ago I couldn't have sat here like this,' she confided, leaning forward with her elbows on the table and touching her upper arms. 'I was grotesquely fat. Sometimes I forget for a few minutes and think I still am.'

Her candidness – how many women, after all, would admit to such a thing? – charmed Matt completely.

When their drinks had been served and the meal ordered, Camilla reached into the vast haversack she had brought with her and drew out two photograph albums, clearing a place for them on the table.

'You want to show me your family snaps?' said Matt, sitting back in his chair and looking alarmed. 'If you're planning to show me pictures of your devoted husband . . .'

Camilla smiled. 'I'm divorced. Would I be sitting here with

you now if I were married, Mr Lewis?' she added playfully.

His tone altered, became serious. 'There's no reason why you shouldn't. It is only a business lunch, after all. Isn't it?'

Two spots of colour appeared in Camilla's cheeks. 'Oh, yes . . . of course it is. How stupid of me . . .' She faltered, covered in confusion and Matt burst out laughing. Her innocence was absolutely enchanting. No wonder he found himself so strongly attracted to her, when all he ever seemed to meet these days were all-knowing, highly lacquered, sharply calculating girls who never missed a trick.

'You're teasing me,' Camilla reproached him, sagging with relief.

He tapped her left hand, bare of rings, with his fork. 'I knew you weren't married.'

'I might have been one of those women who don't wear a wedding-ring,' she countered, pretending to be affronted, and the expression in Matt's eyes sent a shiver down her legs.

'Ah,' he said with slow deliberation, 'but you're not. I've figured that much out already.'

To cover the awkward moment that followed, during which she couldn't think of a single thing to say, Camilla busied herself opening the photograph albums and pushing them across the tablecloth towards Matt. Business, this is a *business* lunch, she told herself, knowing that it really wasn't. Matt Lewis was looking at her in a very unbusinesslike way indeed.

'Take a look at these. Each of our models has a complete portfolio, of course, but it'll be quicker and easier if you look through the albums and choose three or four to narrow it down. Now, Katy, Eloise and Anne are already booked, Marcie wouldn't be able to work tomorrow because she has to take her daughter to the dentist and Linda,' she turned to the appropriate pages and pointed, 'has got tonsillitis, but all the others are available, so just take your time and see who you think would be most suitable. I can phone them as soon as you decide, and confirm the booking straight away.'

'Our food's arriving. I'll have a look at them afterwards,' said Matt gravely, having made up his own mind at least an hour ago, but realizing that Camilla might need a little more time in which to get used to him. 'That lobster looks amazing. Do you know, I asked the hotel receptionist to recommend a good restaurant. When we first walked in here I thought of clubbing her to death with my nine iron, but it's thanks to her that I'm sitting here now with this lobster, and with you. I may recommend that she should get a raise instead.'

'Ask the waiter if he knows her,' said Camilla, spearing a plump Mediterranean prawn with her fork and rolling it slowly through the creamy, garlicky mayonnaise with which it was served. 'He'll probably tell you that he's her boyfriend's sister's cousin's son.'

Matt watched her while she ate, scarcely able to concentrate at all upon his own meal. By asking her questions about the agency he was able to sit and listen to her, and to realize with pleasure and relief that his first instincts had been correct: she was perfect.

The quality she possessed, and which he found so entirely irresistible, he decided, was that of innocence. She was simply unaware that she was a beautiful, sexually very attractive woman. She had absolutely *no idea*.

And that was so rare these days. Matt had glanced briefly at the photographs in the album, pretending interest while all his thoughts had been absorbed in listening to her low-pitched, slightly hesitant voice, and while he recognized that maybe the

244

models were a fraction more physically perfect ... more classically beautiful ... he had known that Camilla was the one he wanted. These beautiful women, apart from the fact that they earned their living by their looks, were conscious of their beauty anyway. Some, he had discovered over the years, were aware of it only most of the time; others, constantly. Each movement, each gesture was geared to that fact, each thought and word dictated by it.

Camilla, on the other hand, with her shy, self-deprecating sense of humour and that guileless smile, coupled with her aura of beauty, had hit him like a bolt out of the blue. She was unique, as far as he was concerned, and he wanted her more than he had ever wanted anything else throughout the course of his entire charmed life.

The sudden appalling thought that she might not want him in return sent an icy shiver of panic down Matt's spine, made him realize that he could not afford to waste another second. He had to be reassured that Camilla at least *liked* him. That would be enough to keep him going throughout the rest of the meal ...

'The girls in that album,' he said abruptly, nodding his dark head towards it as if it were a coiled snake, 'I don't want any of them. None.'

'I'm sorry?' said Camilla, dismayed. What was going on? He had been silent, listening with apparent absorption while she told him about Zoë and her daughters, and now he was cancelling the assignment? 'But you didn't even *see* all of them. Have another look ...' Embarrassed, as appalled as if he had said, 'Your baby is ugly', she pushed the album back towards him, almost toppling over his wine glass as she flipped open the cover.

'. . . see, that's Daisy, one of our most popular girls, she's just completed a photographic assignment for *Vogue*, she's done TV commercials, catwalk . . .'

'But I don't want a catwalk model,' he intercepted, moving the wine glasses out of danger. 'I want "a date". It's practically mandatory, Camilla; all the other guys will be there with their wives or girlfriends – maybe both,' he added with a wink, 'and I couldn't think of anyone I wanted to ask. You can't just pick anybody, so I decided to go to the professionals and hire someone for the day; that way at least I know I won't have any hassle afterwards. Doesn't that make good sense?'

'It makes sense,' said Camilla with the slightest touch of annoyance, 'but I still don't understand why none of our models are good enough for you. Look here, at Miranda . . . she speaks four languages and she's *beautiful* . . .'

As her trembling fingers struggled to turn the pages of the album, Matt's hand reached out and grabbed them. Camilla had smooth, elegant hands. She wore no nail polish, and no rings. Her face, when he glanced up, was a picture of irresistible confusion.

'Camilla, I want you.'

'Oh,' she said finally, gazing past him – just over his left shoulder – with such apparent concentration that Matt was forced to turn and look round, to see who had caught her attention. That middle-aged man eating langoustines with his fingers and letting the juice run down his chin? The two girls frantically fending off a lazy and disinterested wasp? Those pink and cream roses in their tub?

Camilla, seeing nothing at all, was thinking. She didn't even dare to examine Matt's reasons for inviting her, but, since meeting him she had felt as if she was walking effortlessly along a narrow beam, convinced that it was less than a foot from the ground. It had all been so easy. Now, hearing the unmistakable meaning in his words, it was as if she had suddenly looked down and found that the beam was in fact a tightrope, and that it was stretched across the Grand Canyon.

'I'm sorry. I say what's on my mind, I guess.'

He neither looked nor sounded sorry. Camilla dredged up the remains of her previous confidence. Loulou wouldn't have been floored in this situation; she tried to think how her friend would react now.

'You . . . want . . . me,' she repeated his words slowly, making them sound like a challenge. 'Are you talking about tomorrow's assignment?'

'That'll do for a start,' he said, the laughter lines deepening around his eyes as he realized that she was deliberately playing him at his own game.

'You want *me* to do it? Be your "date" for the day? Are you sure?'

'Positive.'

'OK,' said Camilla, amazing herself even as she said it. She had meant to refuse outright. 'I will. But I'd already made arrangements to spend the day with someone else. Would it be OK with you if they came along too?'

Matt stared at her astounded.

'Oh, sure,' he managed to say eventually. If Camilla was bringing her goddam boyfriend he'd shoot himself quietly afterwards. 'Whatever you like, Mrs Stewart. No problem.'

Chapter 30

It wasn't the British Open, but it was just as popular with the crowds, who loved the easy, carnival atmosphere of Pro-Am tournaments and who had flocked in their thousands to see their favourite actors, singers and comedians playing to the gallery, competing with the professionals and thoroughly enjoying themselves.

Caroline, sprawled across the bed in Janet Reger charcoal grey silk knickers and nothing else, watched the TV coverage of the tournament and admired the neatness of it all. The stars of stage and screen were enhancing their image, the pro golfers got free publicity, the crowds had a great day out and the benefiting charities made oodles of money from the event. Everybody won, nobody lost. If only life were that easy, she thought, reaching for the remote control and turning up the sound. There was her mother's favourite singer, partnering Greg Norman and exchanging banter with those watching him. Ballesteros, on an adjoining green, was arguing comically with his caddy while two of the British Ryder Cup team built sandcastles in the bunker. There, wearing a false nose and shocking pink plus-fours, was the New York comedian whose name Caroline could never remember, playing against his fellow American, Matt Lewis. When she had been over in the States she had been persuaded by a golf-mad girlfriend to go along to the US Open Championship. Together they had followed Lewis's progress through an entire round because Donna was convinced that he had winked at her before teeing off at the start. Tall, broad and deeply tanned, he was a big man, yet effortlessly graceful. Caroline watched idly as the TV camera panned in for a close-up. He had his arm casually around the waist of a blond woman of about thirty, attractive but not as flashy as most of the players' girlfriends. The woman smiled as he inclined his dark head and whispered something into her ear, then applauded enthusiastically as the comedian putted into the hole for a birdie. Matt covered first his own eyes, then hers, in mock despair. The crowd, easily amused, fell about laughing at the expression on his face, then applauded once more as a small, dark-haired boy ran over to the hole, retrieved the ball and solemnly presented it to Matt.

The scene switched to the fourteenth green and Caroline, losing interest, turned off the TV and lay on her stomach with her chin resting on the cupped palms of her hands.

Staring at the blank screen, she realized that witnessing people being happy together had a tendency now to make her feel faintly nauseous. It was a new symptom which, coupled with the cold, inner well of loneliness and the sensation that she was somehow enclosed within a clear, plastic bubble, sound-proofed and separated from events going on around her, only seemed to confirm what she already knew.

Her spontaneous marriage was failing as rapidly as it had come about. What had seemed like a smart move at the time – practically a fairy-tale come true – was in fact not smart at all.

She really had made a truly horrible mistake.

And it wasn't only sad, it was ridiculous, she reflected with impatience. Who, after all, would believe that she could possibly be unhappy, being married to a stunningly good-looking, sexually perfect man who as an added bonus was not only a rock star but a rock star with more money than she could ever seriously imagine?

She had even received *hate*-mail, for Christ's sake, from teenage girls distraught by the news that their beloved Nico had taken a wife. How had she dared to *do* it to them? ... She didn't *deserve* someone like him ... they'd never forgive her for doing this to them ...

Caroline closed her eyes, willing the loneliness to go away. She *should* be happy to be one of the most envied females in Britain, but they simply didn't know what it was really like to be married to someone who was kind, generous, funny, not to mention great in bed ... and to feel that they, too, were sealed inside a plastic bubble just as silent and impenetrable as her own.

At first it had all been so thrilling. Maintaining the pretence that she had no idea who he really was had been a doddle. Listening to Nico's reluctant explanations – as if he'd been half afraid that they might put her off! – she had feigned astonishment, disbelief and finally serious acceptance of the situation. She had assured him that it wouldn't alter her feelings towards him, that she loved him for himself rather than for who he was in the eyes of the public, and that she was *glad* she hadn't known about it beforehand because then he might have worried needlessly that her motives were less than genuine.

Nico had been profoundly relieved and she had congratulated herself on her performance. As long as she remembered not to sing along with his old songs when they were played on the radio – and she knew most of them off by heart – she would be safe.

And so far she had managed to pull it off. She had also managed to become accustomed to the fact that almost anything she wanted, Nico could give her. Provided, of course, that those things were purely material ones.

She knew she had behaved badly, deceiving Nico from the word go, but she had seen her chance and grasped it. And it hadn't meant that she didn't love him, either. Because she did, with all her heart.

Which was why the situation she now found herself in was so tragic and so very bizarre.

Twisting the massive, square-cut diamond ring he had bought her from Cartier on their return to London, Caroline opened her eyes and gazed at it, trying hard to find pleasure in the glittering whiteness of the exquisite stone. Instead, hot tears threatened to spill on to her cheeks at the desperate tragedy of it all, because Nico was only able to give her *almost* everything. He tried, but nothing, nothing in the world could make up for the fact that every once in a while she would glance up and catch him looking at her as if she were a total stranger. And at other times, she recalled, he looked as though he knew only too well who she was, and was appalled with himself for having so impetuously made her his wife.

How could she possibly be expected to make it a happy marriage when Nico was so obviously unhappy with *her*?

By tilting her head sideways she was able to see the time by the narrow, diamond-studded Rolex he had bought her last week. Ten past five. If she strung it out with a long bath it was about time to start getting ready for the charity dinner they were supposed to be attending together at eight. Nico's manager, making the best of what he clearly thought was a very bad job indeed, had decided to milk the marriage for all it was worth and the gossip columns had been filled for almost three months now with photographs of Nico and herself attending galas, concerts and every party imaginable. It wasn't that much fun – Nico always looked to her as if he would rather be lying on a bed of red-hot nails – but Monty Barton insisted that they be *seen* and Caroline felt she might as well go along with it because anything was better than being alone at home, or alone with a husband who tried too hard but clearly didn't want to be there.

Camilla and Matt were in bed. 'I don't believe I'm doing this,' exclaimed Matt, one strong brown arm flung across his face. 'If the news ever got out I'd be ruined – do you hear me? My reputation would be in shreds.'

'I won't tell if you don't,' Camilla assured him, smiling into her pillow. 'And stop *talking*; we're supposed to be getting a well-earnt rest before tonight. I'm tired even if you aren't.'

'Matt Lewis, sharing a room with a delectable female and sleeping eight feet away from her. Who the hell invented twin-bedded hotel rooms anyway?'

'Hotels. They're more expensive than doubles. Go to sleep.'

'It just isn't natural,' he complained, admiring the back of her neck from a distance. 'Couldn't I come into your bed and give you the best massage of your life? Hell, I wouldn't take advantage of you if that's what you're worried about.'

'I'm asleep,' said Camilla, enjoying herself because she knew he didn't mean it. Matt let out a tragic sigh. 'This is like some goddam Rock Hudson and Doris Day film. Don't you have *any* respect for male hormones?'

'Far too much respect to allow them into my bed. *Sleep*, Mr Lewis. We have a long evening ahead of us. You may be used to walking around a golf course all day, but I certainly am not.'

'You're a terrible woman, Mrs Stewart. A cruel and terrible woman.'

'I am, I am.' Camilla pulled the bedclothes over her head. Beside her Marty slept, his angelic cheeks pink, his dark hair brushed back from his forehead, and his closed fist resting against Camilla's left shoulder.

'Oh Marty, Marty,' murmured Matt, watching them together. 'You just don't know how lucky you are.'

Roz still couldn't quite believe what a mess she had become, yet at the same time she was unable to do a single thing about it. Here she was now, at six in the evening and still in the dressing-gown she had put on when she first got out of bed. Since she had had neither the time nor the energy to wash her hair it stood up in ugly dark spikes all over the head, and since there were no beauty salons in Littleton Grey her unwaxed legs displayed a regrowth of fine dark hairs. She didn't dare take a razor into the bath with her these days; it would be too tempting.

'Shut *up*,' she muttered, lighting a cigarette and pouring black coffee with a shaking hand as Nicolette's wailing increased in volume and intensity. Surely no baby in the history of the world had ever cried as much and as loudly as this one and she seemed to specialize in timing her onslaughts to coincide with the exact moment when Roz herself had only finally managed to snatch a few minutes of fitful sleep.

It wasn't surprising that she had gone through three nannies in as many months, although Roz had decided that they were all incompetent fools anyway. She couldn't be expected to know how to keep a baby quiet, she was new to all this, after all – but that was what nannies were paid for, and none of them had been able to do a damn bit of good either. The first had stayed for three weeks until Roz had screamed at her to do something about the bloody noise. The second had handed in her notice

253

after only a fortnight, announcing that she was too used to Knightsbridge to be able to adapt to life in the country. A feeble excuse, Roz had told her coldly, for the fact was that she quite clearly didn't have a clue about caring properly for young babies.

Maria, the third, had lasted the longest – almost five weeks – and Roz had almost become friendly with her. Until one night when they had drunk half a bottle of brandy together and Maria had informed her that she was a complete mess.

'You might not think it my place to say so, but you drink too much, you show no affection towards Nicolette, and you've let yourself go. Why don't you visit your doctor?'

Roz had eyed the girl with suspicion, outraged at her words. Maria returned the look with a conciliatory smile.

'You're quite right,' said Roz slowly, placing her brandy glass on the coffee table and rising to her feet. 'It is *not* your place to say so. You're fired.'

It was good in a way that all three had left quickly, but the drawback was that it left her holding the baby – the eternally screaming baby – all alone. And Roz's adverts in the slender weekly magazine which specialized in placing nannies with employers were fast becoming an off-puttingly frequent sight.

'I need help,' she said aloud, standing in the messy kitchen with both hands clasped around her coffee mug. 'I need someone to help me. Now.'

It was chilling to realize that she had no-one to ask. Loulou was probably her only friend, and she was now so engrossed in her own pregnancy that she wasn't able to give Roz the help and support she badly needed. It was almost unimaginable; Loulou, the woman least likely to succeed in pregnancy, was adoring every single moment of it. She had been transformed, and Roz felt too ashamed of herself to admit to Loulou how hard, how exhausting and how very unlovely having a baby really was.

How about her mother, then? Marguerite had paid a fleeting visit, making very short work indeed of Roz's last bottle of vodka and announcing airily, 'You aren't exactly flavour of the month at the moment, are you, darling? But don't worry about it. Everyone will forget soon enough.'

She had then mentioned in passing, whilst patting Nicolette's chubby knees, that she was going to Antibes for a couple of months with her latest flame, a balding French financier. 'I'll let you know where we'll be staying. Send me some photos of this gorgeous baby, darling. Let me know how she is. Good heavens,' looking at her watch, she swiftly transferred Nicolette back to Roz and rose to her feet, 'is that the time? I must dash. Keep in touch, sweetheart. Lovely to see you and don't worry – I'll see myself out.'

So much for her mother, now safely installed in a Med-side villa with her latest man. Roz dismissed her with a weary shrug, and stubbed out her cigarette as Nicolette's wailing increased. At least she had an appointment with the paediatrician tomorrow; hopefully he would show at least some interest in her catalogue of complaints. Maybe he could recommend something to keep Nicolette quiet – a sleeping pill, a strip of Elastoplast or a slug of Remy Martin . . .

And that was only if she had the energy to keep the appointment. Since losing her licence for drink-driving on the day of the crash, travelling – even without the hassle of a baby – had become more of a problem than she had ever imagined possible.

It had come as a grim shock to her, discovering that now she was unemployed she could no longer afford to order taxis without thinking. Littleton Grey was miles from anywhere, and since Roz refused absolutely to catch the only bus of the day, crammed with noisy teenagers and nosy housewives, she had to plan her excursions from the village with care. Tomorrow, as well as taking Nicolette to the hospital, she would have to fit in a visit to the supermarket and stock up with enough food and drink for the next fortnight.

Struggling on alone was so much harder than she had ever imagined, she no longer knew how she was going to manage. Her only friend wasn't available, her mother was a positive liability, Sebastian was too busy at present to escape from Zurich for even a couple of days . . . and finally, just to prove that bad things came in fours, there was Nico.

Cruel Nico.

After having pinned all her hopes upon him, his attitude had crushed her totally. So much, thought Roz with tired bitterness, for assuming that his so-Italian, so family-orientated heart would melt at the news of Nicolette's birth. He had refused even to see her.

And after she had taken the decision to call the child Nicolette, too. The Press had loved it, confirming as it did their endless speculations, renewing interest in the story of the fallen-from-grace TV personality and the singing star who had rejected her and so suddenly married someone else. Nico was a heartless shit.

And to Roz's fury, she couldn't get over him. The more he ignored her, the greater her longing for him grew. It was so ridiculous, and so very ironic, that it was almost laughable. Here she was, the Ice Queen herself, the very person whom Nico had once begged to marry him – caught in the oldest and saddest trap of all.

* * *

When Caroline nudged open the door she saw that Nico was only half ready. Dress shirt unbuttoned, bow-tie dangling untied around his neck, he lay across the scarlet and grey striped sofa, a cigarette burning in the ashtray beside him, his blond head bent in concentration over a copy of last week's *Sunday Times*.

God, he was beautiful, she thought with a pang of longing. But so very remote that sometimes she felt as if she was unable to even touch him. If she reached out, her hand would pass, ghostlike, right through him.

Whereas in actual fact, she realized sadly, the body was there. It was the spirit that was missing.

'Hi, darling,' she said, as if she had just entered the room. If she didn't always feel so stilted in his presence these days, she would have burst into the room, struck a pose and sung: 'TaaRaaa!'

And then, of course, if she had, Nico would have given her that particular look, the one which made it seem as if for a fraction of a second he didn't recognize her, and Caroline would have felt foolish and embarrassed.

Nico looked up, and his smile suddenly seemed so warm and loving that she couldn't help it. Like a junkie needed her fix, she needed some sign of affection. Crossing the room, Caroline paused when she reached him, then bent down and tenderly kissed his mouth. As she prolonged the kiss, she allowed her stocking-clad legs to rub sensuously against his thigh, while her left hand gently played with the sensitive skin at the back of his neck.

Slowly, slowly she sank down on to his lap, experiencing the thrill of achievement-against-the-odds when she felt how aroused he was.

'So what if we're late for the party,' she murmured, reaching to unzip his trousers and moving her hips against him. 'Oh darling, everything's going to be all right, isn't it?'

'Mmm,' said Nico, breathing in the amber scent of her perfume and touching with sensitive fingers the soft tumbling waves of her tortoiseshell-shaded hair. He couldn't bring himself to say yes – that would be too blatant a lie – but neither could he say no. 'Mm,' he sighed again as she unzipped his fly with practised fingers. 'Let's go up to the bedroom.'

Smiling, triumphant, Caroline shook her head, so that her hair brushed across his cheek.

'No, no, my darling. We may be married, but we don't *have* to do it in bed – it isn't compulsory. Just let me move across a little . . . there . . . now slide down over here . . . what's wrong with a little lovemaking on a rug in front of the fire?'

'We're late,' said Nico abruptly, moving away with such suddenness that Caroline almost rolled over on to her back. Before she could even understand what was happening Nico was standing before her, buttoning his shirt and zipping up his trousers. The grim expression on his face was almost scary.

She can't help it, he thought, suppressing the anger inside him. It isn't her fault, she doesn't *know*. Christ, how was it possible that the memory of that one night with Camilla could still be so fresh . . . and still hurt so much?

Burning tears in her eyes, humiliation and resentment vibrating through her body, Caroline stared up at him.

'What the bloody hell's the *matter* with you?' she shouted furiously, then sagged as the tears began to fall. 'What's the matter with me, then? Don't I attract you? Aren't I pretty enough for you, Nico?'

He looked away, embarrassed by her grief and by his own disinterest.

'I'm sorry. It's me, not you. Come on,' he reached out, took her hand and helped her to her feet. Awkwardly, he dropped a kiss on her forehead. 'Let's get ready. We really shouldn't be late for this thing, should we?'

'I don't know what I've done wrong,' said Caroline in a low voice, wondering if she was prolonging the discord so that she needn't go to the charity gala. Her eye make-up *felt* smudged, and she didn't know if she had the motivation to repair it.

He sighed. 'You've done nothing wrong.'

'Then it must be that I'm just not attractive enough,' she pleaded helplessly.

'Don't be silly,' said Nico, turning to leave the room. 'You look fine.'

Chapter 31

'Well?' demanded Matt, 'do I look irresistible or what?'

'Oh, very,' Camilla reassured him, and Matt turned his attention to Marty, bouncing on her lap.

'Am I pretty?' he glowered at the boy, who burst into fits of giggles and covered his mouth with his fists.

'You're pitty.'

Matt struck a macho pose. 'Stunning?'

'Stung,' Marty managed to say, squealing with laughter.

'Handsome beyond belief?'

'Hands!' Marty waved his fists, recognizing the word, and slid off Camilla's lap. 'Kiss, Matt,' he yelled, running to him, and Matt lifted him easily into the air, covering the top of his dark head with noisy kisses, while at the same time his eyes locked with Camilla's.

'Kismet,' he said, smiling. 'That's exactly what I thought, Marty. Although she had me worried for a moment when she said she had a date with someone else today. Boy, was I relieved when I found out it was with you.'

'Mind he doesn't dribble on your jacket,' said Camilla, hoping she wasn't as pink-cheeked as she thought she was, and pretending she hadn't understood what he was saying. 'Marty tends to drool when he gets excited.'

'He's not the only one. Listen, I'm ready and you're not. Why don't I drive Marty back to the hospital, so that you can have the place to yourself and you don't have to hurry? If we leave now, I'll be back in an hour and a half and we'll be in plenty of time for the gala. Great idea?'

Camilla, to her horror, felt a lump form in her throat. Matt's easy charm, his thoughtfulness, his effortless good humour were almost too much for her to handle and she thought for a minute that she might burst into tears of relief. There *were* still some genuinely nice men around.

How many, after all, would invite a woman out for the first time and not be put out when she turned up with a thoroughly excitable little boy in tow, furthermore a little boy who demanded kisses constantly, slobbered freely and emptied a box of fifty golf balls over the dining-room floor during lunch?

Even now, as she watched the two of them, Matt didn't appear in the least concerned that Marty's chocolatey fingers were clutching at the immaculate sleeve of his black dinner-jacket. Marty – to her, at least – was adorable, but he was also as exhausting as the London marathon.

But if Matt really didn't mind, it would be blissful to sink into a hot bath and take her time getting ready for the charity gala later on this evening. She gave him a grateful smile.

'If you're sure it wouldn't be too much trouble . . .'

'No problem. Give me the address of the hospital and between Marty and me and your wonderful British policemen we'll find it in no time. I'll be back by eight o'clock at the latest, OK?'

'Wonderful,' said Camilla, holding her arms out to Marty. 'Come and say goodbye, darling. Give me a big kiss and a hug before you go.'

'Mrs Stewart!' exclaimed Matt, his dark eyebrows shooting up, his tone deeply shocked. 'You brazen woman! I hardly even know you.'

* * *

It had been such a *happy* day, Camilla reminisced as she tilted her head in order to gauge the line of her eye pencil, gentian violet merging with the shimmering Prussian blue which shaded the sockets of her eyes and made them seem dramatically larger.

It had been quite a time since she had enjoyed herself this much. Marty had adored every moment too, understanding that the big outside-broadcast cameras could 'take his picture', and screaming and waving ecstatically every time he spotted one. The general good humour of the crowd had helped, of course, but Marty had won them over completely, endearing himself to the camera crew, the caddies and the other players. What a normal child was sometimes not quite able to get away with, a grinning, riotously happy little handicapped one still could. Camilla, aware that everyone assumed she was Marty's mother, had scarcely been able to contain her pride and laughter when Matt had introduced him into the conversation while he was being interviewed on live TV. Marty had promptly delivered an untidy kiss to the TV commentator's cheek in full view of the cameras. Not many people had called this particular commentator 'pitty' in front of eight million viewers.

Matt was unlike anyone she had ever met before in her life. Only with Nico had she been able to relax to the same degree, some inner confidence persuading her that her own personality was good enough, and not something to be slightly ashamed of, which was how she had always felt with Jack.

But Matt was more forceful than Nico; an extrovert man who was supremely confident with himself and who quite clearly felt that hiding his own motives or feelings was an appalling waste of time. He wanted her, there was no question of it, yet Camilla still remembered her past life too vividly not to have moments of doubt. Sometimes she forgot how she had changed and imagined herself as the colourless creature who had been cowed by virtually everyone. She needed to see herself in a mirror to remind herself that those days were past, that she was good enough to merit such attentions.

But what *would* happen if Matt continued his bombardment of her emotions? Should she go to bed with him or not?

Fresh, too, in her mind was the memory of that single fateful night with Nico, when she had planned every move and realized only later – too late – how catastrophic her mistake had been.

So, don't go to bed with Matt, she silently informed her reflection in the gold-tinted mirror. Sex hadn't exactly done her past relationships many favours; maybe she should learn from those mistakes. Keep Matt at a safe distance. If he was really keen, he wouldn't give up . . .

Pulling a face at her reflection as she untwisted a creamy-pink Chanel lipstick, Camilla realized that she sounded like every teen-magazine agony aunt she had ever read during those long and painful years of adolescence. The advice might be good, and it was all very well, but what nobody was able to take into consideration was the fact that the man she was supposed to be keeping at arm's length was the redoubtable, irrepressible and quite irresistible Matt Lewis.

It was a glittering evening. Camilla, entering the vast mirrored foyer of the hotel on Matt's arm, was enormously glad that she had taken the trouble to put her hair up; relieved too that she had borrowed Loulou's pre-pregnancy best dress – a slippery silk Benny Ong in midnight blue. The colour brought out the brighter turquoise of her eyes and accentuated the creamy softness of her skin, and when she glimpsed the reflection of Matt and herself in the mirrors surrounding them, amidst the noisy, expectant crowds of beautifully dressed guests, she realized with relief that she looked as if she belonged. Tonight, she was letting no-one down. And she was going to enjoy every single, special moment of it.

Dinner passed by in a flash. Memories of her marriage, during which she had endured so many official functions without enjoyment, came back to her and she recalled them as if they were misty, distant dreams. It had seemed then that she had always chosen exactly the wrong thing to wear, had been forced to smile bravely at Jack's barbed comments when he pointed out that fact in front of everyone, and had always been seated next to someone dazzlingly witty, so much so that she was instantly rendered both speechless and invisible. Not worth talking to, or even noticing.

'It's probably because you're a housewife,' Jack had informed her without intentional cruelty when he had discovered her sobbing in the bathroom at home after one particularly terrifying dinner party. 'You can't expect the managing director of Calcom to be interested in your latest *recipe*, sweetie, now can you?'

Camilla had stared at him, wondering if he truly thought of her as some kind of mental defective, whose thoughts were so limited that they didn't even bear listening to. And the circle had been an increasingly vicious one; the more she dreaded the necessary dinner parties, the more paralysed with shyness she had become. Jack was right, she came to realize. She was utterly incapable of attracting or holding the interest of anyone for longer than it took to say her name. Sometimes even that was pushing it.

But the charity gala here at the Glenroy Hotel was a lifetime away. No longer a pale shadow, Camilla was entranced to realize that now she was meeting people and talking to them quite effortlessly. They approached Matt and herself, introduced themselves and *stayed*. Many asked about Marty whom everyone had seen that afternoon, either uttering his immortal line on TV or out on the golf course. Others admired Camilla's dress, were charmed by her unpretentious air and her shy, dazzling smile, and bombarded her with questions about the modelling agency. She, in turn, quite forgot to be overwhelmed by the people she was introduced to, many of whom were either sporting celebrities or TV personalities, and enjoyed herself thoroughly throughout the exquisite six-course meal, which to her shame she barely even tasted.

She was engrossed in conversation with the wife of an Australian golfer when Matt tapped her bare shoulder.

'Sorry to break up the chat, Louise,' he said, winking at the dark-haired girl, 'but I paid a lot of dollars to hire out this woman for the day and I'm beginning to feel neglected. If she doesn't dance with me within the next thirty seconds I'm asking for a refund.'

Louise burst out laughing. Camilla shrugged. 'He isn't joking. I do have to dance with him.'

'He's really paying you?' exclaimed the girl, her Australian accent becoming more pronounced as her eyebrows rose in astonishment. 'Hey, Camilla, does that mean you're some kind of hooker?'

Camilla grinned at her bluntness. Rising to her feet, she winked and replied, 'Don't worry, he doesn't pay me *that* much.' And taking Matt's hand in her own, she said with mock resignation, 'Come on then, Mr Lewis. Let's dance.'

* * *

'Are you OK?' said Nico, his green eyes mirroring his concern. Caroline squeezed his arm and nodded, her own, slightly swollen eyes the only tell-tale sign of her recent tears. No-one else would guess that she had been crying; he just hoped she wouldn't do it again, at such a conspicuous event. Tomorrow she had an interview lined up with a weekly magazine, ironically entitled 'The time of my life'.

As they made their way across the hotel car-park, he said again, 'Sure you don't want to change your mind?' Earlier, she had told him, amidst the tears, that she didn't want to come tonight. He would have liked to have opted out himself, but the gala, following on from the golf tournament during the day, was in aid of the charity he publicly supported and he had promised the organizers that he would attend. However, Caroline had decided that she would go with him after all, and now they were here. Two hours late – her face had needed time to settle – and they had undoubtedly missed the dinner, but at least he hadn't let them down.

'I'm all right,' she assured him, her voice low but controlled as she attempted a smile, and Nico felt a spasm of guilt. He wasn't used to making people unhappy, but despite all his efforts to the contrary he was making a superb job of it with his own wife.

'It'll be fun,' he said, forcing a note of cheerfulness into his voice. 'We'll have a great time, you'll see.'

There must have been 600 people in the ballroom, some still sitting and savouring their liqueurs, some madly table-hopping and others dancing. It never failed to amaze Nico that such splendid, such very *expensive* events always managed to make so much money for charity. Then he recalled the last one to which he had been invited, and the fact that he had found himself, after many extraordinarily potent Brandy Alexanders, bidding £3,000 at the auction for a small Rupert Bear sketch executed by Paul McCartney. It had remained unframed and pinned to one of the oak cabinets in the kitchen for six weeks before disappearing. When Nico had mentioned it to the efficient Hazel Hampton and learnt that she had thrown it away, he diplomatically forbore to explain to her who Paul McCartney was and put the loss down to experience and his own laziness. Next time he spent £3,000 on a sketch, he would take the trouble to have it properly framed.

And it had been for charity, after all.

Nico Coletto hadn't survived almost ten years in the music business without learning to cope with the unexpected. Whether dodging the sudden onslaught of fans, reacting smoothly to the unpredictable caprices of manic record producers, or side-stepping the most provocative journalists' questions without skipping so much as a quarter-beat, he had a quicksilver mind and unbeatable reaction times. Outwardly, nothing appeared to faze him; he could cope with any situation without turning a hair.

Which was how, when he spotted Camilla on the dance floor, he managed not to turn pale, exclaim aloud, or falter in the slightest as he and Caroline made their way towards the top table where the charity organizers were waiting to greet him.

Inwardly, he felt as though he had been hit in the chest with an iron fist. No longer was it easy to breathe. His heartbeat appeared to have slowed to a heavy, funereal pace. The vague aura of unhappiness which had clung to him for months, surreal, grey and unformed, abruptly solidified in his gut. Camilla was here, and her presence was so unexpected that he couldn't even

267

begin to evaluate his shocked emotions. But it wasn't going to be easy, and it had to have happened tonight of all nights . . .

The next hour passed with interminable slowness as, switching on to automatic pilot, he was introduced to the event organizers, to other celebrities, and to the hotel management team who were there in force. Apologizing for his lateness and promising to do his best to help make the gala a success, Nico charmed everyone he met and was distantly aware that Caroline, too, was doing her utmost to appear normal.

But while he shook hands, kissed cheeks, posed for photographs and agreed to draw the tickets for the raffle, his mind worked ceaselessly in other directions. In Camilla's direction. He had taken care not to glance across at the dance floor, nor even towards any of the tables where she might be sitting, but had she seen him, or heard that he was there, or known in advance that he *would* be there tonight? If she didn't know already, then she would find out shortly. He was a so-called celebrated guest and they simply weren't allowed to hide in quiet corners.

And what, he wondered, would Camilla do? Maintain a discreet distance throughout the evening? Simply say hello? Or would she come up and speak to him as if nothing had ever happened between the two of them?

But then, Nico realized as a slow blade turned in his stomach, nothing particularly earth-shattering *had* happened as far as she was concerned. She had simply slept with her employer, found the experience disappointing to say the least, and – to save any further embarrassment – quietly and discreetly removed herself from his life. Seeing Camilla again for the first time since that night might be earth-shattering for him, but for her it would probably do no more than stir a faint, maybe slightly embarrassing memory. And he had had enough one-night stands in the past himself to know how totally unimportant they could be.

Caroline tugged his sleeve. 'Shall we dance, darling?' Her eyes conveyed the signal that they had spent enough time talking to their hosts.

Nico smiled and shrugged. 'My wife's trying to make me young again. Would you excuse us?'

'Rubber-necking, Mrs Stewart?' Matt admonished her as Camilla glanced over her shoulder in mid-waltz and her step faltered. 'I thought I was the brash American sightseer around here. You're the ice-cool Englishwoman, remember.'

'Sorry,' said Camilla, her apology automatic, her mind suddenly reeling with memories. She wasn't sure, she wasn't at all sure . . . but she thought she might just have spotted Nico.

'Could we sit down?' said Caroline, a faint note of complaint in her voice. Nico glanced at her, puzzled.

'I thought you said you wanted to dance.'

'That was forty minutes ago. I didn't mean all night, non-stop for heaven's sake. My feet are aching and I need a drink.'

'Sorry.' With reluctance he led her off the dance floor, where he had felt – for want of a better word – safe. As Caroline tugged at his sleeve once more he realized that it was a habit of hers which could easily become irritating.

'I don't want to sit at the top table again. Those bloody people bore me to tears. Why don't you go and get us another bottle of champagne and I'll find a seat at this end?'

Nico nodded, anxious to keep the peace and appalled at the relief he felt when Caroline released her hold on his sleeve. 'I'll

269

be back in two minutes,' he said guiltily. And in his mind added: make that ten.

Caroline felt better on her own. She *functioned* better as a solo act, as on the day when she had met Nico in Las Vegas. For some reason, becoming his wife had made her feel useless, nothing more than a not particularly important appendage. Everywhere they went people were more interested in Nico than they were in her. Oh, she had a certain amount of curiosity value, but that was all. He was the important one, the half of the partnership who *mattered*, and she was the pale shadow at his side.

And the fact that she herself was intimidated by Nico hardly helped, she knew that. She was intimidated by his lack of love for her, had failed him by being incapable of forcing that emotion out of him. It just made the situation more rickety, more sorry and uneven than ever.

Which was why she was only ever able to function normally, as her old self had done, when she was alone.

Cheering up considerably at the sight of Matt Lewis, sitting with his attractive girlfriend at a nearby table, Caroline headed towards them. They were the only two seated at a table for ten, which gave her the perfect excuse to join them. Matt Lewis, this would be something to tell Donna next time she wrote.

'Phew! Hi, is it OK if I sit here?' she announced, collapsing on to a chair and pretending exhaustion. The golfer picked up a bottle of white wine, filled a glass and solemnly held it towards her.

'You look as if you need it.'

Caroline rewarded him with a smile of bewitching intensity, and was interested to observe that the girlfriend wasn't reacting to it with the usual instant suspicion. Clearly not a run-of-the-mill jealous blond bimbo, thought Caroline, and stuck out her hand in appreciation.

'How do you do. My name's Caroline.'

'And I'm Camilla.' They smiled at each other, Caroline instinctively liking the woman who wasn't jealous of her, Camilla admiring the girl's good bone structure and wondering if they had ever met before. Somewhere in the dim distance, a very faint chord of memory was struck.

'I know who you are, of course,' said Caroline, turning to Matt. 'I was at the US Open last year. My friend Donna dragged me round the course, convinced that you'd winked at her while you were teeing up on the first.'

'That's entirely possible,' said Matt, his dark eyes crinkling with laughter, the wonderfully sexy bags beneath them becoming more pronounced as he took Camilla's hand and kissed it. 'But of course that was in the wicked old days before I met my wife.'

Camilla, with a look of horror, snatched her hand away. 'Take no notice of him, Caroline. I only met him yesterday.'

Matt looked unperturbed. 'I can live in hope.'

'You seem very happy together anyway,' said Caroline, finishing her drink and after a moment's hesitation allowing Matt to refill her glass. 'Thanks. My husband will be back in a minute with some champagne. We can share that when he gets here.'

'What's your husband's name?' asked Camilla, her memory beginning to clear. The girl's face . . . she *had* seen photographs . . . she'd also been right earlier when she thought she'd spotted him amongst the crowds.

'Nico,' said Caroline, thinking as she did so that this was the moment when her own personality began to fade, like an old sepia photograph left too long in the sun. 'Nico Coletto. He's a singer.'

'Oh,' said Camilla, and in the brief silence that followed realized that she had already left it too long to say, 'I know him'. Instead she added lamely, 'How nice.'

Caroline, staring at her glass and finding it yet again empty, twirled the stem between her thumb and forefinger and said with forced brightness, 'That's really rather a matter of opinion.' Then, seeing the expression of shocked surprise on Camilla's face, and realizing that it was neither the time nor the place for True Confessions, shook her head and laughed. At least neither of them had bombarded her with questions about Nico, as everyone else always seemed to do. They had reacted, in fact, as if they'd never even heard of him. She was still a whole person and she would damn well make the most of it while it lasted.

'I saw your little boy on TV this afternoon,' she said cheerfully. 'What a darling! How old is he?'

'Hello,' said Nico, placing two bottles of Lanson with great care upon the table and wondering how the hell he was supposed to react, faced with this set-up. Caroline had been deep in discussion with Camilla and what they were talking about was anybody's guess. Still, the chances were that they hadn't been comparing his prowess in bed and marking him out of ten, so to hell with it, he decided. Inadvertently, Caroline had precipitated his meeting with Camilla. It was clearly better to get it over with.

'Camilla, how nice to see you again,' he said, and watched in amazement as she turned first pink, then deeper pink, and finally an unmistakable shade of red. His spirits lifted; did this mean she still felt something for him after all?

'How extraordinary,' remarked Caroline, watching the transformation with fascination and not a little intrigue. 'Camilla, I didn't realize that you *knew* my husband. Why on earth didn't you say so before?'

Oh, dammit to hell, thought Nico. Bloody, bloody *hell*.

Ironically, Caroline became more animated and more talkative than she had been for weeks, as if the intrigue she sensed had overcome her habitual reticence. When she pulled Nico back on to the dance floor after twenty minutes of incredibly difficult small talk – thank heavens for Matt Lewis's easygoing, ebullient manner – her eyes were bright and her hips swayed provocatively against his in time with the music. She had also, in that short space of time, finished an entire bottle of champagne by herself.

'So.'

'So what?' he countered shortly, wondering why her pouting mouth no longer entranced him.

'So, are we really expected to believe that the lovely Camilla was your . . . housekeeper?'

'Of course she was. What's so bloody extraordinary about that?'

Caroline licked her lips. 'And were you lovers, too?'

'No!' Christ, even now while they were dancing she was managing to tug at the sleeve of his dinner-jacket like a bloody leech.

His discomfort was almost palpable; Caroline was enjoying herself enormously. For the first time in their short, unhappy marriage she had him at a disadvantage. Jealousy mingled with curiosity because it wasn't as if Nico shouldn't have had an affair with another woman – by his own admission he had slept with dozens in the past – so why was he so vehemently denying this one? Why had Camilla pretended that she didn't even know him? Interesting.

And upon returning to the table she observed that Camilla and Nico were still as jumpy as a couple of cats on a red-hot roof, the conversation flowing like concrete, the expressions of their faces equally stone-like. Very interesting *indeed*.

'My friend Donna would just *die* if I could tell her that I'd danced with you,' Caroline announced boldly, giving Matt another of her dazzling smiles. She switched to Camilla. 'You wouldn't mind, would you, if we had just one quick dance together?'

Camilla, stripping a crimson rosebud from the table decoration of its leaves, said, 'Of course not.'

'And you and Nico must dance together,' insisted Caroline, her eyes flicking from one to the other, laser-like, missing nothing. 'Come along, let's really enjoy ourselves . . .'

Which was how Nico and Camilla found themselves in the middle of the dance floor, dancing together to the slow, sensual music, but scarcely touching at all, joined by only the lightest possible contact.

Camilla still wore the same perfume, Nico realized. She smelt wonderful, and was looking spectacular. Christ, he thought, for a one-night stand he could still recall every moment of it in amazing detail. But that was probably because for him it *had* been amazing. Camilla was the one who had been disappointed, not him.

We have to talk, she thought wildly. I have to say something to stop all this desperate awkwardness. Nico's green eyes were unreadable, his expression quite blank. Only the terrible silence indicated that something was not right between them.

'I'm . . . sorry about what happened,' she blurted out, unconsciously moving closer to him so that she couldn't see his face, his reaction.

'It doesn't matter,' said Nico quickly, forestalling her. The last thing he needed right now was an explanation . . . details . . . her pity . . . 'That's all in the past. I'm married and you're here with Matt.'

'But I wanted to . . .'

'No!' he told her urgently, his fingers tightening against the warmth of her bare shoulder. '*I'm* sorry too, so let's just forget it. We're just friends, OK?'

'Are we? Can we still be friends, really?'

Not getting what he wanted didn't come easily to Nico, he simply wasn't used to it. But he couldn't have Camilla and it would surely be easier to get used to it if they were at least on speaking terms. His life for the past three months had been pretty bleak, after all. Right now he needed all the friends he could get.

Taking a step backwards so that he could see her clearly, and reading the guilt and self-recrimination in the eyes which slowly met his, he gave her a firm, reassuring smile.

'Nothing can stop us being friends, Camilla. Now, for heaven's sake, cheer up and let's make the most of the rest of this bloody awful evening. Tell me what you've been doing lately. Tell me one of your terrible jokes. Tell me,' he said, a strange hollow churning sensation gripping his stomach, 'all about you and Matt Lewis.'

Chapter 32

The telephone call two days later came like a bolt from the blue. Caroline was out, visiting the hairdressers, and Nico, having just got rid of Monty Barton, was celebrating his manager's departure with a large Remy Martin and a packet of digestive biscuits. Feet up, he was watching a rerun of the Addams Family on Channel 4 while at the same time flipping through a copy of *Cosmopolitan* left by Caroline on the floor.

'Five reasons why you shouldn't fake it!' screamed a headline in the magazine, and Nico winced, rapidly turning the page. 'Old lovers – why can't they be new friends?' enquired the header of the next article he arrived at, and he almost smiled. On screen, Gomez ran a trail of kisses up Morticia's arm and she answered him with a wickedly enticing smile. Nico downed his cognac and wondered if Morticia ever faked it with Gomez.

Before he could contemplate the answer, the phone rang.

'Nico, it's me.'

He knew who it was. 'Who?'

'Roz. Roz Vallender,' she added with exaggerated impatience. 'The mother of your child.'

'Sure about that?' he said, more nastily than he had intended but unable to stop himself. 'You know what they say, Roz. Don't believe everything you read in the papers.'

'She bloody well *is* your daughter!' shouted Roz, 'and you'd better listen to me. I can't cope – Nicolette's seriously ill and I can't manage on my own any more. I *need* you, Nico. You've got to help me.'

He jackknifed into a sitting position. 'What's happened? What's the matter with her?' It hardly mattered whether Nicolette was his; if she was that ill he could still respond to Roz's cry for help. Anyone would, after all.

'I've got to speak to you,' she said urgently. 'Can I come round now?'

'Well . . . I suppose so. Where are you?'

'Phonebox,' said Roz, concealing her triumph at having cleared the first hurdle. 'I'll be there in five minutes. Thank you, darling.'

As she made her way up the gravelled drive towards the front door, Roz recalled the occasion of her last visit, when she had found Camilla here. That very day, according to Loulou, Camilla had packed her bags and left, and had refused to explain why.

Today, of course, there was the chance that Nico's wife would be here but somehow she doubted it. She bloody well hoped not, anyway – this reunion definitely didn't need any outsiders standing by to witness it, and particularly not a new little wife who, as she understood it, Nico had only acquired in order to spite *her*.

She looked down at Nicolette in her arms. At least the doctor at the hospital had been sympathetic to Roz's complaints and had prescribed a sedative for the child, one which quietened her enough to stop the incessant screaming. Nicolette was fast asleep now, looking adorable in a tiny, exquisitely embroidered pale pink dress and well wrapped up in a heavily fringed pink and white shawl. Who could resist her, for heaven's sake, or not *want* to be the parent of such a beautiful baby?

As for Roz herself – well, she was looking pretty damn good as well. The appalling black cloud of depression which had settled over her within days of Nicolette's birth had dispersed as abruptly as it had arrived, exorcising itself with miraculous agility the moment Roz had broken down in a storm of tears in the consultant's office at the hospital after hearing the news about Nicolette.

'Believe me, Mrs Vallender, I do understand how you must feel,' he had said, passing her a box of white hospital tissues and patting her hand in an awkward gesture of reassurance.

But for Roz her tears, the first she had shed in many years – for weeping in her opinion was only for the very weak – performed the miracle she had given up even hoping for. As she wiped her eyes with the tissues and heaved great, shuddering sighs of exhaustion and relief, she could feel the dank, black clouds become weightless, lift away.

Still gulping and sobbing intermittently, she clutched the eminent doctor's strong hand and cried out, 'Oh God, I've been . . . so . . . *miserable* . . .'

It had gone. Now her energies were poured into the task of sorting out her life, and Nicolette's sad little life as well. There were plans to be planned, and Roz, though still deeply shocked by the news, found that at last she had the energy to carry these plans out.

And Number One, she thought briskly as she cradled Nicolette in one arm and rang the front doorbell with the other, was to sort things out with Nico, once and for all.

He opened the door himself, his green eyes dark and guarded but as spectacular as ever. Seeing him again for the first time in almost ten months, she experienced a jolt of emotion and sought to clarify it. But it was nothing so difficult or complicated as love, she realized with relief. It was merely honest to goodness lust. Nico was still one of the most attractive men she had ever met in her life, that indefinable aura of sexuality emanating right through his scarlet and green cashmere sweater and faded denims as clearly as cologne.

But what she felt for him was not love, so she could deal with it. At last she was in control again.

His gaze swept over Roz and remained as enigmatic as it always had when that was what was required, but she smiled to herself when she saw his eyes come to rest upon Nicolette, that fluffy pink and white bundle in her arms. He softened visibly, as she had known he would.

Meet your namesake, darling, she thought, optimism prickling her skin. Aloud, however, she said, 'It's nice to see you again, Nico. After all this time. May we come in?'

The house seemed different; lighter, less cluttered and more cared-for than Roz remembered, as if to prove that Nico was now a respectably married man and no longer a semi-wild, carefree, infinitely eligible bachelor. A year ago he had asked Roz to marry him and she had laughed, gently refusing because her life was so perfect that she didn't need that too. Now she did.

In the sitting-room she made herself comfortable on the settee, adjusting the pencil-slim black skirt from Galliano which had cost far more than she could now afford, and stretching out her Dior-stockinged legs in high black Gucci stilettos. It hadn't been so long, after all, that she couldn't remember what Nico liked.

As he stood before her, she held Nicolette up towards him.

'At least hold her,' she said in a low voice. 'She doesn't bite. See, no teeth.'

Without even hesitating, Nico took the sleeping baby into his arms, supporting her small downy head with natural expertise and touching her soft pink cheek with one finger.

'She's fast asleep. When you said she was ill I thought you meant she was in hospital. She doesn't look ill at all.'

He glanced at her with suspicion, comparing the serene Roz before him with the woman who had sounded so desperate over the phone.

'I wanted to make sure you'd see us,' she informed him calmly. 'She's your daughter, Nico, your own flesh and blood after all, and she *is* ill. I wasn't lying when I said I couldn't cope on my own.' Her dark eyes filled suddenly with tears and she touched the settee beside her with a trembling hand. 'Sit down.' Warily, maintaining a distance between them, he sat. Roz was wearing a heavy, musky perfume which he didn't particularly like. It was incredible, he thought distantly, how indifferent he was to her presence. And the baby was just . . . a baby. If she were his, then he simply couldn't feel it, not a thing. And if she wasn't his, he thought wryly, then it was hardly surprising.

'It's not like you to cry,' he said with a touch of cruelty. It was like talking to Caroline. He didn't have the patience to be nice any more. Being nice had caused him too much trouble in the past.

Roz said nothing and Nico felt a fresh surge of impatience. 'So why *are* you here?'

'Think how good we were together,' she burst out passionately, tears still glistening on her smooth brown cheeks. 'We were *perfect*, Nico – but the timing was all wrong. Everything's different now, we've both changed, made mistakes and learnt from them . . . *Now*, darling, we could really make a go of it. We've got a ready-made family; it couldn't be better. We'd be so happy, don't you see?'

'Bullshit, Roz,' declared Nico, wondering whether she was entirely sane. The situation was so bizarre it was almost laughable. Except that Roz wasn't laughing . . . she was deadly serious.

'Think about it,' she urged forcefully. Nico handed the sleeping baby back to her as if it were a grenade. And in a way, of course, that was what Nicolette was. Ammunition.

'These mistakes we've both made,' he mused, his thickly lashed eyes assuming a dangerous glitter. 'I assume you're referring to my marriage? I have a *wife*, Roz. You were right, everything *is* different. I'm no longer interested in you. Now is that a good enough reason to ask you to leave?'

She stared at him, aghast. He had changed so much. The Nico who had occupied her thoughts with an intensity bordering on obsession was an entirely different person, not this cold-eyed stranger with nothing but contempt for her and her terrible plight.

'Nicolette needs a father . . .'

'And I drew the short straw? Come off it, Roz, you can't blackmail me, for Christ's sake.'

'But she's ill!' Roz yelled at him, realizing that she was trembling with the unfairness of it all. 'I can't cope on my own. You have a responsibility towards her . . . towards both of us . . .'

'I'll organize blood tests,' said Nico wearily, holding up his hands against the onslaught of her shouting. 'If I'm her father I'll pay maintenance – enough to cover whatever you need. But that's all. I'll give you money, Roz, if that's what you want, but me you can't have. I just don't want to know, any more.'

'You bastard, I don't *want* your money. Haven't you learnt yet that hard cash can't solve all your problems? Just who do you think you *are*?'

It was a nightmare. Nothing was going as she had planned, yet she couldn't prevent the terrible diatribe . . . Nico had to understand what he was doing to her . . .

'I'm a bastard,' he replied in bored tones.

'Bloody right. And you've got your values screwed up as well,' she hissed at him, her arms tightening around the still-sleeping form of her daughter. 'Take Camilla. You went out of your way to help that stupid fat cow, when all she'd done was lose the husband she couldn't even manage to keep. Gave her a home, didn't you? And a nice little job? Help Camilla, help her get her act together, that must have made you feel really good. But then *I* have a problem, a *real* problem, and you don't even want to hear about it. I've been through *hell* because of you and you just aren't interested. What's so different between us, Nico? What's Camilla got that I don't have?'

And then she glimpsed the pain in his eyes and guessed. A knife twisted in her stomach and she laughed aloud, incredulous and appalled. 'Oh no. That's too much. That's exactly what you did do, isn't it? *Take Camilla.* You screwed her. Really Nico, isn't that taking the good Samaritan act just a little too far?'

'You foul bitch,' said Nico, dangerously slowly. For the first time in his life he wanted to hit a woman, but he wouldn't give Roz the pleasure of wearing his bruise, parading it like a trophy along Fleet Street, selling it to whoever would do him the most damage.

Besides, he knew how to hit her where it *really* hurt. 'Yes, I slept with her,' he said evenly. 'It wasn't screwing, though, not like you and I used to do. It was the real thing. The two of you don't even compare. Camilla's better than you in every sense, Roz, and I do mean every sense. She's a far nicer person and she's better in bed than any other woman I've ever known. So you can forget about the good Samaritan bit, because it really couldn't be further from the truth.'

Roz, white and shocked, stared at him as if she'd just been shot. With hatred in his heart, Nico gazed stonily back at her until she spoke.

'I'm going.'

'Good idea,' he said calmly. 'I'm sure you can find your own way out.'

Vampires was losing a great deal of money, fast. The rapid downhill slide was staggering and it was all Loulou Marks's fault. Worse still, she didn't even appear to be concerned about it. It was a catastrophe. Sharing a bath with a razor-happy AIDS victim was preferable to visiting Vampires these days, it seemed, yet there wasn't a single thing anyone could do to reverse the slide.

Loulou wasn't any fun any more.

She had lost the knack of abuse.

She was happy.

As far as Christo Moran was concerned, it was an altogether desperate situation, the very worst kind of disaster. Loulou had been the spark, the catalyst bringing Vampires exploding into life for as long as they had both been there. Now, incredibly, more beautiful than ever, the spark had gone to be replaced by an almost incandescent shimmer of loveliness.

It really wouldn't surprise him, Christo thought darkly, if she'd caught religion. It was that particular kind of shimmer.

* * *

While Christo pondered over these murky thoughts and polished glasses which would most likely not be used in the almost empty bar that day, Loulou sat cross-legged upon her settee upstairs and practised her breathing, immersed in her own thoughts.

As if watching herself from a comfortable distance, a detached observer, she marvelled at her calmness. Who would have thought it possible that here she was, awaiting the knock on the door which would signal Mac's arrival, and she wasn't even panicking?

Mac! Remember Mac? Second husband, *almost* fourth, and possible father of your child? Taunting herself, attempting to goad herself into some kind of reaction, Loulou exhaled slowly without even trying. It was no good. Whatever happened would happen, but nothing could stop her feeling like this. A cocoon without end. Wasn't nature miraculous to be able to make her so happy?

As thoughts of Mac drifted away – prolonged concentration these days was beyond her – she pulled open the wide neck of her giant white sweatshirt and held it away from her body, gazing down with absolute, unwavering absorption at the pale gold swell of her stomach. A tiny movement, either a foot or a fist, disturbed the smoothness for a second and Loulou smiled, slowly exhaling once more. Clever, clever baby.

And clever me, she thought with peaceful satisfaction, for being able to hold you inside me.

When the knock came at the door she let the neck of the sweatshirt spring back into place and gave her stomach a reassuring pat.

'Mac's here,' she whispered. 'Come on, baby. We'll show him, shall we?'

In some small, sneaky corner of her subconscious nestled the treacherous thought that maybe, just maybe all this excessive goodness was a ploy; that it formed part of a pact. If she was good, *really* good, then God would reward her by making the baby Mac's. Occasionally the thought bothered her. Most of the time, however, she was too busy enjoying her newfound serenity to be concerned.

It will be interesting, she thought idly, to see what Mac makes of it all, anyway.

'Hi,' said Mac, his eyes straying instantly to Loulou's stomach as if to ensure that the photographs he had seen in the papers were true.

'Yes, I really am,' Loulou promised him, amused. 'Come in and sit down, Mac. It's lovely to see you again. You're looking well.'

'So are you.' Christ, she did too; the silver-blonde hair he had always loved was longer than ever, brighter than ever. Barefoot and dressed all in white she looked so angelic it wasn't true. Despite the harsh words he had dealt himself before setting out, reminding him what a lying bitch she was, he could feel himself weakening already.

But he was, at the same time, wary. Phoning Loulou and arranging to meet her had been a spur of the moment decision and he was still acutely aware of the circumstances of their last meeting. Travelling down to the Cotswolds, whisking her away with him in a helicopter at dawn had been his last spontaneous gesture, and that had turned out to be a disaster of epic proportions.

The trouble was, Loulou *made* him act illogically. She always had. Today, he was on his guard.

'Drink?' she said, waving a bottle of his favourite St Emilion.

Mac shook his head. The flat brought back so many memories that he felt instantly ill at ease. It was Loulou's home now, her territory. Disadvantages like that he could do without.

'It's a nice day. I thought we could go out. Are you up to a walk or are you supposed to be resting?' He had only the haziest ideas about pregnant women. Were they allowed to go for walks or were they supposed to lie with their feet up?

Loulou suppressed a smile. 'Oh, I think I can manage a walk. Hang on a sec and I'll find some shoes.'

And she certainly could walk. Eschewing Mac's suggestion of a gentle stroll in nearby Hyde Park, she pulled him in the other direction, away from the glittering shops of Knightsbridge, along Sloane Street then cutting through to the Chelsea Embankment. A heavy mist hung low, shot through with autumn sunlight; a perfect London morning.

And as they walked, they talked.

But, wondered Mac as they reached Parliament Square, awash with burnished copper leaves, had they actually *said* anything?

There had been no mention, for a start, of Josh, whose existence she had so blithely denied, so conveniently forgotten on the night of the ball. No mention, either, of who the father of her child might be. She was treating him like a long-lost brother, for Christ's sake. And while he might not know much about the subject of pregnancy, he could still count on his fingers. There was a chance, there had to be at least a chance, that the baby was his.

Loulou meanwhile, stepping easily along beside him, looking for all the world like an elegant puffball, was admiring the view of the Thames and reminiscing about a more distant past.

'When I was sixteen or seventeen, visiting London, I always used to come here,' she said quietly. 'This was my favourite walk. I wanted so badly to *become* someone . . . it was like an obsession. One day I'd be back and everyone would know who I was. God only knows how I thought I was going to do it, although I have a sneaking feeling that I did harbour a secret plan to marry an MP and turn him into prime minister. Can't you just see it?' she smiled up at Mac. 'The perfect prime minister's wife?'

'You've done pretty well on your own,' he said, longing to touch her hair. 'You're successful. For a girl who couldn't even pass her maths O level you're a bloody miracle. And you seem happy,' he added, searching for an entry into the conversation he really wanted to be having. 'Are you, Lou?'

She glanced sideways at him, amusement playing on her lips, seeing through him at once, as she always had.

'Ridiculously happy.'

'You've changed.'

She shrugged. 'I just don't feel that I have to fight any more.'

'Am I the father?' he blurted out, desperate to know, and Loulou squeezed his arm.

'I can't tell you that. I'm sorry.'

'You can't tell me or you don't know?' demanded Mac, struggling to control his impatience. Goddammit, how could she *be* so changed? So bloody calm?

'Well, both. If I knew, then of course I'd tell you.'

'Christ!'

'I'm sorry, darling,' she said again, sympathetic but unrepentant. 'But don't worry, if it does turn out to be yours I won't sue you for child support or anything like that.'

'Who are the other contenders?' he said, jealousy surging inside him. Loulou shrugged.

'Only one other. You met him.'

'Jesus.'

'No, not him.'

'It isn't bloody funny!' he exploded, his dark eyes narrowing with anger, and Loulou shook her head.

'Of course it isn't. But there's nothing I can do to change it. And there's no need to shout at me, either, because it really doesn't affect you. It isn't as if I'm begging you to marry me, Mac. Don't think that, please, because that's the last thing in the world I'd do. So just calm down.'

They walked on in silence for several minutes, entering Birdcage Walk. Loulou admired the perfect autumn trees bordering St James's Park while Mac attempted to come to terms with her words. She *had* changed. He had gone to meet Loulou today mentally prepared, knowing exactly how she would react. She was going to fling herself into his arms, beg his forgiveness and plead for his support. He, in turn, would be kind but firm, making sure that she understood the situation from both their points of view. Further than that he had been unable to plan since a great deal, obviously, had depended upon the answer she gave him to that all-important question.

So much, thought Mac numbly, for his carefully laid plans. Gone with the bloody wind.

'Money!' declared Loulou unexpectedly, shaking back her hair and enjoying the sunshine on her face. 'Do you realize, Mac, that the root of all my problems has always been money?'

To show that he could keep up with any change in conversation instigated by his crazy ex-wife, Mac said, 'Bullshit. You have plenty of money.'

'That's just what I mean,' she replied, her expression thoughtful. 'I have too much. It's a problem.'

Stopping in his tracks, Mac pulled her round to face him. Nobody had ever been able to accuse him of beating around the bush. 'Lou, listen to me. If you really don't know what your problem has always been, and if you really *want* to know, I'll tell you. It's men.'

Loulou looked as if she was going to burst. With a glittering, triumphant smile she exclaimed, 'That's *exactly* what I'd always thought – but I was wrong all the time! *Think* about it, Mac. You were too proud to let me help you when I had more money than you did. You hated the fact that poor Omar left me Vampires because you couldn't stop wondering what I must have done to earn it. Then there was Hugh, who only gambled as much as he did because he knew I could afford it. Bang go two marriages straight away, you see? And Joshua, of course, was simply more interested in my money than in me. All of them, Mac.' She gestured with her arms. 'They all either wanted my money or couldn't handle the fact that I had so much of it. It's so obvious I just can't understand why I never realized it before.'

In her enthusiasm she looked like a young girl. Mac understood with a jolt how much he still loved her. What a totally crazy state of affairs.

'So what are you going to do?' he said, fighting the urge to take her into his arms and kiss that beguiling smile off her face.

'It's obvious,' Loulou declared cheerfully. 'Get rid of it, of course. Now, do you think we could go and get an ice-cream? A chocolate one? Before I starve?'

Anaesthetized by shock into terrifying, icy immobility, Roz sat at the kitchen table clutching a glass of water and staring at Nicolette's feeding bottle. The brown teat looked like a tiny upraised thumb. The container of milk formula beside it bore a picture of a contented, smiling normal baby, cradled in its mother's arms. Outside, it was growing gradually light, the wavering shadows of the ash trees darkening against the grey backdrop of the sky. The only sound in the kitchen, in the entire house, was that of the relentless clicking of the grandfather clock in the hallway which only served to accentuate the otherwise total silence.

Struggling to the surface, searching for some practical course upon which to steer her numbed thoughts, Roz reached for the bottle and the box of powdered milk and rose jerkily to her feet. Crossing the kitchen to the bin, she took a shallow breath and dropped them into it with deliberate care.

There was no need for them, after all, now that Nicolette was dead.

She wanted to cry, but no tears would come.

It was so dark, so quiet that it was almost possible to think that she was the one who had died, instead.

Where, she wondered vaguely, *was* everyone? Then, remembering the journey home from the hospital in the doctor's car, she recalled also the fantastic ease with which she had manoeuvred her solitude. He had tried to persuade her to telephone a friend or relative from the tiny office behind the children's ward. She had told him that the relevant phone numbers were all ex-directory, and written in her diary which was at home.

He had brought her here, then, and she had excused herself, telling him that she would make the necessary calls from the bedroom. Sitting on the edge of her bed she had picked up and replaced the receiver three times, so that he could hear the pings on the extension downstairs. When several minutes had passed, she had returned to the sitting-room to assure him that her mother, her aunt and her very best friend were all on their way, refusing his offer of a sedative and explaining that she was fine, that what she most needed was twenty minutes alone before her mother arrived.

It had been a relief when the poor, well-meaning, exhausted man had gone. How, after all, could she have explained to him that her parents were both abroad and unable to be contacted, and that she only had one friend, who was herself on the verge of giving birth? Such a dearth of friends was positively embarrassing.

When the doorbell rang, shattering the silence, she thought it must be the milkman calling to present his bill and took her purse with her to the door. She was already fumbling for a £5 note and some coins before realizing with vague astonishment that it was the GP from the village.

'Dr Logan, what are *you* doing here?' It was like bumping into one's dentist at a night-club. 'I'm . . . I'm afraid I have some very bad . . . very sad news for you.'

'Let's go inside, shall we, Roz?' said Dr Logan, his deep, kind voice loud and reassuring as he placed his arm around her narrow shoulders and led her back towards her chair. 'My dear, the hospital contacted me. They told me about your daughter. I'm here to make sure you're all right. Do you want to talk about it, or shall I give you something to let you sleep?'

Almost with a sense of relief, Roz felt the grief well up inside her. The taut, gritty pain in her chest seemed to move and her chin shuddered with the effort of control. The rough tweed of the doctor's jacket grazed her arm as he helped her sit down and she gasped for breath, her eyes blinded by the tears now streaming down her cheeks, reaching for him in an overwhelming spasm of loss and desperation and sheer, bleak desolation.

'There now, Roz. My poor girl, I'm so sorry. It's a terrible thing that's happened to you,' murmured Dr Logan, holding her tightly in his arms and letting her sob. 'Good girl, cry as much as you want, don't you worry, we'll get you through this ... there there ... go on ... good girl ...'

Chapter 33

Matt had always been the kind of person who knew exactly what he wanted. A firm disbeliever in fate – although since meeting Camilla he was willing to reconsider that one – he had planned his life down to the last detail at an astonishingly young age and never even thought for a moment that what he had decided would happen might not.

Matt's mother, coming across the sheet of paper containing his Life Plan one day while she was tidying his room, had been amused and touched by her elder son's presumption. That her tousle-haired, over-active, sports-mad nine year old could have compiled such a thoroughly organized and forward-thinking list was simply the cutest thing . . .

1. Finnish college.
2. Work at a top-class golf club.
3. Become a proffesional golfer and win the US Open.
4. Travel the whole world and win lots of tornaments.
5. Have fun.
6. Find a really baeutiful and nice girl.
7. Go and live in England.
8. Get married to her (the girl) and have five children and three dogs and maybe some other pets too.
9. Teach my children to play golf and other sports like tennis and baseball.

10. Enjoy myself until I am very old.
11. Die

'But why d'you want to go and live in England?' his mother had asked him when he'd returned home from school that evening. He was, after all, the most all-American boy she'd ever known.

Matt had shrugged, an untidy sandwich in one hand and a milkshake in the other. 'I've seen it on TV. I've read books about it and they have some great golf courses. England's neat and I just want to live there. But don't worry, Mom,' he'd immediately reassured her with characteristic generosity and panache, 'you and Pop can come over and visit me as often as you want. I'll pay for the plane tickets, OK?'

By the time he was thirty-five he'd reached number five on his list, the only disappointment so far having occurred when he'd been runner-up in the US Open, narrowly beaten into second place by a blisteringly on-form Tom Watson.

But that was almost more than made up for by the fact that he had fulfilled the sixth goal. He had met the woman who was indisputably the beautiful and nice girl of whom he had dreamt so very long ago.

All he had to do now was buy a house in England, marry Camilla and hope to God that she wasn't allergic to dogs.

As the friendship between Loulou and Mac was tentatively renewed, both working desperately to hide the strength of their true feelings for each other for fear that they would destroy its cobweb fragility, the relationship between Matt and Camilla became more intense, and happily knew no such caution. Matt, larger than life in every way, knew that he had found the woman with whom he wanted to spend the rest of his life. And happier than she would have ever believed possible, Camilla allowed him to sweep her totally off her feet. There were no obstacles in the way of their idyllic, laughter-filled, sex-satiated love, even Toby and Charlotte liked Matt and for the first time she learnt not to question her right to such happiness.

It was hers. It wasn't all a mistake or a dream that might disappear at any minute. She deserved it.

Especially, she often thought with unbounded glee, the sex.

Jack, she now realized – although it had taken her long enough to find out – was not one of the world's great lovers. He had been selfish, at times little more than perfunctory, and totally lacking in consideration for her needs. Maybe he had made more of an effort with Roz, but Camilla, in her ignorance, had not known enough to expect or demand more from him, innocently accepting that what she got was all there was. Nico had opened doors for her but for some reason she had – equally naïvely – assumed that he was an exception. Incredible as he had been, she had somehow come to the conclusion that he was a one-off, an experience that could never be repeated.

It was a source of incredulous joy to her to learn that Matt was equally talented. Tender, teasing, exciting and exhilarating . . . he had awoken in her a sensuality she hadn't known existed.

The most difficult part, she found, was keeping the news of her wonderful discovery to herself. Loulou, who was still being perfectly saintly, but who managed to retain her old forthrightness had winked knowingly and said, 'Good in bed, is he?' but other than that, no-one else knew. It was, Camilla decided, the only aspect of the affair which was frustrating, unless you counted the slightly irritating fact that she had wasted two whole weeks by holding out before being persuaded into Matt's bed.

Oh, but it had been worth waiting for, she remembered now as she soaked in a hot bath before getting ready to meet Loulou at Lorenzo's for lunch.

And it wasn't as if she had set out on purpose to delay the big seduction scene; events had always seemed to conspire against Matt, and she had been privately relieved each time they had.

Once a fat lady always a fat lady, in your mind, at least, she thought ruefully, sinking down in the Badedas-scented water so that the foam spilled over her breasts.

It took some adjusting to; she had to make a conscious effort each time she thought of her body to remind herself that she was no longer overweight, and that instead of unsightly fat there were now generous but firm curves, all in perfect proportion with each other.

But the image that she had long been used to was what tended to remain uppermost in her thoughts. And that, coupled with the knowledge that she was woefully inexperienced with men, particularly for a woman of thirty-two, had been the reason for her reluctance to consummate this thrilling new relationship.

Smiling to herself, Camilla thought back to the long-delayed seduction. The first time they had shared an hotel room Marty had been there, bouncing and giggling between them, blissfully unaware of Matt's good-humoured frustration. Later that night, following the charity gala, he had driven her home and still unsettled by the unexpected meeting with Nico and Caroline, she had accepted an enormous brandy. Intuitively, Matt had understood that that aspect of the evening was something she preferred not to discuss and she had been profoundly grateful. So grateful that she had fallen asleep on the settee.

And after that it had become a kind of joke between them, at times an almost farcical one. When Matt kissed Camilla the phone invariably rang, or Zoë arrived unexpectedly with a troupe of friends, or Fee and Gussie burst into the room to show them the jam jar of spiders they had so painstakingly collected from the overgrown garden.

'We'd have had more privacy in the Royal Enclosure at Ascot,' complained Matt when what was supposed to be an intimate lunch at his hotel was gatecrashed by three of his fellow golfers, hell-bent on celebrating their morning's win. 'Those guys were supposed to be on my side, for God's sake.'

'I liked them,' Camilla protested, laughing at his indignant expression.

'And they liked you. That's something else that makes me nervous. What are you doing at the weekend?'

'Working.'

'Swap with Zoë. I'm taking you away. We're going to have some time alone together if it's the last thing I damn well do.'

But even then events did their level best to conspire against them.

'Alone together,' Camilla mouthed at him as they boarded the packed shuttle from Heathrow. A delegation of Japanese businessmen had taken up all the available seats. She and Matt were three rows apart.

'Alone together,' she reminded him as they queued amidst the babbling French and Japanese crowds to squeeze through customs at Orly.

'Alone together,' she whispered as they tried to claim their room at the glamorous Paris Hotel on the Rue St Jacques, only to be apologetically informed that due to an over-enthusiastic new clerk, they had been double booked with an Australian sheep farmer and his young secretary who had arrived half an hour earlier and promptly hung their 'Do not disturb' on the door. The manager explained that he was dreadfully sorry, but the rest of the hotel was full. There were no other rooms available at all.

'*Oh merde*,' said Matt, very loudly. 'And on our honeymoon, too. This is *très tragique, m'sieur. Très tragique* indeed.'

'Alone together,' said Matt, a hint of smugness and a great deal of relief in his voice when an hour and a half later they found themselves installed in the honeymoon suite of the even more glamorous Hotel Bristol. 'At bloody last. Come here,' he entreated, reaching for Camilla, 'and give your clever old golfer a big hug.'

'Don't be such an old lech,' she protested, neatly side-stepping his arms. 'We're in *Paris*, Matt. Let's go and *explore* it.'

But eventually, of course, late that evening following a stupendous dinner, they had returned to their suite, and to the vast, velvet-canopied bed which awaited them.

All Camilla's shyness, all her doubts and fears were swept away in the slow, exquisite hours that followed as time and time again they made love, learning the secrets of each other's bodies and giving each other more pleasure than they had ever imagined possible.

'Alone together,' she whispered at last into the soft, wonderfully scented hair of his chest. 'I'm so glad you brought me to Paris, Matt.'

'Not half as glad as I am,' he murmured, dropping a kiss on to the back of her neck. 'But you didn't honestly think I was going to give up, did you? I'm just about the most persistent old bastard on this earth. And now that I've finally succeeded in persuading you into my bed I have only one other thing to say to you.'

'Oh yes?' Camilla lifted her head and grinned at him. 'What's that?'

'I hope,' said Matt, slowly, 'I really and truly hope . . . that you haven't got me pregnant.'

Lorenzo's at lunchtime was crowded and noisy, but everyone still noticed Loulou when she made her entrance. Her trademark silvery blonde hair cascading in ringlets down her back, her scarlet taffeta dress bearing the unmistakable Emanuel hallmark, she glided between the tables like a small but very stately galleon, smiling at people she recognized and waving at Camilla when she finally spotted her. Clasped incongruously in one hand was a very businesslike black leather briefcase which she placed with great care beside her chair before sitting down.

Camilla waited until the *maître d'* had finished making a fuss of her before saying, 'You're looking fantastic. It must be love.'

Loulou smiled. 'I've given it up for Lent.'

'Still seeing Mac?'

'He dropped by this morning, brought me two dozen white roses and a copy of *Baby and Child* by someone called Penelope Leach.'

'It *must* be love. Why the briefcase?'

'Business. This afternoon I have to spend two hours being grilled by my accountant.' Loulou waved the inconvenience away with a dismissive gesture. 'But listen, I heard some terrible news this morning. Roz phoned me.'

'Oh yes?' Automatically, Camilla stiffened, her tone becoming guarded. She would never, she thought, be able to associate any news relating to Roz as good.

Loulou's smile had dropped away and the expression in her eyes was bleak as she leant forward across the table.

'It's awful, Cami. Her baby died last night. A cot death, apparently.'

'Oh no.' Camilla felt sick, and deeply ashamed. Poor Roz. What an appalling thing to happen. 'She phoned you. Is she OK?'

Loulou shook her head. 'I don't know. I think she's still in shock. When I offered to go down to see her she refused, said that her mother would be arriving later today. I felt guilty because I was so relieved. I just don't think I could cope with something like that right now.'

'Of course you couldn't. Poor, poor Roz. That little baby . . .' Camilla's voice trailed off as she recalled how, shortly after Charlotte's birth, she had watched a TV programme about cot deaths. For weeks afterwards she had woken six or seven times each night to check that her daughter was still breathing. Jack had irritably accused her of over-reacting and, exhausted from lack of sleep, she had burst into tears and screamed back at him. The icy, ensuing silence had lasted several days.

But Charlotte had thrived and gradually the worrying had receded.

Roz hadn't been so lucky.

'She told me something else,' said Loulou, twisting a napkin between her fingers and indicating to the hovering head waiter that they would not be ordering just yet. 'Apparently Nicolette hadn't been all that well for weeks and the hospital ran a series of tests. Last week they told Roz that Nicolette sustained some kind of brain damage when she was born.' Loulou paused, frowning as she struggled to understand the tragic unfairness of it all. 'Apparently Nicolette would never have been . . . well, normal. Roz didn't contact me when she found out because she thought it would be too distressing for me. She said she was so upset she didn't want to see anyone. And now, just as she was beginning to come to terms with the idea, this happens. Her baby, poor little Nicolette, is dead. And Roz is absolutely distraught.'

'Of course she is,' said Camilla, taking Loulou's hand and choosing her words with care in deference to her friend's vulnerable condition. 'But maybe it was Nature's way. Lou. If Nicolette was badly brain damaged, perhaps it was the best thing that could have happened. Some parents cope brilliantly in that situation, but others just can't. And if we're honest, we'll both admit that Roz would have found it more difficult than most. It's been awful for her, and she'll need time to get over it, of course, but in the long run it's probably going to be less painful for her than if Nicolette had lived. But you mustn't worry about it happening to *you*,' she urged, meeting Loulou's troubled gaze. 'Only a tiny, *tiny* percentage of babies don't grow up to be perfectly normal. And you've taken such good care of yourself the odds are even more in your favour. Your baby will be fine, Lou. Just fine.'

'I know it will.' Loulou smiled and shook back her long hair, clearing the tension from the air around them. The restaurant noises which had seemed to fade away earlier now resumed their former level. She signalled to the waiter to bring their menus and ordered the drinks, peach juice for herself and a gin and tonic for Camilla.

'I know my baby will be OK,' she added when they were alone once more, 'but a cot death is such a tragedy, we really ought to try and do something to help. I don't have anything definite planned just yet, but I'm thinking of holding a charity night at Vampires to raise money for research into it. Will you and Matt come along, when I do?'

'Of course we will,' said Camilla with enthusiasm. 'Just say the word. Wild horses couldn't drag me away.'

Loulou grinned and raised her glass in salute. 'Good,' she said, a teasing note in her voice. 'Just so long as a wild American doesn't drag you away before the big event.'

Sitting curled up on the settee at home, Camilla tore yet another sheet of paper from the pad on her lap and threw it past the wastebin to nestle with the others. Her last letter to Roz had been difficult enough, and that had been the one she had written shortly before bumping into her in Harrods.

This one was proving to be far worse. Yet something within her drove her on. She didn't like Roz, but felt that sending a short note of condolence was the least she could do. The letters she had received from friends and relatives had helped her so much when her own parents had died within a year of each other; she had read and reread them, gaining an amazing amount of comfort from the knowledge that people thought enough of both her and her parents to make the effort to write such difficult words. Roz deserved that much from her at least, she told herself as she sucked the top of her pen and struggled to choose her own words of sympathy.

But that didn't mean it wasn't bloody hard.

In the end, after over two hours of false starts, she wrote straight from the heart. What had been intended to be a few short lines became a three-page letter from one mother to another, with no mention of the difficulties which had estranged them. Tears welled in her eyes as the grief which Roz must be enduring was shared by Camilla. When she reached the end she folded the pages and pushed them into an already stamped and addressed envelope without even rereading them for fear that the spontaneity of the deeply felt sentiments would be lost.

Chapter 34

November 5th. Firework night. Or more appropriately, thought Loulou with satisfaction and mounting excitement as she hugged the secret to herself, bridge-burning night. All systems were go and she could hardly wait for the fire to be lit.

With professional pleasure she gazed around at the preparations. Christo and the girls had worked so hard. The now-imminent approach of her baby's birth had prevented her from helping them as much as she would have liked but she had done her bit, organizing everything and delegating like mad wherever possible. Until midnight last night she had issued instructions from the comfort of the Number One settee, ensuring that no detail, however tiny, was forgotten and Daisy, Lena and Christo had cheerfully carried out all the physical work of which she was no longer capable. Feeling like Cleopatra and enjoying herself immensely, Loulou had not even stopped to wonder what would happen after tomorrow night. It simply hadn't concerned her.

It still didn't. It was, after all, such a *right* thing to be doing.

And now Vampires was transformed. Hugging her trusty briefcase to her enormous stomach she allowed herself a smug smile. It was going to be a truly spectacular night.

'Loulou certainly knows the right people,' Camilla whispered to Matt as they found themselves a small table beyond the bar. 'If this doesn't put Vampires back on the map, nothing will.'

The whole place was buzzing, alive with laughter and excitement. The pop of champagne corks and the clink of glasses mingled with the erratic clatter of the bouncing silver balls at the two roulette tables set up in the centre of the room. Around them, less noisy but engendering just as much interest were the smaller tables where croupiers in scarlet satin deftly dealt out the cards for *chemin-de-fer*, blackjack and poker.

Clutching the small stack of chips with which she had been presented upon arrival, Camilla watched with admiration as Loulou, good humouredly insulting everyone who approached her, sold further bags for £20 each. Anyone could buy as many chips as they liked. At midnight, the player who had amassed the most number of chips won a holiday for two in Barbados, paid for by Loulou herself.

'Come on, you miserable old sod,' she heard Loulou cry as a well-known actor pulled a handful of notes from his wallet. 'If Patrick Lichfield can buy two hundred chips you can afford twice that amount. Bloody hell, he's only an impoverished photographer – you're rich beyond his wildest dreams! Let's see your gold card, sweetie. Sign over all your dosh.'

And of course he did. Everyone was doing the same. When Camilla made her way over to Loulou's table, her friend flashed her a wicked grin and waved her bucket of money at her with glee. 'Cami, we're doing so *well*! I thought that by inviting two hundred of the richest people I know, I'd end up making twenty grand. If this carries on I'm going to double or triple that amount. Everyone's spending an absolute fortune.'

'You're terrifying the money out of their pockets,' said Camilla with affection. 'They're all scared to death of you.'

'Good,' said Loulou, shaking her bucket once more. 'That means more money. Have you seen Roz yet?'

'Is she here?' Camilla knew that Loulou had invited her and the news had made her edgy, but she was determined not to allow it to spoil her enjoyment of the evening. There was, after all, no longer anything Roz could do to hurt her.

'I haven't seen her,' replied Loulou, deftly sorting chips into even piles, 'but she told me she would definitely be coming. It's the first time she's been out since Nicolette died, so we'll have to look after her.'

'Mmm,' said Camilla non-committally. Writing to Roz to express her sympathies had been one thing; somehow she couldn't imagine herself looking after her. That was a different matter entirely.

'Lena,' Loulou called out, waving a slender arm in the air, 'can you come and take over? I'm going to mingle and help everyone lose all their money. Where's Mac?'

'Helping everyone lose all their money,' said Lena, sliding into Loulou's seat. 'And a girl called Poppy's just come in. She wondered where you were.'

'Poppy!' Loulou exclaimed, clapping her hands. 'That's great. But how could she possibly have missed me – aren't I the fattest woman in here?'

'The second fattest,' observed Matt, appearing at Camilla's side and helping Loulou through the gap between her seat and the table. 'There's an enormous opera singer playing blackjack. I swear she's sitting on three chairs pushed together.'

'Thank you, Matt,' said Loulou gravely. 'In fact I only invited her because she makes me feel positively sylphlike.'

* * *

306

'Bloody hell,' declared Poppy, when Loulou found her at the bar with Jamie, the boyfriend who had unwittingly caused so much trouble at the Easter Ball. 'A lot can certainly happen to a girl in nine months, darling.'

'More than you think,' said Loulou as she leant forward and kissed her. 'It's lovely to see you again. I didn't even know if you'd remember who I was.'

'It was a memorable night,' Poppy laughed. 'Jamie and I are married now, and I've already spotted your gorgeous man here. Have you two tied the knot?'

'Still unravelling the old one,' whispered Loulou. 'It's all a bit complicated, but I'm very happy and that's what matters at the moment. I've got to say hello to a few people but I'll join you in a minute. We'll have a good gossip, and this time it won't be in the ladies' loo.'

Camilla, having bet cautiously at the roulette table and lost whilst Matt consistently piled chips on single numbers and won, paused to take a drink and saw Roz arrive. The chilled wine froze in her throat as she realized who was with her.

Jack.

And Roz certainly didn't appear as if she needed looking after. Her short dark hair was spikily elegant, her gypsyish eyes heavy with make-up. Impossibly slender in a plunging, emerald green satin dress that shimmered with a life of its own, she sauntered on Jack's arm through the mass of people, flashing her crimson and white smile at faces she recognized and graciously acknowledging their greetings as she passed them. The news of Nicolette's tragic death had been well publicized in the Press and Roz had received the public's sympathy. Exonerated for her 'sins' of just a few months ago she had been forgiven and welcomed back to the charmed celebrity fold. And since she was no longer a single mother her job had been returned to her and her new TV series, Camilla had read, was about to go into production.

Well, she thought with a trace of bitterness, Roz certainly didn't look like a grieving mother tonight. And she was back with Jack. It was like a cruel, double betrayal.

Jack, she had to admit, was also looking good. Following the break-up of their marriage he had put on a fair amount of weight which hadn't suited him. She had seen him from time to time since then, of course, when she was picking up the children or when he dropped them off to her but now, dressed in a well-tailored dinner-jacket and with his light brown hair combed severely back from his face she realized that he had improved a lot in the last few months. The extra weight was gone and he had a good tan. And he certainly looked happy enough to be here with Roz tonight.

Selfish lover, unfaithful husband, deceitful man, she told herself, deciding that she didn't want to speak to him tonight and reaching for the reassuring contact of Matt's hand. He turned and winked at her. Jack bothered him not at all.

'We're doing pretty well, sweetheart. Fancy a holiday in Barbados?'

'Lovely,' said Camilla, relaxing and squeezing his warm hand, the realization of how little either Jack or Roz now mattered to her flooding through her like a drug. 'But whoever would I choose to take with me?'

'Who on earth is that?' she whispered to Loulou half an hour later, as a man standing a few feet away turned and stared coldly at them for several seconds without smiling. Then, with slow deliberation, he turned away once more, resuming his scrutiny of the roulette table at which Matt was still amassing vast quantities of chips.

'Laszlo de Lazzari,' said Loulou loudly and with mild contempt. 'He's a mean bastard, but loaded. I'm amazed he even turned up.'

'Sinister,' observed Camilla with a shiver. The man was tall, fortyish, elegantly constructed and immaculately dressed, but his face was decidedly piratical. A black eye-patch covered his right eye. His thick black hair was shot through with silver and his cheekbones were twin scimitars, incredibly prominent and as sharply defined as the hard, uncurving line of his mouth. His large nose was Roman in design and when he lifted his glass to drink, Camilla saw that he was wearing the largest diamond ring she had ever seen.

'Italian?' she asked, wondering why such an openly hostile stare had been directed towards them. Loulou shrugged. 'God knows, but it's a dangerous mixture. If you value your virginity, keep away from him. I wish Nico could have been here tonight,' she said, changing the subject. 'I hope he gets back from Italy before I drop the lump. Did I tell you that he's going to be godfather?'

Camilla smiled. 'He'll spoil it to pieces.'

'That's why I need a sensible godmother to make sure my child doesn't end up a complete brat. Did I tell you, by the way, who I wanted to be godmother?' Wincing slightly, she placed her hand over her stomach as the baby kicked out.

'No.' Camilla had assumed she would choose Roz.

'You. If you'd like to be, of course.'

'Oh Lou . . .' So overwhelmed by the compliment that she could hardly speak, Camilla embraced her friend. 'I'd love to.'

* * *

Laszlo de Lazzari was definitely a man to be wary of, Camilla decided as she watched him at the roulette table. During the course of the evening she had caught him favouring Loulou with several more of those intimidatingly icy stares. Now he was betting heavily, and winning.

His one visible eye, she realized, was of the shade which under any other circumstances she would have described as baby-blue. Instead she shivered inwardly at the unblinking intensity of that steadfast gaze and could only liken it to the deadly eye of a cobra.

Matt, seated opposite him, roared with laughter whenever he lost a bet, but de Lazzari remained virtually silent throughout, ignoring the spinning wheel, moving only to place and replace his chips after each game.

By eleven fifty-five they had roughly equal numbers of chips and everyone who had long ago lost theirs was crowding around the table to watch the game.

Finally, Laszlo de Lazzari spoke.

'You are clearly a gambling man of good fortune and good humour,' he announced, addressing Matt. 'Would it not be interesting to settle the game on a single spin of the wheel? Rouge or noir. You may choose your colour, sir.'

Camilla, standing behind Matt, watched her fingers dig into the shoulder of his dinner-jacket and heard him drawl with lazy amusement, 'Sure. Why not?' as if the man had offered nothing more than a cigarette.

The atmosphere grew tense. Camilla held her breath. With an economical gesture de Lazzari indicated that Matt should make his choice of colour and Matt in turn twisted round in his seat to smile at Camilla and lightly run his finger over the crimson silk taffeta of her dress. Across the room she was aware of Jack's eyes upon her and determinedly didn't look back at him.

'My lady is wearing red,' said Matt, slipping his arm around her waist and drawing her against him, 'so I guess that's what I'll go for. Will you spin the wheel, Lou?'

'With pleasure. Good luck, Matt,' she said, flashing a look of disdain in de Lazzari's direction. 'Here we go.'

Two hundred and fifty people held their breath as the winner of the evening's prize was decided by a small, spinning, clattering silver ball racing around inside a wheel. Loulou stared at it, utterly mesmerized. Camilla closed her eyes. Matt winked at one of the journalists balancing precariously on a chair at the back of the room and said, 'Bernie, are you *sure* you want to be a tightrope walker when you grow up?'

De Lazzari, for the first time that evening, watched the wheel turn.

The ball slowed, skipped, jumped and finally settled. Everyone in the room exhaled in unison. Camilla opened her eyes.

'I guess you should have worn your black dress tonight, honey,' said Matt, giving her waist a squeeze. 'Never mind. Maybe we can afford a weekend in Yorkshire instead.'

'My game, I believe,' commented de Lazzari, his inscrutable blue eye fixing upon Loulou and ignoring Matt totally. 'But I would be happy to play another, Miss Marks. With you.'

'You don't say,' she replied shortly. 'I know you're new to this country, Mr de Lazzari, but you really should know that we don't play those sort of games over here.'

'Not even for your beloved charity?' he questioned, his voice dry with irony. 'Come, come, my dear. I wonder how concerned you really are beneath your charmingly benevolent façade. Double or nothing, that is my proposal. For two wealthy people such as ourselves the risk is hardly –'

'OK,' blurted out Loulou, her fists clenched at her sides, her breasts rising and falling with each breath. 'OK, we'll play. Double or nothing. That's ten grand.'

'She must be mad,' muttered Mac, appearing beside Camilla and Matt. 'Lou's the worst gambler in the world. Every horse she's ever laid a bet on in her life has run backwards.'

Matt grinned, attempting to lighten the atmosphere. 'Well, she's playing with a dark horse now, that's for sure.'

'Tell her to stop,' said Camilla, and Mac threw her a meaning-ful look, his dark eyes signalling despair.

'Since when did Loulou ever take notice of anything I said?'

Seconds later they watched once more as the wheel spun with the ball.

When it stopped, Laszlo de Lazzari permitted himself a small, terrifyingly controlled smile.

'Well done, my dear,' he said to Loulou. 'You are very lucky. Your precious money is safe.'

Camilla, feeling almost sick with relief, turned hurriedly away and headed for the toilets. By the time she returned, hopefully, Laszlo de Lazzari would be gone and the party could continue happily through the night without him.

When she emerged from her cubicle, however, she found Roz re-doing her lipstick in the mirror which stretched across the length of the four ivory-marbled basins. By the dead-pan expression in her eyes Camilla realized that she had come here purely in order to speak to her. Her dark eyes reflected in the mirror, Roz watched her without turning, then slowly recapped her lipstick and dropped it into the evening bag which lay open beside her. Whenever she wished to do so, Roz had always been able to veil her true feelings behind an inscrutable outer mask. Camilla, she thought with a trace of scorn, had never possessed that facility; her thoughts and emotions were *there*, plastered all over her face, and Roz took pleasure in registering each one in turn. The initial shock – almost fear – had already given way to uncertainty and this in turn was now replaced by a wavering anxious smile, the overtures of a non-existent friendship. Finally, as Roz watched her remembering the letter she had written a few weeks ago, came the expected flicker of sympathy. Typical of Camilla, she thought, to have written such a gushing, all-girls together letter. And typical too, that she was now moving towards her, forgiving her for the past in order to sympathize with her in her present grief.

'Roz, how are you?' Camilla said, and Roz registered that the anxiety in her voice was due to a mixture of genuine concern and uncertainty as to how she would react.

'I'm very well, thank you,' she replied evenly, and watched Camilla hesitate.

'Did you get my letter?'

'I did.' Lighting a cigarette, she blew a perfect smoke ring and watched it drift towards the door.

'I can't tell you how I felt when I heard about Nicolette. It must have been so terrible,' continued Camilla, warming up. 'Are you coping all right? If there's anything at all I can do, you know, of course, that you only have to ask . . .' Her voice trailed away beneath Roz's blank stare and the sympathy died from her eyes to be replaced by that scared-puppy expression Roz remembered so well from school. Camilla might have changed, she thought with cold triumph, but she hadn't changed that much.

And it was both fascinating and reassuring to know that she could still set her on the edge of that precipice of self-doubt and inferiority.

'That's very noble of you,' she said in a low, controlled voice, 'but all I ask is that you drop the pretence. It makes me feel quite sick.'

Camilla turned pale, stunned by the words, and Roz felt a surge of power. She felt more alive, somehow; more enervated now that she was finally ridding herself of that poisonous build-up of jealousy. Camilla had turned Nico against her, had taken him from her, and it was only right that she should feel pain in return.

'You hate me for what I once did to you,' Roz continued, grinding her cigarette into the wash basin. 'You never wanted to see me again, and that certainly didn't bother me. I went along with that. But now, simply because my daughter is dead, you think that my loss gives you the right to sympathize with me, to forgive me for what happened in the past. Well, it doesn't. I have not become a *nice* person, I am exactly the same as I was before and we really both know that. Pretending otherwise is sheer hypocrisy, so don't even try it. So there's no need to treat me any differently because I neither need nor want your forgiveness. I'll just carry on sleeping with your ex-husband and you can carry on sleeping with Nico if you want. Let's leave it at that, Camilla. OK?'

How could Roz be so vindictive, Camilla wondered, as she watched her stalk out of the cloakroom with her spiky dark head held high. Stunned, she sank into the only chair and tried to understand what she had done to deserve such a bitter reaction.

Roz was still distraught over Nicolette's death, there was

that; but was it the whole reason, or simply an excuse?

And yes, it *was* an excuse. Roz's final words had given her away, and that was something else which hurt for a different reason. Roz knew about Nico and herself, which could only mean that Nico had told her. Camilla felt betrayed. How could he have done that?

Minutes later, she left the cloakroom and made her way back to the party, more determined than ever not to let Roz spoil her evening. The two of them would never be friends. She knew that now.

She would just ignore her in future. One cautious overture of friendship had been thrown back in her face. There would be no need for any more.

What hurt most of all was the discovery that Nico had betrayed her.

That hurt a lot.

Seeking the reassurance of Matt's smile, his strong arm around her shoulder, Camilla made her way back to the party. Vampires was still crowded; everyone was enjoying themselves immensely and the noise level had soared.

Christo Moran pressed a glass of champagne into Camilla's hand as she passed him at the bar, and gave her fingers a sympathetic squeeze. Dear Christo, she thought with a rush of gratitude. He didn't say much, but like the excellent barman he was, he missed nothing.

'They've both left,' he said in an undertone which enhanced his smooth, southern Irish accent. 'Don't let the woman upset you, darlin'. She simply can't bear the fact that you're doing better than she is.'

'Better?' There was a catch in Camilla's voice. 'What does that mean?'

'Everyone likes you,' Christo stage-whispered, a smile curling at the corners of his wide mouth. 'You have real friends. That's what really counts and Roz Vallender's only just begun to realize it.'

'Oh,' she said, surprised and cheered by his words. Impulsively she kissed his pale, freckled cheek. 'What a nice thing to say. Thank you.'

'It's the truth,' said Christo simply. 'Be happy.'

Loulou was seated opposite Laszlo de Lazzari. They were playing poker now. Mac, looking distinctly alarmed, whispered to Camilla that in the ten minutes she had been absent, Loulou had lost £150,000. Camilla stared at him in disbelief.

'Why?' she said at last, so horrified that it was the only word she could formulate.

'She's flipped. That pirate's wiping the floor with her. She hardly even knows how to *play* poker.'

'Then stop her!'

Mac looked grim, his dark brows drawing down into a straight line. 'I tried to. She said it was her money. Jesus . . .' He broke off, appalled, as Loulou threw down a pair of tens. De Lazzari regarded her blankly for less than a second before placing his own cards face-up on the green baize. A royal flush. Loulou smiled and shrugged, and watched him write a new figure on the pad beside him.

Camilla, unable to simply stand by and watch, said: 'Loulou, what the hell do you think you're doing?'

'Having fun,' Loulou replied cheerfully. 'Now don't nag, Cami. I'm enjoying myself.'

'What did I tell you?' murmured Mac through clenched teeth.

He shook his head. 'She's flipped. Gone mad. I can't watch any more.'

As he turned and made his way through the mass of people behind him, Matt reappeared at Camilla's side and trailed his finger down her bare back. Minutes before, she had yearned for such a gesture to break the dark spell of Roz's vindictiveness, but that was forgotten now. She clung to his arm and said nothing, her gaze fixed unswervingly upon the cards which de Lazzari was dealing out with long, expert fingers and a bleak, dangerously intent smile.

At two o'clock exactly, the very last rocket exploded overhead into an inky, starry sky and Loulou sat back in her chair with a sigh.

The game was over. At last. And any minute now, the game would also be up.

'An exhilarating evening,' commented Laszlo de Lazzari, his voice barely making itself heard above the clamour of the crowd. Studying the writing pad with care, he added, 'You owe me two million pounds. This is, I believe, the current market value of Vampires. I would, therefore, be happy to accept this property in lieu of cash.'

'Just as well, really,' said Loulou, grinning across at Camilla, who felt sick. 'And since it would take far too long to sort out all the legal work now, here are some deeds which I had drawn up earlier.'

With due solemnity, Christo handed her the black briefcase from which, recently, she had seldom been parted. Adopting the teasing air of a magician, Loulou slowly drew out a sheaf of documents and laid them across the table. A dawning suspicion began to uncurl in Camilla's mind and when she glanced across at Mac, who had been drawn helplessly back to the table to watch and had been chain smoking and drinking straight Scotch, she saw her suspicions reflected in his own face. Poppy, who had been glued to the game from the beginning, leant so far over Loulou's shoulder in order to see the documents that her breasts came perilously close to escaping over the front of her white sequinned dress.

'His name's already printed on the deeds,' she squealed, and Loulou burst out laughing, holding her swollen stomach with both hands. A fresh buzz of noise broke out from the people clamouring around the table; some began to laugh with her. Laszlo de Lazzari rose to his feet and raised one hand for silence.

'Ladies and gentlemen,' he began as a flashbulb exploded. 'I arrived in England only a few months ago, but it did not take me long to realize that the famous character of the English is still very much alive. Loulou is by blood only half-English, but I think that no-one will disagree with me when I say that she is a lady of true, and quite magical, character.'

Still not entirely sure what was happening, everyone nevertheless cheered and applauded. Camilla, riveted by de Lazzari, slowly began to realize that his former aloofness had melted like mist. His voice, too, was warm. And the terrifyingly bleak smile had been replaced by an almost shy, natural one.

'When she sold Vampires to me four days ago, it was on the understanding that this little game should take place tonight. Both fascinated and bemused by such an unusual stipulation, I was compelled to agree. It was to be good entertainment for her guests, she explained, although I have to confess,' he paused, his good eye sweeping the circle of faces around him, 'that I began to be concerned for the health of some of you as the game progressed.'

Matt laughed uproariously at this although Mac, Camilla observed, was still looking concerned. But then he was also digesting the news that Loulou had sold Vampires. For the life of her she couldn't imagine why Loulou should have taken such a drastic step; the famous wine bar and restaurant had been her whole life. And what on earth would she do with the money?

'So I hope that you have all had the enjoyable evening she worked so hard to achieve,' continued de Lazzari. 'And I trust that you will put your hands together and applaud your lovely hostess, particularly when I tell you that the money raised by the sale of Vampires – *all* the money raised by the sale of Vampires – has been donated by Loulou to the charity for which this evening was arranged. Funds for the much-needed research into the tragic condition known as Sudden Infant Death Syndrome, or Cot Death, have been boosted by over two million pounds, thanks to this magnificent young lady. So will you please join me . . .'

Tears were streaming down Camilla's cheeks as she applauded wildly along with everyone else. She couldn't get close to Loulou; at the moment she was being engulfed by hugs from people congratulating her. It was several minutes before she could manage to disentangle herself and make her way over to Mac, who had hung back. Camilla watched as she approached him, almost shyly, and held out one hand.

'I did it for you, too,' Loulou told him, her voice husky. 'Vampires was the cause of our splitting up. I decided that I could do without it.'

Wordlessly, Mac took her into his arms and held her.

'And if you tell me off for playing such a lousy game of cards,' Loulou added some time later, 'then all I can say is how well would you play if you'd been in labour for the last two and a half hours?'

'Jesus!' exclaimed Mac, his black eyes filled with horror. 'You really *are* mad. You should be in hospital . . .'

Loulou hesitated for a second, before asking the most difficult question of her life. 'Mac, I was wondering. I know it's an enormous favour to ask . . . but would you come with me? Please?'

Chapter 35

Pacing the tiny, smoke-filled waiting-room, Mac watched a murky grey dawn break over the spires and roofs of London from his eighth-floor window. Earlier, another man had paced with him, accentuating his own tormented anxieties.

'Your first baby?' he had asked Mac, and Mac had felt a tightening in his chest as he sought a suitable reply. How on earth could he say: 'It might be,' to this equally agitated stranger?

In the end he had nodded and prayed that a nurse would not erupt into the room announcing 'Mr Mackenzie, your ex-wife has given birth to a fine healthy black baby.' If she had to say it, then at least let it be when he was on his own . . .

And thankfully, when the nurse did at last arrive, she had beamed at the other man. 'Congratulations, Mr Rowlands, you have a handsome baby son. If you'd like to come along with me now . . .'

Mac had shaken hands with the stranger, had wished him and his family well. 'A son,' the man had said over and over again, pumping Mac's hand and shaking his head with disbelief. 'I have a son. Well, good luck,' he had added over his shoulder as he left the room with the nurse.

'Thanks,' said Mac awkwardly. Good luck. That was something he needed. He might be just about to become a father himself. And on the other hand, he thought with dismal uncertainty, he might not. He might be just about to become . . . nothing at all.

He would know, of course, from the expression on the nurse's face when she arrived. What he would do after that he had absolutely no idea.

At nine twenty-four on the morning of 6 November the nurse returned.

He knew, of course, from the expression on her pink face. And turned away to gaze fiercely at the pale green wall.

'Mr Mackenzie?' she enquired, and with reluctance Mac turned slowly back to look at her.

'Yes?' He felt sorry for her. It couldn't be easy, having to alter the format. She spoke carefully. 'Miss Marks has a beautiful baby girl. If you'd like to come with me . . .?'

He felt as if he were being slowly torn apart. His whole world had collapsed. For a brief moment the sea green walls swam before him. He wasn't a new father. The nurse knew that. He was *nothing*.

'Miss Marks asked to see you,' said the young nurse, embarrassed by his silence and by the entire situation. She had only been working in obstetrics for four months and it was the first time something like this had happened. The mother should have told them, she thought with a trace of resentment, then at least they could have been more prepared.

Mac wanted to say, 'Give me five minutes on my own first', but he knew that if he did, he would never go in. Still without saying a word, he moved towards the door and indicated with a slight nod of his head that she should lead the way.

Loulou lay back, propped up by half a dozen pillows, strands of blonde hair clinging to her damp forehead. Her enormous silver-grey eyes, Matt noticed, were filled with incandescent joy and for just a fraction of a second he felt a surge of hope.

It was dashed for ever, a moment later, as Loulou folded

back the white blanket in which the baby – not *his* baby – was wrapped. Mac, trying hard not to look, briefly glimpsed honey-coloured skin and a tangle of delicate black hair. Loulou reached out to him with her free hand, just as she had last night at Vampires, and fighting the sick, stone-like sensation in the pit of his stomach, Mac went towards her, forcing himself to plant a dry kiss on her temple.

'Oh darling, isn't it incredible? I've done it . . . actually *done* it,' breathed Loulou, and he straightened, stood awkwardly beside the bed, avoided looking at the baby cradled in her slender arms.

'Congratulations.'

'Isn't she fabulous? Don't you think she's just the most gorgeous thing ever? Would you like to hold her, darling?'

How was it possible to feel this empty? wondered Mac, his mouth set with pain, his fists clenching. How could he be grieving for the loss of a baby which had never existed, not even for a moment? And how the *hell* could Loulou lie there and ask him to hold this baby, this cuckoo which had lain so long in the nest of her womb, and which was nothing to do with him at all?

The grief and unfairness of it all threatened to engulf him and he turned away. 'I have to go. I'll let Camilla know . . . she'll come and see you . . .'

'Mac, wait,' said Loulou, but he had gone. So quickly that she hadn't even realized he was leaving. She sighed and sank back against the pillows, stroking the dusky, petal-soft skin of her daughter's perfect cheek. Mac didn't understand, she realized. He was upset. She could understand that, because she had expected to feel the same way herself, after hoping for so long that the child would turn out to be his.

But what she hadn't expected was the incredible tidal wave of rapturous, uncomplicated, delirious joy which had swamped her at the exact moment of birth. Nothing had prepared her for that, and it was presumably why Mac had been unable to understand, as she did with an incredible, perfect certainty, that it didn't *matter* who the father of her baby was. The fact that she had been born was all that mattered . . .

Nico and Caroline were having a monumental row when the phone rang, the first really major one of their relationship. It was almost a relief, Nico realized, to hear her screaming out her grievances, to know that she, too, had recognized the faults in their marriage.

And how ironic, he thought to himself as Caroline yanked a nicely framed Hockney print from the wall and hurled it across the room, that the source of this fight should be Loulou, of whom Caroline had so reminded him when he had first encountered her on that hot, dusty street in Las Vegas.

At least she had gone up in the world, he decided, struggling to keep a straight face; then she had been throwing a packet of soap powder around. Now it was an expensive bit of artwork.

'You care more about that tart than you do about me,' she yelled, reaching for the next print along the wall. Nico lunged forward and grabbed both her hands, his green eyes fiery with anger.

'She is *not* a tart, and if you throw one more picture I'll . . .' Words failed him; he didn't know what he would do. And how could he deny the former accusation when they both knew it to be true?

'Of course she's a tart.' Caroline winced as his grip on her wrists tightened, but the expression on her face remained

ferocious, mean with jealousy. The healthy tan she had worn
when she first met him had faded now and her pale skin looked
tired and dull. Even the striking dark blue of her eyes seemed to
have dimmed in the months since they had been back in
England. Only the thick, tawny brown hair and her spectacularly
curving figure were unchanged, he realized. And they no longer
thrilled him.

The attraction – it had never been love – had withered and
died.

'I'm your *wife*,' she was shouting now, pulling against the
iron grip of his fingers, 'and you told me on the phone last
night that you couldn't get back from Paris until the weekend.
Oh but then, this morning,' she went on, her voice awash with
sarcasm, 'you somehow managed to hear that your precious
Loulou had given birth. And *somehow* you managed to drop
everything and catch the first plane back here. And without
even letting me *know* that you were back you went straight to
the bloody hospital to see her. You bastard, can't you understand
how that makes me feel? Hasn't it even occurred to you to
wonder what other people are going to make of it all . . . not to
mention the Press?'

Nico shook her, not hard enough to hurt her, just enough to
make her listen.

'Lou's been a friend of mine for years. A damn good friend.
She's just had her first child. She isn't in the easiest of situations,
and at the moment she *needs* her friends. The last show in Paris
was cancelled because of a television strike and maybe, just
maybe, if you had just given birth to your first child I would
have flown back and visited *you* first.'

'Well, that really would be a miracle,' shrieked Caroline, her
mouth stretching into a furious narrow line, 'because I don't

know how they think it happens in bloody Italy, but over here you have to have some kind of a sex-life before the woman gets pregnant.'

In the loaded silence which followed they realized that the telephone on the table beside them was ringing. Caroline jerked away and lashed out with one foot in its direction. With a swift movement Nico released her and picked up the phone. Any excuse to interrupt the argument. Even if it was Monty Barton, he thought grimly, calling to complain about the striking French technicians, he would keep him talking for half an hour.

'Yes?' he said curtly into the receiver.

'Hi,' said Mac, his own tones equally curt. 'It's me. Isn't life a bitch? Are you busy tonight or would you keep an old friend company while he really ties one on?'

'I'll join you,' said Nico, relieved. 'Hang on; I'll be there in fifteen minutes.'

Chapter 36

The usual gaggle of papparazzi were hanging around outside Luigi's when Nico and Mac arrived by taxi, but at least once they were inside they would be undisturbed. Having had an armful of fan mail flung into his face by Caroline earlier, accompanied by a wailed; 'If they knew what a sod you really were they wouldn't write this crap,' Nico had chosen the evening's watering hole with care. As soon as they had run the gauntlet of exploding flashbulbs at the door, Luigi himself would ensure that they had privacy and the freedom to behave as badly as they liked.

'Hey, Nico . . . how's the wife?' shouted one of the photographers, and he turned and gave him a flashy smile.

'How was Paris?'

'How's Loulou Marks?'

'How's Roz Vallender?'

'How would you like your neck stretched?' murmured Nico through gritted teeth, making sure that only Mac could hear. 'Come on, let's get inside. I can't stand the sight of blood.'

Three bottles of wine and half a bottle of Remy Martin later, both men were feeling better, alcohol having blurred the edges of their respective troubles. Luigi had joined them earlier, falling briefly asleep at the table, and two unsubtle young actresses had slid into chairs opposite them, staying for three glasses of wine before realizing how unwelcome they were.

Now they were alone, Mac pulling desultorily at a lobster claw and Nico pouring a hefty measure of cognac into his coffee.

'I don't even know what she's calling it,' said Mac gloomily, swallowing the succulent lobster meat without even tasting it.

'Liliane. Lili. It was her grandmother's name, apparently.'

'The old woman would turn in her grave.'

'Come on, Mac. It isn't a crime.'

Mac nodded, looking thoughtful. 'Ah, but you haven't been married to Loulou. You don't know how I feel. She's done some crazy things in her time, but this is the craziest. Giving two million pounds to that charity runs it a close second. Jesus – if that baby had been mine I was going to ask her to marry me. Again. *Despite* everything she's put me through.' Now he was shaking his dark head. 'I'm the one who must be crazy. What a mess.'

'Getting married doesn't help,' declared Nico, lighting a cigarette with the air of one who knows. 'I only did it to get Roz off my back. Finding someone who had never even heard of me, someone I knew wasn't only interested in me for my money . . . that was a bonus. I thought it was fate.' He raised his cup, draining it. 'Now I know it was bloody fatal. Even marrying Roz couldn't have been worse.'

'Shame about Nicolette. Hers . . . yours . . . do you think she really was yours?' asked Mac, who was fast becoming obsessive where paternity was concerned and who knew he could ask Nico anything. They had known each other for several years now and their friendship had been so effortlessly and instantly forged that it seemed much longer than that.

Nico shrugged. 'Who can say? It was a possibility, I suppose. I felt as guilty as hell when she died, but when I heard what was wrong with her . . . I didn't know until afterwards . . . it sounds terrible, but I was almost relieved. Is that sick?'

'Of course it isn't. Only natural. Roz was looking OK last night, anyway. She turned up with Camilla's ex-husband of all people and apparently had a real go at Camilla before she left for having the nerve to write to her after the baby died.' He sighed heavily. 'What a bitch.'

Nico couldn't help it; the mention of Camilla's name jolted him. She could still have that effect. He hadn't got her out of his system yet. For a moment he was unable to speak without giving himself away, and his confused feelings for Camilla were about the only secret he had kept entirely to himself. Mac had no idea.

'Poor Camilla,' went on Mac, refilling his glass and failing to notice the pause. 'For some reason or other Roz has given her a pretty hard time over the past year.'

For a moment Nico wondered whether to confide in Mac, then through the haze of alcohol remembered why he hadn't done so before. He had failed Camilla in bed. Those kind of details he preferred to keep to himself.

The next afternoon when Nico finally arrived home, he had come to one conclusion. Dinner at Luigi's followed by four bottles of Dom Perignon at Tramp, chased down by the remains of Mac's drinks cabinet had steadily clarified his dilemma and its obvious solution.

Having spent the night in Mac's spare bedroom, and awoken with a bone-crushing hangover, much of the previous night's conversation had faded into merciful oblivion.

Only the idea – and subsequent decision – remained clear, crystallized and necessary in his mind. His marriage was over – if it had ever truly existed. The sooner he put an end to it, the easier it would be for both Caroline and himself.

It was the best thing all round, without question.

And in Caroline's present mood, he realized, it should be easy enough to persuade her that he was right. Undoubtedly it would cost him a great deal of money . . . he wasn't naïve enough to think otherwise. Equally undoubtedly such a very short marriage, and on the heels of his disastrous liaison with Roz, would result in scandal, bad publicity, general loss of favour. Monty would flip when he heard the news. The Press would speculate wildly, probably put it about that he was gay.

His mother would be distraught.

It was raining slightly as he stepped out of the car, a grey chilly drizzle which clung to him, coating his blond hair and white cotton shirt with a layer of dampness too light to permeate. The gravel, gleaming wet, crunched beneath his feet as he turned towards the house.

Was Caroline even there, he wondered, after last night? He hoped she would be reasonable and listen calmly to what he had to say. Any more appalling fights like yesterday's and his modest art collection – with a pang he recalled Camilla's innocent joy when he had brought home the five Hockney prints – would be lost.

Caroline was waiting, if that was the word, in the sitting-room. Nico ground to a halt in the doorway when he saw her. His first thought was that she had been on the vodka and tonic with a vengeance.

'Darling, thank goodness you've come home,' she said, rising from the settee and moving towards him with a slow, sinuous sway. Naked but for cream silk knickers, a matching bra and suspender belt, her excellent legs encased in the sheerest silk stockings and ivory high-heeled shoes, she pressed herself against him and in his state of shock all Nico could say was, 'It's raining; I'm wet.'

'Good,' murmured Caroline, sliding her arms around his neck and burying her face against his open shirt front. 'Nico, I'm sorry about last night. I love you so much; it was crazy to fight like we did. I don't know what I'd do if we broke up. I was jealous but I know now how wrong I was. Loulou's your friend and I had no right to interfere. Forgive me, hmm?'

As she spoke she was moving against him, her barely contained breasts rubbing sensuously across his chest, her pelvis sliding against his own. Despite himself, Nico felt his body responding. Caroline was running her hot, wet tongue along the line of his collarbone, her hair brushing his skin. The sex between them – before he had begun avoiding it – had always been fantastic. Inhaling a delicious waft of Caroline's perfume he felt himself weakening, remembering how erotic it felt to be undisguisedly seduced by a woman, and allowed her fingers to trail down towards the front of his black denims.

This wasn't what was supposed to happen, he thought, his mind dazed by lust, his own fingers expertly unfastening her bra so that those generous breasts could spring free . . . but it had been so long . . . and this was his wife, after all . . . and he knew he could please *her* . . .

'Don't leave me,' whispered Caroline against his neck, as he slid her panties down to her trembling knees. 'Forgive me, stay with me, I swear I won't ever make you angry again. Just make love to me, Nico . . .'

Chapter 37

'Christo, if you tell me now that there is no hot water I shall make *you* babysit all night, and it will serve you bloody well right for being so mean with that immersion tank. I'm going to a wedding, for Chrissake . . . I can't go smelling of baby-sick.'

Christo swept the baby, Lili, from her mother's arms and held her high in the air to gurgle contentedly above him.

'Electricity costs money. Happily,' he said, teasing her, 'today is Tuesday and I still have some. So you may have your bath, Cinderella. Did you really think I'd let you go to the wedding of the year without one?'

'You're an angel.' Loulou dropped a kiss on to his russet head, then pulled a face at Lili whose black saucer eyes were only inches from her own. 'And so are you,' she murmured lovingly, addressing her daughter and tweaking one of the pink ribbons which had by some miracle stayed in her fine candy-floss hair for over ten minutes. 'Just be good for Christo while Mummy has her bath and then we'll get you dressed. Seven weeks old and you're going to your first wedding. Who's a lucky girl?'

It was Christmas Eve and Loulou had never been happier. As she sank into the hot bath she reflected for the hundredth time how absolutely right she had been to give up Vampires.

Vampires had been fun, but it was also a lot of hard work and an enormous responsibility. And while some women managed to carry on in business when their children were born, Loulou wondered how they coped. Lili took up not only all her time, but her emotions too. Loving someone with such intensity, she had discovered, left no room for anyone or anything else. And loving a tiny human being with ravishing black eyes, a perfect rosebud mouth, irresistible dimples and the most adorable fingers and toes she had ever seen was *so* much more fun than loving a wine bar – or even a man – that she was completely hooked.

Thank heavens, she thought with a smile, for darling Christo.

By closing her mind to the possibility that Lili might not have been Mac's daughter she had blithely assumed that once she had given up her business and her home, he would invite her to live with him. They had been getting on together so wonderfully that it had seemed the obvious thing to do. They would live together, a proper family, and be disgustingly happy for the rest of their lives.

But Mac had taken the news of Lili's undoubted paternity extremely badly and as a result had missed out on all the happiness in which Loulou was so luxuriously wrapped. Instead it had been Christo who, having had the foresight to consider what might ensue, had come to Loulou's rescue. He had been renting a small flat in Kensington with an Australian who was now returning home to Sydney, he explained to her. A room was therefore available, the rent was reasonable and the landlord was agreeable. Christo, who had arrived from southern Ireland three years ago with nothing, had never forgotten how Loulou had given him a job and installed him in her spare room until he could find a place of his own. They had always got on well together. Now it was his turn to help the impulsive, generous, wayward girl who had done so much for him in the past.

Touched beyond words, Loulou had hugged him so hard that

his lungs almost collapsed. Four days after Lili was born they had both moved into the tiny flat with Christo and from the sale of her own furniture and other possessions she raised enough money to pay her share of the rent for almost two years. Further ahead than that she couldn't think. Fate, she had told Camilla airily, would take care of her. Money wasn't important, after all.

Hair dripping, slender body gleaming wet, she stepped out of the bath and considered her flat stomach with pride. Then her glance fell upon her watch lying in the soap dish and she saw with horror that it was one o'clock. In less than an hour Nico and Caroline would be arriving to give her – and Lili of course – a lift to the Register Office. The wedding was scheduled to kick off at two fifteen.

No-one who chooses to get married on Christmas Eve has any right to expect good weather. When the day dawned frosty-white, sparkling and sunny, Matt kissed Camilla and said with a grin, 'Just lucky, I guess. Someone up there must like us.'

'Stop gloating,' Camilla told him, deftly removing the glass of champagne from his hand and placing it safely on the table. 'Save your energy for catching Marty. It sounds as if he and Toby are murdering Charlotte and I don't want blood splattered all over her new dress.'

'Ah, this is the life,' said Matt cheerfully, pinching her bottom as he went past. 'My future wife and I, alone together at last. With three wild children all hell bent on killing each other. Bliss.'

'Alone together,' murmured Matt at two o'clock as they travelled in the pale grey, chauffeur-driven Rolls, which he had insisted on hiring, to the Register Office in Knightsbridge. On

334

his left, squeezed between himself and Camilla, sat Charlotte. Toby was perched on the very edge of the seat on his right, polishing his new shoes with a clean handkerchief. Sprawled across Matt's lap and singing a wordless song at the top of his voice was Marty. Across the top of Charlotte's head his eyes met Camilla's and his heart leapt. He couldn't wait to marry her and make her noisy, quarrelling, loving collection of children – both real and borrowed – at least partly his own. He couldn't wait to make her pregnant and add to the brood. He wanted it all, now. He couldn't wait.

'. . . I now pronounce you man and wife,' concluded the Registrar and Marty, who knew only that Matt had at last released his firm grip on his hand, broke into a fresh chorus of song in celebration. Matt burst out laughing and lifted him into the air. Suddenly everyone was kissing everybody else. Charlotte, planting a shy kiss on Matt's cheek, whispered, 'Are you my daddy now?' and he melted.

'No sweetheart, you'll always have the same daddy. I'm your stepfather, but I think it's easier if you just call me Matt.'

'Oh,' said Charlotte thoughtfully. 'Will you buy me Christmas presents, though?'

'Definitely,' Matt assured her and she brightened. Initially truculent, she had metamorphosed in recent weeks into a kind, if somewhat bossy, ten year old. 'That's OK then. Do you want me to look after Marty for you so that you can kiss some more people?'

Nico hung back, wishing that he hadn't come. Watching Camilla marry someone else – someone who so obviously made her happy – wasn't easy and the fact that he couldn't find anything about Matt Lewis to dislike didn't help. Besides, he thought unhappily, standing witness to all this undiluted joy only brought home to him how messed up his own life was. Caroline had made a terrific effort in the last couple of months and had been particularly understanding since he had been racing to finish his new album.

The only trouble was, he reflected as he watched Loulou fling her arms around Matt's neck and give him a noisy kiss, the nicer Caroline was, the more guilty he felt because he couldn't love her. If only she would do something *wrong* . . . give him a reason not to love her . . . it would be so much *easier* . . .

Caroline, at his side, gently nudged him. 'You haven't congratulated them,' she said in a low voice, carefully controlled, determined not to betray the fact that she was desperately jealous of Nico's past relationship with Camilla. Only the fact that he had been so reluctant to come to the wedding told her how much he still cared, and that made Camilla far more of a threat than Loulou in Caroline's eyes. Or she would have been, if she hadn't just married that gorgeous Matt Lewis.

Camilla, who had just dismantled her bouquet of white roses and baby's breath and tucked the delicately fragrant flowers into the hair of first Charlotte then Zoë's children, Gussie and Fee, glanced up and saw Nico making his way towards her. She straightened, felt a moment of awkwardness and hoped it didn't show in her smile. It had been Loulou's idea, of course, that Nico should be invited. He would be hurt, she had insisted, if he weren't. And Camilla was quite unable, without going into very private details, to persuade her otherwise. She had half-hoped that he would have been unable to attend. Even loving Matt as much as she did hadn't killed her feelings for Nico. And after the way she had treated him she should be grateful, she supposed, that he had had the decency to come to her wedding.

'Congratulations,' said Nico, inclining his head and kissing Camilla's cheek. She breathed in the familiar scent of his after-shave and longed suddenly to hug him.

'Thank you, Nico. And thank you for coming. I'm glad you did.'

'Why wouldn't I?' He smiled, and the lie came easily. 'We're friends, aren't we? Matt's a lucky man.'

'I'm lucky, too,' she told him simply. 'When you think what I was like only a year ago.'

And when you think of everything that has happened since then . . . the thought sprang, unspoken, between them both and Camilla smiled, reached out and touched his hand. The spon-taneous gesture had far more effect than the sterile kiss which had preceded it and instantly she regretted making it. Nico looked uncomfortable and she drew back, glancing past him at Caroline who had now been drawn into conversation with Matt's younger brother, Lloyd.

'There's probably another wedding party outside, the Regis-trar's looking twitchy. I think we'd all better start making a move.'

Grateful for the change of subject Nico relaxed, his green eyes sparkling with humour as he glanced across at the fidgeting man. 'Loulou thinks he's on speed. Apparently he officiated at one of her weddings – it must have been the last one – and he was just as twitchy then.'

'He probably got nervous when he saw Loulou,' said Camilla. 'Maybe he thought she was going to get married again.'

Eventually the Registrar's office was cleared and everyone piled into their cars. Despite Camilla's horrified protest at the thought of what it would cost him, Matt had decided that the reception had to be held at the Ritz. He had also booked a suite there for the week, after wisely informing his excitable golfing friends that he would be spending his honeymoon at the Carlton Towers.

Jack, it had been arranged, would turn up at six o'clock to take Toby, Charlotte and Marty back home with him. When Camilla had informed him of her imminent remarriage they had sat down together to discuss the children's lives. Making no mention of the night he had turned up with Roz at Vampires, she had persuaded him that their shared custody should now become more equal. Jack needed a certain amount of free time and she needed her children. Now that Matt had bought a large five-bedroomed house in Belgravia, they were well able to accommodate them. She had been terrified that, seeing how much it mattered to her, he would create difficulties, but to her surprise and relief Jack had agreed. Both children, he admitted, had missed her. They weren't always easy to cope with, although he was pleased with the way Charlotte was maturing. And besides, he added, he wasn't one to hold a grudge.

'*He* doesn't hold a grudge!' Matt had exploded when Camilla related the conversation to him afterwards. 'How bloody noble can the lying bastard get?'

It had all been amicably sorted out and Camilla wondered if it was possible to be any happier than she now was. From persuading Jack to share the children with her, it was a relatively easy step getting him to accept Marty. Like both Charlotte and Toby he had had initial reservations, but meeting him swiftly overcame such flimsy obstacles. With his new, spiky haircut, irresistible, ever-present smile and gradually expanding vocabulary – he could now say Tom and Jerry, hug me, hole-in-one, champion and shit with embarrassing fluency – he had bombarded the family with affection and an infectious giggle.

Marty's mother, struggling with six other children and a 'husband' who seldom came home, was pathetically grateful to Camilla for giving Marty the love and attention she was unable to afford herself. Charlotte wiped strands of saliva and smears of chocolate from Marty's mouth with the practised ease of a nurse, assuming as she did so a slightly bossy, long-suffering air which reduced Matt to fits of laughter. Toby spent endless hours trying to teach the distractable Marty how to play football. 'Mum,' he complained eventually, 'Marty doesn't understand about goals. He keeps pulling up the posts and saying "Champion". He's even worse at football than Charlotte.'

Camilla watched them now with pride as they played together at a circular table in the lavish, high-ceilinged ivory and gold Berkeley Suite at the Ritz. The day was perfect and realizing it, tears of happiness sprang to her eyes.

Hastily blinking them back and taking a sip of pink champagne, she gazed around the room, observing the other guests. Matt's parents, Paula and Tom, were laughing at one of Nico's dead-pan jokes. Caroline was deep in discussion with Lloyd, not for the first time that afternoon. Her sleek, honey-brown head bent close to his dark one and from time to time she glanced sideways at Nico to see if he was paying attention. Zoë and Loulou also seemed to be enjoying themselves with two of Matt's friends. The ultramarine dress Loulou wore was borrowed, for hardly any of her pre-pregnancy, notoriously close-fitting clothes fitted her post-pregnancy chest. Camilla was one of only a few people who knew that the nationwide publicity following Loulou's donation of 'all her wordly goods' to research into cot deaths had resulted in a wave of smaller donations being sent not only to the same charity, but also to Loulou herself. Quietly, and without fuss this time, she had written to each of these kind-hearted donors, thanking them and explaining that while she was grateful, she was passing the money on to the charity. Not a penny had been kept back for herself. And Camilla had found *herself* in the happy position of being able to lend Loulou her clothes for a change, their bust sizes now being almost identical.

Soon, more people would be arriving, she realized. Half a dozen or so of Matt's closer friends on the international golfing circuit were catching a flight over from Spain and spending Christmas in London. The English family with whom Paula, Tom and Lloyd Lewis were staying would be here, as would several of the models from Sheridan's, with whom Camilla had become friendly. Christo was holding the fort at Vampires tonight, but Daisy and Lena had both managed to take the evening off and would be arriving at any moment, dressed up to the nines in the hope of ensnaring a couple of the golfers.

And there was a possibility that Mac would turn up, too. Camilla had phoned him a fortnight ago, mentally prepared for a curt refusal. He hadn't seen Loulou since the morning Lili was born. She knew, because Nico had told Loulou who had in turn relayed the information to her, that Mac was bitter. And if there had been any chance at all of him forgiving her, it had apparently been dashed beyond hope by the news that Loulou was now living with Christo Moran.

'Typical,' he had told Nico with disgust. 'That woman isn't capable of living without a man. I would have thought that Christo at least might have had more bloody sense.'

He refused absolutely to believe that Loulou's relationship with Christo was platonic. 'She's a tart. She sleeps with anyone. And don't try and tell me she's changed because I *know* her. I know her only too bloody well.'

Thinking also that he might have arranged to spend Christmas up in Scotland Camilla had phoned him anyway, but to her surprise, Mac had thanked her and accepted the invitation. 'I'll bring my camera and take some thoroughly indiscreet, informal photos for your wedding album,' he had said cheerfully. 'Nico's going to be there too, isn't he?'

'Yes,' said Camilla, wondering whether her decision to invite Mac had been prompted by Loulou's insistence that Nico should be there. It was all so complicated, she barely understood it herself.

'Great,' said Mac. 'I'll see you there, then. But just don't expect me to speak to Loulou,' he had added in warning tones. 'Because I couldn't.'

Having just autographed a dozen gold-embossed menu cards for one of the waitresses, Nico tucked his pen back into the inside pocket of his suit jacket and watched Camilla and Matt dance together at the other end of the room.

Taking care to conceal his feelings, although why he felt it necessary when Caroline was continuing to flirt outrageously with Matt's good-looking younger brother, he realized the truth of Camilla's statement earlier that afternoon. She had come a long way.

Camilla was clearly one of those people, he thought with a flash of envy, who could put the past firmly behind them and if the events were not forgotten they were at least relegated to a level of such unimportance that they could cause no further pain.

Unlike his own, which occupied his thoughts night and day and refused to fade. If anything, he realized, the mismatch with Caroline only accentuated the unhappiness, made the might-have-beens more poignant and desirable. Life's a bitch, Mac had recently grown fond of informing him. And Nico was beginning to understand exactly what he meant.

Camilla was looking stunning tonight, the silky material of her dress shimmered beneath the warm silvery glow of light from the chandeliers, her eyes sparkled and she never seemed to stop smiling.

Radiant was the word, he supposed and shook his blond head slightly, mocking himself. I must be bloody mad, he thought, coming here today.

Loulou was infuriated to find herself glancing across the room each time the impressively carved, golden oak doors swung open to admit new arrivals. But Mac had told Camilla that he would be here and no matter how many times she told herself he no longer mattered, still her heart leapt and her head swung round like a bloody metronome whenever the doors moved.

Of all the lousy men in the world to have fallen in love with, she thought, Mac was the worst. He was so moody, so jealous and unpredictable ... and by renewing their friendship, but resolutely refusing to sleep with her, he had only enhanced the fascination, that mysterious aura of desirability. Not that she *would* have gone to bed with him, she reminded herself, but it would have been nice to have the chance to say no, particularly to Mac who appeared to believe that it was a word outside her vocabulary.

Hugging Lili to her, she caressed the wondrous curve of her daughter's cheek as she slept contentedly amidst the noise and celebration. Any minute now Daisy's sister, who had volunteered to babysit for the rest of the evening, would be arriving to take Lili back to Christo's flat. And any minute now, thought Loulou wistfully, since Camilla had warned her with gentle tact that he would probably ignore her, Mac might arrive.

'I saw you on TV the other afternoon,' Daisy was saying to one of the Spanish golfers, wondering if he would notice that she had undone an extra button on her shirt when he wasn't looking. 'I was very impressed with the way you handled your nine iron.'

'As I am impressed with *you*,' insisted Manuel, gazing at her pale cleavage with devotion.

At that moment, in the reflection from one of the enormous gilt-edged mirrors lining the walls, Daisy saw Mac arrive. Sliding off the edge of the table upon which she was perched, she nudged Lena furiously.

'Guess who's turned up?' In unison their heads swivelled to the left.

'And look what he's brought with him,' said Lena loudly, her voice betraying both admiration and dismay. 'Bloody hell. I bet Lou wasn't expecting this.'

Loulou wasn't. For some ridiculous reason, she told herself, the idea that Mac might bring someone with him had not even occurred to her. If she *had* been prepared, she would have been able to carry on without even missing a beat. As it was, however, she had to turn abruptly away and stare hard at a large bowl of creamy white lilies, willing her eyes not to fill with tears.

The hope, so faint that she had scarcely dared to acknowledge its existence, that she and Mac could somehow be reconciled and reunited, was dashed to smithereens like the champagne glass lying unnoticed beneath a chair.

Mac kissed Camilla on the cheek and shook Matt's hand. He looked relaxed and cheerful, almost triumphant as he introduced Cecilia Drew.

Camilla felt a stab of sympathy for Loulou, whose faint hope she had mutely shared. Cecilia Drew, with her hip-length ebony hair, topaz tiger's eyes and svelte six-foot figure was a formidable opponent, a force to be very seriously reckoned with. Even Loulou, no slouch in the looks department herself, could scarcely compete with such ferocious glamour.

The copper and gold bugle-beaded dress she wore, strapless and slit to the thigh, was incredibly over-the-top, yet if anyone could carry it off Cecilia Drew, *Vogue's* favourite model, star of a thousand catwalks and of a far grander agency than Sheridan's, could.

Her grip as she shook Camilla's hand was surprisingly firm. Her wide, gold-slicked mouth curled into a smile.

'Congratulations on your marriage,' she said in a low, carefully modulated voice strangely at odds with her startling appearance. 'Mac has told me a lot about you.'

Camilla didn't make the obvious reply but Matt, typically, had no such reservations.

'Well, Mac has certainly kept quiet about you,' he declared with open admiration, winking at Mac. Camilla nudged him in the ribs. Didn't he realize that Loulou, at the far end of the room, had turned back round and was now silently watching them? She looked as if someone was slowly pulling out all her toenails with steel pliers.

Mac, wickedly handsome in a white tuxedo, his pristine white dress shirt undone at the neck and his black bow-tie dangling, ran a proprietary hand down Cecilia's bare brown back. His black eyes, catching the light from the chandeliers as he tilted his head, glittered like coal. Helplessly, Camilla glanced across the room once more. Loulou's eyes were desolate with longing and pain. At that moment she could have kicked herself for inviting Mac. This wasn't what was meant to have happened. In trying to help, to be a good friend, she had only succeeded in making things a million times worse.

'We can't stay too long, I'm afraid,' said Mac. 'I do realize that you weren't expecting both of us, but I wanted Cecilia to meet you.'

'Stay,' urged Matt, reaching for a bottle of Krug and searching for a couple of glasses. Camilla realized that he simply didn't understand her frantic signals for him to shut up. He had got on well with Mac on that fateful night at Vampires and he couldn't see any reason why he should leave now that he was here.

Across the room, to her relief, she saw Nico leave Caroline's side and go to Loulou, placing a comforting arm around her slender shoulders.

Mac shook his dark head. 'No, really. Camilla understands why we have to leave.' He looked at Cecilia and Camilla saw with a sense of foreboding the odd expression of triumph in his eyes as he did so. 'We just wanted you to be the first to know. Cecilia and I have decided to follow your excellent example. We're getting married in the very near future ourselves.'

This time, even Matt was momentarily caught off balance. He finally realized what was really going on. Camilla felt as if she had been kicked in the stomach. In that slow second before Matt recovered and began a fresh round of handshakes, kisses and slightly forced congratulations, Camilla's gaze locked with Mac's and they exchanged a look which told her everything.

Nothing could have stopped him, she realized, and Loulou wasn't the only one who would suffer. Both Mac and Cecilia were victims, too, of his desperate compulsion to hurt her as she had hurt him.

But for the moment Mac was happy. He genuinely thought this was what he wanted. And he had done exactly what he had come here tonight to do.

Chapter 38

Being married again was wonderful, thought Camilla as she unpacked the last of the suitcases and shook sand out of a white silk skirt, but Loulou's unhappiness still hung like an ominous cloud over the horizon. The change in her was appalling and Camilla was genuinely concerned. Her friends were all standing by her, helping her as much as they dared – for she still had her pride and tried as hard as possible to present a brave front – but there was only one person who could cure her of the terrible depression and he was equally proud, equally determined to keep well away from her.

Mac and Cecilia were the darlings of the gossip columns. Everywhere you looked there they were, immortalized in black and white, presenting dazzling smiles to the cameras, whooping it up in Paris, Mustique, London and Gstaad. Camilla urged Loulou not to read the papers. Compulsively, Loulou devoured every one, hating herself for doing it and wondering why it hurt so damn much.

'I can't understand it,' she confessed when she had last seen Camilla and Matt. 'I'm *never* like this. It's pathetic. You can laugh your head off at me, Cami . . . remember all the brilliant advice I gave you? Remember how I bullied you, gave you a couple of weeks to get over Jack? And now here I am, not having even spoken to Mac for months, dripping like a hot tap all over your settee. Go on,' she added bitterly, 'have a good laugh.'

'We aren't laughing,' Camilla reassured her, taking her thin cold hand, 'and I feel terrible – I should never have invited Mac to our wedding reception.'

Loulou shook her head; even her hair looked tired these days, lacking its normal bounce and lustre. 'He would still have done it. But it's so *stupid* . . . nothing bothered me after Lili was born. I floated round on a cloud. I was happy and I didn't care too much about Mac doing his disappearing act. It wasn't until he turned up with Cecilia bloody Drew that it suddenly hit me. And who could compete with someone like her even if we were starting out on level pegging?'

It was as if she had given up, Camilla realized. Her fighting spirit was gone. Nico, to Caroline's semi-concealed fury, had carted Loulou and baby Lili off to his sisters in Bath, staying there with her for a week. That had really got the Press going. Speculation was rife. Neither Nico nor Loulou cared. The short break was pleasant enough and the mayhem which always reigned in the homes of Nico's beautiful sisters and their noisy families diverted Loulou's attention to a degree, but it didn't really help.

Laszlo de Lazzari, after a discussion with Christo, offered her a managerial position at Vampires, in the hope that working again would cheer her up. Loulou refused to even consider it. She needed time, she said, to think things through and sort herself out.

Roz invited her down to Gloucestershire and dragged her out to parties every night. People who had longed for years to meet the glamorous, effervescent Loulou Marks did so and were sorely disappointed. After five days Loulou escaped back to London, feeling like a hedgehog in search of somewhere to hibernate.

But Camilla wouldn't allow her to hibernate. With relentless determination she phoned Loulou, visited her at the flat and whenever possible dragged her and Lili back with her to the new house in Belgravia.

Lifting an ivory chiffon cocktail dress from the suitcase on the bed and slipping it on to a hanger, she decided to call Loulou as soon as the unpacking was finished and persuade her to come and stay for a few more days, at least. It had taken all Matt's efforts to persuade Camilla to go with him to southern Spain for the golf tournament in which he was competing. She had enjoyed herself enormously, but she was also glad to be back. Loulou needed her, having confessed that at least with Camilla she didn't feel she always had to put on a front. Camilla only wished that there was more she could do to help. Gin and sympathy sometimes simply weren't enough.

'Where's my wife?' demanded Matt loudly and Camilla met him halfway up the staircase, where he kissed her so thoroughly that they both ended up leaning against the elegantly curved banister rail.

'Hmm, not bad,' he remarked when they had regained their balance. 'For a newlywed, anyway.'

'Maybe I need a little more practice,' suggested Camilla, squirming with pleasure as he gently nuzzled her neck.

'Fifty or sixty years should do it. Shall we start now?'

He was easing her back up the stairs. Laughing, she ducked away.

'You're due at the television studios in less than an hour,' she reminded him, and Matt groaned in protest. Having missed several of the international tournaments during the relatively quiet season of the golfing calendar in order to spend more time with Camilla, he had agreed to allow his agent to step up the personality promotions. Public and TV appearances were lucrative and relatively hassle-free, and together with several new advertising deals they ensured that as Matt became more familiar to the public his popularity increased. His tousled good looks, easy-going personality and occasionally outrageous remarks endeared him to the general population and in the space of four months his fanmail had tripled.

This afternoon he was taking part in a light-hearted sports quiz show for the third time and the only drawback, as far as Matt was concerned, was having to wear television make-up.

'No time for a quickie?' he wheedled, trailing a finger up the outside of Camilla's tanned thigh.

'Absolutely not,' she replied firmly, although it was an exciting thought. 'Go and get ready. I'm going to phone Loulou, see if I can persuade her to come over.'

Matt headed towards the bathroom, pulling his black sweat-shirt over his head as he went. 'Tell her that if she does,' he said, his voice muffled by the folds of material, 'she can have my autograph.'

Still smiling to herself, thinking how lucky she was that Matt didn't mind Loulou's frequent visits – particularly when she was so often in low spirits – Camilla descended the stairs and made her way slowly across the hall to the sitting-room.

Pausing in the doorway, she admired the sun-filled L-shaped room, temporarily free from the clutter of the children's toys and games. It was really coming together now, all her hard work had paid off. The scent of roses, from two enormous bowls of creamy white blooms, one on each windowsill, filled the room.

Picking up the phone and punching out Loulou's number, Camilla wandered over to the mantelpiece and gazed with affection at the painting hanging above it. Matt, like so many

Americans, was obsessed with the history of England. Having developed a love affair with antique shops, he regularly returned home with hopelessly woodwormy cabinets, bookcases and curly-legged tables, exclaiming over their age and history. This painting, not woodwormy at all, displayed another aspect of his heritage; commissioned by him a week after their wedding, Toby and Charlotte had almost disowned him as a result.

'We're a family,' he had informed them, so bursting with enthusiasm that he failed to comprehend their lack of it. 'We've got to have a family portrait. It's an heirloom, you ignorant bunch of heathens. In a hundred years' time we'll all be gone but our painting will live on.'

Camilla had cringed at the time. Really, Matt did have the oddest ideas. And Toby and Charlotte had wriggled and complained for hours each time they had been press-ganged into sitting for the young, rather intense artist. Marty, refusing to be left out, had adored every moment, his endless singing almost driving them insane. But Matt had kept them going, encouraging them and adopting an enormous variety of suitably paternal poses.

And of course he was right; the family portrait was a miraculous success. Now even Charlotte could be persuaded to admit that it was perfect.

Camilla had fallen in love with it. There were Toby and Charlotte curled up on the settee, mischievous childlike smiles captured forever, with Marty grinning up from his beanbag on the floor between them. Camilla, perched on one arm of the settee, was smiling down at the children, and Matt, standing behind them all, was linking fingers with her as if it were a secret gesture, his own expression one of quite magical joy and pride.

It was a wonderful family portrait and now that Camilla had overcome her initial reluctance at the idea, she adored it.

'So you *are* there,' she exclaimed happily when Loulou at last picked up the phone. 'Are you coming over here for dinner this evening or do Matt and I have to wade through an entire side of beef on our own?'

'Sounds great,' said Loulou with more enthusiasm than Camilla had heard from her for a long time. Then she added shyly, 'OK if I bring a friend?'

Simon Mortimer was without doubt one of the most unsuitable men Loulou could possibly have chosen to help her back on to her feet emotionally, thought Camilla, trying very hard to find something likeable about him and realizing as she caught Matt's eye across the dinner table that he felt exactly the same.

Loulou, in her fragile state, had reverted to her old ways, finding the one man most likely to kick her while she was down. Attractive in a languid, Sebastian Flyte kind of way, Simon clearly found it amusing to slide obliquely snide comments into almost every sentence. Camilla couldn't believe that Loulou let him get away with it. When Simon ran a hand over her knee with a possessive gesture then remarked that it was about time she shaved her legs – which was patently untrue – she merely sat there and smiled. Camilla could remember a time in the not-too-distant past when Loulou would have brandished a knife at the offender's throat, and listened appalled as Simon ran down her dress sense, her laugh and her choice of scent which he declared made her smell like a whore's handbag.

Unable to help herself, she lied sweetly, 'I gave Loulou that scent for Christmas,' and waited for Simon to show some small sign of remorse.

Instead, he winked at Matt and said, 'Oh well, anyone can make a mistake.'

It was one of those very rare occasions when Matt was lost for words.

The evening dragged on interminably. When dinner was over, they moved from the dining-room to the sitting-room and Camilla held her breath as Simon lazily approached Matt's treasured family portrait. If he said one word . . . just one condescending word . . .

And it seemed as if he was able to detect the tension in the rose-scented air, or maybe he caught a glimpse of the expression in Matt's eye, for he turned and nodded at him. 'It's a good painting. Pick the right artist and you can make damn good investments these days. Ever thought of going into wine, Matt?'

It was the nicest thing he had said all evening. Matt grinned and replied, 'Almost every night, before dinner.'

Luckily, Simon had to be up at five the following morning; at midnight he left, alone, leaving Loulou – and Lili, asleep upstairs – to spend the night with Matt and Camilla. Kissing Loulou's forehead and affectionately patting her cheek, he said his goodbyes and disappeared into the night in his turbo-powered Porsche.

'I bet you hated him,' said Loulou with a teenager's defiance as she tucked her legs beneath her on the settee and accepted a small Sambucca from Matt. 'But he's very kind. He looks after me. And at least I know he isn't after my money.'

'I'm sure he's very nice,' said Camilla, casting helplessly around for something tactful to say. Sensing her hesitation, Loulou went on eagerly, 'He treats me like a lady. He hasn't even tried to get me into bed yet.'

'Probably as gay as a daisy,' muttered Matt under his breath. Aloud, he said, 'Lou, he treats you like shit. You can do a million times better than that.'

Camilla winced; Matt's normally endearing bluntness was sometimes downright alarming, although luckily if anyone could take it, it was Loulou.

'Maybe I can,' she replied with a spirited toss of her blonde mane, 'but right now, he's what I need. Look at Mac – everyone likes him, but he still dumped me. And I paid out two million for that pleasure. At least Simon accepts me for what I am.'

'He's still a shit,' said Matt, calmer now but wishing Loulou wouldn't simply accept her fate as if she had no control over it. Some women, he thought with frustration, he would never understand.

'And that's my trademark,' Loulou explained, draining her Sambucca and watching the coffee beans slide lazily down to the bottom of her liqueur glass. 'I always fall for the bastards. I'm too old to change my ways now.'

'How did the TV thing go this afternoon?' said Camilla, to change the subject. By the time Matt had got back from the studios it had been a rush to get ready for dinner and she had had no time to ask him about it.

'Fine. Jerry's leaving and they want me to be team captain for the next series. Guess who I saw in the canteen there?'

He glanced across from Loulou to Camilla and with a dull thud of premonition Camilla said, 'Roz.'

'Right,' said Matt, visibly impressed.

'Did she say anything?'

'She looked like she was in a hurry. All she did was smile and ask me if I was still married.'

'Bitch,' hissed Loulou, far more upset by Roz's behaviour

than by Matt's criticism of Simon. 'She's been really good to me, too. What on earth makes her act like a cow wherever Camilla's concerned?'

Simple, thought Camilla, averting her eyes. Nico.

Chapter 39

The applause was deafening as Nico moved into the last number of the evening, the finale to a two-hour concert which had electrified a wildly enthusiastic audience. Blue-white spotlights arced gracefully across the stage, panning out every thirty seconds or so over the crowds, now all standing, who had danced their way through the evening.

Roz, in the second row, smoothed her tan suede skirt over her hips and touched the breast pocket of her cream jacket to check that the mini tape recorder was still there. In the other pocket were her notepad and fountain pen. She didn't really need anything; her excellent memory could cope with any facts or figures she might learn, but she was able to acknowledge to herself now that they weren't the real reason for her presence here tonight. Officially, she would be interviewing Nico after the concert and assessing the feasibility of a ninety-minute TV documentary to be made, charting a week in the life of a rock star.

Unofficially, she was simply determined to get him back. Into her bed and into her life.

Hopefully, she thought with a secret smile, both projects would be successful.

Never having watched Nico singing live in concert before, she paid close attention now, admiring the skilful way he was able to keep the audience enthralled. Every single person there this evening had been totally won over by the brilliant production, the magical lighting system, the professionalism of the backing musicians and, most of all, by the way Nico talked to his audience, joked with his musicians and projected his charismatic personality throughout the auditorium. Blond hair gleaming, green eyes flashing, he moved around the vast stage with an athlete's grace, his tanned skin glistening with perspiration and his beautiful voice caressing every woman personally. In his plain white shirt and white Levis, he held the audience in his gentle grasp, teasing them, swaying in time with the beat and casting sensual glances in the direction of the front row. In that sea of faces, each one was convinced that he was directing those sultry looks at them alone.

The audience screamed with delight.

The concert was a dazzling success.

Roz eased her way through the side door as milling crowds yelled for an encore. Since they were pretty certain of getting one it was relatively easy for her to explain to the security guards who she was, to show them her passcard and be escorted to Nico's dressing-room without getting crushed in the process.

After the intense heat of the concert hall, and the clamour of a thousand different perfumes jostling for attention, the air-conditioned coolness of Nico's room was blissful. Pushing up the sleeves of her jacket and rapidly checking her appearance in the mirror above the make-up table – now littered with half-empty lager cans, a Walkman, two toothbrushes and a copy of last week's *Sporting Life* – Roz perched on the edge and took a sip from one of the cans of lager. Her pulse was racing, her knees were like jelly, and she realized that she hadn't experienced such a buzz of anticipation for years. It was almost like being sixteen again.

Ducking her head once more in order to glance at her reflection in the mirror she reassured herself that she was looking good. Modesty aside, very good ... This time Nico wouldn't be able to resist her.

On the last occasion, when she had gone to his house with Nicolette in her arms, she had been in a position of weakness. That had been so alien to her character that she hadn't been able to pull it off.

But a fortnight ago Sebastian had phoned her, his call as always coming out of the blue, and had informed her that he was coming over for a long weekend. No business meetings, no conferences to attend; he was simply going to spend three whole days relaxing with Roz at the cottage.

And it had been a blissful three days. Her toes still curled at the memory of their lovemaking. When Sebastian decided to relax he did so with as much dedication as he afforded his high-powered business in Zurich. They had eaten wonderful meals, drunk glorious wines, lazed in each other's arms, talked almost non-stop and indulged in the most delicious sex, blocking out the outside world completely and revelling selfishly only in each other.

Sebastian was the biggest ego-boost of all time and his visits to Roz seemed to be all the more precious because they were so limited.

And now, she thought with renewed confidence, examining her manicured fingernails and drumming them experimentally against the formica-topped dressing-table, now she was strong again. Which was how Nico liked her. So there would be no more begging or pleading, she reminded herself as she lifted her spiky, dark head and smiled at her reflection. This time she was going to get what she wanted.

And preferably, this time, for good.

As the dressing-room door was kicked unceremoniously open, Roz slid down from the ledge upon which she had been perched. Monty Barton, sweating and joyful, burst into the room with one of the backing singers plastered against his plump side.

He was beaming like a Cheshire cat, delighted that the concert had gone so well. Roz had caused her share of problems in the past – he had been fending off the Press for weeks over that controversial pregnancy of hers – but that was in the past now. He felt sorry for her, losing the baby so tragically, and she was, after all, a damn good TV presenter.

'Roz, it's great to see you!' he bellowed, as the rest of the band poured into the room behind him. Suddenly the place was heaving with stage crew, lighting and sound technicians, singers and musicians. Everyone was there except Nico.

And then suddenly he was there too, and Roz caught her breath. On stage he had been brilliant. Close up he was even more spectacular. She watched, unnoticed, as the two girl singers hugged and kissed him with the abandonment of post-concert euphoria. Champagne corks popped, flying through the air, and the noise level soared.

Without moving a muscle, she waited for him to notice her. Not even Nico at this moment had as much adrenalin pumping through his body as she did.

When their eyes at last met it seemed to Roz that the room had suddenly gone quiet. Her gaze fixed, she watched him move slowly towards her past Paddy the guitarist and the blond backing singer, his expression as inscrutable as ever. At the last moment, she allowed her mouth to relax into a faint smile.

'Hi, Nico. You're looking good.'

And almost as if she had willed it, the old glitter of interest was there in his narrowed green eyes once more.

'I didn't think you'd be here so soon.' He had known, of course, about the interview. It was when he had agreed to it that Roz had had her first inkling that their stormy relationship could be on the turn.

'Oh, I was watching you. Second row, right at the side,' she said, gazing now at his mouth. 'I didn't want to miss a thing.'

He nodded at the crowded room. 'They'll be going strong for hours. Do you want to stay or shall we go somewhere quiet to talk? The limo's outside.'

Roz, joyfully back in command again, realizing that she knew all she needed to know, automatically dropped into a lower gear. The sweet rush of adrenalin slowed to a steady stream. Nico wanted her and she was back in control.

'Oh, this is fun. Let's stay,' she said in a low voice, and registered the flicker of uncertainty in Nico's eyes. It wasn't what he had expected her to say, which was what made the situation so absolutely perfect.

'Right,' he said, his manner deliberately off-hand. 'Can I get you a drink?'

Roz smiled again. 'That would be nice. And then I'd like to talk to the band. I need some quotes to take back with me. Maybe you'd introduce me to that tall, rather gorgeous drummer of yours . . .'

The drummer's name was Shaun and he was about as quotable as Guy the Gorilla, but Roz strung out their conversation for as long as possible, savouring the buzz of anticipation. Briefly she spoke to the other members of the band, explaining to them the projected format for the documentary. All the time she was aware of Nico watching her across the smoke-filled room. The sensation it induced was like an addictive drug and Roz, frantic with lust inside, totally ignored him for over forty minutes.

When she eventually returned to his side he was emptying the remains of a bottle of indifferent champagne into a pint glass. A cigarette drooped from the corner of his exquisite mouth and his expression was less than sunny.

'Let's go,' she murmured, removing the glass from his hand. 'I don't want to be here any more.'

They slipped out without being noticed. About a hundred teenage girls were still hanging around by the stage door, but Nico's driver, Ken, was an old hand. Spotting Nico, he revved the engine. The security guards swiftly formed two lines and Nico and Roz ran between them, jumping into the back of the car and slamming the door shut behind them. Expertly nosing his way through the screaming crowds, Ken turned and winked at Roz.

'Easy when you know how. Where to, Nico?' Normally he said 'Straight home?' but then normally, he thought with a chuckle, the boss didn't have a bird with him. He doubted whether Mrs Coletto would appreciate it if Nico turned up at the house with a girl as gorgeous as this one on his arm. And he'd only had a quick glimpse of her, but wasn't it Roz Vallender, the one who had caused so much trouble with the boss last year?

'My hotel?' said Roz in an undertone designed to send shivers down Nico's spine. 'I gave up the flat last year. Whenever I'm in London now I stay at the King's, off Shaftesbury Avenue. We'd be undisturbed there.'

Nico thought of Caroline, waiting at the house for him. He

wasn't late home yet. He knew exactly what would happen if he went with Roz to her hotel. It wasn't too late to change his mind and instruct Ken to drop Roz off there before taking him back home to his wife . . .

'Fine. King's Hotel, off Shaftesbury Avenue,' he told Ken, then sat back and felt the great weight of fidelity fall away from his chest like an avalanche.

Roz slid out of her jacket, tossed it over a grey velvet armchair and turned towards Nico, her dark eyes glittering in the dim apricot light.

He could smell the sweet, heavy scent of her perfume – not his favourite, but always reminding him of Roz – and sense her need as strongly as his own.

Why am I doing this, he wondered. And with Roz of all people?

Oh, but it was hard staying faithful to a wife one didn't love, and somehow being unfaithful to her with Roz, with whom he had once imagined he *was* in love, made it less terrible. It would be worse if it were someone new, surely?

And there was the guilt over Nicolette. Maybe this was a way of saying sorry.

But most of all, he realized, she had arrived back in his life at the right time, just when he was feeling so lonely and incomplete that he would have fallen into bed with a stranger anyway.

Without saying a word he reached out and touched the thin silk strap of her vest, watching it slide down her narrow shoulder like a raindrop. He could see how much she wanted him. And since he wanted someone as well, why not Roz?

The other strap fell. She wasn't wearing a bra. Realizing that he still had on his battered leather flying jacket, he shrugged it off, unbuttoned his shirt and watched Roz's scarlet fingernails snake lightly down his bare chest.

And finally she was in his arms, kissing his mouth and teasing him with her tongue.

Breaking away for a second, Nico said, 'I thought you were supposed to be conducting an interview.'

'I am,' Roz assured him, her voice husky with longing as she undid his trousers. 'And I know all the right things to say, too.'

At four thirty in the morning, after two hours of the purest misery as he lay awake and – more alone than ever – realized with increasing clarity what he had done, Nico slid out of bed, found his clothes in the dark and silently let himself out of the room.

Last night, high on champagne and the powerful blast of post-concert adrenalin, it had seemed like a good idea.

Now he simply couldn't face Roz, the worst person in the world he could have slept with. The final straw had been when, just before slipping into an exhausted sleep, she had curled her arm around him and whispered, 'Don't tell me *that* wasn't as good as it was with Camilla Stewart.'

Rigid with self-loathing and disgust, Nico had stayed awake, smoking endless cigarettes and castigating himself for his stupidity. The scent of Roz's perfume revolted him now. The sordidness of his presence in her bed sickened him still further.

After the first bout of lovemaking she had said, 'You married Caroline because of me, didn't you?' and he had nodded in the darkness. 'It's been a disaster, hasn't it?' she had continued, and there had seemed to be little point in denying it. He had nodded again, and felt Roz's smile against his shoulder.

'I did warn you, darling. We know each other too well. You should have listened to me at the time. Still, it's not too late.'

Managing to make his way out of the hotel without encountering anyone other than an ancient night porter who clearly didn't recognize him, Nico stepped into the road and flagged down a cab. Happily, in this area of London, there were still some about at such an ungodly hour.

Oh, but it *was* too late, he thought as he collapsed on to the back seat and realized that he was going to have to pay the fare by American Express. Far, far too late. He had been a bloody fool but he wasn't going to allow himself to be made an even bigger one.

Going to bed with Roz had been like eating snails for the first time; something to try once and never repeat. Well, he hadn't been doing it for the first time, but at least he knew now that he would never do it again. She was exorcized, out of his system for good, and he need never wonder in future what might have been, because now he knew.

There was no love there.

Nor was there any in his marriage of course, but while Caroline was making such superhuman efforts to keep it intact he hadn't the heart to dump her.

Nico rested his head against the window and watched the empty streets flash past as that familiar black cloak of loneliness surrounded him once more. He would tell Caroline that he had gone out with Monty and Shaun to a club, and then on to a Chinese restaurant – not Indian or Italian, he didn't smell garlicky enough – and even if she didn't believe him she wouldn't show it. Hurt silences and hysterical outbursts were things of the past now, replaced by determined smiles and endless understanding.

God, he thought wearily, if only I loved her we could have had the happiest marriage in London.

His thoughts strayed then to Camilla, who appeared to hold that particular title at the moment, and he resolutely veered away from it. It came as some small consolation – even though at the same time he hated himself for realizing it – that just now Loulou was as miserable as he was. Funny how it had never even occurred to either of them to jump into bed together, considering how close they had been over the past few years.

Not for the first time Nico considered the situation – and the possibility – but for the life of him he simply couldn't imagine it. The affection they felt for each other was that of good friends, nothing more.

And thank God for that, he thought with a ghost of a smile. At least it was one less relationship that could go disastrously wrong.

' 'Ere you are then, guv,' said the cab driver, pulling up outside the front gates of Nico's house. 'That'll be twenty quid to you. Any chance of a couple of autographs for me daughters while you're 'ere?'

'No problem at all,' said Nico politely. 'Er . . . I don't seem to have any cash on me. American Express OK?'

'Bleedin' 'ell,' sighed the cabbie. Then he turned and winked at Nico, and threw across a pen. 'Nah, no problem, mate. No bleedin' problem at all.'

Chapter 40

Matt pulled Camilla into his arms and kissed her so thoroughly that she thought she might faint right there on the sun-drenched terrace overlooking the back garden. The realization only served to convince her even more that her suspicions were correct and in a blaze of love and joy she almost told him there and then.

It took all her strength not to. Tonight was the night and after hugging the secret knowledge to herself for over three days now she was determined to hang on to it for just a few hours more.

June 24th. It had been Matt's idea to celebrate their half-anniversary in style and he had produced the tickets for *Phantom of the Opera* on Saturday morning with justifiable pride. They were like gold-dust at the moment.

'Buy yourself a spectacular dress,' he had announced, leering wickedly. 'The less there is of it, the better. We're going to see *Phantom*, then have dinner at Le Gavroche, maybe take in a few clubs, then come back here and take all our clothes off and indulge in a few hours of post-marital screwing. And I'll warn you in advance that I paid a visit to Cartier yesterday and we're now broke. That's so you'll know that I'll be expecting a little surprise present in return,' he added, his expression grave. 'I thought I'd better tell you so you won't find yourself in one of those embarrassing situations . . .'

'I would have run upstairs, pulled a couple of pairs of socks out of the airing cupboard, wrapped them up and given them back to you,' said Camilla sweetly, wriggling out of reach as Matt began biting her earlobe.

'No-one can say that my wife isn't economical,' he murmured, his strong white teeth increasing their pressure.

'She needs to be,' Camilla protested, 'the way her husband flings his money around . . . ouch!'

Well, she had her surprise present all right, she thought as they made their way, arm in arm, through to the front of the house. And it hadn't been easy keeping it a surprise either. It had always amazed her when she watched those old black-and-white films on TV and the young wife announced coyly to her husband that she had something to tell him . . . Why on earth, she had wondered, hadn't he guessed? Was the man stupid or something?

But by some miracle and a small amount of trickery she had managed to deceive Matt. Thanks to the memories – still clear in her mind – of how she had felt when she was pregnant with first Charlotte and then Toby, she had known almost straight away this time. The faint nausea, the suddenly acute sense of smell . . . much of it had been indefinable, but Camilla recognized it and clung to the realization with all the joyful fervour of a drowning man being thrown a fully-equipped yacht.

And when Matt had informed her of his planned semi-anniversary celebrations she had decided that then would be the perfect time to tell him. Placing a box of Tampax in pole position in the bathroom, she had taken to clutching her stomach occasionally and complaining vaguely of period pains. By tonight though, she had intimated, all would be well again. They could make love to their hearts' content.

'Don't get stuck at the bar this afternoon,' she warned him now as they exchanged a final kiss on the front steps of the house. Matt was playing in a pro-celebrity match at Sunningdale which was being televised, and he and Jacko were partnering two comedians notorious for their drinking prowess. The last time he had played with one of the celebrities he had rolled home in a taxi at two o'clock in the morning and his hangover the next day had been one of the all-time greats.

'Orange juice,' declared Matt with a sweeping gesture, 'is all that shall pass my lips. And I shall be home by five thirty, to escort my gorgeous wife to the theatre. How often, after all, does one get the chance to celebrate one's six-months' anniversary?'

'Dahlink,' breathed Camilla, doing a passable imitation of Zsa Zsa Gabor. 'As often as possible, of course.'

She stood and waved as Matt reversed the new dark green Mercedes – his pride and joy – across the drive and then edged his way out into the early morning traffic. When he was out of sight she gazed with satisfaction at the banks of roses which scented the whole garden – beating even the intrusive petrol fumes – and the riotously tumbling honeysuckle which enveloped the high stone wall separating their garden from next door. When she had cleared the breakfast dishes from the terrace she would return and cut an armful of roses for the sitting-room.

After that, she had an appointment with her hairdresser, then a lunch date with Zoë at a new Italian restaurant in Wimbledon. She only hoped Zoë wouldn't be too intrigued when she discovered that she was avoiding alcohol. Matt had to be the first to know. If Zoë found out it would be all over the city by sundown.

Smiling, she glanced down at her stomach then turned and made her way back into the cool, flower-scented hall.

Tonight, during their celebration dinner amidst the glorious elegance of Le Gavroche, she would break the news to Matt that he was going to have a baby.

Really, thought Camilla at four thirty that afternoon, this family was expanding by the minute.

The latest addition, having just peed for the third time on Zoë's kitchen floor – in a small gap *between* the sheets of newspaper which had hastily been thrown down – now launched itself at Camilla's ankle, its back paws scrabbling frantically for leverage against her shoe. Bending down, she picked up the six-week-old puppy – billed as a collie-labrador cross but clearly endowed with other dubious connections – and buried her face in the soft, sherry-gold fur of his neck. Rocky snuffled and squirmed in ecstasy, his legs still paddling crazily in mid-air, and Zoë yelled, 'Put him down, Cami. He's going to pee again, I know it.'

They stood and watched the puppy attack a corner of newspaper, an expression of such ferocious determination in his tiny yellow eyes that he clearly felt his whole existence depended on the outcome of this battle. Zoë had named him the moment she had set eyes on him at Battersea Dogs' Home, cannoning against the wire mesh of his kennel. And Camilla had fallen instantly in love with the tough, wonderfully affectionate puppy.

Before Rocky had even noticed them, his future had been decided. He would live with Matt and Camilla and the children, and vacation at Zoë's house whenever they had to travel abroad. It was the perfect solution.

'Do you think Matt will really like him?' said Camilla, and Zoë scooped him up into her arms, watching fondly as he immediately picked a fight with her cascading, wayward red hair.

'He'll really *adore* him. No question. I'll bring him over to you at about ten o'clock tomorrow, so he can pee all over your carpets and make himself at home.' She glanced at her watch. 'You'd better make a move if you're going to tart yourself up for tonight. Now aren't you glad I made you come with me to Battersea? Wasn't it my best idea ever?'

'Very glad,' said Camilla solemnly, watching as Rocky hurled himself down to the ground and hurriedly relieved himself against the nearest leg of the kitchen table. 'Absolutely your best idea ever. Whatever would we do without them?'

By five thirty she was finally ready, having showered and changed into the Nicole Farhi amethyst silk dress which was belted at the hips by a wide band of shimmering violet and rose quartz beads. And Matt wouldn't discover until much later the exquisite, quite outrageously seductive rose silk lingerie which caressed her skin beneath the outer trappings.

Since he would be back at any moment now she took a bottle of pink champagne from the fridge and carried it out on to the terrace where she had already placed two glasses. The white wrought-iron garden table and chairs were warmed by the sun and the garden itself had never looked more lovely.

Waving away a lazy bee, Camilla clasped the neck of the champagne bottle in both hands and inexpertly pushed out the cork. Foam spilled over her fingers as she watched the cork sail through the air and land at the edge of the terrace. Licking the back of her wet hand and taking care not to spill any on her dress she poured the fizzing, pale pink liquid into one of the slender, tulip-shaped glasses. Having only drunk apple juice at lunchtime she felt she could justify half a glass of champagne now and raised it into the air with a flourish. Smiling, suffused with happiness, she toasted herself.

And why not, she decided, taut with excitement. She was pregnant and in love. She deserved it.

By six o'clock, when Matt still hadn't returned, she wondered if she should phone the clubhouse at Sunningdale, then decided that it would be a waste of time since Matt would obviously have left there by now. The traffic must be heavier this evening than he had anticipated.

By six thirty Camilla was feeling distinctly uneasy. Matt was now an hour late and she felt sure he would have called her if he had been held up. Phoning the clubhouse, she got the engaged tone. She tried calling his mobile but it was switched off so she left a message.

Agitated, she paced the house, pausing at every window overlooking the drive. If Matt had stayed late at the bar for a drink with his golfing companions, she thought helplessly, she would be really cross with him. If he wasn't back within five minutes they were definitely going to miss the first act of *Phantom*.

At exactly seven o'clock, the telephone finally rang, making her jump.

And at seven o'clock, the nightmare, the terrible, terrible nightmare began.

The journey to St Thomas's Hospital, Westminster, was a nightmare in itself. The early evening traffic was appalling and twice she had to stop herself leaping out of the taxi as it crawled along the Thames Embankment, hemmed in by other traffic. Across Westminster Bridge she could see the hospital . . . surely it would be quicker to reach on foot.

'Cars overheating, stopping and holding everyone else up,' volunteered the cab driver, having glanced in his mirror and seen the agonized expression on her white face. He pulled out to pass, and moved into third gear. 'Here we go, love. We'll be there in a jiffy. Which entrance shall I head for?'

'I don't know,' said Camilla, realizing that her whole body was shaking. It was impossible to keep her voice steady. 'Casualty? I'm sorry, I just don't know. It . . . it was a car accident . . .'

'Then that's where he'll be,' replied the cabbie reassuringly, putting his foot down. 'Don't you worry, love. I'm sure he'll be OK.'

When he brought the taxi to a halt outside the entrance, Camilla had to hand him her purse. After a moment's hesitation he pushed it back into her bag and patted her arm. 'Never mind about that, just go and find him. Best of luck, love.'

'Oh, thank you,' she said, overwhelmed for a second by his kindness. 'Thank you so much . . .'

Matt had been taken to the intensive care unit, the receptionist informed her, and gave her directions which Camilla struggled to understand. The wide, grey corridors hung with colourful artwork echoed with the sound of footsteps. Shiny painted lines in different colours led to different destinations. Camilla eventually reached the intensive care unit and pressed the buzzer set into the wall beside the double doors.

A tall nurse wearing a high, intricate white cap opened one of the doors a few inches and slid through it sideways so that it closed again before Camilla could even glimpse inside.

'Yes?'

'My husband has just been brought in,' said Camilla, trembling and breathless. 'Matt Lewis. A doctor phoned me.'

'Of course,' said the nurse kindly. Taking Camilla's arm she edged her away from the doors. 'If you'd take a seat in our waiting-room for a minute or two I'll send someone out to speak to you. They'll explain everything.'

Camilla stared at her in horror. 'But can't I see him now? He's in there, isn't he? I want to *see* him.'

'And you will, Mrs Lewis,' the nurse told her, her expression sympathetic, but professional. 'But I'm afraid the doctor must see you first. He really won't be a minute.'

For a muddled moment Camilla wondered if they thought *she* was ill. Why on earth did the doctor want to see her? But the nurse was leading her towards a small, empty waiting-room and on to a beige plastic chair.

'Would you like a cup of tea?'

This time Camilla was sure the nurse had gone mad.

'No,' she said slowly, aware that her heart was pounding like a hammer against her ribs. 'I just want to see Matt. Now.'

Five minutes later the young Scottish doctor led her into the all-white unit, humming and ticking with machinery. Her legs like jelly, her fingernails digging into her palms, Camilla followed him to the third bed along.

Matt was there.

One of the nurses, who had been checking a drip-line running into his arm, brought a chair for her and pushed it to the side of the bed. Weakly Camilla collapsed on to it as the doctor began to explain the functions of the machines surrounding them. The tube in his mouth was attached to a ventilator which was doing Matt's breathing for him. The shoe-box-sized monitor was recording his heartbeat, respiration and blood pressure. The drips were there to maintain the balance of body fluids.

Camilla, dazed by the network of tubes and wires and electrodes, ignored them and concentrated instead on Matt's face.

It was ridiculous, she thought unsteadily, that he could be so desperately ill yet still look so healthy. Ill people didn't have deep tans and clearly defined muscles.

Matt looked as if he were fast asleep; his dark lashes shading the lines beneath his closed eyes, his tousled dark hair curling on to his forehead as it always did. Yet according to the doctor his car, when it had swerved to avoid another which had gone out of control, had hit a low wall and overturned, and in the process Matt had sustained a severe head injury. It was a closed injury, which meant that there were no visible wounds apart from a small amount of purplish bruising to the left side of his neck where his seatbelt had prevented him crashing through the windscreen.

But it was still a very severe injury, the doctor had explained in a deliberately neutral voice, and Matt was deeply unconscious, his condition at the moment critical. The medical team were doing everything they could to stabilize him, but as his wife she had to understand how serious the implications might be.

Cautiously, taking care to avoid the lines of tubing attached by strips of plaster to his wrist, she cradled Matt's warm hand in her own icy ones and watched the mechanical rise and fall of his chest as the ventilator pumped air into his lungs. He was so brown against the glaring hospital whiteness of the starched sheets. His dark hair was so glossy . . . how could they know whether he was in pain? Could he feel anything . . . did he *know* what had happened to him?

'I'll be here on the unit all evening,' said the young doctor eventually, reaching up to adjust a dial on one of the monitors, 'if there's anything else you'd like to ask me. And Nurse Simpson is looking after your husband,' he added, nodding at the plump, auburn-haired girl who had brought her a chair. 'So he's in very good hands.'

Pulling his stethoscope from the pocket of his white coat he disappeared to the far end of the ward and the nurse gave Camilla a reassuring smile. 'It must all be such an awful shock for you at the moment. Everything in here looks so strange as well, which doesn't help.'

Camilla nodded slowly, tears sliding down her cheeks. She watched them splash down on to her hand, entwined with Matt's, and felt a great chasm of grief and pain open up inside her. How could this be happening? And how could it have happened to Matt of all people?

He had planned tonight's celebrations with such care, and she had been going to break the news to him that she was pregnant. It was all so unfair, so desperately unfair that she couldn't bear it . . .

'Can he hear me,' she asked in a low, unsteady voice, 'if I speak to him?'

'We don't honestly know,' said the nurse, coming round to stand behind her and placing a comforting hand on Camilla's trembling shoulder. 'But he might. Talk to him as much as you want – it certainly won't do any harm. Just don't be disappointed if there isn't any outward reaction.'

An hour later she brought Camilla a cup of hot, strong tea.

'Look, does anyone else know you're here? Are there friends or relatives you'd like to contact?'

Unable to think clearly, Camilla shook her head. 'No-one else knows. Matt's family live in the States. I've got their number at home. I can't go and get it,' she blurted out, her eyes wide with panic. 'I can't leave him.'

'Of course not,' said the nurse soothingly, 'I wasn't going to suggest you did. Why don't you call a friend and ask them to come here and pick up your house keys, then they can go to your home and bring you whatever you need. Address book, a change of clothes, that sort of thing.'

'Of course,' said Camilla, glancing down at the amethyst silk dress with its glittering belt and matching high-heeled shoes. 'Different clothes. We were going out tonight,' she added, needing to offer some kind of explanation, her pale tear-stained face dreadfully at odds with the bright glamour of her outfit. 'To celebrate being married for six months . . .'

Loulou arrived at ten o'clock, equally pale and shocked. Camilla's words had barely been discernible over the phone, but as soon as she was able to understand what had happened she had left Lili with Simon at the flat, jumped into his car and come straight to the hospital.

'Oh, you poor thing, you poor, poor thing,' she murmured, holding Camilla tightly in her slender arms as her friend gave way to her first real tears and collapsed in a storm of heaving, grief-stricken sobs. They were in the waiting-room since Loulou couldn't enter the intensive care unit which only permitted visits from relatives. Camilla, persuaded outside for a few minutes whilst a team of doctors carried out some tests, was frantic to get back to Matt.

'It's so awful, he's just lying there and he looks OK, but he's unconscious,' she sobbed, her tears soaking Loulou's shirt. 'Oh Lou, I just don't know what to do . . . I feel so helpless but I can't bear to leave him and the doctor told me to be prepared for the worst. If Matt dies . . . if he *dies* . . .'

Loulou, tears streaming down her own cheeks, clasped Camilla's hands tightly between her own. 'He won't die,' she said fiercely. 'He's got so much to live for. Matt can't die, he'll get better. Now tell me what you want me to bring from the house. I'll phone Jack and tell him what's happened so he can keep the kids with him for a few more days.'

'Phone numbers. In the book by the telephone. I've got to call Matt's family.'

'I'll phone them if you like,' said Loulou, her mind racing. The awful task was clearly quite beyond Camilla's capabilities at present. 'And you need an overnight bag. I'll find everything. You go back in there and stay with Matt. I'll be back in about an hour and a half.'

The nightmare worsened.

By the time Loulou returned the doctors were carrying out more tests, this time designed to assess brain function. When she was shown into the tiny office where Camilla was sitting in an attitude of total shock and despair, she didn't know what she could possibly do except stay with her.

'I got through to Matt's parents,' she said, inwardly reliving the terrible minutes when she had had to break the news to them. 'They're flying out tonight on Concorde.'

'They might be too late,' said Camilla quietly, too far gone now even for tears. 'Lou, it's all happening so fast. I can't keep up. I can't understand what they're telling me half the time.

Reporters keep phoning up wanting to know how Matt is and the nurses just say critical. But one of the doctors brought me in here and asked me if I knew how Matt felt about kidney transplants. He wants me to consider it and I simply can't concentrate . . .'

Her voice trailed away as she turned to gaze out of the window. Below them, the city glittered with lights beneath an indigo sky. Loulou sat down beside her and tried to take her hand, but Camilla was twisting her wedding-ring jerkily round and round.

'I don't *know* how Matt feels about kidney transplants,' she went on despairingly, 'and I can't ask him because he's unconscious. Oh Lou, how can I live without him if he dies?'

Loulou swallowed hard and this time could not reassure Camilla that Matt wasn't going to die. But praying – and at the same time sure that she was doing the right thing – she said slowly, 'You're his wife, you know him best, but if you really can't think about it at the moment I'll tell you. I know Matt well enough to be able to say that if he did have to die he would want his organs to be donated to someone else who needs them. Of course he would, Cami. He wouldn't hesitate for a single second. He'd be happy to think that he could help other people.'

Camilla nodded and pushed her hair wearily away from her face. 'You're right. I'll tell the doctor when he comes back that they can have whatever they want.' Glancing at the overnight bag which Loulou had dropped on to the table, she added, 'It looks as if I might not need that, after all. When they've finished doing the tests they'll come and tell me. They've said that I can stay with him for a little while afterwards to say goodbye . . . if I have to . . . It hasn't happened yet. Maybe there'll be a miracle . . .'

But the consultant's grave expression when he entered the room told Camilla at once that there had been no miracle. Slowly, and with great compassion, he explained to Camilla that Matt's injury had been so devastating that there was no possible hope that he could ever recover. The brain function tests, which had been carried out by two separate teams of doctors, proved beyond any shadow of a doubt that all brain function had ceased. He was terribly sorry to have to break such tragic news to her . . .

Camilla held up her hand, the one with the wedding-ring on the third finger. 'Thank you for being so kind. I know that Matt would want . . .' She hesitated, swallowing hard, then said, 'Would have wanted his organs donated for transplant purposes. Do I have to sign any form for that?'

'I have a form here. I'm sure you'll gain some comfort in the months ahead from the knowledge that your husband's tragic death hasn't been completely in vain. Thanks to him, and to you, Mrs Lewis, others will live.'

Silently, Camilla took the fountain pen from his fingers and signed the form. Then she rose unsteadily to her feet and looked at Loulou. 'Will you wait here for me?'

Beyond words, the solid ache in her throat almost unbearable, Loulou nodded.

'Are you sure you want to go back in there, Mrs Lewis?' asked the consultant with evident concern. Camilla stared at him in astonishment.

'Oh, I'm quite sure. I didn't tell him earlier . . . I was saving it as a surprise for him when he woke up . . . but I have to let him know now. He would have been so proud. You see, I'm pregnant. I'm going to have Matt's baby.'

Chapter 41

Small, icy waves lapped against the rocky shoreline with lazy irregularity. When the tide eventually receded a crescent of silver sand would arc across the bay, glistening in the late afternoon sunlight, and Camilla would take Rocky for a walk across to the little town of Drumlachan.

But for now, while the tide was still in and most of the sand hidden, she was content to sit in the old wooden rocking-chair in the warm shelter of the glass conservatory which fronted the cottage, and allow her mind to wander.

It had to be a step forward, she realized, to be able to *allow* such thoughts. Now, almost a year after Matt's death she could cope with them, but for many months it had been a physical impossibility. Fighting the memories, willing herself not to remember those so very happy times, she had backed away as much as possible, withdrawing like a snail into its shell from the pain they so acutely evoked.

But at last, it seemed, that pain was beginning to recede. She could remember Matt without being engulfed by grief. Having told herself over and over again that she was lucky to have had him and to have been that happy for a short time was better than never having known him at all, she was managing to overcome the bitterness she felt at such tragic unfairness, and such terrible, terrible waste.

The guilt too, had been overwhelming at first. In the days following the funeral, now mercifully hazy in her mind, she had become convinced that the accident had been her fault. If Matt hadn't been driving back along that particular road and at that particular moment, *to be with her*, there would have been no accident. If she hadn't told him not to stay with his friends in the clubhouse he would still be alive.

And nothing anyone could say to her had been able to persuade her otherwise.

Losing the baby a few days later, miscarrying in the same hospital where Matt had died, had convinced her still further. That her last link with Matt had been broken, wrenched from her grief-stricken body with vicious clawing spasms of pain, had proved to her beyond all doubt that she had been to blame. The miscarriage was her punishment. She didn't deserve to give birth to his child.

Calmly now, she rocked in her chair and gazed out over the blue-green water bordering the west coast of Scotland. Rocky, dozing in the shade, stirred slightly as Camilla reached for the iced spritzer on the table beside her.

It had taken a long time before she had believed what everyone had told her, had realized that guilt was a natural extension of grief and that the accident had not, after all, been her fault. Until recently, every time someone had said, 'Time heals all wounds', she had wanted to hit them. It had seemed like a conspiracy to keep her alive, and she had known that they were lying, trying to make her feel better. Haunted by grief and guilt and the most appalling loneliness, she had refused to listen to them, hating everyone for lying to her. Nothing could make her feel better. Matt was dead. He was no longer with her. How could she ever feel better, knowing that?

But somehow, like a very slowly unfolding miracle, she understood now that some degree of recovery was possible.

And Squirrel's Gate, the tiny cottage perched on the edge of the sea three miles from the small Scottish town of Drumlachan, had played its part in the healing process. Remote, backed by purple mountains and fronted by water, it had been offered to her by a friend of Matt's who would be away in California for that time. Initially planning to stay for just a couple of weeks – the solitude and silence had been what Camilla had craved following the ghastly crowding of her life in the first weeks after Matt's death – she had closeted herself there for almost two months. Toby and Charlotte had come to stay throughout August with Marty joining them for the second fortnight. When it had been time for them to return to school for the autumn term Camilla had gone back with them, but the house in Belgravia brought back such vivid memories of Matt that it had been an effort to remain there. Toby and Charlotte understood what had happened, but when Marty, who had no comprehension of death, ran from room to room in the house shouting, 'Where Matt?', Camilla had been consumed each time with fresh, unbearable grief.

So she had stayed in London with the children on alternate weeks. On those Friday afternoons, as soon as she had kissed them goodbye at Jack's house, she would drive up to Scotland and retreat into silence.

As autumn passed and winter drew closer, the cottage became more demanding and she welcomed the diversions. The plumbing was erratic, the central heating system downright temperamental and the electricity supply extremely susceptible to the vagaries of the weather. In December, when the bad weather came, snow obliterated the tiny lane leading to the cottage and banked around it like an eiderdown. Kept busy from morning until night digging the snow away from the door, cooking by candlelight over a tiny paraffin stove and battling to keep warm, Camilla had no time to think of anything else. When the children were there, she was equally diverted but maintaining a pretence of cheerfulness for a week at a time was an appalling strain and much as she loved them it was a relief to be able to return to her own thoughts and weep as much as she wanted without interruption when they weren't there.

The bleak, harsh winter months had matched her mood. When spring arrived and the snows melted, however, she was appalled at first to realize that the tender green new buds on the trees and the glittering sunlight on the water lifted her spirits. This had sparked off a fresh round of guilt, since she was by now so accustomed to grief that it seemed disloyal to Matt to feel even an inkling of happiness. She was betraying his memory . . . he was beginning to fade from her thoughts . . . Terrified that she would forget him and castigating herself for such treachery she returned to London and watched, for hours and hours, video tapes of the TV programmes in which he had appeared, reassuring herself that she hadn't forgotten the timbre of his voice, his exuberant gestures, his wickedly beguiling smile.

Matt's beloved family portrait made her cry. Too clearly she recalled his words when it had been painted: 'We have the rest of our lives together, sweetheart. And when we're gone, there will still be the portrait to remind everyone that we were here. We'll be immortal.'

But the rest of their lives together had been less than five months and the unfairness of it all was so heart-breaking that eventually Camilla had taken the portrait down from the wall, packed it carefully in a box and put it away in the loft.

Matt was still there in the room, framed photographs of him

stood on every table and on the mantelpiece, but the sight of the portrait and the particular memories it evoked was more than she could cope with at the moment.

Now, as Rocky rose to his feet and padded towards her, tail wagging in anticipation of a walk, she realized that she was at last beginning to come to terms with her grief. She no longer panicked, thinking that she would forget Matt, because she knew that that would never happen. The guilt, too, had faded. It had been a natural reaction, according to her doctor in whom she had eventually confided, but one which was entirely illogical. Gradually she had come to see that he was right.

Rocky bounced off the steps leading down to the path and set off towards the beach at a frantic pace. Camilla smiled at his incredible enthusiasm; he had been such a comfort to her in the past year. At first his puppy-helplessness had required her attention, then as he grew and his ebullient personality became even more forceful, she found herself panting to keep up with him. He adored her unreservedly, showering her with affection and sloppy kisses at every opportunity and diverting her constantly with his antics. During those moments Camilla forgot her unhappiness and was able to laugh, to feel normal again.

Lazily, enjoying the afternoon sun, she followed Rocky along the beach, throwing sticks into the water and watching him hurl himself after them as if they were the crown jewels. Emerging from the waves with the stick in his mouth, shaking himself so violently that the air was filled with spirals of salty spray, he would drop the prize at her feet and leer up at her, poised for flight until she threw the stick once more.

When they reached the sleepy town of Drumlachan he assumed a more sedate, adult role and waited with a show of obedience outside shops while Camilla replenished the stocks.

There wasn't much to buy since she made this trip each day, but it was pleasant to chat with the locals who had unbent considerably since realizing that she wasn't just a short-term summer visitor. Knowing nothing of her past, they treated her normally and spoiled the children, particularly Marty, 'the laughing wee laddie', with bars of chocolate and wickedly fattening doughnuts whenever they came to stay.

It was five o'clock by the time Camilla and Rocky began to make their way back to Squirrel's Gate and since the tide had receded further and there was now more beach for Rocky to explore, the walk took almost two hours. Tiny crabs scrambled at his approach, haughty seagulls taunted him, waiting until he was only feet away before squawking and rising into the air, and long wet ribbons of dark brown seaweed wrapped themselves like serpents around his paws.

It wasn't until she was climbing the steps to the cottage that Camilla spotted the sleek, metallic grey nose of a car parked on the grassy verge behind it.

Surely not tourists, she thought with faint surprise. The beach was deserted, the heather and bracken-covered hills rising up behind the cottage silent and still.

Whistling for Rocky, who was loitering on the water's edge engaging in perilously unarmed combat with a sea urchin, she paused on the top step and waited for him to join her. Although if it were burglars, she thought with a tiny smile, their make of car indicated that they would be sadly disappointed by the contents of her modest second home.

Inside the cottage, Nico had been waiting for over an hour for Camilla to return, assuming that she had not gone far since neither the front nor the back doors had been locked when he arrived. After some hesitation he had let himself in and made himself a cup of tea in the tiny, but well-equipped, kitchen. Then, nerves getting the better of him, he had emptied the tea down the sink and poured a Scotch from the slightly dusty bottle standing on the oak sideboard in the sitting-room.

Stretching out on the soft leather sofa, he had settled down to wait, resisting the urge to explore the rest of the cottage which had become Camilla's isolated retreat from the world. This sitting-room, however, contained items which reminded him of her so strongly that the last two years seemed to slide away . . . six or seven bowls of wild flowers filled the room with their sweet scent, opened books lay on the floor beside the right-hand corner of the settee and a jar of the almond-scented hand cream she always used stood on the coffee table. The photographs of Toby and Charlotte which had taken pride of place in her room at Nico's house were here now, together with new ones in plain silver frames of Toby playing cricket, the little boy Marty, and a more grown-up Charlotte wearing a white jumpsuit, plaits and a beaming smile. There was also a photograph of Loulou looking angelic with Lili in her arms, and another of all four children together, rolling around on a sunlit lawn. There were no photographs, he observed, of Matt.

It wasn't until he heard Camilla's whistle that he realized she was back. Instantly he leapt to his feet, spilling droplets of Scotch on the crimson rug. His heart pounding, wondering if he had been right to come here and hoping that he wasn't about to scare the living daylights out of her when she realized there was someone in the house, he waited uneasily for the door to open. For such a long time he had wanted to see her again . . . now he was about to and he didn't have a clue how she would react.

And he didn't get a chance to see her initial reaction either, for before he could move out of the way a dripping wet, conker-brown animal leapt up at him writhing and whining with delight, its whiplash tail going like a propeller blade, spraying salty water in every direction.

'Bloody hell,' spluttered Nico, struggling to remain on his feet as the creature ricocheted off his chest and crouched, pink tongue lolling, on the rug in front of him. Only then, in that moment of respite, did he have the opportunity to look over towards the doorway and gauge Camilla's reaction to his unexpected appearance. And when he saw her she was doubled up with laughter.

'I have to tell you,' said Nico, as Rocky licked his hand, searching it for biscuits, 'that you have one lousy guard dog.'

Camilla, struggling to contain her laughter, shooed Rocky out through the door. 'I saw the car outside. I thought I might have extremely wealthy burglars. The expression on your face when Rocky launched himself at you . . . oh, your trousers are soaking . . .'

'I was so scared I probably wet myself,' he said, grinning, and suddenly Camilla was right in front of him, her arms hovering, tears brimming in her eyes.

'Oh Nico, it's lovely to see you. I'm so very glad you're here.'

The emotion in her voice, the unexpected tears, hollowed his stomach with love and he held out his own arms, taking a step forward so that they came together in one fluid movement. Camilla hugged him tightly and he stroked her dark blonde hair, which smelled of shampoo and sea salt, and held her against him in silence for several seconds.

The awkwardness which had hovered between them for so

long might never have existed. Holding Camilla as he had *longed* to for so long seemed so natural and right that Nico didn't want it to end.

Finally, unwillingly, Camilla stepped back and smiled up at him, wiping the tears from her cheeks with the back of her hand.

'Sorry about all this. I seem to cry for the most ridiculous reasons these days. Now your shirt's wet too. What with Rocky's antics and mine you could drown.'

Nico silently blessed the crazy dog who had defused such a potentially awkward meeting. Glancing down at his white cotton shirt and pale green trousers splattered with salty water and sandy paw prints, he shook his head and brushed at the sand. 'They'll dry. Sit down and stop apologizing. And I just happen to have brought with me a couple of bottles of your favourite wine, so if you could just point me in the direction of the nearest corkscrew . . .'

They sprawled at opposite ends of the settee, barefoot and facing each other, and demolished the first bottle of satin-smooth St Emilion within half an hour whilst Rocky slept, intermittently twitching in his dreams, upon the rug beside them. Outside the sun was setting, turning the sky first apricot-pink then violet. Camilla rose to switch on two rose-shaded lamps and fetched the second bottle of wine from the kitchen. Listening to her talking, her soft voice just as he remembered, Nico realized afresh how much she meant to him. Steady, he warned himself. He had to take great care, remain firmly in control of his emotions. This wasn't Caroline, or Roz, or any of the other now faceless women with whom he had temporarily abolished the interminable loneliness. This was Camilla, whom he loved and who thought of him as nothing more than a good friend.

She was also a widow who had adored and worshipped her husband and who evidently still worshipped his memory. Which meant he was going to have to tread very carefully indeed if their fragile relationship was to remain unspoiled and intact.

'So what made you trek all the way up to Drumlachan?' asked Camilla, refilling his glass and pushing a lock of streaky blonde hair away from her face with her little finger, a gesture he remembered so well. 'I do travel down to London every other week you know.'

'I had to come up to Edinburgh to see a record producer,' Nico shrugged and winked. 'Practically on your doorstep. Loulou suggested I pay you a visit. She's convinced you're living in a cave, existing on acorns and seaweed.'

'Food!' she exclaimed, glancing at the willow basket in the corner by the door where she had dropped it. 'You must be starving. Shall I cook you something? How long can you stay?'

As long as possible, thought Nico, but aloud he said, 'I'm in no hurry. We could go out to a restaurant if you'd prefer.'

Camilla shook her head with the overemphasis of someone unused to four glasses of wine in quick succession. Taking Nico's drink from him and placing it on the table beside her own, she caught his hand and rose, slightly unsteadily, to her feet.

'Come on, you can chop the garlic and keep me company in the kitchen. I haven't had spaghetti carbonara for so long I've probably forgotten how to make it.'

'You're far too thin,' Nico scolded her as he dropped the slivers of garlic into the pan of melted butter and turned up the heat. In the steamy, fragrant warmth of the tiny kitchen he felt he could say almost anything now. Camilla turned to him and grinned.

'So my daughter informed me not so long ago. She said that if Matt was watching from heaven he'd be shouting at me to put some weight on.'

It reassured him that she could speak so easily of Matt. 'Well, I'm watching you too,' he said with mock severity, eyeing her narrow hips and slender thighs in their faded Levis and observing the white leather belt pulled in to the last notch in order to hold them up. 'And I agree. A few more curves are definitely in order. They suit you. You aren't the same without them.'

The garlic was golden brown now. Camilla stirred in half a pint of double cream and added the strips of cured ham.

'I'm not the same anyway,' she said quietly. 'I thought I was devastated when Jack and I split up; it seemed the worst thing in the world that could possibly have happened. Oh, but losing Matt was so very much worse. I really didn't know if I could carry on without him.'

'And now?' asked Nico, taking the motionless wooden spatula from her hand and stirring the sauce in the pan.

She sighed. 'And now ... I've begun to realize that I can. Life isn't much fun at the moment, everything seems such hard work. And when something interesting or funny does happen, I keep wishing that Matt could be here to share it, to make it *more* fun. Like now, for instance,' she added with a weak smile. 'It's so lovely to see you. If Matt was here as well, the three of us could have such a great evening ...'

'I'm having a great evening,' interrupted Nico firmly, reaching for her fingers and giving them a squeeze. 'You mustn't feel as if you're only half a person, Cami. The two of us are having a great evening together and I'm very, *very* glad I came here. I shall be even more glad,' he went on, 'when you drain that spaghetti, hand me those eggs and pour me another glass of wine.'

'Slave driver,' she complained, laughing. 'Really, some ex-employers *never* change.'

Together they demolished the creamy, garlicky carbonara and the second bottle of St Emilion. Nico enthralled Camilla with wickedly exaggerated tales of his show-business friends' antics, agreed with her that Loulou could do far better for herself than Simon, whom she was still seeing, and brought her up to date with Mac's relationship with Cecilia. They still had not married, but although their arguments were legendary – last week at the Hard Rock Café she had thrown a bowl of green salad over Mac and flounced out on the arm of a celebrated actor – they were still living together. Camilla and Nico were both of the opinion that Mac and Loulou were crazy about each other, but that both of them were too stubborn and proud to admit it. It was quite infuriating to know it, yet be unable to do anything about it.

Camilla talked about the children and marvelled at their resilience. She avoided mentioning Matt as much as possible, since she always felt she was in danger of boring people when she spoke of him, but Nico brought his name into the conversation from time to time so naturally that eventually she stopped worrying.

'I don't think I ever thanked you for the flowers you sent to the funeral,' she said suddenly, remembering and covering her mouth with dismay. Nico had written her a letter of condolence, she now recalled, and sent a beautiful wreath of white lilies.

'And your letter. It was so nice of you to take the trouble to write.'

'I am nice,' teased Nico, to lighten her mood, but tears were welling in her eyes once more at the memory of the funeral. They were sitting close together now and he slipped a comforting arm around her shoulder. Camilla produced a handkerchief and wiped her cheeks.

'I'm sorry, here I go again. This is what I'm like. It just happens . . .'

'Don't worry about it. I think you're very brave,' he assured her, breathing in her subtle scent and telling himself he was a complete animal because despite everything her closeness was arousing him. 'I haven't any idea how you must have felt. I can't even imagine what it must have been like for you.'

Turning her head and gazing up at him, Camilla said, 'Just think how you'd feel if you lost Caroline. If suddenly you were on your own, knowing that you'd never see her again.'

She watched those famous slanting green eyes of his grow cloudy, like jade. His fingers absently rubbed the soft skin on the inside of her elbow as he considered her words, and she realized belatedly with something close to shock that although they had talked non-stop since his arrival, Caroline had scarcely been mentioned all evening.

'I think,' said Nico finally, his voice low and toneless, 'that what I would feel in those circumstances would be far less than you felt. You and Matt were happily married. You loved each other. Caroline and I are just . . . married. Unfortunately, not all marriages are happy ones.'

'Oh, Nico,' whispered Camilla, appalled. 'That's terrible. I'm so sorry.'

He allowed himself a half-smile. 'There you go, apologizing again. It's my fault, not yours.'

'But it's so sad,' she exclaimed, her eyes wide with dismay. 'And here I've been whingeing on about my own problems when you've got enough of your own to worry about. When did things start to go wrong? Maybe if you tell me about it we could find a way to sort everything out for you. If you want to talk about it, of course,' she concluded with an apologetic gesture. 'If it's too personal and you don't want to, I'll understand.'

Nico laughed and lit a cigarette. Camilla was sounding exactly like her old self now, using the same ploys and mannerisms to get him to talk as she had always done when they had shared the house and he had come home with a problem. Whether that problem had been Monty Barton or a persistent female, a recording contract or disagreements over how a new album should be produced, Camilla had urged him to talk it through and even if she didn't always understand the technicalities she came up with enough new ideas to make the talking worthwhile.

She had always been the best listener he had ever known, and never having discussed the problem of his marriage with another living soul, Nico felt a great wave of relief wash over him. If anyone could understand, it would be Camilla. So long, he added carefully, as he left out her unwitting involvement in the whole sad affair.

Outside, the soft breaking of waves on the beach could just be heard. The sky, inky black now, was dotted with bright stars. The curtains at the windows remained open because there was no need to close them. They were completely and utterly alone together, and Nico felt more at peace than he had for years.

393

He regretted now having allowed such a length of time to elapse before coming to see Camilla. She was definitely good for him, he decided, on any terms. And if he couldn't have her as a lover then he would accept her as a true friend. It was, after all, far better than nothing at all.

'When did it begin to go wrong?' Idly he repeated her question. 'Probably the moment I met her. I was homesick in Vegas and she took my mind off it. When Roz hassled me, Caroline simply suggested that we get married. I had a free day, so we did.'

'An impulsive gesture,' observed Camilla, nodding wisely, 'but some impulsive gestures have happy endings, so what went wrong after that?'

'I didn't love her,' he said simply, stubbing out his cigarette. 'I tried, God knows, but it wouldn't happen. And I don't honestly know whether Caroline loves me, which just goes to show what terrific lines of communication there are between us. She says she does, but maybe she feels she *has* to say it . . . Christ, we can't even talk to each other without sounding like a couple of strangers thrown together at some awful dinner party. I listen to us and wonder why the hell we're bothering, but Caroline keeps on trying. She tries so hard, Cami, but that's just what it seems like – trying. And it doesn't ring true. So you see, we've never really had the kind of relationship you and Matt shared. But what am I supposed to do? Caroline hasn't done anything wrong and she refuses to admit that anything *is* wrong. And since I'm the one who got us into this mess, I feel obliged to try and stick it out, even though I know it's hopeless.'

'Hmm.' Camilla allowed herself time to think and Nico watched her, admiring the sweeping twin curves of her eye-lashes and the high cheekbones which her loss of weight had accentuated. She bit her lower lip, considering his words, and he wanted suddenly, desperately, to kiss her soft, pink mouth. The urge was so great that he had to look away and was slightly disconcerted to find Rocky gazing straight at him, as if the dog knew exactly what was on his mind.

'Before, you were impetuous,' she announced, tilting her head to one side in order to gauge his expression. 'Impetuous is exciting, irresistible almost. Now, though, you're being noble and it's about the most boring thing anyone can possibly be. And since I went through a brief phase of it myself I can promise you that it's a bloody hard state to snap out of. Before you know it, it's become a habit and everyone gets sick to death of you.'

'I'm not noble, I'm just guilty,' he protested, shying away from the idea that he might be boring.

'So you've assumed all the responsibility for that guilt,' Camilla told him with wicked accuracy. 'And I bet poor Caroline's bored to tears. You're no fun any more – when you're with her, I mean,' she added hastily, catching the mutinous glint in his catlike green eyes. 'You have to snap out of it, stop blaming yourself and make a real effort to *enjoy* yourself instead. You have a brilliant life, a lovely wife, and so much money it's coming out of your ears. Give it a chance. Take her away on holiday and concentrate on all her good points instead of your big mistake. Failed marriages are so miserable and such a dreadful waste of time, and you're so nice you don't deserve to be unhappy.'

Deeply touched by her speech, Nico said gently, '*You're* so nice, Cami. If anyone doesn't deserve to be unhappy it's you, yet you've had more tragedy in your life than most people. Why is life so unfair?'

And it was at that moment, when her eyes filled with

uncontrollable tears at his tender words, that Nico kissed her. Unthinkingly, he bent his head and found her mouth with his own, all the emotions held in check for so long exploding inside him as he pulled her into his arms and felt her body trembling in response. Her hot tears touched his cheeks, ran down and added their poignant, salty wetness to the kiss. He no longer knew whether he was doing this for her sake or his; the incredible rightness of holding and kissing Camilla, the culmination of a two-year dream, was tangled in his mind with the desperate need he felt to drive away at least some of her terrible grief. If he could only banish it and make her happy for a few minutes, a few hours, a whole night, then that was all that mattered. His own happiness was secondary.

But at this moment he realized as his hand slid down her back and she gave a small moan of pleasure against his mouth, he had never been happier in his entire life.

By shifting slightly on to his side he manoeuvred them both into a more comfortable position. Without taking his lips from hers he ran gentle fingers along the sleek curves of her waist and hips then lightly played along the slender line of her thigh. He was so aroused that he knew she must be able to feel him against her other leg, now stretched between his own. Slowly, very slowly, taking care not to alarm her, he outlined her lips with his tongue and allowed his hand to travel back up to her waist. Beneath the shell-pink cashmere sweater he encountered the irresistible silky warmth of her skin. God, she had lost weight. But her breasts were still as gorgeous as they had always been. His mouth brushed her cheek, then her faintly scented neck. When it touched the sensitive hollow above her collarbone she sighed, her fingernails raking his shoulder, her hips moving imperceptibly against him and he thought he would explode with joy. Camilla wanted him, really wanted him.

And this time, he vowed silently, he wouldn't let her down.

Then he felt the wetness of a teardrop on his temple.

'Nico, we can't,' she whispered, her voice husky. 'We really can't. It isn't right.'

'Of course it's right.' He was licking her salty cheeks and dropping light butterfly kisses around her mouth. 'I just want to make you happy.'

Camilla managed a faint smile. 'I thought I told you to stop being noble,' she said with a feeble attempt at humour.

His eyes glittered with answering amusement.

'Well, maybe I'd be making myself happy too.'

But his heart sank as, with infinite regret, she stroked his cheek. 'We still can't. *I* can't,' she said softly, and it occurred to him all of a sudden that she hadn't slept with anyone at all for almost a year, since Matt had died. She was probably afraid of breaking that link with him. It was a traumatic hurdle to overcome.

'I understand, Cami. I know how much you loved Matt,' he said with difficulty, 'but he wouldn't want you to lock yourself away. Don't think that you'd be betraying him . . .'

'Oh Nico, I didn't mean that.' She was half laughing now, through her tears, and squeezing his arm. He shifted slightly on the settee, realizing that she was turning him down and wondering why a certain part of his anatomy still hadn't got the message. 'It's not me, it's *you*. We've just spent half an hour sorting out your marriage, thinking of ways to save it. How is sleeping with me going to help that, you fool? You can't be unfaithful to Caroline.'

'If it'll help you change your mind,' he said, unwilling to

give up this easily, 'it wouldn't be the first time.' No need to mention the fact that the first time had been with Roz. He would spare her that unnecessary detail.

'Well, that has to stop,' she told him firmly. 'A bit of fidelity might work wonders for the two of you.'

'OK. After tonight?' he suggested, making one last-ditch attempt and giving her his most beguiling smile.

'Don't Nico.' This time she laughed aloud, in control of herself again. 'I would never sleep with a married man. I know only too well how it feels to be the jilted wife, remember. We shouldn't even have gone as far as we did tonight, but you caught me at a vulnerable moment. And I'd had more wine than I'm used to,' she added, glancing at the two empty bottles on the coffee table. 'But thank you for the offer. It was very generous of you.'

Generous, Christ! thought Nico helplessly. How could she not know that he was crazy about her? Since he couldn't think of anything else to do, he lit another cigarette and watched the blue smoke spiral towards the ceiling.

Ah well, he decided ruefully, at least he and Camilla could still be friends which was, when you came to think of it, all he had been expecting anyway when he had turned up here. For a few glorious minutes he had believed that there would be more, but those hopes had been smartly dashed.

He would be a good loser. He would not sulk. It was just so very *unfair* though, he reflected with a wry sideways glance at Camilla, that the only woman in the world he really wanted was practically the only woman in the world who didn't want him back.

'I know it was generous of me,' he said, teasing her as she had teased him. 'It's because I'm such a wonderful guy.'

'Nice,' corrected Camilla shrewdly. 'You're basically a *nice* guy. Wonderful is stretching it a bit far. You'll be wonderful when you stop cheating on your wife.'

'I've already stopped,' he reminded her with feeling. Then he winked. 'Don't tell me you didn't notice?'

It wasn't until several days later that Camilla realized she had finally turned the corner. It came home to her as she was driving down the M6 back to London, when she heard herself singing along with a song on the radio. She was looking forward to being back in London. She was happy.

And thanks to Nico, she could even contemplate the idea of sex once more.

It had been one of the things she had badly missed after Matt's death. Not that she had *wanted* to leap into bed with anyone – there was no question of that – but the fact that their sex life had been so wonderful made it all the more difficult to accept that it was over.

Then she had lost the baby and the frustrations had subsided as if in sympathy with her double grief. Since she couldn't have Matt, she would have no-one. Her hormones seemed to put themselves on indefinite hold. She didn't need them. Sex was no longer a part of her life.

But Nico had reawakened those feelings and their intensity had stunned, almost alarmed her. At the time she had panicked slightly, concealing her alarm with humour and, luckily, a damn good excuse.

But she knew now that she had wanted him to make love to her. She had wanted to make love to him. If he hadn't been married she would have done so.

What she couldn't work out was whether, if he hadn't been

married and she had gone to bed with him, she would have been doing the right thing.

Camilla came to the conclusion that maybe it was just as well they hadn't. For now, it was enough to know that her body was returning to normal. Welcome back, she thought, breaking into a smile and turning up the volume on the radio. It had been a good week and it deserved to be celebrated. Once more she broke into song.

Thoughts of Nico, however, continued to occupy her mind. On arriving home she had infected Toby and Charlotte with her newfound happiness, whisking them off to the fair which had materialized since her departure on Hampstead Heath and treating them to dinner at McDonald's afterwards, since that was their particular idea of heaven.

Back at the house in Belgravia, when the children were asleep in bed, she poured herself a small glass of Cointreau, put on a much-loved Roxy Music album and curled up at one end of her favourite settee.

Nico had been such good company, she reflected lazily, her mind drifting. There had been no awkwardness after their potentially very awkward encounter. When she had reminded him that he was miles from anywhere and over the limit to drive he had said, 'That's what I was counting on', but had cheerfully slept in the spare room, yelling at her the following morning to get her ass in gear and come downstairs this minute because he had cooked breakfast. They had explored the beach with Rocky after that, then driven into Drumlachan where he caused quite a stir. The townspeople who normally exchanged pleasantries with the quiet English girl staying at Squirrel's Gate were struck dumb when the grey Lamborghini roared into the market place and she emerged with the singer whose face adorned a good many of their daughters' bedroom walls.

Later that afternoon Nico had left to return to London. She had urged him to remember what she'd told him about Caroline and with great decorum he had kissed her goodbye on both cheeks, European style.

'I will. Who needs an Italian mother when they have you around?'

'I'm serious,' she'd protested, laughing, and he had given her a quick hug.

'So's my Italian mother. You should meet her. Nice earrings,' he had added, touching one of them with his index finger. 'Real?'

'Real,' she'd replied, smiling. And he had jumped into his car and left.

Putting down her liqueur glass she touched the diamonds in her earlobes, a rapid, habitual gesture to check that they were still there. That was another small triumph, she reflected. It had been on the morning of Matt's funeral, whilst she was wandering in a completely dazed state around their bedroom, that she had opened the smallest drawer of an ornately carved Victorian oak chest bought by Matt from one of his beloved antique fairs and found the tiny red box from Cartier. Her surprise semi-anniversary present.

The brilliance and perfect simplicity of the twin diamond studs, each weighing almost two carats, had seared her very soul. She had teased him so often about his terrible taste – he couldn't help it, he adored intricate detail on clothes, jewellery . . . everything. The flashier the better, as far as Matt was concerned.

But he had obviously listened to her good-humoured criticism. Realizing that she did not share his own exquisite eye, he had taken care to choose a gift which he knew *she* would love. And he had chosen the unadorned, oval diamonds realizing that she would adore their uncluttered elegance.

It was this thought which had made them so very precious to her, proving beyond all else the depth of his love. She had slipped the glittering diamond studs into her pierced ears and worn them ever since, day and night, removing them for only a few minutes every week in order to clean them.

And when Nico had remarked upon them, for the first time in almost a year she had not developed a lump in her throat in memory of the morning of their discovery.

That sign, more than anything else, had made her realize that she was finally on the road to recovery.

Chapter 42

When Loulou arrived on her doorstep a fortnight later, Camilla knew at once that something was very wrong. A huge, puffy bruise was beginning to form along one cheekbone, a trace of blood was visible beneath the froth of silvery hair at her temple and her black T-shirt was torn at the neckline. She was trembling, her enormous grey eyes opaque with terror.

'Come inside.' Reaching for Loulou, she pulled her into the house. 'Do you need a doctor?'

'I need a lawyer,' wailed Loulou, stumbling into the sitting room. 'That bastard – I think I've murdered him!'

While Camilla sponged the blood from her hair, applied an ice-pack to her cheek and plied her with cognac, the story came out. Simon, it appeared, had celebrated the closure of a particularly lucrative business deal with far too much champagne. Summonsing Loulou to his flat in Kensington so that they could continue celebrating, he had started picking on her almost immediately. She looked like a tart. She was sleeping around. She was wearing stockings – that proved it.

He had hit her, hard. Defending herself, she had fought back and Simon, unsteady as a result of all the alcohol, had fallen against the dining-room table, hitting his head. Lying there, he hadn't moved. His breathing was alarmingly erratic, his eyes closed. Loulou had panicked and run away, coming to Camilla's house for sanctuary.

'Oh God, I bet I've killed him,' she moaned, clutching the

ice-pack to her cheek and looking anguished but unrepentant. 'That sonofabitch would die just to pay me back for pushing him. He'd do it out of spite, to make me suffer. Do you *know* what he called Lili?'

'What's his number?' said Camilla calmly. 'Why don't I phone him first and find out if he's dead?'

'Alive,' she announced, replacing the receiver. 'He sounds like a bear with the proverbial. I told him that if he was extremely lucky we wouldn't press charges and that you never want to set eyes on him again.'

'You told him that!' wailed Loulou. 'But Cami – I love him.'

'He beat you up.' Camilla inwardly despaired of Loulou's hopeless attraction to men who treated her badly. 'Next time he could murder *you*. Lou, it's over.'

Now Loulou was looking even more alarmed than she had when she thought Simon might be dead.

'He won't do it again,' she said quickly. 'It was probably all my fault anyway and he was only—'

'Trying to break every bone in your face,' snapped Camilla, her tone deliberately brutal. 'If you went back to him he could do it to Lili. Anyone who'd hit a woman would have even more fun beating up a young child. That's even easier – they can't put up so much of a fight.'

'Don't!' moaned Loulou, agonized. 'OK, OK . . . I won't see him. I suppose you're right. Shit.' She gazed absently at her fingernails. 'We were going to go and live with him next week as well.'

'You'll be far happier staying where you are,' Camilla told her firmly. 'And Lili adores Christo, after all.'

'Hmm,' said Loulou. 'The trouble is, Lili isn't the only one.

404

Christo's girlfriend adores Christo too. She's moving in with him, and although they're both far too nice to say so, I know they'd really prefer not to be part of a *ménage à quatre.*'

'Lou, sometimes you really are the absolute limit,' exclaimed Camilla, fizzing with exasperation. 'Don't you ever even *think* of your friends?'

Loulou looked hurt. 'What have I done now?'

'Come on, get up.' Pulling the melting ice-pack from her friend's hand, Camilla dragged her to her feet. 'We're going over to Christo's flat right now to pick up Lili and your things – God knows, you don't have enough even to fill the car. And don't argue. You're coming to live with me. Now.'

They stayed up late into the night, talking non-stop, both so excited about being there together that they didn't even notice the grandfather clock chiming first twelve, then one and two.

'I can make sure you eat properly,' said Loulou, adding with a gleam of triumph, 'I can *cook* for you!'

'I want to gain weight, not lose it,' Camilla reminded her.

Their conversation ricocheted from one subject to the next. Whilst Lili, Charlotte and Toby slept peacefully their mothers discussed their upbringing, then moved on to men. Nico, Camilla learnt, was taking Caroline away to Barbados. Caroline had confided to Loulou that they were hoping to start a family. Loulou was aware that their marriage wasn't perfect, but since she evidently had no idea of the extent of Nico's unhappiness Camilla thought it prudent to keep the news to herself. Likewise, she censored her own account of his visit to her cottage in Scotland, saying only how nice it had been to see him.

Loulou was delighted and relieved to see that she was overcoming her desolation following Matt's death. The grief had lessened and Camilla was obviously more cheerful. She was regaining her old sparkle, at last.

They also discussed Mac and Cecilia and it rapidly became clear to Camilla that Loulou had regarded Simon as a form of retaliation, a weapon with which she had hoped to make Mac think again.

'He doesn't love her,' she said, twisting a long strand of blonde hair around her fingers. 'It's been almost eighteen months now and he still hasn't even *married* her, which must mean something. They have the most appalling fights – far worse than he ever had with me – yet for some reason they stay together. The photographer and the model,' she enunciated with disgust. 'They're only doing it because it boosts both their careers.'

All Camilla could do was agree with her because that was what Loulou wanted to hear.

Then their conversation turned to Roz, who was also having a less than happy time at present. Apparently she was at loggerheads with the new producer of her TV show and as a result the ratings were suffering. As the well-publicized mother of a cot-death baby, Roz had wanted Loulou to guest on the show. Loulou's enormous contribution to the charity devoted to its research had also generated a vast amount of publicity at the time and Roz felt that this show could renew public interest in the charity and its continuing need for funds. The producer, a raving homosexual, had flatly informed her that such a pro-gramme would be morbid, dull and of no interest to anyone apart from the parents who had been affected. Instead, he suggested, she should be doing a fashion special, concentrating on the talents of the new designer, Marco Ciati.

'Who by some incredible coincidence,' concluded Loulou

with heavy irony, 'is young, gorgeous and also gay. Roz evidently had a ring-ding stand-up show-down with him in the middle of the studio canteen and called him a freak-show faggot ... well, that's about the most polite thing she called him ... so now he's doing his best to get her kicked out again. I have to admit that I feel just the tiniest bit guilty. Doing a programme about cot-deaths was my idea after all, and now Roz has got herself into trouble because of it. And I know she won't give in.'

Camilla considered her friend's words. Roz was a total enigma as far as she was concerned; one minute she was going out of her way to be unpleasant, the next she was risking her job in order not to let Loulou, or the charity, down.

'She's very loyal,' said Loulou, reading her mind. 'I know she's been the most frightful bitch as far as you're concerned, but she's always been a good friend to me.'

Chapter 43

Roz was indeed less than happy at the present time. She loathed Murray Irving, her ghastly producer. He seemed determined now to make her life as miserable as possible, and he wasn't doing too badly either. Work was no fun at all these days, thanks to that goddam fairy.

Her social life, too, was less than gripping. No men interested her. Since her carefully planned reunion with Nico had failed so dismally – he had fled home to his boring wife and taken great pains to avoid Roz ever since – she had failed to unearth a single *interesting* man. Or a married one for that matter, she thought with a vague attempt at humour. Sex was sporadic and unsatisfying and she invariably wondered afterwards why she'd even bothered. At this rate, it was a toss-up whether she'd die of boredom or AIDS.

Altogether a very boring situation to be in, she decided. But what on earth was she supposed to do about it? Advertise in *The Times* for a white knight?

Both these situations, however, paled into insignificance compared with the new bombshell now facing her.

The letter lay in her lap, and she ran her index finger along the top edge of it rather than pick it up again. There was no longer any need to do so, since she knew the contents by heart. Since its arrival this morning she must have read it fifty times and on every occasion she had experienced the same twist in the pit of her stomach.

At first she had assumed it to be a belated birthday card. The large, fuchsia pink envelope had fluttered through the letter box and Roz, just leaving the cottage, had stuffed it into her bag without even glancing at the front of it. Which meant that it wasn't until she was comfortably settled on the Intercity train heading towards London that she pulled the envelope out and saw that it had been addressed initially to the TV studios. The fact that URGENT, EXTREMELY PRIVATE AND PERSONAL, and NOT TO BE OPENED BY ANYONE OTHER THAN ROZ VALLENDER was plastered across the top in black ink had evidently prompted her secretary to redirect it to her home in Gloucestershire, since she hadn't been due to visit the studios until next week.

Roz had smiled when she saw it. Probably some star-struck teenage boy confessing his undying love for her. Sometimes they wrote poems, or included photo-booth pictures of themselves. She doubted, in view of the pink envelope, whether it was an obscene letter.

The smile had faded from her face when she opened it and began to read.

Dear Miss Vallender,

First of all, I think you should sit down because what I have to tell you may come as a shock. I hope you will think it's a nice shock.

I could have written to you months ago but I waited until today – my eighteenth birthday – because I thought you might be more fully prepared. It must have occurred to you that this could happen, now.

Have you guessed yet?

Yes, I am your daughter, Natalie.

I'm sorry I haven't done this through the proper channels, but I was too impatient – and too afraid that if the official woman contacted you, you might refuse to have anything to do with me. A letter from me to you seems better, more personal somehow. And more persuasive too, hopefully.

Anyway, my adopted mother knew your name. Six months ago I overheard her talking to a friend and discovered that you were my real mother. It was weird, because not long before that we'd been watching you on TV and I'd said how much like you I looked. We are very alike, you know.

Mum knows I am writing to you. She and Dad are great and I love them both very much but I have always longed to meet my *real* parents. I don't resent you for giving me away – I can count on my fingers and I realize that you were very young when you had me. And I have had a nice life so far, so no complaints.

But I *would* like to see you. The reason I haven't enclosed a photograph is in the hope that this will make you curious enough to want to meet *me*.

I am interesting, intelligent (nine GCSEs) and have a good sense of humour. I like Indian and Chinese food. My favourite television programme – creep, creep! – is yours.

Please, *please* write back to me. It'll be even worse than waiting for exam results, so do it as quickly as possible. Every morning I shall be lying in wait for our poor old postman.

Yours very sincerely,
Natalie Purnell.

PS I was so sorry about Nicolette. I didn't even know then that she was my half-sister, but when I heard that she had died, I cried for ages.

It was one of the very few occasions in her life when Roz had felt utterly helpless. The child she had conceived when she was fifteen and to whom she had given birth on her sixteenth birthday had never completely faded from her thoughts, but to have this proof of her existence thrust at her so abruptly had knocked her for six. Her daughter was impatient to re-enter her life and she was hopelessly unprepared. She was, naturally, aware of the adoption laws enabling eighteen year olds to seek contact with their natural mothers, but somehow Roz had never imagined that it could happen to her.

Natalie, however, had obviously decided otherwise.

But Roz, who had functioned on auto-pilot for the last twelve hours, still did not know what to do. She was confused, torn . . . afraid . . . and although it made no sense to her whatsoever, for some unfathomable reason there was only one person in the world whose advice she wanted to hear.

It wasn't until Lili winced and flailed her chubby bare brown arms that Loulou realized she was holding her too tightly. Her daughter gazed at her reprovingly, then beamed forgiveness and nestled her head against Loulou's neck, the whimpering which had prompted her late-night arrival downstairs now a thing of the past.

Loulou, absently kissing her hair, made a final circuit of the kitchen and gazed out at the wet blackness of the night. Rain was sliding down the windows and the wind howled around the house like a swarm of indignant ghosts.

Sighing with impatience she turned and headed for the stairs. Lili was ready for bed once more and at least if she was putting her back into her cot she couldn't be listening at the closed door of the sitting-room, frantically attempting to eavesdrop on the conversation taking place inside.

What on *earth*, she wondered with burning, tortured curiosity, could possibly be going on in there? Roz and Camilla, together?

'I came to say I'm sorry,' said Roz, 'for everything. My behaviour has been unforgivable and I'll understand if you want me to leave, but I had to say it anyway. I've been a prize bitch. I was jealous of you. Now I know how wrong I've been, and I'm so ashamed of myself . . .' She shook her dark head and searched for the words which she had been practising for hours. 'I'm just very, very sorry,' she ended simply, and lifted her head so that Camilla could see the truth and sadness in her eyes.

Camilla, listening to the slow, steady thud of her pulse and the rattle of rain against the windows, could think of no words to say. That Roz could be here, apologizing and asking for her forgiveness, was so improbable that she still wasn't entirely sure she wasn't dreaming. She glanced out of the window at the rain, then at the clock. Ten past midnight.

It was no dream.

And how, in all honesty, could she refuse?

'I'm glad you came.'

'I'm glad, too, I think,' said Roz, a glimmer of a smile touching her lips although her slanting dark eyes still registered anxiety.

'Lou kept telling me how good a friend you were to her, so I knew you couldn't be all bad.'

'Loulou spends her entire life reeling from one disaster to another. She isn't happy unless she's got something to be really unhappy about. I wasn't jealous of her.'

'Were you really jealous of *me*?' said Camilla incredulously. 'I can't believe it. Why?'

Roz's black eyebrows straightened with concentration. 'Not at first. I didn't know that Jack was your husband, but I suppose I didn't care *that* much when I found out. Oh, I cared that he'd tried to trick me, but I wasn't too bothered about how badly it would affect you. And then there was the thing with Nico. You'd really pulled yourself together by then –'

'Thanks to Loulou,' interjected Camilla.

'– you'd gained confidence, you looked great, and you virtually told me to get stuffed. That's when I first started to feel jealous. And after that, it seemed you could do no wrong. You were rocketing ahead and at the same time I was sliding further and further downhill.'

Roz paused, lost in thought, then gestured impatiently with her hand. 'When Nicolette died I had nothing left and you had everything, a brilliant career, a wonderful man, two perfect children . . . everybody seemed to *love* you. And no-one at all loved me. The letter you wrote to me was the final straw. I'm afraid I went a bit crazy when I read it.'

With sudden clarity Camilla realized that Roz's words were echoing Christo's almost exactly. Dear, perceptive Christo had realized just what was going on that night at Vampires when she and Roz had last met. How incredibly astute he was, she thought with a rush of affection for the red-haired Irishman. The idea that Roz might *envy* her would never have entered her head in a thousand years.

'And you must still have been terribly upset about Nicolette,'

413

she murmured, but Roz stopped her.

'You see?' she demanded with a trace of exasperation. 'You're too *nice* – making excuses for me already! I said some hateful things. Do you really think you can forgive me?'

Camilla smiled. 'I really think I already have.'

'How could you *leave* me outside!' wailed Loulou, perching on the arm of the settee and jiggling her tulip-shaped glass, demanding an immediate refill of the slightly warm champagne. 'I was practically climbing the walls out there. You abandoned me for *hours*.'

'You would have been interrupting every five seconds,' pointed out Camilla reasonably, accepting a rare cigarette from Roz.

'I would not!'

'Of course you would,' Roz joined in. 'We *know* you, Loulou. And besides, with what I had to say, I didn't want an audience.'

Loulou sniffed loudly. 'That must be a first.'

'Oh, shut up and drink your drink. We're together, we're celebrating and we're happy for Christ's sake.'

'Happy?' yelled Loulou, struggling to stay dead-pan. 'Happy! How can you *say* that? How on earth can we be happy when we don't have a single man between us?'

Chapter 44

It wasn't until eleven o'clock the following morning that Roz could bring herself to broach the subject of Natalie with Camilla. Loulou was upstairs in bed nursing both Lili and a hangover. But it was Camilla whose advice she sought, whose opinions she needed. She knew without asking what Loulou's would be.

Camilla, who had taken Toby and Charlotte to school over two hours earlier, was dressed in a lilac cashmere golfing sweater which had been Matt's, and close-fitting denims.

Roz still found it difficult to believe how totally Camilla had changed. She was scarcely recognizable now as the anxious, overweight housewife who had fussed and panicked her way through a dinner party, unaware that within hours her comfortable, sheltered little life would be lying in smithereens at her feet.

All Roz had to do now was retrain her mind to admire rather than envy her.

Draining her coffee cup, she said, 'Thanks for letting me stay last night. I really didn't feel like going back to the hotel.'

'We were up until three thirty,' Camilla reminded her with a smile. 'There didn't seem much point in your leaving. It's lovely, anyway, to have more people in the house. Especially friends. More coffee?'

'No thanks, it's coming out of my ears. Actually, I need to

ask your advice about a very personal matter.'

'Me?' Camilla looked surprised.

'You. Because you know what I'm really like. More than anyone else,' she said wryly, 'you're aware I'm not always the nicest person in the world, or the easiest to get along with. And that needs to be taken into serious consideration in this case.'

Camilla poured herself a refill of fresh, strong coffee and sat down opposite her, watching as Roz dug in the pocket of her scarlet jacket and pulled out an envelope. After a moment's hesitation, she handed it across the table.

'Read this. I'll wait outside in the garden.'

The grass was still wet from last night's rain, but the sun was out and the scent of roses hung in the air. At the edge of the patio Roz stooped to retrieve a small white sandal and a pair of knickers abandoned there by Lili. Just like her mother, she thought with affectionate amusement, then wondered whether Natalie was like *her*, and how Camilla was at this moment reacting to the news that Natalie existed. The knot of tension in her stomach was growing inside her like a living thing, the waiting becoming intolerable.

Less than five minutes later Camilla joined her, the expression on her face grave.

'Why do you need my advice?' she asked slowly, and Roz averted her gaze, staring intently at the dew-laden roses which covered the old stone wall bordering one side of the garden.

'Because I'm afraid.'

'You don't want to meet her?'

'I do, I do. I'm afraid she'll be disappointed.'

Camilla took her arm and they began to walk slowly together

around the garden, the imprints of their footsteps trailing in the wet grass behind them.

'She's seen me on television. She thinks I'm like that,' said Roz in a low voice. 'How can she accept the *real* me?'

'Oh, the real you isn't too bad,' Camilla assured her with a squeeze and a smile.

'What if she meets me and realizes that she hates me?'

'Why should she?'

Roz turned to her, her dark eyes filled with pain. 'And what if I get to know her, then discover that I'm *jealous* of her?'

'You won't,' said Camilla positively. 'There is no reason on this earth why you should envy *anyone*. Instead there's every reason why you should love her. She sounds terrific.'

Roz managed a smile at last. 'She does, doesn't she?'

'And in many ways she's like you,' Camilla continued, willing Roz to understand. 'She certainly used her initiative, writing directly to you like that. And she must be mature, to be able to consider your feelings enough to wait until now before sending the letter.'

'She's certainly got character,' said Roz with growing pride and enthusiasm. Thank God she had been able to talk to Camilla about this. She was so right – you didn't envy your own daughter for all her good qualities, you loved her instead!

'And a sense of humour.'

'She's clever. Not sending a photo of herself . . .'

'And determined.'

Roz grinned. 'In fact,' she said slowly, and with triumph in her voice, 'she's a lot like . . . no, *exactly* like . . . me!'

Natalie ran her fingers through her spiky, shoulder-length dark hair and glanced at her watch for the hundredth time in an hour.

In just a few minutes now the train would be pulling into Paddington station; already a few of her fellow passengers were organizing themselves, arranging their bags and cases around their feet. Hastily she kicked her empty Coke can and three apple cores under her seat and brushed an apple pip from her skirt.

God, she was so excited she didn't know what to do with herself!

How many times had she replayed the scene in her head? Meeting her real mother. And since yesterday, when Roz Vallender's letter had arrived, she had had to adapt it, for in her imagination the meeting had always taken place indoors, in someone's house.

Instead, it was happening at Paddington station, amidst crowds of strangers and hissing, roaring trains. Natalie approved. She was adaptable, after all. Railway stations sounded very romantic, very *Brief Encounter*.

And totally, totally mind-blowing.

She hoped she was wearing the right clothes. Having watched her mother on television she knew that she was an extremely sharp dresser. Designer stuff, the real thing. And she had been tempted at first to go for contrast – torn Levis, the black micro T-shirt which revealed her midriff, the biker boots sprayed yellow.

At this point, however, her adoptive mother had stepped in. 'You want the poor woman to take one look at you and deny all responsibility?' she had challenged Natalie with the ease of long practice. 'Good heaven's girl, whatever would she think she'd given birth to? Wear something that won't frighten her to death, at least.'

Natalie knew she was lucky. She had read enough problem

pages to know that most adopted children wanted to contact their real mothers, yet many were afraid of upsetting the family which had brought them up as one of their own.

Few women were as totally secure as Christine Purnell. She and her husband Tom were a loving, down-to-earth couple who had faced the situation with generosity and understanding. When Natalie, after many rehearsals, had broached the subject, she had kissed her tall, dark-haired daughter and said, 'I'd want to know if it were me, love. You do whatever it is you have to do.'

'I still love *you*, Mum,' Natalie had insisted, remembering the article she had read in *Woman's Own* about adoptive parents feeling rejected. Christine roared with laughter.

'I love Tom, and you, and those two noisy brothers of yours, and there's no rule to say I can't. We don't each have enough love for only one person. I daresay you'll have enough for two mothers, if you're careful with it.'

Roz, shivering despite the heat on the station platform, was beginning to regret her rashness. Urged on by Camilla, she had written to Natalie explaining which train to catch and where to meet her. She wished now that she had suggested instead a more private venue. Apart from Wembley Stadium or centre stage at Covent Garden there was almost nothing less private than Paddington station. Greeting long-lost lovers there was OK, but long-lost daughters was quite another matter.

And despite her black sunglasses and voluminous high-collared trench coat three people had asked her for autographs already. Any minute now, she thought wildly as her teeth chattered with nerves, a film crew would pop out of the nearest siding, fix up a few spotlights and set the cameras rolling.

Finally, the train slid into the station and Roz rammed her fists deep into the pockets of her white St Laurent jacket. It was scarcely behind schedule at all yet those three minutes had seemed like three hours.

And all she could do now was stand and wait. Natalie had the advantage. It was up to her to seek out her mother and introduce herself.

Shit, thought Roz helplessly. This was like preparing to go on the air without a script. She had no experience with greeting grown-up daughters for the first time. She didn't know what to *say* to them.

As a stream of passengers poured out of the carriages she scanned them with anxious eyes from behind the safety shield of her dark glasses. There was a plump girl with dark hair and terrible acne ... she breathed a sigh of relief when the girl flung her arms around an equally spotty boy. Maybe that girl, whose eyes were brown but whose hair was bleached white? She was painfully thin and a hand-rolled cigarette drooped from her mouth as she dug in her jeans' pocket for matches. Oh please, prayed Roz, realizing that the girl looked distinctly unwashed, *don't let her be Natalie* ...

'Hello,' said a voice to her left, and Roz felt time stop. Slowly she turned to see a tall, slender girl with hauntingly familiar eyebrows, dark catlike eyes and razor-cut shoulder-length hair, wearing an absurdly adult navy blue suit and carrying a huge plastic rucksack sprayed gold. 'I'm Natalie. How do you do?'

To her astonishment Roz found herself shaking her daughter's hand. Natalie, it appeared, had her own ideas about mother-daughter reunions.

Glad that at least someone appeared to have a vague idea

how the script should run, she said, 'It's good to see you. Er . . . how was your journey?'

Natalie shrugged, giving her a breezy smile. 'The pits. Whoever said it's better to travel hopefully than to arrive must've been off his trolley. I'm just glad to be here . . . at last.'

'I'm glad you're here, too,' said Roz, praying that she sounded less awkward than she felt. Realizing that she was fiddling with her dark glasses she shoved them into the pocket of her trenchcoat and tried to look decisive. 'Shall we go and find a cab?'

Where, she berated herself as they made their way out of the station, were her maternal feelings? This still felt like a blind date on the verge of going terribly wrong. Surely there should be something *more* between them than this stilted English politeness?

When they were settled in the back of a taxi, Natalie leaned over her gold rucksack, unzipped it and drew out a bunch of drooping yellow freesias.

'These are for you,' she stated matter of factly. 'They're from my mum, actually. She thinks of things like that.'

'They're lovely. How kind of her,' said Roz, feeling more helpless than ever as she accepted the wilting blooms. Then she watched in horror as a large tear rolled down Natalie's smooth brown cheek.

'I'm sorry, I'm sorry,' sobbed Natalie, searching wildly for a tissue. 'I planned all this for so long. Right up until the train stopped I was going to run up to you and give you the biggest hug in the world and you were going to burst into tears and it was all going to be so . . . wonderful . . .' She paused, sniffing loudly and gulping for breath. 'And then I got scared and thought you might not like it because we don't even know each other so I decided to be all polite and businesslike instead . . . and now I *hate* it. I feel like I'm here for a job interview. Oh shit . . . didn't you ever *miss* me in all those years? I've wondered for so long about what my real mother was like. Haven't *you* ever wondered what might have happened to *me*?'

'Oh my God, Natalie . . .' Roz felt her defences crumble. The fear and passion in the girl's voice clutched at her heart and without even realizing what she was doing she reached for her. 'How can you even think that I wouldn't? Of course I thought about you. *Always*. And now . . . I'm just glad you contacted me so that we can both find out about each other. If you hadn't done it, I wouldn't ever have been able to learn anything about you.'

It had been an exhausting day all round.

By the time Camilla, Loulou and the children returned home at six – having vacated the house for the day so that Roz and Natalie could have some privacy in comfortable surroundings – their feet were aching and the Science Museum definitely knew that it had been visited.

When they entered the sitting-room they found Roz alone, smoking a cigarette and looking drawn.

'She didn't turn up?' said Loulou, horrified.

'Natalie's upstairs having a bath. I'm down here having a guilt attack.'

Camilla shooed the children into the kitchen. 'How's it going?' she asked, pouring out gin and tonics.

Shaking her dark head, Roz murmured, 'Nothing like the movies. I had to lie a lot. I don't *feel* like her mother – I haven't had the practice, for God's sake.'

'It'll take time,' said Camilla reassuringly, handing round the drinks. 'What's she like?'

A glimmer of humour showed in Roz's eyes. 'Me, I suppose. With a bit of a Geordie accent.'

Chapter 45

It was certainly not like the movies, thought Camilla later that evening as she watched Roz struggling to conceal her unease. Natalie was chatty, likeable and openly demonstrative towards Roz. It was fascinating to compare their striking looks and the inescapable similarities in their characters, but the differences were equally interesting. Roz had always been naturally reticent, an intrinsically private person. Within the space of one hour, they had all learnt Natalie's entire life history, her likes and dislikes, her views upon almost everything and her aspirations for the future.

It also rapidly became clear that she was star-struck. Which wasn't, of course, unusual for an eighteen-year-old girl, but it made Roz edgy, that much was very apparent.

Since discovering her mother's identity Natalie had scoured the gossip columns like a stockbroker devouring the FT Index. She *adored* Nico Coletto, was quite *au fait* with Loulou's recent adventures and was a great admirer of Mac and his work. And whilst she was clearly thrilled to be reunited with her natural mother, the fact that Roz was a celebrity was a wonderful bonus. It was so exciting. She knew so many famous people. And the small Tyneside town where Natalie had grown up couldn't compare with the glitter and glamour of London. Natalie was due to go to university in September – a degree course in Geology – but that was *so* boring . . . she had always wanted to be a model or an actress . . . and London was the only place to be if she wanted to really make something of her life . . .

'I can't believe it,' groaned Loulou, having followed Camilla into the kitchen on the pretext of helping her make the coffee. 'Any moment now she's going to ask Roz for her autograph.'

Camilla tried not to smile. 'Or worse, ask for Nico's.'

The following morning Roz and Natalie came dangerously close to having their first row, with Natalie pressing hard to be allowed to go to the TV studios where Roz was preparing a programme and Roz reacting violently against the suggestion.

'Are you ashamed of me?' demanded Natalie with wounded eyes, and Camilla realized that she was expecting too much, too soon, of the woman who had so recently been thrust into the role of mother to such an ebullient teenager.

'Of course not,' parried Roz, agitated and unprepared. 'But I need to finish two days' work in one if we're going to leave for Gloucestershire tonight, and none of it will get done if I have to waste time introducing you to the world and his dog. Some other time, OK?'

'Will you introduce me to Nico Coletto?' said Natalie with a smile that was both challenging and sly.

Roz's eyes narrowed dangerously and Camilla stepped into the breach.

'Stay here with me today,' she said firmly, thinking that Roz would certainly have her hands full when she took Natalie down to her cottage in the Cotswolds for a few days. Natalie was testing her mother, seeing how far she could go and what she could get away with. Roz would have to make sure she didn't allow her guilt to overcome common sense.

At two o'clock that afternoon, with all the desperate compulsion of an alcoholic, Loulou slid surreptitiously into the Kendall

Fordyce gallery in Kensington. For days she had been telling herself she wouldn't come here. Last night she had even thought she might have won. This morning, of course, she realized that she hadn't a hope in hell.

No self-control, she thought gloomily. The story of my life. And taking care to adjust the charcoal grey fedora over her eyes – every strand of her rippling blonde hair was crammed beneath it – she purchased a catalogue from the reception desk by the entrance and made her way into the gallery itself where the exhibition featuring Mac's latest work was being held.

Loulou was able to look back and marvel now at the cocoon of serenity which had eased her through pregnancy. At the time she had been unable to recognize it – it had just felt so wonderfully, perfectly *right* that she hadn't questioned the strangeness of it all.

But now she was back to quite her old self and very frustrating it was too.

Here I am, she thought with indignation bordering on despair, chasing after Mac again and knowing full well that he's only keen on me when I'm *not* chasing him.

And would he even *be* here today? She was terrified that he would, yet the prospect of coming here and *not* seeing him was equally appalling, just as she had been unwilling to come here, but unable to stay away.

Which was why she had borrowed Camilla's grey fedora and Roz's baggy white trenchcoat, donned a pair of very black glasses and was sporting unfamiliar pillar-box red lipstick. Hopefully she looked like an Italian banker's wife and not a bit like Loulou Marks, idiot extraordinaire.

The gallery was more crowded than she had expected, which was good. Holding her catalogue up to her face she squeezed between a couple of portly, fragranced men and came abruptly face to face with Cecilia Drew.

Not the real Cecilia, although the image still managed to leave her breathless.

Taking a step backwards Loulou stared at the enormous black-and-white photograph of her rival, clad in shorts and a miniscule camisole top, curled up in a wicker chair. Sunlight, streaming through a torn lace curtain, dappled her long, slender body with shadows and light. Her long hair gleamed and her eyes were directed just above the camera, capturing yet more light and an exquisite sense of longing for whoever stood behind it.

Loulou didn't see it as exquisite. She found it nauseating. And you could see her dark nipples through the thin camisole, she thought with disgust. Why, it was practically pornographic.

A young man with incredibly muddy training shoes paused beside her, studied the picture and nudged his friend.

'Wouldn't mind giving her one,' he said, grinning, and Loulou sniffed loudly.

'I doubt if she'd be interested,' she said, tilting her hat and turning away. 'She's a raving dyke.'

There was no sign of Mac anywhere, when she finally dared to look. Wandering around the well-lit gallery she began to relax and enjoy herself, although there were far too many pictures of Cecilia around for her liking, and the sight of each one pierced her with jealousy.

He's only using her to advance his career, she told herself, but it was disheartening all the same. No woman wants her man to go off with an ugly girl, but Cecilia was right off the other end of the scale. Loulou, who had never considered herself unattractive or lacking in physical attributes – although bigger boobs would have been nice – realized that each time she surveyed a new photograph of Britain's current highest paid model she felt as if she were shrinking. The cuts and bruises, legacy of her disastrous liaison with Simon, had completely cleared now – at least she had that to be thankful for – but her crazy, spiralling blonde hair couldn't compete with Cecilia's sleek black mane, her wide grey eyes seemed merely childish next to Cecilia's exotically tilted topaz ones, and to add insult to already considerable injury she was several inches shorter.

No-one ever called me a jungle animal, she thought gloomily as she gazed at a photograph of Cecilia in a skin-skimming bodysuit lounging gracefully along a tree branch and overheard someone say, 'What a tiger.'

At that moment she heard a commotion behind her, a rising swell of excitement amongst the knowledgeable crowd who had attended this exhibition because it was undoubtedly set to be one of the most successful of the year.

Without moving, Loulou felt the back of her neck prickle and knew that Mac had arrived. Instantly she wished she hadn't come. It was a ridiculous disguise . . . Mac would spot her immediately . . . please God don't let him have Cecilia Drew with him . . .

Cigar smoke attacked her throat and she stifled a cough. Turning round – because it would look odd if she didn't – she saw through the black glasses that Cecilia was indeed with him, clinging elegantly to his arm while with his other Mac shook hands with a variety of guests, admirers and journalists. Everyone was congratulating him. It was a magnificent show. Now Mac was truly being recognized as one of Europe's great photographers.

Silent and still, Loulou watched from her position at the

back of the crowd, remembering how different it had once been. The years of struggling when Mac had bought films rather than food, the terrible little bedsitters they had shared with mice and cockroaches, the furious rows when Mac was too proud to let her support him, the happy, *happy* times when a small cash prize in a photographic competition had meant a night out celebrating, the way Mac had always been able to make her laugh . . . the wonderful sex they had shared . . .

Without warning two helpless tears rolled down her cheeks and she pushed them fiercely away, taking a deep breath in order to calm herself.

The man standing in front of her puffed energetically on his King Edward cigar and clouds of smoke billowed past him, catching in Loulou's lungs once more. She coughed loudly, tried to quell the irritation and coughed again, tears streaming down her face now as she gasped for breath. People were turning to look at her, she realized, and doubled over as another choking fit seized her by the throat. This was terrible . . .

Suddenly the young man with the dirty training shoes was beside her, slapping her on the back. She tried to knock his arm away – Christ, a slap on the back was the last thing she needed – and staggered forward as he hit her again.

Then her hat flew off and she felt her hair tumbling down over her shoulders. The famous, silver-gilt, waist-length hair which was so unmistakable.

And so impossible to miss.

Mac watched the fedora cartwheel along the black, polished floor and felt his insides contract. For a second the old familiar longing for Loulou had engulfed him, mingling with other, conflicting emotions whose nature he didn't dare pin down. She had hurt him, caused him more pain than any other woman he had ever known and he had too much pride to allow himself to forgive her for that.

But she was *his* Loulou, he realized. She was his ex-wife and she had as many good points as faults; it just wasn't always easy coping with either of them.

'Isn't that your ex-wife?' asked Cecilia in a low voice as Loulou, pink with humiliation, crammed her hat back on to her head and turned deliberately away from them.

Mac nodded, his jaw tense as he watched her march off towards the opposite end of the gallery, a youngish man with indescribably filthy trainers and a navy blue T-shirt at her heels.

She was looking bloody good, anyway, he thought. It was eighteen months now since he had last seen her – at Matt and Camilla's wedding reception – and all he knew about her was what he had managed to glean from Nico without appearing too interested.

Glancing down at Cecilia's exquisitely manicured, vaguely predatory fingernails upon the sleeve of his leather jacket, and at the figure-skimming yellow skirt she was wearing, he felt a moment's dissatisfaction.

One of the things he had always admired about Loulou was her style. She had a careless, slapdash elegance and never took longer than two minutes to put together any outfit. She always looked good, *effortlessly* good, and never wasted any time in doing so, which Mac appreciated.

Even now, he thought, in that ridiculous oversized white trenchcoat reaching practically to her ankles, a white vest and leather trousers, she looked . . . perfect.

Of course, Cecilia looked perfect too, but only now was he able to truly appreciate Loulou's economy with time, if not money. Cecilia, to his knowledge, had never spent less than two hours preparing to greet the outside world, agonizing over which clothes she should wear and which of a million accessories would most enhance them.

He was fond of Cecilia, and despite her hugely successful career she badly needed looking after, which he liked, but he didn't love her. When the initial dizzying lust had worn off he had gradually realized how very little they actually had in common. Unwillingly, he had found himself comparing her with Loulou. Cecilia was probably more classically beautiful, but she wasn't an adventurous person. Everything she said or did was planned. She hardly ever made him laugh.

The trouble with Loulou, on the other hand, was her over-adventurous spirit. She had scarcely ever allowed him to look after *her*. He never knew what she would do or say next, and while sometimes that had amused him, her wild unpredictability also drove him to distraction.

Life with Loulou had been like flying in a monoplane with a circus pilot, up and down, looping crazily in all directions. Being with Cecilia, by contrast, was sailing on an ocean liner, as straight and calm as a spirit level.

She was the most unspontaneous person he had ever known, and he spent a great deal of time persuading himself that she was the antidote to Loulou he so badly needed. No surprises. No risks. No threat to his masculinity. And absolutely no fun. But then, Cecilia, he reminded himself for the thousandth time as she smiled professionally for a photographer, would never arrive home with another man's baby . . . and expect him to fucking well adore it.

Another flashbulb exploded and Mac realized that a woman wearing hideous mock-sapphire earrings and carrying a notepad was trying to attract his attention. Pretending not to notice, he watched Loulou covertly. He could almost feel the waves of shame and frustration emanating from her as she studiously avoided the attentions of the man next to her and rammed her rolled-up copy of the exhibition catalogue into one of the deep pockets of her trenchcoat.

Mac knew exactly how furious she was with herself right now. He knew, too, that she wouldn't leave straight away because that would seem to her like running out. But she was insecure. Her cover had been blown, and she had lost her psychological advantage as a result.

Her acute vulnerability touched a nerve within him and despite himself, Mac smiled, sympathizing with her predicament. But maybe now at least she would understand how he had felt when she had in the past hurt him.

'Martin Stacey-Thompson,' said the young man in the filthy trainers and the Robbie Williams T-shirt. He stuck out his hand for Loulou to shake and inspected her shamed features with beady pale blue eyes which missed nothing. When she tried to pretend she hadn't heard him he shook his head and tut-tutted. 'I thought you had more guts. Wouldn't it help for him to see you engaged in animated conversation with another man rather than shivering all alone like a frozen whippet? Being caught out like this can't honestly be the most awful thing that's ever happened to you.'

Realizing that he was right on all counts, Loulou willed herself to relax. Turning to look at him – his voice was surprisingly deep and mature and didn't match his appearance one bit – she gave him a slightly forced but nonetheless dazzling smile. Before he realized what was happening she had kissed him on both cheeks.

432

Across the room, Mac felt his blood pressure soar. The bitch, he thought furiously. The bloody, bloody cow. She was only doing it to irritate the hell out of him.

'Your move, smartass,' she said, without allowing the words to disturb her smile, and Martin Stacey-Thompson slid his arm around her waist, beneath the voluminous white trenchcoat, and drew her tightly against him.

Mac gritted his teeth and found to his disgust that he was quite incapable of turning away. His warring, ambiguous emotions felt as if they'd been thrown into a blender on high speed and in less than five seconds he had lost *his* advantage.

That terrific sense of superiority had gone right down the pan. Loulou, the little tart, was kicking him in the groin, exerting maximum pain as only she knew how.

'Is that her boyfriend?' said Cecilia, struggling to make conversation with her tense, silent lover. She knew how important it was to appear friendly – people always leapt at the opportunity to call extremely beautiful women bitches – and she genuinely admired Loulou, who had given away a considerable fortune to a very deserving charity. 'Shall we go over and say hello?'

'Are you out of your mind?' said Mac brutally. 'I have nothing to say to her. She's nothing but trouble.'

Cecilia wilted like a flower in the desert and with a stab of guilt he realized that he was playing a cruel game with her. If he had said that to Loulou she would have marched over to the offending party and introduced herself just to show him that he couldn't bully her. And while her impetuosity in the past had sometimes made him wince, he admired her for being so gutsy.

He was playing the two women off against each other in his mind, he knew that. And unfairly, neither of them could win.

When the eager woman with the notebook dragged Cecilia away for a 'girls' talk' he felt relieved. He didn't want Loulou to make mincemeat out of her; now he could tackle her alone. Or almost alone, since that leech with the T-shirt still had his arm around her waist as if it was glued there.

'Loulou.' He announced his presence curtly, gratified to see the startled expression in her grey eyes when she turned round.

'Mac,' she replied evenly, and waved an arm at the exhibits hung behind her. 'Quite a nice show. You've done well. How are you?'

'Fine.' He glared at her companion, presumably the latest in her endless queue of lovers. 'Surprised to see you here.'

'Oh, we thought we'd pop by,' she said airily. 'Martin wanted to come. Darling, why don't you zoom round the rest of the gallery? I'll have a little chat with Mac and then we can shoot off.'

Martin, watching the exchange of bravado with interest, shrugged and kissed her cheek. 'Five minutes then,' he said, sounding almost amused. 'But our table's booked for three fifteen and you know Peter hates it if we're late.'

'Don't remind me,' exclaimed Loulou, giving him her society smile and pinching his wrist hard. 'Now run along.'

When they were alone the atmosphere between them changed so abruptly that Loulou shivered. The air was electrically charged. She felt exhilarated, and afraid and slightly out of control. Fate was an incredible thing, she thought wildly. Anything could happen now, anything at all. So long as she played it *cool*.

'Run along?' mimicked Mac, his dark eyes flashing with derision. 'So that's your latest lap-dog?'

'A wolfhound in poodle's clothing,' she replied demurely,

her heart hammering against her vest. She could smell Mac's aftershave and it was doing incredible things to her senses. 'And you,' she added, nodding in Cecilia's direction, 'appear to have a tiger by the tail. Is she as dangerous as she looks?'

Mac put one hand out, resting it against the cool white wall so that Loulou was hemmed in on one side. She tried not to notice how close he was, nor how he towered over her.

'At least she didn't come here in some ridiculous disguise,' he drawled in a low voice. 'What are you playing at, Lou?'

He watched as her chin came up in a gesture of defiance. At that precise moment, when their eyes locked and all the old memories flooded back, he wavered. It was all up to Loulou now. She was almost everything he had ever wanted, and the little part of her which wasn't was supplied to him by Cecilia.

If only, he thought, she could drop the pretence, confess that she had been unable to stay away because she had to see him – because she'd never stopped loving him – then the rest of their lives would be changed. If she could only *admit* that, he would be hers.

Loulou, also flashing backwards through time, remembered the lessons she had learnt the very hardest way of all. Mac only wanted her when she could take him or leave him. He detested limpets. He liked tigers. She had to play it *cool* or he would be truly lost for ever.

'My disguise?' she said with a casual flip of the hand and a glance in Martin's direction calculated to drive Mac into a frenzy of jealousy. 'Well, if you must know, Martin's quite a fan of your work so he dragged me along here with him. Since I thought it might be awkward if you and I bumped into each other, I stuck on a hat and dark glasses. Less embarrassing for all concerned—'

'Bullshit,' said Mac flatly, his face darkening with anger. She was blowing it. He'd given her the chance, dammit, that all-important chance and she was throwing it back in his face. 'You wanted to see me. You couldn't stay away.'

He watched her spine stiffen as she drew herself up, leaning away from him like a very small and outraged tower of Pisa. At that moment he knew that all was lost.

'I couldn't stay away?' she echoed in a fierce whisper. 'Don't give *me* that crap. I haven't been near you for almost two years – that's how hard it is to stay away from you, you smug bastard. Do you really think you're *that* irresistible?'

Out of sheer desperation, Mac tried again. Softening, he said, 'No, but I'm right, aren't I? You did want to see me.'

I mustn't back down, thought Loulou wildly. Sticking out her chin, she averted her eyes from that dangerous, knowing, mesmerizing gaze. For a moment her mind went blank. She couldn't retaliate because no words would come. The room was too hot and she was dimly aware that almost everyone in the gallery was watching her lose the battle.

Encouraged, Mac reached out and touched her forearm. 'Why can't you at least admit it, Loulou?' he went on in the same low tones. 'I know it must have cost you a lot to come here. Stop being so bloody proud, for Christ's sake, and tell me the truth.'

Something inside her snapped. She hated the fact that he was being condescending in front of all these people. This was Mac's exhibition. They were here because of him, because of his incredible talent. He was a success now, and living with the most sought-after model in England to prove it. She felt like an extremely poor relation, to whom he was forcing himself to be kind because he was that kind of guy.

And bloody hell, she thought furiously, it's because of him

that I *am* poor. But that doesn't give him the right to reduce me to an emotional mess in full view of his adoring bloody public.

'OK,' she said loudly, 'I'll tell you the truth. I did come here to see you, but only to remind myself how lucky I am. I'm happy now, happier than I ever was with you, so there's no need to play your condescending little games with me any more. In fact,' she continued, her voice rising, 'I feel sorry for that woman over there. How the hell does she manage to put up with your bloody awful moods and your obsession with work?'

'Shut up! You're making a scene,' hissed Mac, grabbing her by both arms. Furiously, she shook him off.

'I *like* making scenes. If I'm not happy about something I'll argue – that's the difference between us. And yes,' she yelled, realizing that by now the entire gallery was agog, 'it *did* cost me a lot to come here today, but that's nothing compared with the two million you cost me two years ago. You always resented the fact that Vampires was mine so I got rid of it. For *you*, Mac!' Gasping for breath, hot tears rolling helplessly down her cheeks, she thought she would burst with rage. 'But that wasn't enough for you, either. So don't talk to me about what it cost me to come here because we both know just how much it was. I learnt a very expensive lesson from you, Mackenzie, and I'll never, *ever* forget that!'

Turning away, sobbing wildly and almost blinded now by tears, Loulou pushed through the hypnotized crowd and ran out of the gallery. On the steps outside, like Cinderella's slipper, her grey fedora fell to the ground once more and cartwheeled slowly until it came to rest against one of the stone pillars flanking the entrance.

'Come on,' said Martin breathlessly, when he caught up with her halfway down the street. 'Stop crying. I'll take you home.'

'I haven't got a home,' whispered Loulou, sniffing disconsolately and wiping her cheeks with the back of her hand.

'Don't worry.' Putting his arms around her and pulling her to a halt, he kissed away the salty tears. 'I have.'

Chapter 46

It didn't take Roz long to realize that she was seriously out of her depth. On the phone to Camilla after three days in Littleton Grey with Natalie she said, 'I feel as if I've ordered the Crown Jewels from a catalogue as a joke and now they've told me I can't send them back. I can't cope.' But Camilla only laughed and said, 'Are the Crown Jewels really so bad? Pay for them in instalments. Take your time with Natalie and don't expect too much too soon.'

Roz was trying not to, but Natalie was inexhaustible. She asked endless questions and digested Roz's halting answers so intently that it scared her in case she wasn't doing it right. What if she accidently said the wrong thing? She was a private person used to interviewing others on the screen. Now she had her own interviewer and it was a more nerve-wracking experience than she had ever suspected.

And to her shame, other aspects of Natalie's sudden eruption into her life also irritated her. The terrible adult suit she had worn on the occasion of their first meeting had been kicked into a dark corner of the bedroom and Roz, to her dismay, found herself faced with an eighteen year old who dressed like an eighteen year old. Slashed jeans, massive biker boots, strategically ripped vests and micro-minis were worn with glittering chains looped around neck, waist and hips. The shiny, shoulder-length hair expanded into a gelled, hedgehog mass which didn't even quiver when it hit solid wood. Luckily the

439

vampire-red lipstick Natalie favoured never lasted long, but only because she talked so incessantly. It was a toss-up which Roz least preferred, the horrific lipstick or the endless, probing questions.

And Natalie was as untidy as an eighteen year old too. On the third day Roz went into the spare bedroom which Natalie had made her own and found twelve mugs and glasses lined up on the windowsill. An opened tin of raspberries was gathering mould on the chest of drawers and an ashtray lay upended on the floor, ash and butts scattered all over the thick, pistachio green carpet.

When Natalie returned from a foray to the village shop armed with a bottle of sweet Cinzano, forty Bensons and three more tins of raspberries, Roz blew her top.

'Oh, for God's sake,' complained Natalie five minutes later, hurling herself on to the unmade bed and wearing an expression of such extreme truculence that she looked exactly like Roz. 'Don't *nag* me. We're supposed to be having fun. You're beginning to sound just like my mother.'

That evening, the fight patched over, Natalie asked the question Roz had been dreading for days.

They were sitting together in the garden basking in the warmth of the sun's last rays and lazily brushing away midges. Roz was drinking vodka and tonic, ice cubes clinking as she played with her glass and gazed with lazy pleasure at the garden. The sweet scent of tobacco plants hung in the air and overweight bumble bees gorged themselves on the nectar, the manner in which they edged constantly from one flower to the next reminding her of Loulou in her endless search for a man who could make her forget Mac.

Natalie, halfway down her bottle of sweet Cinzano, was looking lovely tonight, Roz thought with something close to pride. Having spent two hours tidying her room, washing-up the mountain of hoarded mugs and glasses, then ostentatiously dusting the sitting-room with a handful of tissues, she had clearly realized earlier that she had gone too far. Now, by unspoken concession, she was wearing a plain white T-shirt dress which almost reached her knees, her hair was clean, gel-free and shiny once more and she wore no make-up at all. The truculent expression had disappeared and she had been making Roz laugh, regaling her with dreadfully exaggerated tales of the horrors of her old school.

With a jolt of surprise Roz realized that she was actually enjoying herself, and enjoying Natalie's company.

And at that precise moment Natalie asked the question she had been dreading. Glancing sideways from beneath dark lashes she said in a voice which was casual yet utterly determined, 'Roz, I want to know. Who *is* my father?'

There was a long, long silence, during which Roz could feel the steadily deepening thud of her own heartbeat. But when she finally looked up and met Natalie's steady gaze the question was still there; it hadn't gone away.

'If you don't say something soon,' said her daughter, almost kindly, 'I'll start assuming the worst. Perhaps there was something awful about him . . . maybe for some reason you're ashamed of the fact that you ever knew him . . .?'

Numbly, Roz shook her head. Then she stood up, still clutching her drink, and rested a hand briefly on Natalie's sun-warmed shoulder. 'Wait here, I'll be back in a moment.'

When she returned less than a minute later she pulled her chair close before sitting down once more. 'There was nothing awful about your father,' she said slowly. 'And I was certainly not ashamed to have known him. It was just a teenage holiday romance that . . . had unexpected consequences. His name was Sebastian and he was clever and kind, fun to be with and incredibly ambitious –'

'Show me,' said Natalie, her outstretched fingers trembling as she reached for the snapshot lying face down in Roz's lap.

Her dark eyes filled with tears as she studied the creased photograph taken nineteen years earlier on the banks of Lake Geneva. Sebastian, blond and suntanned and shielding his eyes from the sun as he laughed into the camera, gazed back at her.

'Oh, Mum, he looks nice.'

'He was nice,' replied Roz softly, squeezing Natalie's hand as a lump formed in her own throat. 'And it wasn't just a casual fling, either. I loved him. It's important that you should know that I really did love him.'

'Pernod or lager?' Martin had said, as he slid Loulou out of the enormous trenchcoat and threw it over a white rattan chair.

'Better make it lager,' said Loulou dolefully. 'Three Pernods and I'm anybody's.'

He had turned and grinned, and she had been struck afresh by the contrast between his boyish looks and that deep, authoritative, extremely cultured voice.

'Well, since you're mine now anyway, you may as well have Pernod. Poor darling, you look as if you need it.'

That had been a week ago. Martin Stacey-Thompson had seduced her with delicious expertise and had carried on doing so ever since. To her delight and relief she had found herself falling in love again, and this time with a man who was worthy of it. Cheerful and good tempered, he was so much *nicer* than either Mac or Simon. Martin looked after her, adored Lili and made her feel precious again. No barbed insults, no jealousies, no apparent hang-ups. He cosseted her, seducing her mind as well as her body, and encouraged her to talk as much as she liked about Mac, telling her that she shouldn't bottle it up. She needed, he explained gently, to talk it all through, in order to exorcize her mind of hate.

The past week had been idyllic, decided Loulou as she stretched out in the suntrap of Martin's tiny patio garden with Lili sleeping contentedly on a yellow blanket beside her, and there was absolutely no reason why the idyll should end. Martin knew everything about her and loved her anyway, spending long hours discussing their future together, and hinting that his current financial position was about to undergo a drastic change for the better.

Not that money was all-important, of course, but the riches-to-rags novelty had certainly begun to wear a bit thin of late. Almost all her clothes now were old and although she was happy living with Camilla she was aware that the situation couldn't go on indefinitely. An inveterate and unselfish splurger, she longed to be able to buy extravagant gifts for her friends and family, but where once she would have blown a small fortune on first-night theatre tickets, a rented villa in Antibes at the height of the season, irresistible jewellery and flagons of exquisite perfume, she was now unhappily confined to the smallest of gifts and no matter how much Camilla enthused over the delicate rose silk scarf or the new ultra-violet eye-shadow from Dior, the knowledge that she could have bought a hundred of each for herself had she so wished spoiled the joy of giving for Loulou.

And while Lili was perfectly happy wearing the cheapest chain-store outfits and playing for hours with bunches of keys, Loulou longed to shower her with expensive toys and dress her in really good clothes.

Now that Martin had come into her life, she thought with mounting excitement, she sensed that everything was about to change for the better. And if this lucrative deal – about which he was being so deliciously secretive – came off, maybe she would be able to stop worrying about her own appalling financial situation. Not that she wanted to sponge off him, she told herself hastily as she adjusted her dark glasses, wriggled into a more comfortable position on the lilo and glanced across at Lili, who was smiling in her sleep, but the way Martin spoke of their future together gave her such a feeling of security . . . and it would bloody well serve Mac right if she were to marry again. She *was* almost thirty-four, after all . . .

Camilla, in sharp contrast, was having a hideous day, one of the very worst. Having drastically overslept, she awoke to the sounds of a full-scale screaming match downstairs as Toby and Charlotte battled to the death for the last Shredded Wheat. By the time she had staggered into the kitchen Toby was wearing the contents of the marmalade jar and brandishing a pair of scissors at his sister. Charlotte was in floods of tears and her uncombed brown hair was six inches shorter on one side than the other. Rocky, wriggling in ecstasy – such excitement at eight thirty in the morning was a lamentably rare occurrence as far as he was concerned – hurled himself at Camilla and smeared marmalade paw prints over her dressing-gown.

By the time she had thrown Toby under the shower, trimmed Charlotte's drastically uneven hair, fed Rocky, driven the children to school and returned to find practically an entire swarm of wasps feasting on marmalade, she was exhausted. The phone rang three times for Loulou, who was still at Martin's flat. The doorbell pealed, and only when the young man on the front step had been talking for five minutes did Camilla realize that he was recruiting new members for some obscure religious cult. By the time she got rid of him and returned to the kitchen, the wasps had paged all their relatives and invited them to join the party. Feeling hot, sticky and in need of both strong coffee and a cool shower, Camilla pulled off her baggy scarlet T-shirt and switched on the kettle. She had to bake cakes for Toby's school fête, which was being held tomorrow, do at least three loads of washing and buy a birthday present for Zoë.

And all I want to do, she thought irritably, is collapse in front of the TV and watch the men's semi-finals at Wimbledon.

At that moment, Rocky sidled into the kitchen.

'No,' said Camilla sternly as he edged towards a cluster of wasps gathered around his waterbowl. The next moment, he yelped and stamped all over them and the whining insects rose in fury to defend themselves. Stung on the nose, he went berserk. Camilla grabbed him and hauled him unceremoniously through the kitchen door. Like a nightmare, the phone rang again, water was spreading across the floor from Rocky's upturned bowl and a sharp stabbing pain on the sole of her foot told her that she had trodden on another wasp.

Running into the sitting-room, wearing only a bra and a short white skirt and nursing her stings which were surprisingly fierce, she stood in the middle of the room and glared at her favourite photograph of Matt, which stood in a plain silver frame on the mantelpiece.

'Where are you now when I need you?' she yelled, and felt tears of panic and frustration welling up behind her eyes.

And at that moment, by cruel coincidence, the radio began playing a Bryan Ferry song which reminded her so much of Matt that she crumpled into a chair. It was like an unexpected blow in the stomach; just when she had been doing so well, rebuilding her life and beginning to accept that all was not lost . . .

The french windows which led on to the patio were wide open. Nico, standing outside, watched Camilla's shoulders sag and his heart went out to her. Without hesitating he stepped into the room.

Dazed and unquestioning, Camilla rose and slid into his arms, holding him so tightly that he could feel her nipples pressing against the wall of his chest. For several moments the only sounds in the room were the haunting, melancholy strains of Bryan Ferry and her uneven breathing as she quelled the threatening tears.

Finally she drew away, and Nico saw her smile.

'At least I have more clothes on today than when we first met,' she said, glancing down at her white silk bra and short skirt and marvelling at the fact that she felt no embarrassment.

'Only just. I'm not interrupting anything, am I? You don't have a lover lurking in the bedroom?' He spoke the words jokingly, then wondered with a stab of jealousy whether they might be true.

'Hardly.' Camilla laughed at the thought, still clutching his arms. 'But there are enemies in the kitchen. I don't think I've ever been so glad to see anyone before. You must be my knight in shining armour.'

'I knocked at the front door, but there was no reply. Your car was parked on the drive so I came round the side of the house,' said Nico, needing to explain his unorthodox arrival. 'Who have you got in the kitchen – tax inspectors?'

'I have a catastrophe in the kitchen,' she informed him solemnly. 'Please don't think I'm being feeble. I really don't spend my entire life bursting into tears but today so far has been the absolute pits.'

Nico really was amazing, she thought five minutes later when he joined her on the terrace with Rocky bounding joyfully around his legs.

'Crisis over,' he said, resisting the urge to kiss her and falling instead into the chair facing Camilla's.

'The wasps . . .?'

Nico shrugged modestly. 'I lacquered them to death with a can of hairspray. There was a red cloth on the table. I cleaned up the mess on the floor with that.'

My Fiorucci T-shirt, thought Camilla with an inward smile. Who cares?

'So it's safe to go back into the kitchen,' she said with obvious relief. 'Thank God – I have to bake a dozen cakes for Toby's school fete.'

Nico shook his head and reached into the pocket of his blue and green striped shirt. Juggling keys, dark glasses and a folded white envelope, he handed her the envelope.

'You can buy a dozen cakes. I came to see you because I happen to have a couple of tickets for the centre court at Wimbledon and if you say you can't go I'll . . .'

'You've got what!' shrieked Camilla, grabbing the envelope with both hands and tearing it open. Amazement mingled with delight as she studied the tickets and leapt out of her chair. 'You absolute angel! I'd *kill* for a seat on the centre court . . . I can't believe this . . .'

'No need to go to those lengths,' he said mildly, enjoying her reaction. Caroline, totally disinterested, had flatly refused to go. 'But I think you'd better get dressed before we leave. I wouldn't mind, but they're a bit old-fashioned at Wimbledon – they prefer their spectators with clothes on.'

Armed with paper cups, two bottles of chilled white wine and a bag of croissants stuffed with cream cheese, mushrooms and prawns, Nico and Camilla slid into their seats just as the first semi-finalists made their way on court. A roar of approval rose from the crowd, everyone clapping wildly as the dashing, mercurial Croatian and the cool, precise American headed for the umpire's chair. Camilla, cheering at the top of her voice, applauded with such enthusiasm that her sunglasses slipped down her nose and Nico, watching her while he ostensibly fitted a corkscrew into the cork of the first bottle of Chardonnay, realized with a jolt of panic and desire how desperately in love with her he was.

Here, now, wearing a simple white broderie-anglaise cotton dress, her gleaming honey-coloured hair fastened up and her tanned face glowing with happiness, she had never looked more desirable. Her scent was light and flowery, her make-up subtle and her slender curves irresistible. Even the wasp sting on her shoulder, pink and white like a tiny archery target and slightly swollen, couldn't mar her perfect beauty, he thought as he handed her the paper cup.

'I won't have any yet,' said Camilla, scarcely able to tear her eyes from the court. 'I'm too excited to drink.'

Nico grinned. 'Enjoying yourself?' he asked, teasing her, and with delicate precision she pinched the inside of his elbow where it would hurt most.

'Oh, I suppose it's OK. A pretty average sort of day,' she murmured sweetly. 'Although I really was looking forward to a peaceful afternoon at home baking cakes . . .'

'You must hate me for dragging you away,' said Nico, tweaking the back of her hand in retaliation. 'Forcing you here against your will to watch some dreary little game of tennis . . .'

'Shh,' Camilla hushed him, her long-lashed eyes narrowing in concentration as she watched the handsome Croatian's blistering service action.

'Cami,' protested Nico, realizing that he had lost her, that she really was engrossed. 'For heaven's sake, they're only warming up.'

The match was so enthralling and was played with such death-defying brilliance that Nico actually felt guilty. Every single spectator around the sun-drenched court was living and breathing the game and all he could do was think about the woman at his side.

While Camilla yelled and applauded every point, apparently rooting for both men with equal fervour, Nico had only the haziest idea of the score. He clapped automatically whenever she did and prayed for the match to end because only then would he be able to regain her attention. Never having been to Wimbledon before, he had somehow imagined that they would spend the afternoon sitting in the sun, drinking wine and sharing an intimate, loving conversation, oblivious of the crowds around them and the players on court.

He was beginning to wish he'd suggested a picnic on Hampstead Heath instead.

But when the match finally ended after five brilliant sets and the volatile dark-eyed Croatian vaulted the net in victorious celebration, Camilla made the wait worthwhile. Unable to control herself she threw her arms around Nico, gave him a joyful hug and then kissed him quickly on the cheek.

'Thank you for bringing me,' she whispered beneath the roar of the crowd around them, and as he inhaled the mingled scents of her warm body and the flowery perfume she wore he felt the beginnings of an erection beneath the taut, faded denim of his Levis. Camilla, resuming her wild applause as the players left the court, said, 'Sorry, I shouldn't kiss you in public. There are TV cameras all over the place and you're a married man.'

How can she not know how I feel about her, wondered Nico helplessly, taking care to adjust his jeans as he sat back down.

'If it bothers you that much, we could always leave,' he murmured as Camilla collapsed, exhausted, into the seat beside him. 'Then you could kiss me in private.'

Realizing that despite his teasing manner he actually meant what he said, Camilla felt her stomach grow hollow with desire. It was unfair of him, she thought, to say such things, knowing as he did her views on adultery. She wasn't a nun, she had reached the stage now where the absence of a loving – and sexual – relationship in her life was really beginning to prey on her mind, and she was extremely attracted to Nico. If he wasn't married there would be no question of fending him off . . . it simply wasn't *fair* of him . . .

'And you'd still be married,' she replied flatly. Then, seeing that he was about to say something else, she raised her eyebrows in horror and added, 'Besides, what on earth do you mean: "We could always leave?" With another match about to start on court? You must be out of your mind – wild horses couldn't drag me away now!'

Giving in, Nico replaced his dark glasses and refilled his paper cup with wine. Turning to her, his eyes hidden by their twin black shields, he grinned. 'Not even a wild Italian?'

'Wild Italians – no chance,' declared Camilla, then tilted her head and considered for a moment. 'Although maybe that gorgeous Croatian tennis player might be in with a chance if he really asked nicely . . .'

Chapter 47

During the next two days Nico found himself doing more serious thinking than he had in years.

And he had to think fast, because the following Wednesday he was due to leave for Montserrat, that idyllic tropical island in the Caribbean, where he was due to record his next album. The wildly expensive studio had been booked for a month, his band were already out there, grabbing a few days of sun, rum and relaxation before the hard work began, and Monty Barton was on the phone every thirty minutes checking and rechecking flight times, work schedules and musician-hire arrangements like a demented secretary.

But all Nico could concentrate on was the fact that he wanted Camilla. He *had* to have her – she was the only person in his life who mattered and he wasn't going to piss about pretending to be her friend, her good old platonic friend Nico, any longer.

He was going to persuade Camilla to see sense, then he would divorce Caroline. It was the only thing to do – and he didn't want to have an affair with Camilla any more than she did, anyway. It wasn't enough.

He wanted to marry her, and that was quite simply all that mattered now.

'I'm going out,' Caroline announced, coming into the kitchen where Nico was sitting brooding over a strong black coffee which reeked of brandy and pretending to concentrate on the racing results in the paper.

Watching his light-and-dark blond hair fall forwards as he bent his head, and irritated by his lack of response, she added recklessly, 'With my lover', then cringed as Nico looked up at her. There was no disguising the expression of hope, almost eagerness in those jade green eyes, like a caged tiger suddenly realizing that the door has been left ajar.

No chance, sweetheart, thought Caroline, kissing the top of his head as she reached for her denim jacket hanging on the back of his chair. Nico certainly wore the look of a man in the throes of a tortuous affair – he'd scarcely spoken to her at all this week – but she wasn't going to give him the satisfaction of retaliating. She was behaving so bloody perfectly that no way would he be able to shunt any blame on to her.

'Joke,' she said, taking a sip of his coffee and deliberately not commenting on the fact that it was heavily spiked. 'Cecilia and I are going to the Sanctuary. I don't know when I'll be home.'

'Fine.' Nico nodded absently, resuming his scan of the racing pages. He had been surprised when Caroline and Cecilia had struck up a tentative friendship, but now they met each other for shopping expeditions or lunches almost every week. He suspected that they enjoyed gossiping about Mac and himself; it gave them a chance to air their grievances while at the same time presenting a glamorous, united front to the people who saw and envied them their spectacular riches. It was too much to hope that Caroline might really be meeting a lover, he thought with genuine regret.

Madge Pargeter, who had been busily hoovering the master bedroom upstairs, paused to kick a pair of knickers out of its path, then left the cleaner running while she massaged her rheumaticky spine with both hands and watched from the bedroom window as young Mrs Coletto slammed the front door shut behind her and stalked over to the dark green Ferrari parked askew on the gravel drive.

Poor Mrs Coletto, thought Madge with a touch of indignation. That pink mini-dress she was wearing now had cost almost three hundred pounds – she had found the receipt in the carrier bag only yesterday – yet for all her ritzy silk underwear, fast cars and fancy clothes she still wasn't happy. It just went to show.

Madge had cleaned some houses in her time. She'd seen it all; big noisy families who seemed happy at first but who existed on violent arguments and plate throwing; married couples who weren't happy at all unless they were both cheating on each other; even one household where the man was knocking off his wife, his step-daughter and the baby's nanny all at the same time.

Knowing what was going on in other people's lives was what made the job interesting, and she hadn't quite figured out the Colettos yet, which intrigued her.

Having applied for the job at her daughter Shona's insistence – Nico was her current all-time favourite rock singer – Madge was still, after almost three weeks, sussing out the situation. Slowly resuming her cleaning, she considered the facts so far. Mr and Mrs Coletto never seemed to argue, which was odd. Everyone had arguments. Mrs C was unhappy, but she had phases of trying too hard to please, whereas *he* scarcely seemed to notice either way, as if he didn't even care. It seemed likely to Madge that he had other women on the go yet she had no proof of this.

Funny family, she mused, bending down to pick up an emerald earring caught in the thick pile of the carpet. I give 'em six months at the most before the lawyers move in and the real fighting begins. I'll settle for my Albert and our Shona and Keith any day.

Downstairs, unable to stand the inactivity a moment longer, Nico threw aside the *Standard* and went into the sitting-room, picking up the phone and punching out Camilla's number before he could think of a reason why he shouldn't. Mrs Pargeter, the nosy old witch, was upstairs, safely out of the way. He knew that Caroline deliberately chose cleaning women who were so ancient and unattractive he couldn't possibly fancy them and he found it vaguely amusing, but she also took pains to get the old crones on her side, presumably so that if he did do anything wrong they would immediately tell her. Right now he felt too guilty to find that funny.

Not really guilty though, he amended, picking up and glancing at a postcard which had arrived that morning from Montserrat. Shaun, his drummer, had scrawled 'Born to rum' across the back. No, he wasn't really guilty, he just needed to sort certain matters out in advance. As soon as he explained everything to Camilla, and as soon as she told him what he needed to hear – *if*, of course, she told him what he needed to hear – he would square everything with Caroline. She could leave this sad, loveless marriage practically a million-airess in her own right, for God's sake . . . and then be free to find a man who *would* make her happy. How could that be wrong?

'Hello?' The sound of Camilla's voice, slightly muffled and at the same time echoing, convinced him that he was right. He realized how tightly his fingers were gripping the receiver and deliberately relaxed them.

'Hi, it's me.'

More muffled noises – she sounded as if she was changing the phone from one ear to the other – then: 'Who's me?'

Nico's heart sank. He would recognize Camilla's voice anytime, anywhere in the world. Why didn't she know *his* voice, for heaven's sake?

'The wasp killer,' he said lightly. 'You haven't paid your bill.'

'Nico!' At least she sounded pleased to hear from him. 'I'm sorry – my ears are full of shampoo. You sound all bubbly.'

'Have I got you out of the shower?'

Camilla giggled. 'I'm in the bath. Isn't it decadent? Listen . . .'

As Nico heard the splashing of water his imagination ran wild. The idea of talking to Camilla while she was lying naked in a hot scented bath was incredibly erotic. Suddenly it became easier to say what he had to say.

'Sounds fun,' he told her, smiling into the phone. 'Listen, I'm leaving for Montserrat in a couple of days, and I'd really like to see you before I go. Are you free this afternoon?'

Camilla hesitated for only a moment. 'I can be, yes. Where shall I meet you?'

He hadn't properly thought this out. 'I could come over to you,' he said hopefully, but this time she didn't hesitate for even a second.

'No good, I'm afraid. There'll be . . . people here. I could always drive over to your house though.'

'That's out too,' said Nico, admiring her innocence. It would never occur to Camilla that he might not want Caroline to know he was seeing her. And he certainly wasn't going to give Mata Pargeter the pleasure of reporting Camilla's visit back to her.

Then he remembered Cino's restaurant, hidden away in a leafy corner of Kensington. He could reserve their private dining-room and ensure their privacy for the afternoon. And since Camilla had picked him up from there on several occasions when she had been working for him, she knew where it was.

'Cino's restaurant,' he said, crossing his fingers and praying that the room hadn't already been booked. 'I'll meet you there at one o'clock and we'll have lunch in the back room – it'll be more private.'

'I remember it,' Camilla told him, and he heard a splash. 'Damn, the shampoo's fallen into the bath. One o'clock, then. I'll be the one reeking of peaches and almonds.'

'I can't wait,' murmured Nico, already imagining how she would smell. 'Bye, Cami. I'll see you there.'

Interesting, thought Madge Pargeter, carefully replacing the receiver upstairs. Listening in on other people's telephone conversations wasn't something she made a habit of, but once in a while it proved almost irresistible. And very, very occasionally, even profitable . . .

The traffic was appalling as Camilla drove through Belgravia. If she was a little late getting there Nico would just have to wait, but at least it was better than allowing him to turn up at her house, where Roz and Natalie were due to arrive at around two o'clock. She was pleased that there was no longer any animosity between Roz and herself, but Nico had indirectly been the catalyst for at least part of the feud while it had lasted and she wasn't yet up to a three-way confrontation between them.

And Nico didn't yet know about Natalie.

Still, thought Camilla as she opened the sunroof and breathed in the scent of hot tarmac and exhaust fumes, it would be interesting when she returned home to see how Roz and Natalie were getting on together. Roz had booked them both in at an hotel off the Bayswater Road, but Camilla had persuaded her to cancel the rooms and stay with her instead during their visits to London. She enjoyed the company, and it seemed ridiculous to waste money on an hotel when she had empty rooms in her own house. Also, since she had been the one who had persuaded Roz to meet her daughter she felt it necessary now to support her through what couldn't be a particularly easy time.

But she had done the right thing, she decided, in keeping Nico away from the house. According to Roz, Natalie worshipped Nico and was pestering her to see him, and for this amongst other reasons Camilla had left a note with the back-door key – hidden in their pre-arranged spot – saying that she was out visiting Zoë, and that she would be back by four at the latest.

Because the sunroof was open, the crash when it came sounded like an explosion. Camilla jammed her foot on the brake and the car slewed sideways to a vicious halt at the kerb.

Terrified, appalled by the suddenness of the accident, she clutched at her seatbelt with frozen fingers and stared at the crushed, metallic blue tangle of metal that a second ago had been a new Escort XR3i. The lorry into which it had careered head-on had ground to a stop beside the traffic-lights with only a slight dent in its front bumper.

Both vehicles were less than twenty feet away from her and the abrupt silence following the crash rang in her ears.

Without even thinking, Camilla unlocked her seatbelt and stepped out of the car on legs which were shuddering and jerky. The Escort's windscreen was an opaque maze of cracked glass, but there was blood on the driver's window and she could make out the dark outline of a head slumped sideways against it.

Reaching the car at the same moment as the lorry driver, who was unhurt but visibly shaken, she saw that the man inside was bleeding heavily from a head wound, and that his arms were flailing as, panic stricken and confused, he attempted to escape from the crushed confines of his prison.

'He jumped the lights – I couldn't avoid him,' blustered the ashen-faced, overweight lorry driver, pulling at the passenger door.

'Leave it,' said Camilla automatically, but although the door was too buckled to open, the sharp movement brought a shower of glass down from the windscreen on to the man inside.

'Call an ambulance,' she said, as other people began to converge around the car. And moving around to the other side she opened the passenger door and climbed in, not even noticing the cushion of glass fragments which tore at her stockings and dug into the backs of her legs.

'You'll be all right,' she said in a low voice to the injured man, taking his hands in hers and holding them firmly against his chest. He was wearing a pink and white striped golfing sweater splattered with dark blood, and his dark curly hair was so like Matt's that for a confused moment she thought it must surely be a dream.

'I can't see,' moaned the man, shaking his head and struggling to release his hands. Camilla, moving closer, put her arms around him. Now there was blood on her own hands and on her white skirt. As she wiped the warm, sticky liquid from his forehead he coughed and spat out a front tooth.

'You're not blind,' she told him, wondering how she could feel so ill and at the same time sound so calm. 'There's a cut on your head and the blood's run into your eyes. You're not blind, and you're going to be *all right*. An ambulance is on its way. What's your name?'

For a moment he seemed not to be able to remember. His head moved helplessly from side to side and she said urgently, 'Don't move. You're safe. I'm here. My name's Camilla.'

'Eddie. Edward Fairbank. My wife . . . she's expecting me home . . . I was playing golf this morning . . .'

Camilla, her mind flooded with the terrible memories of that evening just over a year ago, felt her chest heave. But I musn't cry, she told herself fiercely. Mustn't cry, mustn't think about that . . .

The urgent blast of the ambulance's siren came as such a relief that she felt sweat trickle down the back of her neck.

'It's OK, they're here. Give me your phone number and I'll call your wife, tell her that you're all right.'

'I'm not all right,' groaned the man, squeezing her hand so hard that Camilla winced.

'You're alive,' she said fiercely, then closed her eyes and willed herself not to be angry with him. In a quieter voice she went on, 'You're very lucky. You've had an accident. But you aren't going to die, are you? So give me your wife's phone number. I'll find out from the ambulance men which hospital they're going to take you to. And just remember – you're *going to be OK.*'

* * *

In the dim, secluded corner of a tiny Greek restaurant across the road Camilla succumbed to the grief and shock which earlier she had managed to stave off. The ancient proprietor, who had also seen the accident occur and who had been the one to call the ambulance, wondered but did not ask why she should have been so deeply affected by it. People, he decided with a shrug, had their reasons and this English woman clearly didn't want to share them. The pain in her eyes, though, was unconcealed.

To help her as much as he could he moved her car from its rakishly parked place on to a meter, plied her with strong Greek coffee and left the telephone at her table.

'I'm phoning on behalf of your husband,' Camilla had told Edward Fairbank's wife as rapidly and reassuringly as possible. 'He's all right, but he has had a minor accident in his car. He asked me to tell you that he's being taken to the Whittington Hospital, but please don't worry, he really isn't hurt badly. Just cuts and bruises.'

Then, when there was no longer any need to remain in control, when her duty was over, she gave herself up to the nightmare. Memories of Matt came flooding back, as vividly as if his own accident had just occurred.

That was what it had been like for him – the unbelievable suddenness of that split second when calm had become chaos. When life had become near-death. And when, later that night, life for Matt had ceased to exist.

For one bewildering, agonizing moment Camilla had thought she was being given a slow-motion replay of Matt's accident. Then, to her shame, she had resented Edward Fairbank for not being Matt, and for being alive. Would he ever truly appreciate how lucky he had been to escape with such relatively minor injuries? Would his wife ever understand the extent of her reprieve?

And why had *they* been spared, when she and Matt had not?

Chapter 48

The restaurant owner watched from his own corner while Camilla wiped away her tears. Despite the heat she was shivering and the coffee sitting in front of her had gone cold. Her white skirt was smeared with blood, her pale stockings shredded. She still looked terribly shocked and upset.

Stiff upper lip English, he thought with mounting incomprehension and frustration and moving slowly, anxious not to startle her, he approached the small table where she sat.

'Is there anything I can do, madam?' he asked, his English good but heavily accented, his dark eyes sympathetic. 'Perhaps you should telephone your husband, for him to collect you. Is that a good idea?'

Nico, sprawling sideways in his chair in the private dining room at Cino's, glanced at his watch for the hundredth time. Two fifteen. Where on earth was Camilla?

He debated ringing her home a third time. Before, there had been no reply and he had assumed she was on her way to meet him. Now, as he pulled off his tie in agitation and tossed it over the chair where his charcoal grey jacket already hung, he was beginning to wonder whether something had happened to her — or whether for some reason she had simply chickened out.

Impatiently, he picked up the phone, cradling the receiver close to his ear to block out the sounds of revelry coming from the main restaurant. The rip-roaring party next door only accentuated the silence in his own private room. When the telephone was picked up, he thought he must have dialled the wrong number. 'I'm sorry, is Camilla there?'

'No, I'm afraid she's out at the moment. Who are you?' enquired a girl with a Geordie accent.

'A friend,' said Nico carefully. 'Have you any idea where she might be?'

'Yeah, she's left a note here. Hang on . . . she's gone to see someone called Zoë. Does that help?'

'Thanks,' he said, puzzled and slightly irritated. 'I'll ring her there.'

Zoë, when he eventually obtained her number from directory enquiries, was equally surprised.

'Oh, hi Nico. No, Camilla isn't here. Why, should she be?'

Telling her that he had only called on the off-chance, he replaced the receiver and looked at his watch again. Being stood up was a new experience for him, but it appeared to be happening now.

Well, she really picked her moment, thought Nico with mounting anger and disappointment. So much for the afternoon planned to change both their lives. Obviously Camilla had realized, at least in part, the implications of today's lunch date and had decided she didn't need the hassle.

She simply wasn't interested, he realized grimly, his stomach churning with the cold, sickening reality of rejection. After hours of delicious, terrifying anticipation the finality and sense of anti-climax was brutally fierce. What might have been was now lost for ever. Shit, shit, shit.

He wouldn't be there, thought Camilla, leaving the car and hailing a passing cab. Not now . . . it was almost two thirty. She should have phoned the restaurant, she thought helplessly, but until a few minutes ago it simply hadn't occurred to her. And as Charlotte had borrowed her mobile without asking, again, she was out of luck. All she had been able to think about in her state of shock had been Matt, and when she had finally remembered Nico, out of the shock and grief had come a resurgence of guilt.

No matter how strenuously she might deny it to herself, deep down she was chillingly aware of the formidable attraction between Nico and herself. He had shown his hand over and over again in different ways, sometimes teasingly, at other times with heart-stopping honesty. Finding himself trapped in a marriage which wasn't all it might be, he freely admitted to having had other affairs, and it appeared now that this was what he had in mind for her, even knowing as he did the strength of her views about such harmful deception.

'Belgravia,' Camilla told the cab driver, then quite helplessly heard herself say, 'No, sorry, Cino's restaurant in Kensington. Do you, by any chance, have a mobile I could borrow?'

'Sorry love, my son left it switched on, the batteries are flat.'

Fate, Camilla thought, just wasn't on her side.

Nico drew her like a magnet. Even though he would almost certainly have left there by now she clung to the thought that he might have decided to stay and eat. He might *just* still be there, and she needed to at least speak to him before he left the country. They had to talk – Nico knew that too. And whilst she couldn't possibly become just another in his long line of affairs, she wanted him to understand how much he meant to her.

He was, after all, the only man on this earth to whom she was seriously attracted. It was plain bad luck, thought Camilla with infinite sadness, that he should be married to someone else.

* * *

As the cab wove through the mid-afternoon traffic Camilla pulled out her make-up bag and rapidly applied powder, lipstick, and a fine mist of perfume. Then, thinking superstitiously that if she was wearing make-up Nico wouldn't be there, she wiped off the lipstick with a tissue.

Nico, flinging his jacket and tie on to the passenger seat of the black Lotus, jammed the key into the ignition and revved like mad, just to irritate a couple of middle-aged women about to cross the road. Pulling away from the kerb at top speed, he saw a black taxi brake to avoid him, the cabbie indicating with an index finger to his forehead what he thought of his bad-tempered driving.

Sod you, thought Nico, raising two fingers in return and hating everyone. What a bloody, *bloody* awful day.

Camilla stepped out of the taxi, glancing down the road at the disappearing Lotus and wondering wildly if it could have been Nico. No, of course it wasn't. He wouldn't drive that recklessly – and besides, when he had taken her to Wimbledon he had still been driving the metallic grey Lamborghini.

Inside the restaurant, Cino stared at her, his professional smile glazing slightly as he took in her blood-spattered skirt and wrecked stockings.

'Mr Coletto was expecting me,' said Camilla embarrassed. 'I'm very late. I shouldn't think for a minute that he's still here.'

'Madame,' Cino's voice expressed genuine Italian distress. 'He leave only one moment ago. One moment! In a black sport car . . . you miss him by *so* much.' With his thumb and forefinger he indicated a couple of millimetres, his dark eyes wide with dismay. The young woman was a mess, but beautiful, and who was he to prejudge her? Her non-arrival earlier had certainly put poor Nico into the blackest of moods, he reminded himself, so she must be important to him in one way or another.

'Damn,' said Camilla, her own tone registering just as much distress. Hastily she scrabbled in her bag for her purse. 'Could I possibly come in and use your phone?'

Caroline, returning home from the Sanctuary feeling pampered and sensual, was annoyed to find Nico out. Here she was, manicured, glowing brown from her session on the ultra-tan sunbed, moisturized all over and about to be parted from her husband for an entire month . . . and he had disappeared.

Dropping her denim jacket over the *chaise longue*, she went into the sitting-room and poured herself a vodka-martini, switching on the answering machine before stretching out along the arm of the nearest chair with her drink in one hand and a joint in the other. Nico didn't like her smoking grass, but since he wasn't here there wasn't a lot he could do about it, she thought resentfully. At least she would be free to do whatever she liked when he flew off to Montserrat on Wednesday, and heaven knows, she reasoned, the way things had been going lately smoking a bit of grass was practically the only enjoyment left to her.

The messages on the machine were predictably mundane. Monty Barton had called four times urging Nico to contact him, the BBC wanted to speak to him, some PR chap from the record company had phoned twice, Nico's sister Bianca once, and *New Woman* magazine once.

How nice, thought Caroline with irritation. Nine phone messages for Nico and none for me. Am I alive? Do I really live

here? Do I even *exist*? And if Nico isn't with Monty, where the
hell is he right now anyway?

The phone burst into life again at that moment. Knowing
that if she picked it up she would only have to pass on another
bloody message, Caroline glared at it and switched the machine
on again. That was what it was there for, wasn't it?

But like most people she couldn't resist listening as the
machine picked up the call.

And when she realized who was speaking her interest grew.
Camilla's carefully nonchalant tone didn't fool Caroline for a
minute as she heard her apologize for not meeting Nico for
lunch. There were unmistakable undertones in her words and
she knew intuitively that it had been no innocent lunch date.
Nico hadn't mentioned it to her earlier, and she didn't doubt
that he wouldn't when he eventually arrived home, which only
made it more significant still.

As she poured herself another hefty drink she erased
Camilla's message of apology and her tentative request for Nico
to return her call. Just because Camilla had been tragically
widowed, she told herself grimly, didn't mean she couldn't fight
dirty. She was only too aware of Nico's feelings for Camilla,
and since chasing after a married man clearly didn't fall outside
her moral code, Caroline had no compunction about retaliating
in kind. Nico was hers, after all. And nobody else was going to
bloody well take him away from her.

At that moment Mrs Pargeter appeared in the doorway, Mr
Sheen in one hand and a duster clutched in the other. She
coughed politely and Caroline quelled the impulse to snap at
her. Good cleaning women, after all, were as hard to find these
days as faithful husbands.

'Come in, Mrs Pargeter,' she said with a smile and as much

grace as she could muster. 'Is there a problem? Anything I can do to help?'

'Bless you duck,' said Madge Pargeter fondly, 'it's kind of you to ask but I'm fine. No, it's a bit of a delicate matter I'm afraid . . . it's just that there's something I felt you really ought to know . . .'

'Mum and I are getting on like a house on fire,' said Natalie, when Camilla returned downstairs after a shower and stretched out on the settee in her favourite white silk dressing-gown.

Camilla, silently observing the 'Mum', exchanged glances with Roz whilst Natalie wolfed down another jaffa cake.

'A singularly inapt expression, I always think,' mused Roz. 'It always reminds me of alarm bells and disaster.'

Natalie grinned. 'OK, we're getting on very well then. Have a jaffa cake,' she urged Camilla. 'They're very good for shock. Are your legs OK now?'

'Only minor cuts,' said Camilla, glancing at them. 'They're nothing. And I phoned the hospital just now – they're keeping the chap in for a couple of days just to be on the safe side, but his head wound wasn't serious apparently, and they've stitched him up. He's lost a tooth and a bit of blood, but otherwise he's OK. He's a lucky man.'

As she spoke, she glanced over at the photograph of Matt and herself which stood on the mantelpiece and her eyes glazed over for a second. Natalie, who couldn't bear awkward silences, leapt headlong into the breach.

'Hey, I almost forgot – the most gorgeous-sounding guy phoned up for you this afternoon. He wouldn't give his name, but he had *the* sexiest voice I've ever heard. He wanted to know where he could find you so I told him you were over at Zoë's house. Who is he?'

So Nico had phoned Zoë's and drawn a second blank, thought Camilla, wondering if he had been home and listened to the message she had left for him.

Avoiding Natalie's curious gaze she said blankly, 'No idea. Probably my ex-husband. Anyway, tell me what the two of you have been up to in the last week. What do you think of the Cotswolds?'

Natalie pulled a face. 'Dull, dull, dull. I like London better. But Mum and I have had loads of time to talk, so it's been OK. She showed me a photograph of my real father yesterday – he was only young when it was taken but he was dead good-looking. I can't wait to meet him – he's almost as dishy as Nico.' Proudly, Natalie glanced across at Roz, who was deeply engrossed in lighting a cigarette. 'I'll say this for Mum: she hasn't half pulled some gorgeous men in her time.'

When Nico emerged from the shower with a scarlet towel around his hips, his magnificent brown body gleaming with droplets of water, Caroline said nothing. She had already asked, extremely casually, where he had been that afternoon and Nico, apparently riveted by a TV programme about earthworms, had replied, 'Working', which only confirmed what she already knew.

Now, she stepped out of her white silk knickers and stood watching him.

'What?' said Nico irritably.

'A journalist called round this afternoon,' said Caroline softly. 'He was kind enough to inform me that you were having an affair with another woman.'

'Journalists! You know what they're like.'

'He also told me that in his opinion your career wouldn't easily stand another scandal. And I'm talking about a really messy divorce scandal.'

'I'm not having an affair,' Nico countered, his green eyes darkening. Reaching for him, pulling him towards the bed, Caroline said soothingly, 'I know you aren't, of *course* you aren't, but once these press people get an idea into their heads . . . they think our marriage is on the rocks and it's up to us to prove them wrong, that's all.'

As she drew him down on top of her, sliding away the ivory towel and winding one curvaceous leg around his hip, Nico realized that there was no longer any point fighting it. Camilla had given him her answer this afternoon, her non-appearance proving once again that she didn't really give a damn. At least Caroline gave a damn, he thought, weakening as she began expertly to arouse him . . .

'We don't have to prove them wrong; it's none of their goddam business anyway,' he said later after a clinical but satisfactory bout of love-making. Caroline, stroking his muscled thigh with a pink-glossed fingernail, smiled. 'But why give them the pleasure of trying to break us up? And the journalist was right – it can only mess up your image. Your fans don't want us to split, do they?'

Nico shook his head. Staring at the ceiling, he willed himself to stop thinking about Camilla.

'So,' concluded Caroline, dropping a kiss on his flat tanned stomach, 'we'll put a stop to those boring old rumours. I packed a couple of suitcases this evening. The day after tomorrow, we're *both* leaving for Montserrat.'

Chapter 49

'Camilla, I've got myself into a terrible mess,' confessed Roz, when Natalie had finally been persuaded to go to bed and they were alone.

Camilla, sipping coffee, curled her feet under the hem of her dressing-gown and met Roz's troubled gaze.

'You sound like Loulou,' she said with a faint smile. 'Come on, tell me about it. Is it Natalie?'

'Who else?' said Roz, blowing a perfect smoke ring, but looking agitated. 'Although I suppose it's really my own fault. You haven't asked me about Natalie's father. Aren't you curious to know who he is?'

'You were sixteen,' said Camilla thoughtfully. 'Presumably you gave birth to Natalie just before you went to Elm House. You always had lots of boyfriends . . . I can't even remember their names now.'

'Remember this one?' Roz passed across a slightly creased Polaroid shot and poured herself another glass of wine as Camilla studied it. The memories flooded back instantly.

'Sebastian,' she said, holding the photograph up to the amber light and admiring the blond good looks of the boy sitting with his arm around a younger, softer-looking Roz on the shores of Lake Geneva. 'Of course. But why is it such a problem? You've shown Natalie this photo. You lost touch with each other years ago, presumably. Just tell her that there's nothing else you can do. She'll understand . . .'

'But she won't,' interrupted Roz, taking the photograph back. 'She's determined to track him down, wherever he is. My daughter thinks she's Sherlock Holmes, for God's sake,' she concluded gloomily, and lit another cigarette from the butt of the last.

'Would that really be so terrible?' ventured Camilla, and watched Roz shake back her spiky dark hair, briefly closing her glittering black eyes.

'Now comes the hard part,' she said at last. 'I know exactly where Sebastian is. We never did lose touch. Once or twice a year he comes over to England to see me and occasionally I go to Zurich to visit him. He's an international banker, as successful as they come, and he's never married. Natalie rattles on about contacting Interpol and all the time his phone number's right here in my head . . . but how the hell can I possibly explain to her that although Sebastian and I have been lovers for almost twenty years, he's never known that he has a daughter?'

Camilla's mind reeled as she struggled to assimilate this startling statement.

'You mean that you didn't tell him you were pregnant?'

'I told him I thought I was,' said Roz evenly. 'He went berserk. Sebastian had very strong views even then and he was violently anti-abortion – and equally violently anti-fatherhood. He blamed me, because I'd told him I was on the Pill when in fact I wasn't. I worshipped him, but he simply refused to tolerate the idea that I might be pregnant. He was only seventeen himself but he called me an idiotic child, and I knew that even if I had the baby and put it up for adoption he'd refuse to have anything more to do with me. He didn't exactly have a forgiving nature.'

'So what happened?'

Roz shrugged helplessly. 'I was totally besotted with Sebastian. He was my entire world; there was only one thing I could do if I ever wanted to see him again. When I returned to England I wrote and told him that it had all been a false alarm. The next six months were spent at a school for naughty girls, and five weeks after Natalie had been born and spirited away, Sebastian turned up in England none the wiser. Somehow,' she concluded with a bitter smile, 'the appropriate moment in which to tell him never arose. He's still not at all keen on children and he'd be as shocked as you are to learn that I've kept that kind of secret from him for this length of time . . . so what on earth can I possibly tell Natalie?'

As Camilla was attempting to formulate some kind of reply, the door swung open.

'Simple,' announced Natalie calmly, although her voice was husky and her cheeks wet with tears. 'You tell her the bloody truth, *to her face*, and let *her* decide what to do. My father might be the biggest, most selfish bastard of all time, but he's not going to spend the rest of his life in ignorance. Someone's got to tell him he has a daughter, and I think it might be best if it were me.'

'It's a double-page fucking feature,' exploded Loulou, still quivering with rage as she sat on the end of Camilla's bed dressed in a child's white vest and creased white track-suit trousers. Waving the newspaper at Camilla she said, 'Read it!'

'I can't,' complained Camilla, blinking as the early morning sunlight burnt her eyes. 'I haven't got my contact lenses in.'

'I'll read it,' said Loulou through clenched teeth. 'Can you at least see the bloody headline? It's big enough.'

' "The Price of Love – £2 million," ' read out Roz, peering over her shoulder. ' "Loulou Marks won the hearts of our nation when she donated two million pounds to research into the tragic syndrome of cot deaths. But all lovely Loulou was trying to do was win back the heart of sexy Scottish photographer 'Mac' Mackenzie, the second of her three husbands.

' "Last week, heavily disguised, she crept into the Kendall-Fordyce Gallery in Kensington where Mac's latest exhibition is currently receiving critical acclaim. All she wanted was to catch a glimpse of the man she loved, the man who rejected her when she gave birth to her daughter Lili. But when Mac arrived at the gallery arm in arm with his new love, the stunning model Cecilia Drew, Loulou went to pieces . . ." Good heavens, Lou, you didn't, did you?' said Roz, gazing at her in astonishment. Loulou, snatching the paper from her, ripped it into confetti and glared back.

'Of course I bloody didn't!' she snapped, her silver-grey eyes blazing. 'And if I did, it wasn't how it *sounds*. Shit, that double-crossing, smarmy, money-grabbing little . . . I told him everything!' she wailed. 'It was *private* and he went and sold it to that bloody scum-bag paper. I didn't even know he was a journalist . . .'

'Who!' demanded Roz and Camilla in unison, and Loulou covered her eyes in despair, waiting for them to say, 'I told you so.'

'Martin Stacey-sodding-Thompson, of course,' she groaned. 'He sold me down the river and got his big break. Do you know how much he was paid for writing this trash?'

'Not as much as he's going to pay out in libel damages,' said Roz, trying not to smile.

'Don't make fun of me,' shrieked Loulou, throwing herself

down on the bed. 'How can it be libel when it's bloody well true?'

'I'll make us some coffee,' said Camilla, who really wasn't up to coping with such drama before breakfast, but Roz motioned her to stay where she was.

'I'll get it. You stay where you are and make sure Lou doesn't throw herself out of the window.'

'Don't panic,' murmured Loulou, lying across the bed with her eyes closed. 'I may not be able to sue the bastard, but I can still kill him. I need to stay alive for that. Oh God,' she moaned, rolling over and sitting upright. 'Whatever is Mac going to say when he finds out about this?'

'He was married to you,' called out Roz as she made her way downstairs. 'He should be used to it by now.'

Two minutes later she was back. 'The stupid little bitch!' she stormed, her dark brown eyes narrowed with fury. Camilla pulled herself upright once more and wished for the second time that morning that she had decent eyesight as yet another piece of paper was thrust into her hands. 'She's only run off to Zurich!' exploded Roz. 'My daughter's determined to ruin my life. What the hell am I going to do now?'

'Zurich?' Loulou, intrigued, abruptly forgot her own catastrophe. 'Why on earth would she go there ... what's she looking for, anyway? A gnome?'

Heathrow Airport was chaotic with excited, height-of-the-season holiday makers; queues were forming in every direction, the tannoy was blaring non-stop and Natalie, sitting on her small suitcase, clutched her one-way Swissair flight ticket to her chest as if it were a rosary. For the first time she began to doubt the wisdom of her action. All she had was the name of her father, and the city in which he lived. Most of her savings had gone on the price of the plane ticket; the number of travellers' cheques in her purse was pathetically small.

Now she was both hungry and thirsty but dared not spend any money. Realistically she knew that she could only afford to stay in Zurich for three or four days. And if she was unable to find her father within that time she was going to be stuck; no money to stay and none with which to get back to England.

What the hell, she thought with mounting trepidation and excitement. This is it. No going back. This is real life!

Gradually she became aware of a commotion at the other end of the great hall. A photographer ran past, cameras flapping against his chest, and she could hear young girls shrieking with excitement. Some kind of celebrity must have arrived.

Anxious for any diversion Natalie rose to her feet and hauled her case into her arms, making her way across the crowded hall. Maybe it was Sting – she was crazy about him – or a film star heading back to the States.

By the time she reached the other end of the hall a sizeable crowd had formed, and several more photographers were flashing away with their cameras.

'Who is it?' she asked one of them, and he paused to glance at her. Pretty girl. Photogenic. Great legs. Shame about the clothes.

'Nico Coletto, on his way to Montserrat,' he told her as he slotted a new film into his camera, and watched the expression on the girl's face change.

'Nico!' she screamed, more loudly than anyone else, and cannoned through the crowd using her case as a battering ram.

'Nico, stop!' Natalie yelled again, pushing her way to the

front and seeing that he had finished signing autographs. He was moving away towards the VIP lounge and she knew he was her only chance . . .

'Please stop, I have to speak to you,' she bellowed, sweat breaking out on her upper lip. By the way he hesitated, but didn't turn round, she knew that he had heard her.

'It's about my mother,' yelled Natalie in desperation. 'You know her . . . it's a matter of life and death!'

At last he turned, his gaze sweeping the crowd until it came to rest upon Natalie.

'Oh please,' she said, her knees almost buckling with relief and ecstasy. 'We really, *really* have to talk . . .'

In the VIP departure lounge, Nico seated himself opposite Natalie, his green eyes watchful.

Unable to utter a word, she returned his gaze, breathing shallowly in her excitement and struggling to convince herself that she was really here. Nico, her mother's lover, and her own long-time hero, was sitting less than four feet away from her, his baggy cream linen jacket screaming Armani and his slender, sun-tanned fingers tapping against his jean-clad thigh. He was wearing white beach shoes, a sea-green T-shirt which matched his incredible eyes, and the most heavenly aftershave she'd ever smelt.

For a long moment he said nothing either, just watched her as if she were a puzzle he couldn't quite work out. Glancing behind him, Natalie saw Caroline, his wife, speaking in an undertone to an overweight middle-aged man who was pouring lager from a can into a slender champagne glass.

'So,' said Nico finally. 'A matter of life and death. Was that a very over-the-top exaggeration or a downright lie?'

Natalie felt a hideous blush crawl up her cheeks. 'A slight

478

exaggeration,' she amended with an embarrassed smile. 'But it *is* important.'

'Maybe you'd better tell me who your mother is,' he said slowly, tilting his blond head. 'I think I can guess; it's just very hard to believe.'

She grinned suddenly, and shook her head in a manner which so reminded him of Roz that he knew he was right. Jesus, it was uncanny how much she resembled her.

'Say it,' commanded Natalie. 'And don't look so worried – I'm not going to tell everyone you're my old man.'

'You're Roz's daughter,' said Nico with a faint, incredulous smile which lit up his face. 'Does *she* know?'

This time Natalie burst out laughing. 'Of course she does! Yesterday she told me who my father is. That's why I'm here, to go over to Switzerland and meet him. Have you seen Mum lately?'

'Not recently,' Nico said, thinking fast. This was, without a doubt, the voice which had answered the phone yesterday afternoon when he had tried to contact Camilla, so she and Roz had to be staying with her in Belgravia.

He longed to ask this girl – Christ, those dark, slanting eyes were *so* like Roz's – about Camilla, but it would only complicate matters. And right now he was supposed to be getting away from all that. Asking questions would only make things worse . . .

'So what's the emergency?' he asked, glancing at his watch and nodding at the blonde waitress who was hovering discreetly with a pot of coffee.

'A favour.' Natalie held her breath for a second then plunged in. 'I've paid for my ticket, but now I'm skint. If you could lend me some money I wouldn't have to sleep in Swiss doorways.'

'Why didn't Roz make sure you had enough?' intercepted Nico, outraged. Then he sank back in his seat. 'Oh, don't tell me. She doesn't know you're here.'

Cringing from the resigned expression and the disapproval in his thickly-lashed, onyx-green eyes and terrified that he might be about to send her home under armed escort, Natalie said with a touch of defiance, 'She knows I'm here because I left her a note. She just didn't know about it beforehand, that's all.'

Nico saw the determination which tautened every line of her slender young body, and knew that nothing he could say would sway her. It occurred to him at that moment that if he had married Roz this teenager would be his step-daughter. Jesus, Roz could only have been about fifteen when she'd had her.

It occurred to him too that Roz had caused her fair share of problems for him over the years. When they had been together she had treated him in the most off-hand manner imaginable in order to keep his interest alive. And afterwards she had abruptly reversed tactics, using every dirty trick in the book to win him back.

Nico, with his family-orientated Italian blood, couldn't think of one good reason why this girl shouldn't meet her real father, and it caused him some small amount of satisfaction to know that Roz was opposed to the idea.

What the hell, he thought, glancing across the tables to where Caroline and Monty were sitting, both studiously pretending not to be watching him. Let's give the girl a break and show Roz that she can't always have her own way.

'How much do you need?' he said to Natalie, and as he reached inside his jacket for his wallet the look of wonder and relief in her eyes melted his battered, emotionally scarred heart. His own life might be a Godawful mess at the moment, he realized, but that didn't mean he couldn't still help to make someone else's happier when the right opportunity arose.

Chapter 50

For three days Roz had been like a cat on scalding hot bricks, twitching each time the phone rang and snapping at anyone who tried to speak to her. Refusing to contact Sebastian and quite unaccustomed to being on the wrong end of a waiting game, her temper grew steadily shorter and she made heavy inroads into Camilla's drinks cabinet.

Sebastian, reflected Camilla as she made a pot of coffee, bundled a load of washing into the machine and cleared the kitchen table of breakfast debris, must mean a hell of a lot more to Roz than she was prepared to admit. And whilst she herself was quite unable to comprehend the allure of a man who obviously disliked children so much that Roz had been forced to keep the news of his own from him for eighteen long years, she sympathized with Roz's agitation now.

She was also deeply thankful that she didn't have to work with her. From what Roz told her about the screaming rows she was having with her producer, with her researchers and even with the director himself, the TV studios were not a happy place to be at the present time. At this rate, she decided, Natalie's antics were in danger of bringing an entire networked show to an expensive, grinding halt.

Damn the little bitch, thought Roz that evening as she speared a buttered courgette and realized that her fork was trembling. Why couldn't she at least phone and let her know what was going on? This interminable waiting was playing havoc with her nerves.

Broodingly she glanced across at Camilla, looking so calm and unruffled it wasn't true. At least Loulou, who was only pretending to eat, was as rattled as she herself was; it comforted her to know that she wasn't the only one going through hell at the moment, even if Loulou did only have herself to blame for her current ridiculous predicament. Roz hadn't met Martin Stacey-Thompson, but he sounded exactly the slimy sort of toad who could only ever cause trouble.

When the phone rang, everyone jumped as if the four-minute warning had sounded. Roz felt her heart thumping unpleasantly against her rib-cage, but it was only Christo ringing for Loulou. Glad of an excuse to abandon her dinner Loulou disappeared into the sitting-room with Roz's cigarettes, obviously settling in for a long cheering-up chat.

'Who *was* that who phoned for you the other afternoon?' asked Roz idly, just to make conversation. 'The man with the sexy voice who wouldn't give Natalie his name.'

Camilla looked uncomfortable for a moment.

'Nico,' she admitted finally, trying and failing to sound casual, and sensed rather than saw Roz's raised eyebrows.

'Really,' drawled Roz, curious to know more. Despite everything, she still felt that Nico was hers, and had never fully come to terms with the way he had rejected her. As far as she had been able to work out, Nico had dropped her simply because she had been an innocent pawn in the break-up of Camilla's marriage to Jack.

'I thought he'd gone to Barbados,' she went on with deceptive languor as she toyed with a piece of chicken on her plate. 'Didn't I see something in the papers recently?'

'He left the day after he phoned,' said Camilla hesitantly. 'We were supposed to have lunch, but I got involved in that accident and didn't make it to the restaurant.'

Right now, Roz observed, Camilla was trying hard to appear unconcerned . . . and failing abysmally. In a flash it became apparent that she was still crazy about Nico, and Roz suppressed a small triumphant smile. Maybe if her own situation had been different she would have let the matter rest in deference to Camilla's hopelessly unhidden feelings, but after three days of torture and chain-smoking, her own emotions were jangling like prisoners' chains. All the old jealousy rose up within her, along with anger as she recalled Nico's summary dismissal. And she would never forget that terrible afternoon when he had destroyed her with his taunt that Camilla had been better in bed than she had. Whether or not it was true didn't matter, but the fact that he had said it shot a great hole in her pride. Nobody, not even Nico, was allowed to say something as derogatory as that and get away with it.

'Oh dear,' she said sympathetically. 'Poor you, you have got it bad, haven't you?'

'Wha . . .?' began Camilla, her eyes horrified as she prepared to leap in with a denial. But Roz was too fast for her.

'And don't think I don't understand,' she continued smoothly. 'God, I should know what it feels like, after all. But it really isn't fair of him to involve you, Cami. You of all people don't deserve that kind of treatment.'

'But I'm n-not . . . it's not . . .' stammered Camilla, flushing pink.

'Naughty, naughty Nico. Up to his old tricks again,' said Roz with a sorrowful shake of her dark head. 'I'm just glad I finally outgrew him. Do you know, he started chasing me again last year? We even ended up in bed together one night – it was at the end of his last concert tour and I'd had a little too much champagne – anyway, I was pissed and he was persistent.' She smiled to herself and twirled her wineglass between her fingers, observing Camilla's aghast expression. Poor thing, this was really crucifying her.

I'm a bitch, thought Roz without even the slightest pang of remorse. But I can't help it; and Camilla has no right to Nico, anyway. He was mine first. And for what it's worth – which is nothing – he's married to Caroline now.

'I don't know how his wife puts up with him, screwing around all over the place the way he has almost ever since the wedding. As far as I can make out, Nico was faithful to her for almost three weeks. And now he's come back to you.' Roz paused and smiled sadly at Camilla. Then, in a conspiratorial tone, she said, 'Well, of course he *is* the most marvellous lover, but I just hope you don't get hurt. I had to tell Nico that it was over between us – I simply don't need the hassle any more – but I can understand why you're hooked on him. He can be irresistible when he sets his mind to it . . .'

'I'm not having an affair with him!' blurted out Camilla, breaking the spell of Roz's low, mesmerizing voice. 'There's nothing like that between us, really there isn't.'

She was telling the truth, Roz realized with satisfaction, but from her distraught expression the words had hit home nevertheless. She had achieved what she had set out to do . . . and it made her feel just great.

'Well, thank God for that,' she said, changing tack and raising her glass in salute. 'Good for you, Cami! Men like Nico need to be rejected now and again . . . it brings them back down to earth and makes them realize they can't always have everything they want. Nico's been an absolute bastard where Caroline's concerned. Maybe now he'll sort himself out and make a real go of it with her. Cheers, Cami. I only wish I'd had your strength of character years ago. Well done!'

Until this moment, reflected Natalie with a shiver, it had all been a marvellous adventure. Her happy but uneventful life back in the North of England seemed insignificant now, having been tumbled out of the way by the sheer thrill of finding Roz and coming down to London, where everyone her mother knew seemed to live in vast, glittering houses, drink champagne and speak beautifully. Even Loulou, who had no money, was still inherently glamorous, bearing no relation whatsoever to the downtrodden single parents who lived sometimes in appalling squalor in the least attractive parts of Natalie's own home town.

And meeting Nico, of course, had been one of her all-time great moments. Probably the greatest moment, she decided, with only a slight sense of shame that it should rank above meeting Roz. But then there were an awful lot of mothers in the world; they were everywhere and almost everyone had one, whereas real-live rock stars of Nico's calibre were a different matter altogether, a far rarer commodity. There was only one Nico . . . how could meeting him not be the greatest thrill of her life?

But now, as she sat in the Bergstrasse café stirring her frothy hot chocolate and gazing through the steamy windows at the bank opposite, she was preparing to fit the last piece to the puzzle. And remembering Roz's overheard conversation with Camilla, she wasn't expecting the afternoon to be particularly pleasant. Certainly not *thrilling*.

The force which had brought her here was an inherent compulsion and she had to go through with it. But she was prepared this time for rejection. Coming to Zurich had been exciting, as well as an act of defiance. Bumping into Nico at Heathrow had been brilliant. Checking into one of the city's smartest hotels had been a new experience too and she had revelled in it, deliberately shrouding herself in dark glasses and mystery for the benefit of the superior receptionist at the front desk. And settling down on her bed with a bottle of wine, a packet of foreign cigarettes and a copy of the Zurich phone directory had seemed a wonderfully adult thing to do. Natalie had felt like some glamorous spy in a Bond movie, calling each bank listed and asking – in French! – whether M'sieur Sebastian Adams worked there.

When, at the seventh attempt the telephonist had replied, 'Oui, madame,' she had felt dizzy with triumph, dropping her cigarette into her lap and slamming down the receiver before the telephonist could hear her shriek, 'Oh shit.'

It had all been good fun, tracking him down. Now, thought Natalie with a touch of panic quelled only by her utter determination to go through with it, she had to brace herself to accept the worst. She knew Roz well enough to be pretty sure that she wouldn't have contacted Sebastian in order to warn him. He would still be quite unaware of her existence.

This, she thought grimly, as she cleared the misted-up window beside her and peered once more at the bank's rather grand entrance and the clerks and secretaries who were now beginning to trickle out into the rainy street, was the ultimate cold-call.

Sebastian Adams, this is your daughter.

* * *

487

Having endured a particularly gritty meeting with an important but nonetheless difficult client, Sebastian Adams was not in the sunniest of moods. When he emerged from the bank at five thirty with his sports bag and briefcase he was even less amused to find that it was still raining. The wet streets glistened, a sea of multi-coloured umbrellas bobbed erratically along the pavements and the rush hour traffic was crawling along at less than walking pace. It would be six o'clock at least before he reached the Sheraton, where he went three times a week to swim, take a sauna and work-out. Eight thirty before he returned home. At nine o'clock he was supposed to be picking up Danielle, the sleek tri-lingual secretary he was currently seeing, and taking her out to dinner at a much recommended new restaurant in the Bahnhofstrasse. The thought left him cold; a far more inviting idea was that of calling Danielle and explaining apologetically that he was caught up in a business meeting which was likely to drag on until midnight.

Merde, thought Sebastian as he turned and headed for the car park. I'm making the kind of excuses used by married men and I don't even have a wife . . .

Frozen by fear and uncertainty into briefly suspended animation, Natalie waited too long at her table inside the café. By the time she got outside her quarry had disappeared from sight. Then she noticed a sign indicating an underground car-park adjacent to the bank and realized that to have vanished so quickly, he must have gone to retrieve his car.

What goes in must come out, she thought, dragging her dark glasses out of the pocket of her scarlet denim jacket and realizing as she ran towards the exit that her palms were damp. This was it . . . any moment now she would be talking for the

first time to her father . . . that was, if he didn't run over her
first.

Sebastian swore again – in German this time – and had to brake
sharply in order to avoid the young girl who had stepped into
the path of his Mercedes. Half these kids were on drugs
nowadays – what the hell was the matter with her? Now she was
standing right in front of him, staring intently through the tinted
windscreen as if it were all *his* fault she had nearly been hit.

Irritably he lowered his window. 'You're asking for trouble,
young lady, wearing those ridiculous glasses in this weather.
Now move out of my way, I'm in a hurry.'

Since he had addressed her in German, Natalie didn't understand a word, although his abrupt tone was less than encouraging. Feeling her heart thumping at a heavy, funereal pace, she
said in English, 'Are you Sebastian Adams?'

'Why?' he demanded suspiciously, and she flinched, shifting
from one foot to the other as she struggled to remember what
she had planned to say next.

'I'm sorry I jumped in front of your car, but I have to see
you, speak to you. It's very important.'

For a wild moment, Sebastian had wondered if she were
some kind of terrorist. Now, somewhat reassured, he peered
more closely at this clearly apprehensive, olive-skinned girl
who spoke with a north-country English accent and who was
wearing a cheap jacket, torn jeans and a red and white baseball
cap. At the same time, however, he was pretty sure that her
white silk shirt was from Dior, and that her very dark glasses
were also extremely expensive. She looked faintly familiar,
too. Maybe, despite her scruffy teenage appearance, she was a
client of the bank.

'I can't possibly see you now, and the bank is closed,' he explained with slightly less abruptness. 'Why don't you phone my secretary tomorrow morning and make an appointment. If it really is urgent I could probably fit you in after lunch.'

He was very good looking in a chiselled, elegant way. Natalie, devouring every detail, realized that he must be very fit; not an ounce of fat contaminated his lean, muscular frame. The sports bag on the passenger seat bore witness to that fact. But his grey eyes and forbidding expression still terrified her. She took a deep breath and tried again.

'It isn't about business. This is a very personal matter. Please . . . it's raining . . . couldn't I sit in your car?'

Now he looked frankly startled. Then, for the first time, she saw a ghost of a smile hover around his mouth.

'Didn't your mother ever tell you,' he said slowly, 'not to sit in cars with strange men?'

Emboldened by the oh-so-faint smile and the unwitting perfection of his cue, Natalie took the plunge. Removing the dark glasses which she had borrowed from Roz, she grinned engagingly back at him.

'My mother is Roz Vallender,' she told Sebastian. 'And you aren't a strange man, you're my father. So I think under the circumstances it would be OK, don't you?'

Chapter 51

'Just look at the two of you,' cried Loulou, bursting into the sitting-room and finding Camilla and Rocky sitting disconsolately at opposite ends of the sofa. Rocky, his liquid brown eyes piteously mournful, thumped his tail against one of the silk cushions. Camilla didn't even turn round.

'Has Rocky done something terrible?' said Loulou, glaring at him. Finally, Camilla shook her head. 'I'm being depressed. He's just keeping me company, that's all.'

'Well, don't expect *me* to,' declared Loulou, then put her arms around Camilla. 'But you can tell me what's made you depressed, if it'll help. It isn't Roz, is it?'

'No.' Camilla managed a faint smile. She wasn't going to confess her confused feelings for Nico to Loulou, whose ability to keep secrets was on a par with her recent choice in men. No, this particular secret was one she had to keep entirely to herself, but Roz's revelation earlier had hit her hard. Everything that had passed between Nico and herself seemed cheapened now; it was probably his standard patter for persuading women into bed. Her fragile ego had been cruelly battered and with that had come a renewal of all her old insecurities. This afternoon she had felt lonely and horribly alone. The coming-to-terms with that sensation, which she had hoped she was finally beginning to master, was clearly not yet complete. The situation wasn't helped, either, by the fact that she was no longer working. When Matt had died and she had retreated to Scotland in order to come to

491

terms with her grief, Zoë had taken over the day-to-day running of Sheridan's on a purely temporary basis. Upon returning to London, however, Camilla had realized that she was no longer needed. The agency was continuing to flourish. And having already decided that she wanted to be able to spend more time with her children – and Marty – it had been with some relief that she had passed her share of the business over to Zoë.

The arrangement had suited both of them and Camilla had revelled in her newfound freedom, but on days like today she almost wished that she still had something concrete upon which to concentrate. Anything would be better than this awful, endless, self-recrimination . . .

'I know,' said Loulou sympathetically, assuming that Camilla was upset about Matt, and waving at Lili as she waddled into the room wearing nothing but a smile and one blue sock, 'you don't have to tell me. But I can try and cheer you up, can't I? Christo and Laura are getting engaged tomorrow night, and it's Laura's twenty-first birthday. Her family are holding a massive party at their home in Bath. I've just phoned Roz at the studios and she doesn't want to go – she's too wound up about Nat at the moment – but she suggested that we stay at her cottage that night. Good idea?'

She gazed challengingly at Camilla, daring her to refuse.
'Well . . .'
'It'll cheer you up,' wheedled Loulou, lifting Lili onto her lap and kissing her bare shoulders.

Camilla thought about it. Refusing Loulou was going to be far more difficult than giving in gracefully, she realized. And parties one didn't want to go to were almost always better than those to which one looked forward.

'OK,' she agreed with reluctance. 'It'll be a change of scenery, anyway.'

'And lots of new, uncharted men,' said Loulou serenely. 'What more could two desperate single old women possibly wish for . . .?'

Sebastian Adams had always led an immaculately controlled life. He was the most organized person he knew and he took great pride in that fact. His body, his career, his home and his social life were just as he liked them, just as he had *made* them, and when a woman had once told him that he was chasing perfection he had taken it as a compliment. Imperfection, in Sebastian's logical eyes, was quite simply an unforgivable waste of time.

Which was why he was so totally thrown by the sudden appearance in his ordered world of Natalie.

To say that this was a situation he wasn't prepared for had to be the understatement of the century. And simply as a defence mechanism at first he had refused to even contemplate the idea that what this young girl was telling him might be true. Fixing her with his most imperious glare, then gunning the engine of his car with quite uncharacteristic ferocity, his immediate instinct had been to pretend that she hadn't even spoken, and to simply drive off and leave her.

As if guessing his intention, Natalie had stepped calmly once more in front of the car. Unable to believe the incredible nerve of the girl, Sebastian had jammed his foot down on the accelerator, revving wildly but moving forward only a couple of inches. Despite his panic – engendered by the fact that what was happening now was something over which he did *not* have total control – he had been forced to register admiration for her steadfastness. She wasn't going to move, not even if he *did* run her over. And there was no fear in her eyes at all. All he had seen there was that astonishing, nerve-wracking likeness to Roz.

And now here she was, he thought, still wary but at the same time curious. She had appeared into his life just a couple of hours ago and he still didn't have a clue why he had allowed her to do so.

Although appeared wasn't the right word, he considered as he sipped his iced Perrier and watched her gnawing the end of a chicken bone. She had erupted rather than appeared and even in this short space of time the evidence of that eruption was all around him; the gold canvas bag spilling its contents on to the dark blue carpet, dark glasses rakishly adorning a prized Art Deco figurine . . . yet strangely their presence bothered him less than he would have imagined, just as Natalie's own incongruous appearance irritated him marginally less now than when he had first seen her. That spiky, wet-gelled hair suited her elfin looks and her jeans, although faded and torn, were actually very clean. Really, he considered as if from a great distance, she looked perfectly OK. But then maybe, he amended with habitual care, he was still in deep shock.

'Look, this *has* to be some kind of mistake,' he said for the second time. Unperturbed, Natalie grinned.

'Of course it was a mistake. Roz didn't get pregnant on purpose, did she? No fifteen year old would.'

Irritated by the way she was deliberately twisting his words, Sebastian glared at her. 'You know precisely what I mean. It's obvious that you're Roz's daughter, but why should I believe you when you tell me that I'm the father?'

'*My* father,' corrected Natalie, more seriously now. 'I've

explained all that as well. You really aren't paying attention. Roz didn't tell *me*; she hedged and prevaricated and kept changing the subject. I only found out because I overheard her talking to Camilla.'

Sebastian, though loathe to admit it even to himself, had to concede that Natalie's reasoning was entirely logical.

'But she could have been lying even then,' he persisted, clinging to the vestiges of his organized bachelor existence like a convict on death-row praying for a reprieve. In his heart he knew already that it was all over. 'She might have been lying to her friend.'

'Now *you* listen,' said Natalie firmly, and he realized afresh that she wasn't even afraid that he would refuse to acknowledge her. 'And I mean *really* listen to me. If you aren't my father, can you think of any reason on earth why she has never *ever* even told you that she gave birth to me? She knew you didn't want children so she kept it a secret from you, but if I had been anyone else's child it wouldn't have made any difference to you, at all. So you're my father; you know it and I know it and it's about time you bloody well accepted the idea.'

Sebastian stared at her in amazement. Several seconds ticked by. He couldn't find the words, so he nodded. She *was* right. The game of hide-and-seek was up. And maybe it wasn't quite as disastrous as he had thought it was going to be, after all.

'Why don't you have a proper drink?' suggested Natalie kindly, nodding at his glass of Perrier as if she could read his mind. 'And I'll have a Malibu and pineapple juice if you've got it.'

It was then, quite unexpectedly, that Sebastian started to laugh. The women he entertained in his elegant apartment invariably drank chilled dry wine and were careful not to crease their clothes. Suddenly the utter absurdity of the contrast between them and this scruffy, untidy urchin struck him as incredibly funny.

It crossed his mind that he really should phone Danielle and tell her that their dinner date was cancelled, but with uncharacteristic carelessness, he dismissed the thought, rose from his seat and disappeared into the kitchen.

When he returned, he was carrying a dark green bottle upon which was balanced the red and white baseball cap.

'You really recognized me today from a photograph taken when I was seventeen?' he asked.

Natalie nodded earnestly and continued to chew the last remnants of her chicken leg. 'Really. You don't look all that different, only . . . well, older. But not much,' she amended at great speed, anxious not to offend her father. 'In fact hardly any older at all.'

'Thank you,' said Sebastian, his voice grave as he flung the baseball cap on to the table and expertly uncorked the Bollinger. 'I don't normally drink champagne on a Friday but since you're here I think maybe we ought to be doing a bit of celebrating . . .'

Laura Scott's parents lived in a far grander house than either Camilla or Loulou had imagined. As their taxi snaked along the wide, tree-lined drive they saw a vast Georgian mansion glittering with lights loom ahead of them. Dozens of cars littered the gravelled driveway and plenty of people were milling to and from a massive blue-and-white striped marquee set up on the lawn to one side of the house.

'Christo didn't say it would be like this,' whispered Loulou as they paid off the cab. 'Bloody hell, some of them are in dinner-jackets. And to think I almost wore my jeans.'

'To think that we were going to bring a couple of bottles,' exclaimed Camilla, trying not to laugh.

As they made their way through the hall, towards a vast room crammed with people they didn't know, they overheard one very done-up blonde say to her friend, 'The very worst thing any woman can do when she gets married is let herself go. She should *always* dress up, make up and wear perfume – then her husband won't be suspicious when she has an affair. Suddenly splurging on silk underwear after spending months in nylon knickers and thermal vests is the very worst giveaway.'

'Which is why I never wear knickers at all,' said Loulou clearly, gliding serenely past with her head held high. Then she winked at Camilla. 'It's going to be that kind of party, by the sound of it.'

Eventually they located Christo and Laura. Never having seen her before in anything more exotic than track-suit trousers and one of Christo's enormous Fair Isle sweaters, Laura was a shock. Encased in white chiffon with her brown hair swept up she looked, whispered Loulou, 'very High Society, very *Tatler*.' Christo, who had clearly been coaxed with extreme reluctance into a dinner-jacket, looked decidedly shell-shocked by comparison.

Loulou hugged him with such enthusiasm that the silver combs holding her long hair in a precarious topknot loosened and slipped to the floor. 'You look beautiful,' she assured him. Christo pulled a wry face.

'You'll hate me when I tell you what I've done. Mac dropped into Vampires yesterday evening. He offered to do our wedding photos. I had to invite him here tonight, darlin'. After all, he has been a good friend to me over the years. You both have.'

Loulou's face dropped. 'He's here with Cecilia?'

'Cecilia's in Paris. Mac's coming here alone.' Christo shrugged helplessly at the mass of people around them. 'Or he may already have arrived – I had no idea it was going to be like this. When Laura told me that her father had always worked in factories I didn't realize that he owned the damn things . . .'

Camilla watched Loulou metamorphose before her very eyes. Never one of life's moths, and already striking in a Russian-style black and white embossed leather dress by Fendi, fitted jacket, black stockings and high heels, she seemed now to grow a couple of inches. Her grey eyes grew large and brighter, her cheeks suffused with colour and her shoulders straightened. Even the scent of her perfume appeared to become stronger as adrenalin coursed through her bloodstream.

'I hope Mac's being here won't spoil the party for you,' continued Christo, his Irish accent becoming more pronounced with anxiety, 'but I couldn't not invite him, could I now?'

'I'll be fine,' Loulou assured him, bending to retrieve her silver combs from the polished parquet floor. 'I'd better go to the loo and sort my hair out. Back in two minutes, Cami. See if you can find us some drinks, OK?'

Straightfaced, they watched her disappear up the winding staircase. Camilla gazed at Christo for several long seconds.

Christo cracked first. 'Oh, OK,' he said with a huge smile. 'Maybe Mac told me that Cecilia had gone to Paris before I invited him down here.'

'It might be a disaster,' warned Camilla, trying to control her own rising laughter. 'It's very brave of you to risk it.'

Hugging Laura to his side, he shrugged once more. 'But it may just work out, you know. They're crazy about each other – any fool can see that.'

'Except themselves,' said Camilla.

'We're so happy together,' explained Laura, touching Christo's cheek with tender fingers, 'that we want everyone else to be happy, too. And a little collusion doesn't go amiss, sometimes. Christo would have run a mile when he first met me, if I'd told him about Daddy's money. Sometimes you have to fib a bit to get what you really want in life.'

'And it's about time you had a bit of happiness yourself,' Christo told Camilla with mock severity. 'Since I'm at present sorting out the troubles of the world, we'll have to see if we can't find a handsome gentleman to lift your own spirits. When I've done my duty meeting everyone I'm supposed to meet tonight, I'll introduce you to a few likely candidates.'

Touched by his kindness, and suddenly overcome with a fresh wave of loneliness, Camilla shook her head and gave him a wry smile.

'Don't worry about me,' she said quietly. 'I'm really not looking for a man at the moment.'

'Good,' said Laura with great firmness, as if that settled the matter. 'That's always the best time to find one.'

Several minutes later, Loulou returned.

'I've looked everywhere, even under the beds upstairs,' she said, shivering like an overbred greyhound and spilling most of the champagne Camilla had handed to her. 'Mac isn't here yet. Which would be best – should I be flirting with someone gorgeous when he arrives or standing alone looking soulful?'

'Most of your problems with Mac have been caused by you fraternizing with other men,' protested Camilla, panicking slightly as she realized that either way she was going to be abandoned. 'And if you're on your own it'll seem as if no-one wants to talk to you. Why don't we stick together, then I can discreetly back off when he comes over?'

'You're a gem!' Loulou hugged her, at the same time glancing over Camilla's shoulder and locking eyes with a dissolute boy with a wicked mouth who was lounging against the white marble fireplace. Not a day over twenty-two, she thought, blowing him a kiss. And I'm not even going to *speak* to him because Mac's here, Mac's here, Mac's here . . .

'Bloody hell,' said Mac, feigning surprise. 'The further away from London I go, the more often I seem to bump into you. Is nowhere sacred?'

'Don't give me that bullshit,' retaliated Loulou affably, her confidence bolstered by several glasses of champagne. 'You knew I'd be here for Christo's engagement party.'

'And I came anyway,' he riposted. 'Despite the fact that you've probably got a dozen reporters hiding in the woodwork. What the *hell* possessed you to do that story in the paper, for God's sake?'

'Me!' screamed Loulou, her silver-grey eyes flashing like marcasite. 'I thought you'd organized that . . . I'm going to kill that worm when I get my hands on him . . . and where's Cecilia tonight, anyway?'

'France and you bloody well know it,' retaliated Mac. 'And if you start getting any ideas . . .'

Camilla made a strategic withdrawal. Their helpless sparring, the undeniable explosion of attraction between them, was more than she could cope with. Neither of them were even aware that she was there, and the realization only enhanced her own unease. Nothing would please her more than if Loulou and Mac could somehow be reconciled, but at the same time it left her conspicuously alone and suddenly very, very lonely.

Escaping through the front door she made her way towards

the marquee from which incredibly loud rock music was pounding. As she approached the enormous blue-and-white tent in the darkness, taking care not to let her high heels sink into the springy turf, she encountered a solid object with her toe and almost tripped, losing her shoe in the process.

'Ouch,' protested a male voice and she ground to an uneven halt.

'I'm not a tent peg,' he protested and Camilla giggled, blinking in the darkness and crouching down in search of her shoe.

'You sound nice,' the voice continued. 'How would you like to share my picnic?'

'You have a picnic out here?' Relieved to be spoken to, she paused, only just able to make out the dim silhouette of his body close to hers, stretched out lazily on the grass.

Next moment, a bottle splashed into her lap. 'Bollinger. It's all a midnight feast needs. Who are you?'

'Camilla.' Emboldened by the darkness, she retaliated: 'Why, who are you?'

'Piers O'Donaghue,' replied the voice which had a sensual touch of Irish in it not unlike Christo's. 'And are you pretty? I only buy champagne for girls who are pretty. Otherwise it's lager.'

'Thank goodness it's dark,' said Camilla, raising the bottle to her lips and wondering how Loulou and Mac were getting on. Then she jumped as a warm hand touched her cheek, lightly tracing her profile.

'You'll do,' said Piers O'Donaghue with a smile in his voice. 'Tell me why you're here.'

'I know Christo . . .' began Camilla, but he interrupted her.

'I mean here on this grass, talking to a complete stranger. Had a row with your lover?'

501

'I'm being discreet.' And, for something to say, she explained about Loulou and her hazardous love-life. As she talked, she breathed in the expensive aroma of Dolce & Gabbana aftershave and newly mown grass and after a while her eyes became more accustomed to the summer darkness. Piers O'Donaghue had black curly hair, dark eyes and a deep tan which showed against the whiteness of his shirt. If she deliberately didn't concentrate on the amused, Anglo-Irish voice she could almost imagine that he was Matt, which was quite absurd but made him easier to talk to.

'Two lost souls, then,' he declared, reaching for her bare arm and caressing it with lazy sensuality. 'Our bottle's finished. Do we stay out here like the babes in the wood or go in search of more to drink and risk being disappointed when we each see what the other looks like?'

Camilla trembled, suddenly afraid to break the spell. 'Let's stay,' she said and saw Piers' white teeth gleam. Laughing, he stood up and helped her carefully to her feet.

'You're either very, *very* ugly or enchantingly modest,' he told her, so close now that his mouth brushed her hair. 'But you smell gorgeous and I'm far too curious about you now to wait any longer to find out. Listen, they're playing our song. We have to dance.'

Camilla realized that she was holding her breath as they entered the vast, elegantly lit marquee. All of a sudden, beset by self-doubt and all the old insecurities, she was terrified that Piers would take one look at her and exclaim in horror, 'Christ, you *are* ugly,' before disappearing into the night.

Instead he pulled her round to face him, leisurely surveying the length of her body for several seconds before giving a low whistle of approval and reaching out to remove an imaginary pair of spectacles.

'Why Miss Jones, you're beautiful. Why on earth have I never noticed before?'

Colouring, Camilla glanced down at the ground. Piers O'Donaghue was devastatingly attractive and she was at a loss for words.

Fortunately, he suffered no such inhibitions. 'Come and dance,' he said again, his tone gentle as if he were coaxing a nervous puppy on to his lap. 'I adore women who blush. In fact I didn't know there were any left who still could.'

As they stepped on to the dance floor, alive with whirling couples, the band slowed down and started playing a moody, sexy version of 'Every time you go away'.

'Please don't,' murmured Piers, his warm hand lightly caressing Camilla's shoulder blade. Startled, she met his eyes, which were brown instead of dark blue like Matt's, but otherwise uncannily similar in shape.

'Don't what?'

'Go away.' He smiled, revealing those incredibly white, very even teeth once more. Thinner than Matt, an inch or so shorter and probably five years younger, he nevertheless reminded Camilla of him so intensely that she couldn't stop staring at him. The dark curly hair and the narrowed, perpetually-amused eyes fringed with thick lashes were what really did it, she realized as they moved around the dance floor in graceful unison, scarcely noticing the other couples around them.

'You don't live in Bath,' he stated matter-of-factly. 'If you did, I'd know you. You told me that you know Laura's fiancé so I'd say at a guess you're from London. That means you have to return there . . . but I don't want you to go. And I do mean it,' he added, his expression serious. 'This isn't a line. It's a *coup de foudre*, Camilla. Do you understand what I'm saying to you now?'

503

* * *

Mac was still privately wondering if he had gone mad. Did people *know* when that happened to them or did they just carry on in blissful ignorance of the world around them?

He had been horrified to hear himself accepting Christo's invitation to the party, knowing – as they both did, although it had remained unspoken between them – that Loulou would be there.

He had been even more disturbed to find himself ringing Cecilia at her hotel in Paris and mentioning casually that he was going out to dinner that night with an old photographer friend.

And, driving down the M4 towards Bath later that evening, he had finally considered the possibility that he might benefit from a few sessions on the psychiatrist's couch.

Was he destined, he wondered now, to spend the rest of his life racing down to Gloucestershire for frantic, fated reunions with Loulou?

At that moment, however, the object of his madness returned from her search for Camilla and the familiar longing mixed with love and exasperation hit him hard in the stomach – as it always did. She was like a wayward child, always thinking she knew best, and plunging into predicaments with bright, hopelessly misguided optimism. But at the same time he couldn't help admiring her resilience. The newspaper feature, of course, was what had finally clinched it. Whether or not that ambitious young reporter had realized what would happen, the fact remained that his 'exposé' had been more than instrumental in reuniting him with Loulou. Her secret longing to see him, whether true or not, had gripped him with a need equally as fierce. No longer the ice queen, her exposed vulnerability had affected him more deeply and effectively than anything else could have done.

And now that she had finally dropped her guard, allowing her deepest feelings to surface, she was utterly irresistible.

'I saw her,' she said breathlessly, 'dancing with a divine man. The pair of them wouldn't have noticed if the Seven Samurai had burst into the marquee, they looked so besotted with each other. I'll ask Christo to tell her later that we've gone.'

'Where are we going?' said Mac, unable to prevent himself from reaching for her hand. Loulou gave him a look that was so wicked his knees went weak.

'A hotel,' she whispered. 'Bath's finest. I want us to sign in as Mr and Mrs Smith, so that everyone will know what we're up to.' Tugging at his arm and at the same time draining her glass of champagne, she pulled him towards the front door. 'Come on, I want to be so sinful and naughty that you'll never forget me . . .'

'Don't worry,' said Mac, following her and praying that nobody could see how distorted the front of his trousers had become. 'Whatever else happens, I won't *ever* be able to do that.'

'If there's one thing I absolutely adore,' drawled Piers, pulling Camilla to him, 'it's an insatiable woman. And oh . . . I've made you blush again. If there's one thing I adore even more than an insatiable woman, it's one who blushes at the same time.'

In the coppery glow of the subdued lighting, Camilla admired the sheen of Piers' bare chest, splaying her fingers between his collarbones and trailing them slowly down towards his taut stomach.

'I don't know why I'm like this. I really don't make a habit of it. You're almost my very first one-night stand, you know.' Deliberately she refused to allow herself to remember Nico.

Putting a finger against her lips, Piers silenced her. 'I'm not a one-night stand. We're going to see a lot more of each other than this. *Coup de foudre*; I told you.'

Dreamily she kissed his tanned chest, willing herself not to think too hard, or to hope too much. But it was hard not to hope when their lovemaking had been so exhilarating, so totally perfect.

'I'm going back to London in the morning,' she murmured, testing him. 'You live in Bath. It's too far away.'

Piers rolled his dark eyes and laughed, hugging her against him. 'Camilla, you're incredible. Most women at this stage are saying, "You will ring me, won't you" and "I will see you again, won't I?" He imitated a falsetto whine with devastating accuracy. 'And here you are, at the very *beginning* of our great love affair, doing your damndest to put me off. I'm coming up to London on Wednesday to see you, OK? And nothing you say is going to stop me.'

'Fancy meeting you here,' purred Loulou, flinging her arms wide and wondering if it were really possible to be this happy. She giggled as Mac poured an effervescent trail of chilled Dom Perignon over her stomach and thighs and proceeded to lick it off with exquisite skill and slowness. 'Aren't you glad you came?'

He paused, leaning on one elbow and glancing up at her. 'You're a witch,' he said slowly, and Loulou gave him her most sublime smile.

'But I can make you laugh,' she said, tickling his hip with

her big toe. 'You don't look as if you've laughed much lately. Was Cecilia useless at telling jokes?'

Observing her use of the past tense, Mac replied carefully, 'She has her good points.'

'But mine are better,' murmured Loulou seductively, all her ideas of playing it cool forgotten now that she had finally enticed Mac back into her bed. 'What do you call a man with no arms and no legs who swims the Channel?'

Mac bent and kissed her exquisite navel, then shrugged. 'I couldn't begin to guess.'

'A clever-dick,' said Loulou, smiling and reaching for him once more. 'And since this hotel is bloody expensive and we really should make sure we get our money's worth, you can show me again just how clever you are . . .'

Camilla still found it hard to believe that she could feel so deliciously wanton and free of guilt. Not only had she spent the entire night making love to someone who was virtually a complete stranger, but she had done it in Roz's bed where presumably in the past Roz had slept with Jack. With Nico too, she realized belatedly, and thrust *that* particular thought with great firmness from her mind.

And I feel alive again, she thought, sitting up in bed and basking in the warmth of the sunlight which streamed through the open windows.

Perfect peace, thought Camilla, pushing her hands through her hair in a lazy attempt to loosen the tangles. Peace and happiness and a kind of giddy weightlessness had enveloped her and she was finding it ludicrously difficult to stop smiling. And to think, she recalled idly, that I never thought I could feel properly happy again.

* * *

Later, trailing downstairs in her white silk dressing-gown because getting dressed might break the spell, she found Piers in the kitchen making breakfast and whistling 'White Christmas'. He was naked apart from a black velour towel slung around his hips and Camilla felt her stomach disappear with longing.

'I adore women with wet hair,' he said, handing her a warm croissant and kissing her collarbone where droplets of water from the shower still clung like warm beads. Into her other hand he thrust a mug of strong, aromatic coffee. 'Let's go outside. I wanted to make love to you on the grass last night. Maybe this morning I'll get lucky.'

'The grass will be damp,' protested Camilla, following him to the door.

He grinned. 'Even better. I adore women with wet bodies.'

'And Loulou could be back at any moment.'

Piers regarded her sternly. 'Are you making excuses?'

'Of course I'm making excuses,' said Camilla, wincing as she sat down on the wooden bench beneath a bower of honeysuckle. 'I ache in every muscle and I don't even have the strength to walk straight. My poor old body isn't used to all these ... attentions.'

'Oh God,' he groaned, collapsing beside her with an air of defeat. 'Enforced celibacy. I don't know whether I can stand it.'

'It'll be good for the soul,' Camilla said comfortingly and Piers laughed, his gypsyish dark eyes narrowing just as Matt's always had, an unexpected dimple in his left cheek enhancing his smooth brown features.

'I'm more interested in good bodies than good souls,' he said, tucking his free hand companionably between her knees where the white silk had fallen away. 'But since your poor old body is clearly off-limits, we'll just talk instead. Tell me all about yourself. Tell me about your love life . . . before me, of course.'

Normally reticent to the point of abruptness, Camilla marvelled at his power to relax her. Leaning back so that the sun's rays warmed her cheeks, she said, 'Until last night, the only men I'd ever slept with were two husbands and a single one-night fling.'

And instead of laughing or saying, 'Whose husbands were they?' as some men might have done, Piers leant across and kissed her earlobe.

'How delightfully innocent and refreshing,' he murmured. 'You make me feel very honoured. Now tell me all about *you*. I want to know everything about you, from the very, very beginning.'

'Is this a *joke*?' demanded Loulou, stiffening and drawing back like an angry, bewildered animal.

Mac saw the snapping, fiery light in her silver-grey eyes and knew at once that she was beyond reasoning with. Nevertheless, in desperation, he tried.

'Look,' he said gently, 'we both know now that we should be together. I *want* you; nothing's been right for me since we split up, but because I *had* to carry on somehow, I did. I'm living with Cecilia and –'

'You said last night that you didn't love her!' hissed Loulou, edging still further away from him.

'And it was the truth,' he continued. 'I'll tell her it's over between us, I swear I will. You and I can be together again . . . we can even get married again if that's what you want . . .' He hesitated, then added firmly, 'But I can't tell her just yet.'

'Because it's her birthday next month?' yelled Loulou with vicious mimicry. 'What kind of bullshit is this! Everyone has fucking birthdays, for Christ's sake . . . you hardly ever *remembered* mine when we were married.'

'On Cecilia's twenty-first birthday her mother died of cancer,' said Mac slowly, deliberately heightening the contrast between his own even tones and Loulou's hysterical shrieks. Torn between his desperate love for her and the heavy weight of obligation he felt towards Cecilia, he struggled to find the right words.

'She's so paranoid about birthdays – believing each year that something awful will happen – that she plans them weeks and weeks ahead. I promised her that this year we'd take a trip on the Orient Express. Lou, I don't want to do this any more than you want me to, but I simply can't break that promise. Cecilia isn't strong like you and she couldn't cope with it if I dropped her now – can't you understand that?'

'Oh, poor fragile Cecilia,' ridiculed Loulou, pushing open the window and taking several deep breaths. 'For a start, she's a top model – *the* top model of the moment – and you don't get to a position like that without fighting for it. She'd give Mike Tyson a run for his money, that's for sure. But what *really* gets me,' she continued, reaching for her leather dress and black jacket and rapidly climbing into them, 'is the fact that you're backing out *again*, using her as an excuse to get away. I don't believe you, Mac. It's just so much more bullshit. Why the hell can't you be honest, be like all the other men and simply admit that you fancied a quicky with your ex?'

Mac sank back against the pillows, defeated. Loulou was moving fast now, stuffing her suspender belt and stockings into her handbag and sliding into her spiky high heels.

'Who knows,' she continued, coming to stand at the foot of the bed with her hands on her hips and an expression of deep disdain masking the grief and pain, 'I may have gone to bed with you anyway, just for the hell of it, so there wasn't even any need to swear all that touching, undying devotion.' Then she stepped back again. 'Now fuck off out of my life and go back to your poor, gentle, wimp of a girlfriend. Wish her a happy birthday trip from me . . . and I hope you both drown in Venice.'

Then, leaving him no time to react, she picked up his clothes from the chair and hurled them out through the open window. His shoes followed one at a time, distant splashing sounds three floors down indicating that they had travelled further, landing in the hotel garden's carefully tended lily pond.

'Like that,' pronounced Loulou with a mixture of fear and satisfaction as she darted towards the door. 'I hope you fall into the water and bloody well *sink*!'

Chapter 52

'If you weren't my father,' chided Natalie, watching from the depths of the squashy leather settee as Sebastian made rapid notes in a file and replaced his calculator in the appropriate compartment of his briefcase, 'I'd think you were a stuffy old man.'

He glanced across at her, genuinely puzzled. 'I'm an efficient, properly organized *young* man. The fact that I have a grown-up daughter is merely an accident of nature; it doesn't mean I'm old.'

'OK,' shrugged Natalie conceding the point, 'but it's a Sunday and all you've done since you got up is drink black coffee and work. Don't you ever take any time off and have *fun*?'

Sebastian recapped his fountain pen and sat back in his chair. 'I enjoy working. That's why your mother and I have always got on so well together; she has her career and I have mine, and we aren't afraid of either hard work or the success which results from that. We've always understood each other's priorities.'

'Well, I'm bored,' Natalie countered, her mouth turning sulkily downwards. 'Working with pages of figures isn't my idea of a great time. And Roz – Mum – doesn't do half as much work as you do. I bet she only pretends to be like you so you'll be impressed.'

'Roz doesn't need to try and impress me,' said Sebastian

slowly, stalling for time. Really, this girl had an alarming knack of making rash statements which were uncomfortably incisive. To change the subject, he said, 'And I *do* have "fun" as you call it, but it's not exactly the kind of fun one can have when one's daughter comes to stay.'

'Sex!' said Natalie with such disgust that he almost smiled. 'You don't need those women. What's wrong with my mother?'

'I'm in Switzerland and she's in London. It tends to hamper one's spontaneity, you know.'

Natalie changed tack, shifting on to her side and giving him her most beguiling smile. It was too much like Roz's not to have an effect and Sebastian began to suspect that he was being cunningly manipulated against his will.

'That gives you *more* chance to be spontaneous,' she cajoled, observing the look of discomfort on her father's face. 'It's only eleven o'clock; we could be in London by mid-afternoon. And that really would be an ultra-cool, ultra-spontaneous thing to do.'

'Out of the question,' he said firmly, not realizing that his fountain pen, not properly capped, was leaking black ink through his best Turnbull & Asser shirt pocket. 'Nothing's organized.'

'Don't be so stuffy and *boring*!' cried Natalie, leaping to her feet. 'We drive to the airport, we catch a plane, we take a taxi to Camilla's house. There, I've organized you.'

'But . . .' began Sebastian hopelessly, knowing that he'd been beaten and wondering why it was so easy to be assertive at work and so impossible now.

'Stop it, Dad,' said Natalie swiftly. 'Go and get your passport and stop arguing. And look on the bright side; this is going to be the most wonderful, spontaneous surprise ever for Mum.'

'She doesn't like surprises,' grumbled Sebastian, reaching uneasily for his keys and pushing back his chair. 'She's like me; she prefers everything to be planned.'

Natalie grinned, hugged him and gave him a kiss.

'But sometimes things happen which aren't planned, and they turn out OK,' she said gleefully. 'Like me.'

As Camilla sat outside, shielding her eyes from the bright sun and watching Marty and Toby cavorting around the garden she reflected that it was difficult to be happy when everyone else seemed hell-bent on plunging themselves into misery. Loulou, slippery with oil, was stretched out on a yellow sun-lounger, sulking like mad and intermittently listing aloud all Mac's bad points. Charlotte, who was according to her the only girl in the whole of London missing the Britney Spears concert at Wembley, was out-sulking even Loulou. Rocky, having exhausted himself chasing Marty around the garden, was now suffering from heatstroke and lying gloomily in the shade of the weeping cherry tree.

And Roz, tense and irritable because there had still been no word from Natalie, was upstairs packing to leave for Gloucestershire. At lunchtime, having finally weakened, she had rung Sebastian's number in Zurich and there had been no reply. Snappy, rejecting Camilla's reassurances, she was desperately on edge.

No-one, it had rapidly become apparent, was the least bit interested in hearing about Camilla's new man. Even Lili, her cloudy black corkscrew curls tied up in a daffodil yellow bow, had looked unimpressed when Camilla had pulled her on to her lap for a cuddle.

'Wanna play with Rocky,' she protested, pouting and scrambling back down. Moments later, after tugging Rocky's ears so strenuously that he whined and shot inside the house, Lili burst into noisy floods of tears which only added to the general mood of doom and gloom. Marty ran over, visibly upset, and tried to kiss Lili better but outraged by the interruption, she screamed even more loudly and pushed him away with agitated, outstretched hands. Confused and hurt by the rejection, Marty, too, started to cry.

'Jesus, what a racket,' complained a good-natured, wonderfully familiar voice and Camilla almost leapt out of her seat, her heart thumping like a tom-tom.

'Piers! What on earth are you doing here?' she said breathlessly, aware that Roz had appeared at the open french windows, an expression of deep interest in her dark eyes.

'Couldn't wait until Wednesday, I'm afraid.' He shrugged and laughed at her unconcealed amazement, then solemnly handed her a canister of Ralgex. 'For your poor old muscles, sweetheart. It smells terrible but it'll stop them aching.'

Blushing furiously and realizing that he had deliberately engineered the situation in order that she would do just that, she pushed the can underneath her chair and stood up to introduce him to everyone.

'Roz let me in just now when I rang the bell,' he said, extending his hand and taking in at a glance Roz's slender, tanned figure. 'Of course I recognize you from your TV show. And you must be Loulou,' he went on, taking over with the ease of a politician. 'If it hadn't been for you doing your disappearing act last night, I might not have had the opportunity of meeting Camilla, so thank you. How did it work out with your ex-husband, by the way?'

'The absolute pits,' said Loulou, so cheerfully that Camilla stared open-mouthed at her. 'I threw all his clothes out of an hotel window.'

Piers grinned. 'Good for you, he must have deserved it. Now,' he turned to the children, 'you must be Toby . . . and you're Marty . . . and this beautiful young lady has to be Charlotte.' Entranced they each shook hands with him, until finally he turned to Lili, sitting sucking her thumb on the grass. 'And this gorgeous girl is Lili, am I right?'

He remembers every name, thought Camilla with a surge of amazed gratitude as Lili, tears forgotten, showed her pearly teeth in a smile. Within seconds, Piers' arrival had transformed the atmosphere, a knack which Matt had possessed, but at which Piers was clearly a true master. Glancing sideways, she saw Roz joking with Charlotte. Marty was jumping up on to her abandoned chair with his favourite teddy and Loulou was gathering Lili into her arms so that Piers could admire her more closely.

His smile, when he finally turned to look at Camilla once more, almost stopped her heart.

'You're even more beautiful now than you were this morning,' he said, his voice low and caressing. 'I had to see you again. Do you mind terribly?'

'I was just surprised,' she murmured, still lost in admiration at the way he had recalled everyone's name. He was one of those oh-so-rare men who genuinely listened to people instead of waiting for them to stop talking so that he could start.

And he had driven up to London to see her. What on earth was she going to do with him for an entire Sunday afternoon?

'We'll go out,' he said, as if reading her hopelessly untogether thoughts.

'But the children . . .'

Piers brushed a ladybird from the sleeve of his yellow-and-white striped shirt and pulled a pair of dark glasses from his pocket.

'They come too, of course,' he said simply, as if the idea that they should be left behind hadn't even occurred to him. 'I love kids.' Then he winked. 'Especially casseroled.'

Driven to drink, thought Roz gloomily, gazing at the half-empty bottle of wine on the table beside her. The cottage seemed dark and oppressive, and was almost eerily silent, but outside swarms of midges danced in the last of the evening sunlight and she hadn't the patience right now to tolerate them.

Seeing Camilla with Piers had depressed her still further; it seemed that fate was taking a fairy-tale hand and presenting the good girl with a charming prince whilst at the same time making sure that Roz, the evil witch, got all the punishment she deserved.

And Piers *was* charming, there was no doubt about that, she thought with a resurgence of the jealousy which had gnawed at her throughout her lonely trip home. Once, she wouldn't have thought twice about making a play for him. Now, however, she wondered whether he would even be interested. The look he had given her had been appraising, pleasant, polite . . . and decidedly uninterested.

The interest, thought Roz with guilty envy, had been reserved entirely for Camilla.

And as she took another slug of the not-quite-chilled white Burgundy, she reflected that only yesterday Piers and Camilla had undoubtedly spent a night of fevered, exquisite passion in her very own bed.

I mustn't be jealous, she told herself hopelessly. But it was hard not to be when her own life was so barren, and there had still been no word from either Natalie or Sebastian. In her present mood she could almost believe that never hearing from them or seeing either of them again would be the best thing that could happen. Loving people only caused pain. Losing them was far, far worse.

'I still don't know why I'm doing this,' complained Sebastian as he indicated left to turn off the motorway. Unfamiliar with the hire car he had picked up at Heathrow, the windscreen washers burst into life instead and Natalie giggled.

'Because you try too hard to be perfect. You think Roz is perfect. And so you both lead single, almost-perfect lives and don't even realize that you're lonely. If you and Mum think so much of each other, how can you bear to see her only once or twice a year? It's like eating one chocolate and throwing the rest of the box away.' Enjoying herself, and revelling in the role of Agony Aunt, Natalie grew expansive. 'You think self-denial is good for the soul, and maybe some of the time it is, but human relationships aren't like that. When two people love each other they make compromises and accept each other's imperfections, and *that* makes them happy.'

Sebastian held up his hand. 'All right, all right. If there's one thing I can't stand it's being preached at by a girl almost young enough to be my daughter. Now look, are you quite sure Roz is even going to be at the cottage when we finally get there?'

'Of course,' said Natalie complacently. 'When I phoned Loulou she told me that Mum had left London at around three. Just trust me, Dad . . . and stop worrying!'

'And if there's one thing I never do,' replied Sebastian

ruefully, 'it's place my trust in a girl almost young enough to be my daughter.'

She laughed. 'Make an exception, Dad. Have a little faith. Everything's going to be all right.'

Dusk was falling when Roz heard the car pull up outside the cottage, but she was too depressed to go to the window and see who it was. Having neglected to switch on any lights, she hoped vaguely that the visitor might think the house was empty. If she ignored the doorbell they would disappear again and leave her in peace.

But the doorbell did not ring. Instead, Roz heard a key turning slowly in the lock, and experienced such a rush of relief that she felt momentarily lightheaded. Thank God, she thought with fervent gratitude, Natalie had come back. At least she hadn't lost *her*.

The sight of Sebastian standing silently in the doorway of the dimly lit sitting-room was so totally unexpected that for a second she truly wondered if she was dreaming, that after having thought so hard and so often about him since Natalie's flight to Zurich, her mind had somehow conjured up this apparition.

But Roz was a practical person and she didn't allow her mind to play tricks on her. Besides, apparitions didn't wear Gucci loafers.

Nor, particularly when the apparition concerned was Sebastian, did they sport wayward black inkstains on their pristine white shirt.

'So she did find you,' said Roz, managing to sound almost conversational despite the frantic clamour of her heart. Now, now *at last*, she would know how Sebastian had reacted to the news which she had been too afraid to tell him for over eighteen years.

'Naturally,' he replied, with a faint dry smile. 'It was what she set out to do. Can you imagine anything or anyone defeating that girl?'

'She's certainly strong-willed,' admitted Roz, thinking how crazy it was that she and Sebastian should be standing here like this discussing their daughter with such stilted formality. It was like a parent-teacher meeting at school, for God's sake.

Sebastian, however, seemed not to notice the incongruity, but then that was him all over.

'She nags me,' he was saying now, looking perplexed. 'Can you believe that? *Me*, nagged by a scruffy eighteen year old who doesn't even brush her hair. She bullied me into flying over here today . . . I'm supposed to be at a board meeting first thing tomorrow morning and she simply doesn't *care* about that.'

'And you have ink on your shirt,' murmured Roz, almost in wonderment. The Sebastian she had known for so long didn't allow himself to be bullied by anyone, and his clothes were always entirely immaculate. Although in a curious way the inkstain reassured her more than anything else could have done and because of it she felt able to make her move.

'So why *are* you here, Sebastian?' she ventured boldly, her dark eyes meeting his with a challenging stare, her bare toes tensing against the thick pile of the Persian rug beneath her feet.

He gestured aimlessly, a most un-Sebastianlike feature. 'I don't honestly know. Natalie insisted, I suppose.'

'Where is she now?'

'In the car.' He half-smiled again. 'Probably with a pair of binoculars trained on this window.'

Since a romantic Hollywood embrace didn't appear to be on the cards, Roz sank back down into her corner of the settee, tucking her legs beneath her.

'Were you furious when she told you who she was?' she persisted, bracing herself for the worst.

'Furious?' Sebastian paused, considering the word. 'No, not furious. Stunned, disbelieving at first, amazed . . . and very confused, I suppose. Once it began to sink in I realized I was bitter in some ways, at not having known she existed, yet relieved in others. I've never been interested in babies or children, never wanted any of my own – you knew that of course, which was why you decided not to tell me at the time. I understand that much. But *how*,' he said with a flash of controlled anger laced with resentment, 'could you have kept it from me all these years?'

To her horror Roz, who scarcely ever cried, felt tears brimming against her lower eyelids.

'I didn't want to lose you,' she said, her control sliding away as she realized that what she had most dreaded was now happening for real. With a trembling hand she reached for the bottle of wine and filled her glass. 'You would have thought I was trying to trap you. I couldn't go through with an abortion, so I gave Nat up for adoption and tried to forget her. It never occurred to me for a moment that she'd ever try and find me when she grew up . . . telling you afterwards would only have made you hate me. I couldn't do it, Sebastian. I needed you too much to ever risk losing you.'

'Don't cry,' he said, looking alarmed. 'You never cry.'

'Well, I am now,' Roz almost shouted, as the tears slid down her face. Hating herself for being so weak she glared up at him, desperate for the confrontation to be over. It was humiliating,

Sebastian of all people seeing her disintegrate like this. 'So now you know. I'm a cheat and a liar and I'm not the person you thought I was. I've *never* been that person, so there's no need to waste any more time talking to me because I'm only an imposter. Now *go*,' she said fiercely, closing her eyes so that she wouldn't have to see him do so. 'Just leave me alone. If you go now you won't even have to miss your precious bloody board meeting tomorrow morning.'

Sebastian ignored her. Calmly, his tone mildly curious, he said, 'Have you honestly spent all these years trying to match up to the high expectations you thought I demanded?'

'Oh, shut up!' yelled Roz, burying her wet face in a yellow silk cushion. Leaning across, Sebastian pulled the cushion away and tossed it into a corner of the room. Now he was in control again, the ultra-efficient male who stood no nonsense from hysterical women.

'Tell me,' he insisted, his grey eyes boring into her like lasers. Roz felt fifteen again, immature and cornered.

'I don't even understand the question,' she countered truculently, avoiding his chilling gaze.

'Did you want me to think you were ... perfect?' probed Sebastian with maddening patience.

Oh, why didn't he just *go*, she thought wildly, and realized that he wouldn't move until she admitted it. No one flew this far for a mere ounce of flesh, after all. And Sebastian, it seemed, wanted the lot.

'Of course I did,' she said, sniffing loudly. 'Of course I wanted you to think I was perfect. But I'm not. I wreck every relationship I've ever had. I'm selfish, I'm a bitch, I use bad language, I smoke and I have a foul temper. Jealous? Damn right I'm jealous ... it always tore me to pieces when you used to tell me about your other women, and now I've even got to the stage where I'm jealous of *my* friends because they're happy and I'm not. So there you go,' she concluded with heaving, breathless defiance. 'That's the real Roz Vallender. Aren't you glad I told you about her? Now you can push off with a clear conscience because nobody in their right mind would dream of having anything to do with a selfish cow like me.'

'Oh, shut up,' said Sebastian, moving towards her and pulling her unwillingly to her feet. 'It truly can't be that bad. Our daughter thinks you're wonderful. "Cool" I think was the adjective she used.' He paused for a second, deep in thought. 'Or maybe it was "triff". Anyway, if there's one thing I've learnt recently it's that our daughter is an exceptional judge of character.'

'T-truly?' hiccuped Roz, wondering why on earth Sebastian should be running his fingers slowly up and down her inner arms and regarding her with an expression of such tender warmth. 'I've been awful to her, really. Not motherly at all. I could have murdered her when I found out she'd gone to look for you.'

'Oh, she thinks you're "ace",' Sebastian assured her with a smile that sent tremors down her spine. Surely, thought Roz in bewilderment, he wasn't going to kiss her?

'So you aren't perfect, after all,' he murmured, his mouth now only inches from her own. 'And you're right – it *is* almost a relief to know that. Perfection can be somewhat wearing after a while. But in the meantime, what's "triff" and "cool" and "ace" enough for Natalie is quite good enough for me, and although I never thought I'd say this, would you consider marrying me, Roz?'

'Wha –' gasped Roz, and at that moment Sebastian sealed

her mouth with a kiss. When it ended, he held a finger firmly to her lips, his eyes forbidding her to utter another word.

'Wha –' He echoed consideringly. 'Very good, Roz. Very concise indeed. It sounds like a definite yes to me. Nod your head if you agree.'

Struck dumb, enthralled, still scarcely daring to believe that this was really happening, Roz gazed up at him with reddened, swollen eyes.

And slowly nodded.

'Brill,' said Sebastian cheerfully, kissing her again. 'Now I suppose we'd better call Natalie in from the car and tell her that her entirely ace parents are finally going to make her legal. That is, of course, if she doesn't know already.'

Chapter 53

'How on earth,' said Caroline, sipping disconsolately at her drink, 'can anyone be *this* bored with the Caribbean?'

The ice rattled in her glass as she gestured towards the virgin-smooth beach stretching before them. The hills behind their sprawling white bungalow were a shimmering collage of greens, a hundred different shades of the colour which had given Montserrat its nickname of the Emerald Isle. The sunshine was miraculous and endless, the supply of drink and dope inexhaustible.

'God,' she groaned, shielding her eyes from the relentless perfection of it all, 'this should be enough to keep anyone happy, and all I can do is hate it.'

Susie, who was the long-time live-in girlfriend of Jake, the bass guitarist, chewed a piece of pineapple which she had fished from her own glass and gazed thoughtfully at her pinky-brown stomach, barely swollen by four months of pregnancy. Until this week, Caroline had spoken scarcely more than a few words to her, but now, by virtue of being the only other female in Nico's entourage, Caroline had been virtually forced to make overtures of friendship. Susie at least understood the situation, being what she cheerfully termed a 'lesser half' herself. And although she was perfectly well aware that Caroline's sudden 'friendship' was nothing more than an antidote to loneliness, it didn't bother her. Susie was that sort of girl; she couldn't be bothered to be bothered. Living with darling Jake, carrying his baby and making the most of their life of unexpected luxury was all that mattered. But Caroline was still moaning and she clearly needed an audience. With a barely audible sigh, Susie wriggled down on her sunlounger into a more comfortable position and transferred her baby-blue gaze to Caroline. Although she had eyes as innocent as a Cindy doll's, they were far shrewder than most people gave her credit for. It was this combination of naivety and shrewdness which had carried her from a crowded council house in Bristol to the imposing Georgian residence in Surrey which she and Jake now shared.

'It's not the island,' she said now, her voice hypnotically soft, 'it's because Nico isn't paying you enough attention. Even I can see that.'

'I thought we'd be having a proper holiday,' said Caroline, her inhibitions loosened by her third glass of rum punch. 'Well, maybe not a proper one, but I didn't think that Nico would be working in the studios for more than a few hours each day. The rest of the time we'd be together, having fun . . . I *thought*,' she concluded with heavy sarcasm. 'Do you know, he didn't even speak to me on the flight over? He spent the entire bloody trip gassing with Monty instead, leaving *me* stuck next to some fat greasy businessman from Birmingham called Hubert, for Chrissake.'

'Jakey and I thought about calling our baby Hubert,' said Susie calmly and Caroline shot her a sideways look. The trouble with Susie was that one could never be entirely sure whether or not she was joking.

'But the point is that Nico *ignored* me,' she went on, twisting her almost-empty glass in her hand. 'And that was only the start. Since we've been here he's done nothing but work and sleep. Eighteen hours a day in that goddam studio and the other six sleeping. Needless to say,' she concluded with alcohol-induced indiscretion, 'I am not included in either activity. So much for the weeks of sun, sand, sea and sex that I'd imagined.'

Susie tilted her straw hat over her nose. 'Three out of four isn't bad,' she said with a slight smile, glad that Jake hadn't been similarly affected. After last night's marathon she had wondered if she'd be capable of walking today.

'Only someone with a truly great sex life could say something as ridiculous as that,' retorted Caroline bitterly.

'Nico's wife's pissed off,' said Susie much later that night, when she and Jake were the only two still awake. Shaun, lying out on the verandah surrounded by empty beer cans, was snoring gently. Paddy, the band's keyboard player, slept peacefully on the settee opposite them. It was well past midnight and George Benson was providing suitably laid-back music on the stereo.

'Serves her right for tagging along when she knew she wasn't wanted,' said Jake easily, draping his arm around Susie's plump shoulders and drawing her against him. 'I bet he's still over at the studios now, going over the stuff we did today and keeping out of the old dragon's way.'

'She isn't a dragon,' protested Susie, pinching the back of his hand. 'You can't say she doesn't have the looks or the body. She isn't fat like me.' With ill-concealed pride she gazed down at her slightly swollen stomach, and Jake gave the mound an affectionate pat.

'She's a stuck-up bitch and she's only bothering to talk to you now because she hasn't got anyone else. Back home she knocks about with that bird who does the modelling, Cecilia. I bet she thinks she's really slumming it, having to make do with people like us . . .'

'Thanks!' exclaimed Susie, laughing.

Jake shook his head. 'You know what I mean. She thinks she's better than us, but we know she isn't. And we're a lot happier than her and Nico, aren't we?'

'*I'm* happy. I've got the best fella in the world,' she murmured, resting her cheek against his chest and breathing in the salt-and-honey scent of his skin. 'But I can't help feeling kind of sorry for her. Their sex life's non-existent, she told me today. It's really getting to her.'

'She looks like she needs to get laid,' remarked Jake idly, stroking her hair.

'Does Nico go with other women?'

'Course he does. He keeps pretty quiet about it, but I've seen him sloping off with the occasional bird after a gig, and I shouldn't think it was for a game of chess . . .'

'Poor Caroline,' said Susie sleepily. 'She ought to find someone to give her a good time, then. Sex is so lovely it's a shame to miss out, don't you think?'

'Now you're talking,' said Jake, sliding his hand beneath her loose cotton top and skilfully caressing her breasts. 'Come on, let's leave those two here and go to bed.'

Paddy Laharne waited until they had left the room before opening his eyes. Now there was a challenge, he thought. Caroline Coletto was a damn good-looking girl; he'd always been attracted to that voluptuous body and those catlike dark blue eyes, but she had seemed so distant, keeping herself glued to Nico's side whenever he'd seen her, that he hadn't made the effort to get to know her better.

Ah, but now . . . he grinned to himself in the semi-darkness, his fingers tapping out a three-four beat against the side of the settee. Now he knew the state of play, that presented a definite challenge.

And Paddy Laharne, he reminded himself, could never resist a challenge.

Caroline woke up as Nico slid out of the bed. Other husbands, she thought with a renewed flash of irritation, tried to be quiet out of consideration for their sleeping wives. Nico, she knew, simply didn't want to have to speak to her.

It was six thirty.

'What am I going to do today?' She heard the whine in her voice and despised herself for it.

The look Nico gave her was one of disbelief.

'You can't think of anything to do?' he gestured towards the window. 'Here?'

She pouted. Once he had thought her pout adorable. Now he looked faintly disgusted.

'I'm bored.'

'You're spoiled.'

'I wish I'd never –'

'So do I,' he flashed back at her, before she had even had a chance to regret her own ill-chosen words. Then, guilty because he'd meant it, he weakened.

'I'm sorry. Cutting an album isn't easy. Why don't you drive up to Plymouth and look around the town? Spend some money . . . buy some clothes . . .' He was casting around in desperation for ideas. There was nothing so difficult to please as a woman hell-bent on discontent.

'Yeah,' said Caroline, turning on to her side to look at him and trying to sound cheerful. She knew she had pushed her luck and was grateful for the reprieve. 'I'll do that. Find something to do, anyway. And I'm sorry too, OK?'

His heart turned to stone as he bent to kiss her forehead. Feeling like an impostor, he touched her tousled tortoiseshell hair with the back of his hand. 'OK. Have a good time. And I'll see you tonight. Got enough money for the trip?'

'Better leave me some more,' she said, half teasing, although it came out sounding almost like a threat. 'A wife can never have enough money, after all. Can she?'

Paddy Laharne watched Caroline from a distance, his topaz yellow eyes taking in every detail, missing nothing. Some people were happy with their own company; Caroline was definitely one of those who was not, he decided. She wore unhappy solitude like a cloak. The drink she poured herself was a large one, the cigarette a device with which to occupy herself, to pass lonely time. Several books lay scattered in the sand around her, but remained untouched. Caroline was gazing moodily out to sea, lost in her own unhappy thoughts.

But that body, he reminded himself with a quickening of interest, was still one of the most spectacular he had ever seen.

Paddy Laharne had never been in love. Wild since childhood, adored by hundreds, possibly thousands of girls throughout his tearaway teenage years, he accepted what was offered to him and made a point of never promising anything in return. And the girls, sighing over his long mane of hair, yellow eyes and proud, hawklike profile, were thankful just to be noticed. He was one of those chosen few whose features were so unusual, and so miraculously fitted together, that he transcended the traditional description of good looks. Taken piece by piece, the result should have been plain ugly, yet

Paddy had defied that, attaining instead an appearance so intriguing that mere good looks became irrelevant and uninteresting. And he had exactly the right kind of clever mind to make the most of it.

'Doing your homework?' he asked, glancing at the cover of the book now resting against her thighs. Jackie Collins' *Lethal Seduction*.

Caroline looked up, her expression behind her dark glasses wary. Paddy had scarcely spoken more than a few words to her before and his indifference hadn't troubled her. Now, however, he squatted down on his heels beside her and was showing every sign of striking up a conversation.

'The book makes it all seem far more exciting than it really is,' she said, glad of the chance to talk to someone even if it was only Paddy Laharne. 'Why aren't you over at the studios with the rest of them?'

'Day off.' Paddy grinned at her, his small white teeth startling against the deep tan of his face. 'Jake and Susie have gone over to Antigua. Shaun's disappeared with one of the chalet maids. Nico's running through some new ideas with the sound technicians and Monty's hovering over his shoulder getting on everyone's nerves. I'm all alone,' he concluded, shaking his windswept dark red hair away from his face.

'Welcome to the club,' she replied, sounding disinterested. 'Has Nico taken you to Plymouth yet?'

'Nico,' said Caroline slowly, 'hasn't so much as bought me a drink yet.'

Paddy gave her a naughty-boy wink and rose to his feet, holding a hand towards her. 'In that case, why don't I?'

'Why don't you what?' she parried, suspicion vying with reluctant interest.

'Buy you a drink. In Plymouth. We can explore the town and have fun.'

'Fun,' mused Caroline thoughtfully, a smile playing on her lips as she met his topaz eyes properly for the first time. 'Fun. You'll have to remind me how it goes. I don't have all that much of it these days.'

Paddy had timed his act beautifully. Since helping Caroline to her feet on the beach that morning he had taken care not to allow any physical contact between them whatsoever.

When, finally, they sank together on to a wooden seat outside St Anthony's church, hot and dusty in the dappled sunlight and exhausted by the amount of walking they had done, he stretched his arm across the back of the bench behind her, then very lightly touched the curve of her neck, brushing away damp strands of her hair.

He watched her shiver in response and pretended not to notice.

'This church was completely rebuilt in 1889,' he remarked lazily, admiring the curve of her shoulder and the marvellous swell of her breasts beneath the fuchsia-pink T-shirt. 'A hurricane destroyed the old building. Can you imagine a hurricane, here?'

He had read this in Caroline's guidebook whilst she had disappeared to the loo after lunch, but spoke the words as naturally as if they were etched into his mind.

'You are amazing!' she said, shaking her head and laughing. 'I had no idea you knew about things like churches.'

'I know about lots of things,' confided Paddy, leaning fractionally closer. 'And I know you and Nico aren't as happy as you should be. He neglects you. It's a bloody disgrace, if you ask me.'

Caroline said, 'Mmm,' tilting her head back and closing her eyes. Bathed in sunlight and new happiness, she had forgotten what it was like to have an attractive, attentive man around her. Having always thought of Paddy Laharne as a Beano-reading, ape-like macho-man completely lacking in the social graces she felt vaguely guilty and very pleased to discover that there was so much more to him than she had imagined. This morning he had driven her up into the lime plantations, shown her Galway's Soufriere, the spectacular but dreadfully smelly sulphur crater and taken her to the equally beautiful waterfall at Runaway Ghaut, persuading her to drink the water in his cupped hands because the legend of the waterfall was that those who drank from it would one day return to the island.

Then, despite the blistering heat, he had insisted on escorting her around all the touristy shops in Wapping Village. Nico's eyes always glazed over within minutes of a shopping expedition and Caroline had proceeded with caution, terrified of frightening Paddy away. But he had been brilliant, bursting with knowledge and enthusiasm, persuading her to try on the Sea Island cotton outfits in tropical colours and haggling expertly with the shopkeepers on her behalf when she decided to buy.

Now, at six o'clock, she realized two things. She had gone an entire day without alcohol, and she was starving.

Paddy, seeming to read her thoughts, consulted his watch. 'Maybe we should be heading back.'

'Oh no,' begged Caroline, suppressing another shiver of excitement as his hand accidentally brushed against her bare thigh. 'I'm having fun. Do we have to leave?'

Bingo, thought Paddy, and grinned.

'We could have dinner here,' she rattled on, adding stupidly – desperately – 'I'll pay.'

And now for the first time he made his contact a deliberate one. Taking her hand and raising it to his lips, he slowly kissed the palm, fixing her all the time with his relentless, irresistible gaze.

'You *have* been neglected,' he murmured. 'Poor Caroline. Don't you know that any woman who spends an entire day with me gets dinner on the house, just for putting up with me?'

'Putting up with you,' echoed Caroline wonderingly. 'I was beginning to think that every man was like Nico. Today, Paddy, you've saved my life.'

It was hard – harder than he'd expected – but he managed it.

Dropping her in the jeep outside the elegant whitewashed bungalow she shared with Nico, he allowed several seconds to elapse before dropping a chaste kiss upon her sun-warmed cheek.

'Thank you, Caroline. I won't forget today.'

In the tropical semi-darkness he saw the panic and longing in her eyes and realized that he very probably could, after all, spend the night with her. But it was too soon. He who waits wins, he told himself with the slow, uncurling pleasure of a true craftsman. Besides, if she were to turn him down now, the entire day would be spoiled.

'You could come in for a drink,' whispered Caroline breathlessly, wriggling down in the passenger seat so that her short white skirt edged further up her thighs. All of a sudden she desperately needed Paddy to stay with her. He was kind, attentive, and so ludicrously attractive that she couldn't understand why she had never noticed it before. 'Nico won't be home for hours yet.'

He gestured regret. 'I'd love to, but I really can't. We're

working in the studio all day tomorrow. And if I stayed for even one drink now, who knows what sort of state I'd be in then?'

The words lingered in the balmy night, and Caroline knew what lay behind them. Rejection mingled with gratitude; Paddy was turning her down because he had to and not because he wanted to. He was a real gentleman and she liked him for it, no matter how much she wished they could continue.

'All day?' she said, her tone registering disappointment.

'Until about seven, I guess.' He paused. 'If you don't have anything else laid on, you could come over to my bungalow after that, if you'd like to.' He preferred home matches, particularly when the women concerned had husbands. Less harrowing all round.

'I'd like to,' said Caroline helplessly, shifting in her seat so that she was properly facing him and still half-wishing he would change his mind about tonight.

'Then it's a date. Don't forget now,' Paddy warned her as he restarted the jeep's engine.

'I won't forget. I'm looking forward to it already.'

'Tomorrow,' he said, smiling into the darkness at her unintentional *double entendre*. 'I'll see you at around seven.'

He drove off, leaving Caroline standing alone in the darkness in front of the bungalow. It was practically Jane Eyre, she thought, lost in admiration and unfulfilled desire. What an incredible man Paddy Laharne was. And he hadn't even *kissed* her yet.

Chapter 54

It was bewildering, thought Camilla, in fact almost disorienta-
ting to have one's thoughts so abruptly redirected.

Until now, although she had scarcely realized it, almost all
her spare thoughts had been occupied by Matt. Whenever she
wasn't concentrating upon more immediate matters such as
what the children should eat, what she should be wearing and
whom she should be meeting that day, her thoughts had
automatically flown back to Matt. The accompanying sadness
had become part of her life.

But now, although partly through force of habit he still
entered her thoughts, the visits were brief. The rest of the time,
Piers was there. Effortlessly. Cheerfully. Without causing pain.
He had taken over her mind and she felt so much better that she
couldn't even resent him for it.

'I think I'm in love,' she ventured to Loulou, who was
mindlessly watching 'Blue Peter' with Lili on her lap.

Loulou, despite her own depression and despair, tried to
encourage her.

'I'm so glad, Cami. You deserve it,' she said with only a
touch of wistfulness. 'God knows, I envy you. Here you are
with Piers hammering on your door. Look at me, an unwanted
old spinster. You and Roz are both so lucky . . .'

And I am lucky, thought Camilla, drifting back into the
daydream which had so happily become a reality. Yesterday
evening Piers had driven up from Bath and taken her out to the

theatre. Tonight he had booked a table at Le Gavroche . . .

She glanced up as Charlotte meandered into the sitting-room, eating a banana sandwich and looking unusually subdued.

'All right, sweetheart? Finished your homework?'

Charlotte nodded, slumping into a chair.

'You're sure you're going to be OK this evening? Loulou's staying with you and I won't be late home.'

She was unprepared for Charlotte's attack.

'I don't like Piers,' she announced with brutal suddenness, her long brown hair swinging as she shook her head. 'And why don't you put the picture back on the wall? It's horrible, hiding it away.'

The family portrait, Matt's great pride and joy. Camilla stared at Charlotte, shocked by the determination in her young eyes.

'You don't mean that about Piers,' she countered, as reasonably as she could. 'He bought you that new game only yesterday – you were thrilled with it.'

'That was yesterday,' said Charlotte, squirming in her chair and biting her lower lip. Loulou caught Camilla's eye and shrugged. 'And you could put the picture back,' she persisted defiantly. 'We *liked* Matt. Just because he isn't . . . here any more doesn't mean we can't have the picture on the wall, does it?'

Camilla began to understand. Having weathered her parents' divorce without apparent concern, and having become so fond of Matt, she was resentful now of Piers and of what she saw as his intrusion into their lives. There was the possibility, too, that she felt the need to protect Matt, to preserve his memory.

Glancing at her watch and realizing that she had less than an hour in which to get ready before Piers was due to arrive, Camilla went over to her daughter and gave her a reassuring hug.

'Sweetheart, I'm not going to forget Matt. None of us ever will. And I promise I'll think about putting the picture back on the wall.' But the idea now seemed inappropriate, almost bizarre, since she had so abruptly been swept off her feet by Piers.

Then she had a flash of inspiration. 'Or would you like it in your room? We could hang it over your bookcase next to the window so you can see it when you're in bed. How about that, darling? Isn't that a much better idea?'

Charlotte gazed at her for several seconds. Camilla held her breath.

'No,' declared her daughter with great finality. 'It should be here in this room.' And with a hard, calculating look which tore at Camilla's heart she added, 'Where *everyone* can see it.'

'I'll have a chat to her,' said Loulou, reassuring Camilla as she left the house with Piers. 'And don't worry, she'll be fine.'

'Problems with Charlotte?' asked Piers, concerned. 'Where is she?'

'Upstairs,' said Camilla, still feeling guilty. 'She's a bit upset about something.'

Loulou leapt into the breach. 'You know what us girls are like.' She shrugged and winked in an effort to defuse the tension. 'Probably boyfriend trouble. *Plus ça change.*'

'Well, give her a kiss from me,' said Piers, taking Camilla's hand. 'Come on now darling, we mustn't miss our table at BurgerKing . . .'

Loulou, allowing Charlotte an hour in which to work through her misery uninterrupted, curled up in an arm-chair and tried to concentrate on *Bridget Jones: The Edge of Reason*. It took only a short while before she realized that she was working through her own misery instead.

When Charlotte poked her head around the door, dressed in pink pyjamas and still looking woeful, Loulou welcomed the diversion.

'Come and sit by me, Charley, and we'll cheer each other up. Tell me about the people you hate most at school, make a list of your least favourite food, tell me your worst joke ever, and then we can work our way up to the good stuff.'

Her vague plan to relax Charlotte and edge gradually around to the problem of Piers was forestalled by the unhappy child who squeezed into the armchair beside her and held out her clenched fist. In a resigned, extraordinarily unchildlike manner, Charlotte said, 'I didn't want to show this to Mummy. The other day when Marty was playing in Piers' car he picked up some rubbish. You know how he keeps things and hides them?' She glanced anxiously at Loulou for reassurance.

'I know.'

'Well, this afternoon I found the stuff under my bed. An empty matchbox, a pencil, and some screwed-up sweet papers. It's what he found in the car.'

'And?' said Loulou gently, a knot of apprehension drawing together in her stomach.

'And there was this.' Charlotte opened her fist and dropped a ring into Loulou's lap. 'At first I was just worried because he'd stolen it, and I thought Piers would be cross with Marty. But I keep thinking, it's a wedding-ring, isn't it? And does that mean that Piers is going to marry Mummy? Or is it his?' She frowned, struggling to make sense of what she had discovered. 'Because if it is, I don't understand. I thought only married people wore that sort of ring.'

* * *

Directory enquiries had only one P. O'Donoghue listed in the Bristol and Bath directory and Loulou, after checking that the bedroom door was firmly shut, punched out the number with rapid precision. After three rings it was picked up.

'Hello?' said a woman's voice, and Loulou plunged in.

'Hello, could I speak to Mr O'Donoghue?'

'I'm afraid he isn't in at the moment.' The woman sounded pleasant, well educated.

'Ah. Maybe I could phone again tomorrow then. It's about my carpets, you see.'

'Carpets?' The voice was puzzled.

'They need cleaning,' persisted Loulou, then hesitated. 'I do have the right number don't I, for Mr Patrick O'Donoghue?'

The woman laughed. 'I'm afraid not. My husband's name is Piers and I don't think he's ever cleaned a carpet in his life.'

'Oh well,' said Loulou with resignation, 'I'm sorry to have troubled you. Goodbye.'

When she had replaced the receiver she stared at the wall and thought how wrong she had been to envy Camilla her current good fortune.

And that telling her that Piers was married wasn't going to be easy, either.

Shit. Why were all men such cheating, selfish bastards?

Caroline, in a frenzy of anticipation, could scarcely endure the torture of waiting until seven o'clock before seeing Paddy again. Avoiding Susie, whom she knew would be stretched out in her usual spot, she smoked a small joint in an effort to calm down and spent half the afternoon preparing herself like an Egyptian goddess for the evening ahead. After a long, cool shower she sat naked on the edge of the bed and rubbed apricot-scented oil over every inch of her body. She painstakingly repainted her nails with shocking-pink polish. Then she twisted her heavy tortoiseshell hair into a knot on top of her head – so that Paddy could take it down later – and did her make-up. Light pink lipstick, smoky dark blue eyeshadow, nothing too heavy which might melt in the heat . . .

Sliding into the figure-hugging pink silk dress which finished well above her knees, she twisted and turned before the mirror to see whether it was possible for the casual onlooker to tell that she was wearing no underwear at all. Not that she was planning to be seen by anyone other than Paddy, she thought with an unrepentant smile, but if by some terrible trick of fate Nico should return early, then full make-up and no knickers would be an absolute dead giveaway.

Glancing once more at her full-length reflection, she saw that her erect nipples were clearly visible beneath the pink silk. There was an almost manic glitter in her eyes. To be with a desirable man whom she knew desired her in return was a thrill she had almost forgotten existed. Nico was enigmatic, unreachable. Paddy was genuine, caring, and she knew only too well what he was thinking when he gazed at her with those dark-lashed, slanting eyes of his.

In her present mood she could almost forgive Nico, she decided. Why on earth had it taken her this long to discover that adultery was fun?

'You look . . . sensational,' said Paddy, when he answered the door and found Caroline on his doorstep. Christ, he thought, this was going to be so easy. Where was the challenge? The woman was practically dripping with lust already.

He had to admit, though, that she did look good.

'I'm so glad you're here,' babbled Caroline, suddenly nervous. 'I just passed Shaun going over to the hotel and had to pretend I was on my way back to the bungalow. I've been zig-zagging round the grounds like a sniper.'

Closing the front door behind her and inhaling a lungful of her scent, Paddy realized that the only way he could really have fun would be by working a bit of the old role-reversal.

'I'm glad you're here, too,' he said easily. 'But you don't have to pretend, angel.'

Caroline licked her lips. 'Pretend what?' she asked breathlessly, relieved that he wasn't going to waste any time with boring preliminaries.

Paddy poured her a drink and glanced at his watch. 'Pretend to Shaun, of course. What's wrong, after all, with two friends having dinner together? In fact when I mentioned it to him earlier he said he might join us, so if you want to give Nico a ring and see if he'd like to come along later, I'm sure the restaurant will be able to give us a table for four.'

'A . . . restaurant?' echoed Caroline, staring at him as if he'd just ripped the wings off a particularly beautiful butterfly. 'With Shaun? But –'

'The Rum-Baba,' continued Paddy cheerfully, enjoying the look of horror on her face. Talk about wrong-footing someone; Caroline looked as if she'd just had both legs sliced off at the knees. 'They do great lobster, apparently. Tell Nico that; I know he's crazy about lobster.'

'But . . .' She tried again, taking a hesitant step towards him, her mouth trembling. In those few moments, with her self-confidence in shreds and her disappointment so damn obvious, Paddy almost felt sorry for her. But if he was truly going to enjoy the evening ahead he could only do so by transferring the challenge to her. There was none for him, after all.

'I know,' he admitted gently. 'I know what you thought. I felt the same way myself, yesterday. But angel, *think* about it. You're Nico's wife and I'm his friend. I'm not a complete bastard, you know. I do have some scruples.'

The confusion and sense of disappointment were almost too much for Caroline to bear, coupled as they were with the searing all-too-familiar pain of rejection. Tears glistened in her eyes and she turned away towards the half-shuttered window, clenching her fists at her sides and willing herself not to cry.

Oh shit, not tears, thought Paddy. He drained his glass, poured himself another large Scotch and wondered what he'd do if Caroline simply took him at his word and left. Failing now would almost be funny, if only he didn't want so badly to get laid.

'Don't cry,' he said, moving over to stand behind her and placing his hands on her quivering bare shoulders. 'I'm very flattered, angel, but I hate to see you crying.'

Caroline spun suddenly round to face him, her jaw tense. He saw the tendons sticking out on her neck. 'Nico has affairs,' she said, and it was almost a plea.

'I'm sure he doesn't.' Paddy was really beginning to enjoy himself now. She was one of those rare women whose looks weren't marred by tears. 'You shouldn't say things like that.'

'But he does!' persisted Caroline. 'He's been seeing this woman called Camilla for God knows how long –'

'Sshh,' he soothed, pulling her into his arms to comfort her.

Desperate now, Caroline pressed herself against him, reaching up and finding his mouth with her own. Her hot tongue slid between his lips and Paddy groaned as if weakening, trailing his fingers down her back until they came to rest upon the firm swell of her buttocks. When he realized that she wasn't wearing anything at all beneath her dress he sighed with pleasure. Thank God he didn't really have to turn her down.

'Angel, we mustn't,' he protested weakly, when he at last pulled away. 'You don't know what you're doing to me.'

Caroline smiled, her confidence renewed, her determination now unassailable. 'Oh, but we must,' she said huskily, lightly touching the front of his trousers where his arousal was so clearly evident. 'And I do, I do, I do.'

Piers O'Donoghue was genuinely besotted with Camilla; she was everything his Irish upbringing had taught him a wife should be, and at the same time everything his own wife was not. He had married Juliet three years ago, believing that he was doing the right thing. There were fast, flirty young girls with whom one enjoyed brief affairs, his father had explained at regular intervals throughout his life, and then there was the other kind of girl, whom one married. Juliet Russell came from an excellent family, she would take her responsibilities seriously and she had good childbearing hips. Her personality was pleasant, her temper even and her looks average.

Piers had observed the marriages of his peers and known that his father was right. Those of his male friends who had tied the knot with beautiful, sparky, witty girls were either divorced within a couple of years or suffering all kinds of difficulties, whereas the few who had made 'sensible' matches seemed far more content. A good wife was a definite asset and besides, there were always plenty of less suitable girls eager to supply excitement when it was needed.

Juliet was perfect marriage material and he had never, until now, regretted making her his wife.

Until now.

Until he had met Camilla who was, in his eyes, perfect in *every* way. Beautiful, capable, sexy and a devoted mother, she encompassed all the best qualities of both kinds of women, and since meeting her, he had been unable to prevent himself comparing her with Juliet. Juliet wore clothes which didn't suit her. She seldom bothered with make-up, no longer shaved her legs and hadn't been to a hairdresser for months. She had put on over a stone in the past year. She could carry on a conversation about which he would later remember nothing. She never joked, or teased, or giggled.

And in three years those good childbearing hips had failed to fulfil their promise.

Chapter 55

'You're married,' said Camilla, and he saw the pain and anger in her eyes, heard it in her low voice, and felt his own happiness begin to crumble. He couldn't lose her, he *couldn't* . . .

'Separated,' he corrected easily, whilst his mind raced on ahead. How had she found out? Laura knew, of course, but she and Christo were still away on their honeymoon. 'My wife and I are separated, darling. Surely that doesn't bother you?'

Camilla, searching his face for the truth, shook her head. Unable to remain sitting, she jumped up and began pacing the room with halting, uneven steps. 'You told me you were divorced. It was a lie. And now I don't think you're even separated . . .' She hesitated; that wasn't what she had meant to say. She *knew* – didn't she – that he was still living with his wife?

The significance of that brief hesitation wasn't lost on Piers. He decided to bluff it out. Assuming control, he said bluntly, 'Well, you've been misinformed. Camilla, maybe I was wrong to tell you that I was already divorced, but my wife and I have been living apart for so long that I feel divorced. It simply didn't occur to me that you'd react like this, and as for thinking that I might not even be separated, well . . . if that's what you *think* then maybe there's no point in our seeing each other again. If we don't have trust, what *do* we have?'

He saw her weaken.

'But . . .'

'Tell me,' he demanded more gently, 'why you think that. The explanation will be so simple you'll wonder why you ever even let it concern you.'

Please God, he thought in desperation, let it be something he could explain. He couldn't lose Camilla, couldn't bear to even contemplate the possibility.

In reply she nodded towards the walnut table beside the sofa upon which he sat. Following her gaze, Piers saw his wedding-ring and almost laughed with relief.

'Darling, I was married! I haven't worn that for almost a year. Where on earth did you find it?'

'Marty. He was in your car. You know what a magpie he is.' But she sounded only fractionally less tense and Piers, realizing that more was to come, braced himself.

'Last night Loulou phoned your house in Bath and spoke to your wife,' she said slowly. 'She asked to speak to you and your wife said you weren't at home at the moment.' The emphasis on the last three words was unmistakable, but Piers was gaining in confidence now. He smiled and relaxed, rising to his feet and taking Camilla's cold hands in his own warm ones.

'My darling,' he said tenderly, 'is that what's got you into this state? Of course Juliet said that, she always says that when she's alone in the house. *I* was the one who explained to her how burglars – and worse – operate. A woman alone is in a vulnerable position, but if she makes it sound as though her husband's due home at any moment they'll certainly think twice before paying a visit. And if you don't do the same,' he added seriously, stroking her wrists as he spoke, 'then you certainly should. There are some pretty nasty people out there, you know.'

'Oh Piers,' sighed Camilla, burying her face against his shoulder so that he wouldn't see her tears of relief and swallowing hard as his hold tightened. 'You were right, there was a simple explanation, and I'm just so *glad* . . .'

Triumphant, and equally relieved that for now at least he had successfully quashed her doubts, Piers kissed her damp cheeks and realized how very fond of Camilla he was in danger of becoming. If he was honest, it had already happened, and if he had been the forward-planning kind he would be thinking ahead to what might happen in the weeks to come.

But he never did plan ahead, allowing instead each day to spring its surprises. Less than a week ago it had sprung Camilla into his life, after all. He would cope with the next problem when it arose and meanwhile enjoy what he already had.

'I have to be in the office by nine thirty tomorrow,' he said, his lips moving to her earlobe and then to the sensitive area below it. 'But I could stay here with you tonight if you like, and drive back early in the morning.'

'I do like,' murmured Camilla, winding her arms around his neck and giving him her most irresistible smile. 'I'd like that very much indeed.'

Sitting bolt upright at the kitchen table clutching a mug of tea which was no longer even vaguely warm, Juliet continued to stare at the clock on the wall. Nine o'clock. Thank goodness she had had the foresight to take the phone off the hook – the thought of having to listen to one of Piers' rambling, convoluted excuses was more than she could stomach at the moment.

Glancing around at the pristine beige and white kitchen, every surface gleaming, not so much as a teaspoon out of place, she wondered what more Piers could possibly want of her. Did he even begin to realize the extent of the torture she suffered each time he 'amused' himself with another woman?

Deep down, however, she knew he was *aware* that she knew. That was what hurt more than anything else. She was supposed to be grateful to him for being discreet and accept the situation with ladylike good grace, silently acknowledging it as a necessary part of their life together. It was the done thing, apparently; men had affairs and their wives arranged flowers.

As the thought rattled through her mind, Juliet's gaze fell upon the bowl of flowers adorning the Welsh dresser. Their heady scent mingled with the dusty aroma of pot-pourri and the more clinical odour of Ajax floor cleaner. In a frenzy of hyperactivity she had risen at five thirty and scrubbed the already gleaming quarry tiles on her hands and knees.

The house was perfect, and Piers hadn't come home.

But this time, thought Juliet with bitter triumph, this time she knew where he was.

Pushing back her chair so that its legs grated raucously against the scrubbed stone floor destroying the oppressive silence, she crossed to the dresser and selected a medium-sized, bone-handled knife from the top left-hand drawer.

Then, with systematic thoroughness, she beheaded each of the flowers, scattering them on the floor she had scrubbed so thoroughly earlier.

So men had affairs and their wives arranged flowers, she thought idly, staring at the scattered petals and running the blade of the knife experimentally across her hand. Well, this wife had arranged flowers for long enough.

Surfacing slowly, unravelling her legs from the tangled duvet and savouring its seductive warmth, Camilla half opened her eyes and realized that she was smiling. The memory of last night had stayed with her in sleep; when Piers had left at six thirty he had taken her into his arms and kissed her with such spine-tingling tenderness that she had been tempted to pull him straight back into bed.

'I know,' he had murmured in her ear. 'I don't want to leave either.'

'It isn't fair on you,' she said stroking his just-shaved cheek and breathing in the soap and shampoo smell of him. Then shyly, she had added, 'When the children are staying with Jack, I could always come down to Bath.'

His dark eyes had softened with affection. 'I'll hold you to that.'

When Camilla eventually trailed downstairs she spotted the note Loulou had propped up against one of last night's empty champagne bottles. Ostensibly from Lili, it said, 'Rocky and I have taken Mum off to the zoo. She's borrowed your yellow jacket. Looks to me as if she's tarted herself up in the hope of catching a man. I told her she was far too old for that sort of thing. Anyway, I'll bring her back at about five. Love, Lili. P.S. Hope you had a good bonk.'

Camilla grinned and switched on the radio. One of Nico's songs was being played, a slow and sensual track from his last album, and just for a moment she forgot Piers, remembering instead the happy times she and Nico had shared. Her feelings for him, she realized with a pang of regret, were still as strong as ever, but nothing could have come of them. He was married and Piers was free. Once more, at last, life truly seemed worth living and she wasn't going to waste a single moment of it by regretting what could never be.

And since Charlotte and Toby were away for the next few days staying with Jack's parents in Shropshire, Camilla decided with renewed vigour to drive over to the hospital and pick up Marty. It was simply too good a day to spend alone.

Nico, making his way back to the bungalow at around eight o'clock, reflected that he was doing so with little pleasure and a depressing sense of duty. Since Jake had mentioned to him this morning that Caroline had been talking to Susie, and that Caroline was 'slightly pissed off' by the number of hours he was putting in at the studio, his conscience had continued to nudge him. When the rest of the band had left its cool confines shortly after six, he had planned to stay on as he usually did, but the thought of Caroline sitting alone inside the bungalow steadily prodded away at his conscience. Eventually he had called it a day and left. He would do the decent thing and take her out to dinner; then he would at least be able to reason to himself that he had made the effort.

Jesus, he thought despairingly as he kicked at the dark sand beneath his feet and watched his lengthening shadow move steadily along ahead of him, why did it have to *be* an effort? Why couldn't he be like Jake with Susie, deliriously happy and so relaxed in each other's company that it never even crossed their minds not to be together?

But I could be like that, he thought with a trace of resentment as the glaring white bungalow, flanked by spindly palm trees and thickly banked scarlet hibiscus bushes, came into view. I *could* be like that. With Camilla.

Having made every effort not to think about her since leaving London, the full force of his loss now struck him with savage suddenness. If it could really be termed a loss, of course. But seeing Camilla again in London, feeling that they were finally coming together once more after so long apart and then her refusal to meet him or even contact him the very day before he was due to leave had shattered his hopes more brutally than he had imagined possible. The sense of loss was for something exquisite and fragile, so fragile that it had scarcely even existed.

And now it was gone, but he couldn't accept that it would be gone for ever. If he worked hard he could rebuild it, surely. Maybe a jokey postcard to begin with. Something light and unimportant to re-establish that slender, delicate link between them . . .

Cheered by the idea, Nico ran up the steps on to the verandah. A scarlet towel, hanging over the back of a chair, flapped gently in the sea breeze and a half-empty jug of something-and-orange was gathering flies on the low cane table.

Inside, there was no sign of Caroline. Nico paused for a few seconds, gazing around the bedroom which had been tidied to perfection by one of the cheerful maids. He considered calling on Paddy, persuading him to join him up at the hotel for a drink, then decided against it. He would go alone, pick up some postcards and dream up a witty and suitably casual message for Camilla. God knows, even that would give him more pleasure than having to pretend to enjoy the company of his wife over dinner.

When the cab finally drew up outside the house Juliet sat without moving for a while, rechecking that the number tallied with that written on the scrap of paper in her hand.

This was it, then. This was where the woman lived, and there was her car parked on the gravelled driveway. So Camilla Lewis had money, did she? And plenty of it. What else, wondered Juliet, did Camilla have that other women like herself didn't?

The urge to see what Piers' mistress looked like was almost

overwhelming now. Paying off the cab driver and adjusting her grey suit jacket as she stepped on to the pavement, she couldn't help smiling. This was what she had wanted to do so many times before, and now it was really happening. The man she had hired from the detective agency had obtained the information so much more easily than she had imagined . . . and now she was really here. Instead of sitting at home crying she was doing something about it. The others may have got away with it in the past, but Camilla Lewis wasn't going to.

When Camilla answered the front doorbell she assumed at first that the woman in the flannel suit, American tan tights and sensible low-heeled shoes was collecting for some charity or other. She was already reaching for her handbag, which stood on the hall table, when the woman said in a strangely panicky voice, 'May I come in, please? It's very important.'

Automatically, sensing the urgency in her voice, Camilla stepped back into the hall. Maybe there had been some kind of accident in the street . . .

The woman closed the door quietly behind her and Camilla hesitated, experiencing the first pangs of misgiving as she found herself being stared at with peculiar intensity. The woman was plump, with straight, very shiny brown hair and grey eyes which seemed to be drinking in every detail. Then her gaze switched abruptly to the hall itself, observing the toys which littered the floor and the bizarre flower arrangements on the carved oak dresser beneath the curving staircase. Was this, then, what Piers longed for – not perfectly arranged cultivated flowers but *dandelions*, thrust ludicrously into heavy silver bowls?

'What was it you wanted?' Camilla enquired politely, feeling terribly English and wondering if the woman had some kind of psychiatric problem. She could hardly be a burglar, after all.

'Wanted? What do I want?' echoed Juliet, sounding faintly surprised and glancing once more with evident disapproval at the jumble of toys on the parquet floor. So she had a child – a very young child judging by the toys and the dandelions – and possibly a husband as well. Some women, it seemed, wanted it all: a husband, children, *and* a lover with which to enliven their pampered lives . . .

She was beautiful, as Juliet had expected, although slightly older than she'd imagined.

But still, inescapably beautiful. Glamorous, too, in an obviously expensive white dress with gold chains around her neck and glittering diamond studs in her ears. Her eyes were a dazzling peacock-blue, her streaky gold-blond hair fastened up with gold combs. No doubt her child was equally perfect . . .

'I've come to see you,' she said at last, walking past Camilla into the sitting-room and clutching her handbag tightly in both hands. 'You see, my name is Juliet O'Donoghue.'

'Juliet . . .?'

For about a tenth of a second Camilla was confused. Then it all became horribly, sickeningly clear.

'You're his wife.' It came out as a statement rather than the question she had intended, and Juliet's eyes narrowed with anger.

Feeling ill and frozen to the spot with horror, Camilla said, 'I'm so sorry. I swear I didn't know. Really.'

'Really?' echoed Juliet, pacing the sitting-room and surveying it as thoroughly as she had the hall. An empty coffee cup balanced on the edge of the mantelpiece, more toys littered the floor, scribbled-on paper and uncapped felt pens covered the coffee table . . . the woman was a slut, no doubt far too busy conducting her illicit affairs to have time for a few hours' honest housework.

She might be beautiful, considered Juliet almost pityingly now, and she might live in a big house in Belgravia, but when it came down to it she was still nothing but a slut.

And a lying one too.

'I am a decent person, Mrs Lewis,' she said aloud, marvelling at the steadiness of her voice as she turned to face her once more. 'A decent woman, and an excellent wife. *Look* at me,' she added sharply as Camilla bowed her head in distress. 'Why should Piers keep on doing this? He punishes me when I've done nothing to deserve it. When really I should be punishing him . . .'

'I'll never see him again,' said Camilla rapidly, her heart hammering against her chest, her face pale. 'And please listen to me; I know how you must feel. I *understand* –'

'You do not understand,' snapped Juliet, still clutching her handbag against her stomach. 'How can *you* possibly understand how I feel? Just look at you. You have everything and you don't even realize how lucky you are, because if you did you wouldn't want my husband as well. You have children.' She nodded jerkily at the clutter of toys. 'And I'm sure they're just as perfect as you are. Your husband – he's got to be better than Piers, for God's sake. He certainly can't screw around as much as Piers does . . .'

'I'm sorry,' said Camilla once more, appalled by the entire situation and realizing that she didn't know how to cope with it.

'Oh,' Juliet's eyebrows arched in mock surprise. 'You're sorry. How nice. Doesn't it even bother you, sleeping with a man who is married?'

'But I swear I didn't know . . .' whispered Camilla with shame and mounting desperation.

'Don't *lie* to me! Are your children here now?'

'No, but –'

'Just as well.' Juliet unzipped her handbag and took out the knife as casually as if it were a fountain pen. 'There's no need for them to see this. With you as their mother I should think they've suffered enough already.'

This cannot be happening, thought Camilla, frozen with horror. As if in slow motion she saw Piers' wife move towards her, gripping the handle of the knife with both hands. Trembling violently, she backed away. If she could reach the french windows and unlock them quickly enough . . .

But Juliet was too fast for her. This was what she had come here to do, what she had longed to do so often in the past, and nothing was going to stop her now.

With a strangled yell she flew at Camilla, lashing out with the knife. As the blade slashed through the white sleeve of her dress, a crimson stain grew as if by magic. Camilla screamed, stumbling awkwardly against the coffee table and Juliet laughed, revelling in the rush of adrenalin and launching herself once more at the figure now crumpled on the floor.

'By the time I've finished,' she panted, the words coming viciously through gritted teeth, '*no-one* will want you, you bitch.' And the knife slashed again, at the smooth brown neck hung with gold chains and at the face which Camilla was trying to cover with her hands. More blood sprayed, splattering the table and the thick apricot carpet and Juliet marvelled at its glossy brightness. Shifting her position, balancing herself over the terrified woman beneath her, she wrenched away the hands with brutal force and slid the knife across Camilla's elegant cheek. Such a very sharp knife . . . it was as easy as cutting through butter . . . and so much blood. Well, Camilla Lewis certainly wasn't looking so great now . . .

She didn't hear the door open behind her. When the scream echoed through the room she let go of Camilla's hair and spun round too late to avoid the impact. A heavy china pot slammed into her chest and lukewarm water cascaded everywhere, splashing her face and soaking her clothes. Cursing, blinking the liquid from her eyes, Juliet stared in horror at the screaming boy, naked apart from a T-shirt. Dimly hearing Camilla croak, 'Marty', she looked down at the broken pot lying at her feet and felt a wave of nausea surge in her throat. There could be no doubt that it was an old-fashioned chamber pot. And the lukewarm liquid in which she was drenched wasn't just water . . .

'You filthy animal!' she yelled, gagging helplessly, and the boy let out an unearthly wail, launching himself at her like a small human bullet.

He's handicapped, Juliet realized faintly, struggling to fend him off as he clawed with frantic strength at her arms. Looks like Down's Syndrome . . . not perfect, after all . . .

With the last of her own strength she flung him away, snatched up her bag and ran towards the door. Her eyes burned with tears. Beside her, the phone started ringing. Turning to look back she saw the little boy kneel beside Camilla, and place his arms tenderly around the bloody mess of her head. He was sobbing loudly, making unintelligible noises and taking great gulps of air as he cradled her against his chest, now stained crimson with her blood.

The phone continued to ring.

Slowly, Juliet picked up the receiver and heard a series of long-distance clicks. 'Hello?' said a male voice when she didn't speak. 'Cami, is that you? It's Nico.'

'Camilla needs an ambulance,' said Juliet, her hands starting to shake. 'Please call an ambulance. Now.'

Replacing the receiver, she turned back once more to look at what she had done.

'I'm sorry,' she said through chattering teeth, wiping her sweating palms against her skirt and realizing that it was still soaked with urine. 'I had to do it. I didn't know your little boy had Down's Syndrome . . . I thought he would be perfect.'

Camilla, floating on the grey border of consciousness, managed to raise one hand and rest it upon Marty's spiky dark head. In a voice barely above a whisper she said slowly, 'He is perfect.'

Shaking her head, not understanding at all, Juliet closed the front door behind her.

Chapter 56

Discovering his wife in bed with his keyboards player, Nico realized, was one of the best things that had ever happened to him. Watching them from the doorway, almost admiring the expression of horror and defiance on Caroline's face as she turned and saw him standing there, he felt a great weight of responsibility float away. His green eyes registered wry amusement as she dragged the emerald covers over her perspiring, naked body.

'I *have* seen it before,' he observed mildly.

Paddy lit a cigarette.

'Sorry mate. You know how it is.'

'I know,' said Nico, dead-pan. 'I just dropped by to tell you that I'm flying back to London. Right away. Something's come up. We're booked here until the end of the week so the rest of you may as well stay out here until then. OK?'

Paddy shrugged. 'OK.'

'What about me?' said Caroline, shivering with shock.

Nico, privately amazed by his complete lack of either anger or jealousy, said slowly, 'What about you? You'd prefer to stay here, wouldn't you? Let's face it, Caroline. We've both known for a while that our so-called marriage was over. I'll contact my solicitor when I get back and he can get things moving.'

'It's not a so-called marriage –' she began, automatically defending herself from criticism, but Nico intercepted her.

'When we met,' he said evenly, 'you pretended not to know

559

who I was. That was a lie, and lies aren't the most suitable foundation upon which to build a lasting relationship.'

'But I didn't want you to think that . . .' Caroline broke off, realizing that arguing wasn't going to help. With defiance in her eyes she said sullenly, 'Oh, never mind. How did you find out, anyway?'

'I didn't,' replied Nico, turning towards the door. 'It was just a lucky guess.'

Camilla lay back against the starched white pillows and gingerly lifted the sheet covering her body. Since there were no mirrors in the room she hadn't been able to see what her face and neck looked like, but she could imagine the horror show. If the wounds there were anything like those on her body, she must look ghastly. And they hurt like hell, too, despite the painkillers.

But it could have been worse. The knife had been a small one and the woman's intention had clearly been to scar rather than to kill. By slashing instead of stabbing, many of the cuts were relatively superficial. The median nerve in her left forearm had evidently been spared by less than a centimetre. No major organs had been punctured. The doctor had spent hours repairing her wounds with literally hundreds of painstakingly minute stitches, and had reassured her that the degree of eventual scarring would be far less than seemed possible now, with congealed blood and emerging purplish bruising staining the otherwise smooth tanned flesh.

But scars there would be, nevertheless, and Camilla realized that she was on the verge of panic. Having been heavily sedated earlier, the full horror of the attack was only beginning now, at midnight, to make itself felt. If Marty hadn't been there, if Nico hadn't chosen exactly that moment to call her, if Piers' wife had not for some bizarre reason answered the phone, it could all have been far, far worse.

She should be grateful to even be alive.

So why did she feel so wretched and so very afraid?

Reaching for the bell to summon a nurse, Camilla pressed it and felt the hot tears course down her cheeks. Maybe a sedative or a sleeping pill would help. In the morning, after a few hours of oblivion, she might feel more able to cope.

When the door opened she wiped her eyes with the back of her good hand and blinked as the overhead light came on. Coming through the door was a vast walking bouquet of pink, blue and white flowers. For a single, heart-stopping moment she thought, Nico! then subsided, embarrassed by a tidal wave of disappointment. Of course it wasn't him. The night nurse, a slender girl with a gap between her front teeth, grinned at her as she hauled the enormous basket of flowers on to the top on the bedside locker.

'Special delivery, you lucky girl,' announced the nurse, so cheerily that Camilla winced.

'Is there a card?' she said, pulling herself one-handedly into a sitting position. Maybe Loulou had sent them, or Roz and Sebastian.

'No card. And no visitors either as a rule, but this one charmed his way into the nurses' station and we simply couldn't say no. Are you up to a visit, do you think?'

Camilla stared at her. Surely, *surely* Piers hadn't come here to see her. Horrified, she said, 'Does he have dark curly hair?'

'No, I bloody well do not!' exclaimed an outraged voice on the other side of the door, and this time Camilla's spirits soared. As Nico appeared in the room she realized that subconsciously she had been expecting him, and that there was no-one else in the entire world whom she wanted to see more.

The night nurse melted tactfully away.

'I had to come,' he said, placing his arms carefully around her and kissing her undamaged cheek. Then he stepped back and grinned. 'And here you are, pining away for some gypsy Heathcliffe type. Bloody charming.'

'Serves you right for eavesdropping,' said Camilla with a weak smile as she took his hand. 'And anyway, he was the one I *didn't* want to see. Oh Nico, I'm so glad you're here.'

Tenderly, he lifted the strap of her nightdress back on to her shoulder. 'I'm glad I'm here too,' he said, wishing he could kiss her again. 'Every time I see you you're either scantily clad or stark naked. It's enough to give a man ideas.'

'I'm usually crying, too,' Camilla reminded him, realizing that she was about to do it again. Stupidly, Nico's sudden appearances seemed to have that effect on her. 'And I can't imagine that the sight of me now could give any man ideas.' The words gushed out just ahead of the tears; the next moment she was clinging to Nico, sobbing helplessly, and he was holding her, kissing her hair and murmuring reassurances.

'Sshh,' he whispered, when the heaving sobs at last began to subside. 'The nurses will kick me out if we aren't careful.'

'Let them try,' hiccuped Camilla with a watery smile. 'Oh but Nico, look at my face. They won't even let me see it. Is it really as horrible as I think it is?'

Taking her seriously, realizing how scared and desperately in need of reassurance she was, he studied her closely for several seconds. It *was* horrible, but it didn't seem so to him because she was still Camilla, she was still alive and that was all that mattered. The longest cut swept from her temple along the line of her cheekbone. Another bisected her left eyebrow and several smaller ones ran down her lower jaw and on to her neck.

'This side of your face is a bit swollen,' he said, running his index finger lightly along an undamaged part of it. 'And it all looks far worse than it is because of the blood that's still there. These little cuts down here will heal easily. This big one, *if* it leaves any sign of a scar, will look rather dashing because it's right beneath your cheekbone. I'm serious, Cami. They're really not as bad as you think.' He saw the relief in her eyes and winked, tugging playfully at her shoulder strap. 'Got any more you'd like me to see whilst I'm here?'

'You're nothing but a tart,' she said smiling. 'And thank you. You've cheered me up. I still can't believe that you've flown all this way to see me.'

'I sent you a postcard yesterday, too,' Nico retaliated with mock indignation. 'If I'd known I'd be coming back today I could have saved myself the price of a stamp.'

'The flowers are lovely.'

'Mmm.' He looked vaguely embarrassed. 'Actually they're on loan.'

'On loan?' cried Camilla, trying not to laugh. 'Where did you get them?'

'The hotel across the road. They're the main display in reception. I had to give the receptionist a kiss and promise to return them within the hour. Well, *you* try and buy flowers at eleven thirty at night,' he concluded defensively.

'Nothing but a tart,' repeated Camilla, wiping her eyes. 'Go and return them this minute. Then come back. You haven't even asked me yet how all this happened.'

'I know,' Nico said gently. 'I managed to get through to your house again from the airport in Antigua. Loulou was there, and so were the police. Lou told me everything.'

Camilla bowed her head. 'I feel so ashamed. Nico, I *know* what that woman was going through. I felt so guilty when she told me who she was that I thought I deserved to be attacked. But Piers told me he wasn't married . . . I would *never* have had anything to do with him if I'd known that he was!'

'Well, I can certainly vouch for that,' he said lightly, clasping her cold hands in his own and attempting to avert another crisis. 'You mustn't blame yourself, Cami. He's the one who lied to you. You couldn't be expected to know different.'

'I really liked him,' she whispered, so sadly that he was gripped by a spasm of jealousy. Then she met his gaze and said with hopeless honesty, 'I really liked you, too. Do you think I'll ever really like someone who isn't married?'

Nico, overcome with longing, stared back at her. For a long moment he was stuck for the right words. Finally, praying that when Camilla said 'really like' she meant 'love', and that his lawyers could move that quickly, he cleared his throat and said, 'In about six weeks, I should think.'

Camilla closed her eyes and shook her head, missing the point completely.

'More like six years,' she said in a quiet voice.

Nico tried again. Picking up her hand, he turned it over and kissed the palm, making her jump. 'Six weeks,' he said again, this time more firmly. 'And then, scars or no scars, bright turquoise contact lenses or no bright turquoise contact lenses' – Camilla blushed – 'I am going to ask you to marry me. I know I don't have what my mother calls a proper job but I can –'

'You cannot leave your wife!' shouted Camilla, interrupting him in mid-stream. 'My God, Nico, after what's happened today . . . you *can't* leave her!'

'Oh, shut up, darling,' he said affectionately, adoring the way her grey eyes darkened when she was outraged. 'I already have.'

'Oh, What a Tangled Web!' screamed the headline of the sleaziest paper, and Nico's heart sank when he saw it. Since connecting his frequent visits to the hospital with the stabbing of Matt Lewis's widow by her lover's deranged-with-jealousy wife, the Press had been having an absolute field day, casting Camilla in the role of sultry mistress and speculating with wicked inaccuracy that she and Nico had indulged in a passionate long-running affair. Since Juliet O'Donoghue was now under arrest and Piers had disappeared to 'stay with friends', the Press oscillated between the hospital and Camilla's home, pestering Loulou and driving the hospital staff to distraction. Only Marty was enjoying all the attention; somehow the story of his potty attack had come out and his famous smile was once more plastered across all the papers.

Marty, Nico reflected with amusement, was becoming almost as well known as himself these days. Yesterday he'd been taking him to the hospital to see Camilla and a woman had ignored him totally, pointing instead to Marty. 'There's that little boy I was telling you about, Sharon . . .'

'Bloody gutter press!' declared Loulou, entering the kitchen and catching him with the paper spread out on the table before him. 'The two of us should have an affair now. That would really get them going.'

Nico grinned, pointing at the page. 'Too late, they've already guessed. "Meanwhile, Nico Coletto's spectacular Wimbledon home remains empty whilst he spends his nights at Camilla's house in Belgravia with the lovely Loulou Marks. Who knows what goes on there behind those closed doors? And how will Nico's wife Caroline react when she hears of all this?" '

'God,' Loulou groaned, shaking her head and reaching for Nico's coffee. 'If we told them we play Scrabble they'd never believe us. Are you going in to see Cami this morning?'

Nico shrugged. 'Lawyers first, hospital second. Sorting out the divorce is turning out to be a damn sight easier than sorting out Camilla. Why does she have to be so stubborn, Lou?'

'She's upset. Exercise a bit of patience,' said Loulou kindly, having heard all this a dozen times in the last few days. 'Look,' she continued, seeing the expression in Nico's dark-fringed green eyes. 'You caught your wife in bed with someone else, leapt on to a plane and proposed to Camilla. Meanwhile she's been attacked by a woman for sleeping with her husband. Every day, her bruises and scars look worse. She's *vulnerable*, for God's sake. For one thing she doesn't want to make the same mistake twice, and for another . . .'

'Yes?' prompted Nico, retrieving his coffee cup and discovering that it was empty.

'I think she thinks you feel sorry for her,' Loulou concluded with a helpless gesture. 'She's convinced that no-one could possibly want her, looking as she does now. But she's still shocked by what happened. She'll get over most of that when the scars start to heal. I told you, you just have to be patient.'

'I've been *patient*,' he exclaimed, 'for almost three goddam years, Lou. The last time I was patient Camilla got involved with O'Donoghue. The time before that she married Matt Lewis. So *this* time I decided to lay it on the line. I'd waited long enough and I wasn't going to risk losing her again. And she bloody well turned me down!'

'Poor Nico,' said Loulou, amused by his look of indignation. 'Get divorced. Give her time. And *be patient*.'

'I hate being patient,' he complained. 'And I hate being turned down. And more than anything else,' he concluded, tapping his fingers on the table top. 'I hate other people drinking *my* cup of coffee.'

'Don't you read the papers?' countered Loulou. 'We're having an affair. We're secret, passionate lovers. I'm entitled to drink your coffee.'

Chapter 57

Feeling like some kind of spy, Loulou skulked behind the curtain of potted palms decorating the entrance to the hotel dining-room and watched Roz, Sebastian and Natalie together. It was their very togetherness that was most noticeable and for a second she experienced a pang of such envy that it was almost jealousy. All three of them looked so happy that Loulou wanted to cry. Roz, having lost her hard edge, looked more like Natalie's sister than her mother. Sebastian, laughing at something she had said, seemed relaxed and more carefree than she had ever imagined possible and Natalie, who was wearing a black Rocky Horror sweatshirt and emerald green boots, was positively radiating youthful exuberance, her smile as wide as the Cheshire cat's as her bright gaze darted from one parent to the other.

Lucky them, thought Loulou, her own expression wistful. She then realized that the restaurant manager was watching her.

'Is everything all right, madam?' he enquired, and she gave him a haughty stare.

'Perfectly all right. Why, do I look as though I can't afford to eat here?'

Stiffly, he replied: 'Of course not, madam.'

'Well, I can't,' said Loulou, winking at him. 'Thank goodness someone else is paying, eh?'

'I want you to come on my show,' said Roz.

'Who, me?'

'It was my idea,' put in Natalie, her bracelets jangling in her excitement. 'You are famous, after all.'

'For my lousy choice in men,' Loulou said gloomily. 'Everyone's forgotten by now that I ever did anything.'

'Then we remind them,' explained Roz, sipping her white wine. 'How you built up Vampires, how you gave it all up – we can give the charity a fresh plug at the same time – and you can tell the nation what a little shit that Martin Stacey-Thompson was. Everyone will hear your side of the story. Trust me, it'll be great.'

Loulou continued to look doubtful. Watching the butter melt on her asparagus, she remained silent.

'And then there's the fee,' said Sebastian, reaching across the table to refill her empty glass. 'Which is not insubstantial,' he added as an apparent afterthought.

'Deal,' said Loulou promptly, breaking into a smile. 'You just said the magic word. Let's just hope,' she said, turning to Roz, 'that it isn't a complete disaster. Otherwise *you'll* be fired for choosing me.'

'It had better not be a disaster,' said Roz lightly, resting her hand upon Sebastian's. 'It's my blaze of glory, Lou. I've already handed in my resignation. You're going to be the very last guest to appear on the show.'

'As soon as Sebastian and I are married, we're moving back to Zurich. A TV company there has offered me work, and I'll still be able to do the occasional "special" here as well. We've decided to keep the cottage on so we'll have a base in England as well as Switzerland.'

'That's wonderful,' said Camilla, wincing slightly as she eased herself into her sweater. 'What will Natalie do?'

Helping her, Roz said, 'Happily, she listens to her father. Sebastian made her realize that she should go to university and take her degree. She can fly out to us during the holidays, we'll be able to visit her whenever we're in England, and some of the time, of course, she'll be with her adoptive family. I spoke to Christine and Tom on the phone only yesterday and they're thrilled that we've managed to persuade her to continue with her education. Apparently, when Nat was home with them last week she had her heart set on becoming a singer.'

'There,' said Camilla, striking a pose beside the bed. 'It feels weird to be wearing clothes again. God, it's only been three days, but I'll be glad to see the back of this room.'

'I'll help you pack your things. Look, are you quite sure you don't want me to give you a lift home?'

'Thanks, but I'm being picked up.' There was a trace of awkwardness in Camilla's voice and in that moment Roz realized what she had to say. Placing her hands on Camilla's shoulders, she pressed her gently down on to the edge of the bed.

'Look, I've been a terrible bitch in the past,' she said seriously. 'And I know I've told you that before, but this time you're going to hear everything. I owe you that, at least.'

'You don't –'

'Oh yes, I do,' contradicted Roz swiftly. 'And now I want to set the record straight. There are a couple of things you really have to know. For a start, I was horribly jealous of you and Nico. Nicolette wasn't his daughter, you know. He was right not to believe me when I insisted she was.'

Camilla frowned. 'But why?'

'I thought I could keep him that way,' said Roz, her eyes

downcast. 'At the time, I was desperate. And of course it didn't work. Nicolette's father was just a one-night stand whom I had no intention of ever seeing again, and never did. When she died I thought it must be some kind of punishment for having deceived everyone.'

'Of course it wasn't,' said Camilla with compassion. 'And you didn't have to tell me that anyway.'

Raising her chin, Roz said, 'I'm telling you everything. I *want* you to know. And Nico didn't chase after me when he was married, either. *I* chased him. He wasn't interested. It's particularly important that you know that.'

'It's nothing to do with me,' protested Camilla, turning pink. Roz shook her head.

'He's crazy about you. I clung on to the memory of Nico for a long time because I couldn't cope with the fact that he'd rejected me. It was more an obsession than real emotion but it wasn't until Sebastian reappeared that I understood that. I'm truly happy now and I want you and Nico to be happy too. Together.'

The door swung shut behind them.

'So do I,' said Nico, idly swinging his car keys. Then he winked at Roz and said, 'Camilla! Don't you look different with clothes on. Is that really you inside them?'

'Don't start,' warned Camilla, her toes curling with embarrassment. How on earth was she supposed to react when Nico challenged her like this, in front of an audience. His unexpected flashes of humour had always formed a large part of her attraction towards him, but just at the moment she found it disconcerting. And how could she fully trust him anyway, when he treated the entire matter with such flippancy?

* * *

571

The remand centre on the outskirts of Bristol looked pretty much as Camilla had imagined it; greyish low buildings were bordered by high wire fences, their stark dreariness enhanced by the clear cobalt blue sky above and the surrounding greenness. A bright sun shone, and as their car approached the security-guarded entrance they passed a field of black-and-white cows lazily grazing and enjoying the warmth of the day.

'It's still not too late to change your mind.' Nico, who had volunteered to drive her down from London, seriously doubted the wisdom of Camilla's decision. 'You don't have to do this. Christ, it's a depressing place.'

'We've come this far; I'm not backing out now,' said Camilla, desperately unsettled but doing her best to sound calm. 'Besides, I *had* to come. Nico, do I look OK?'

Bringing the car to a halt in the car park, he turned to look at her, affection vying with exasperation when he realized how much it mattered to her. As far as he was concerned she looked beautiful anyway, with or without the make-up she had taken so much care to apply before they'd left. But then he only ever saw the sweet curve of her mouth, the laughter and compassion in her wide eyes, the sensual tilt of her eyebrows when she was puzzled or concerned about something, and the soft, lush curves of her body beneath her high-necked pale-pink cotton dress.

'So very OK,' he pronounced lightly, 'that I'm considering taking this car somewhere a bit more secluded. Did you know that these seats go right back? Camilla, have you ever made love in a Lotus before?'

'Oh, hundreds of times.' Waving her hand dismissively she took a powder compact from the bag on her lap. Carefully tilting the rear-view mirror, she dusted her nose with powder and re-did her lipstick.

'Too OK, if you ask me,' continued Nico as she sprayed the flowery scent he loved on her wrists. 'Why not let her see what she did to you?'

Camilla surveyed herself in the mirror. The concealing foundation was extremely effective and the scars which remained were barely noticeable beneath it. 'She knows what she did to me. That's why she's here,' she said, nodding towards the grey buildings. 'Besides, the scars aren't why she asked to see me.'

'I still think,' grumbled Nico, 'that she *should* see them. Sometimes, Camilla, you're too damn nice for your own good. And if you dare forgive her for what she did . . .'

'I don't expect you to forgive me,' said Juliet steadily, her hands folding and unfolding in her lap. 'But I am sorry.'

'I don't forgive you,' Camilla replied, thinking that at least Nico would be happy now. She looked the woman straight in the eye. 'I've tried to, and I can't. The scarring will never completely disappear. But I do understand why you did it.'

Juliet shook her head. Her hair, less shiny now, swung around her plump shoulders. 'You said that before, but it still isn't true. We do read newspapers in here – I know everything about you now. Married to Matt Lewis. Long-running affair with Nico Coletto. Now he's divorcing his wife for you. How can you possibly have any *idea*,' she burst out suddenly, 'what it's like being me?'

Glancing across at the prison officer standing with her back to the door of the visitors' room, Camilla opened her handbag and withdrew a brown envelope. Emptying the contents on to the table between them, she pushed them towards Juliet.

'This one,' she said slowly, pointing to the photograph closest to her, 'was taken roughly six weeks before I discovered that my first husband was having an affair with an old schoolfriend of mine. That one is me about a year before that. The other two were taken at around the same time. And I can promise you that they were the best of the bunch. I threw all the less flattering photos away.'

Her face devoid of expression, although her hands were shaking, Juliet examined the photographs in silence. Camilla listened to the distant footsteps and occassional shouts echoing from other parts of the building and stared at the peeling yellowed walls. The decor of the place was as dismal as the faint but permeating prison smell. Somewhere, a door slammed. Through the barred, visiting-room window the sun continued to shine. Finally Juliet looked up.

'What did you do when you found out that your husband was having an affair?'

'I emptied a bowl of chrysanthemums over his head,' said Camilla steadily. 'We were in the middle of a dinner party at the time.'

The faintest of smiles touched Juliet's pale lips. Ruefully, she said, 'That's what I should have done to Piers, I suppose. Then what happened?'

'I left him.' Camilla began to relax. She had been right to come after all. Somehow she'd known that the photographs would be the key. 'A dear friend of mine took me to live with her. She cooked me such terrible food that even when I did feel like eating, I couldn't. She threw away all my terrible clothes and did her fairy godmother act on me. She made me realize that this was the only life we had, that this was *it*, and that I'd better make the best of it. With Loulou bullying me I didn't really have any choice, but it proves that it can be done. Anyone

574

can do anything, if it's what they really want.'

'Can I keep these?' asked Juliet tentatively, prodding the photographs on the table.

'No.' Camilla picked them up, slid them back into the envelope and replaced them in her bag. 'I need them to remind myself . . . and I don't *regret* having looked like that,' she added forcefully, 'because it was part of my life. And I wasn't unhappy then. I'm just a lot happier now.'

She rose to leave and Juliet, on the verge of tears, held out her hand.

'Thank you,' she said, her voice low. 'And I really am sorry, Mrs Lewis.'

'Yes,' said Camilla with relief. This woman might have killed her if it hadn't been for Marty. She wasn't going to forgive her. She wasn't as perfect as Nico thought she was.

Very briefly, they shook hands.

'And I'm sorry I said what I did about the disabled boy,' put in Juliet hurriedly, as Camilla turned towards the door.

'Don't call him that,' said Camilla, and for the first time her tone was distinctly cool. 'He is not disabled. He has Downs Syndrome. And his name is Marty.'

Chapter 58

Roz's last show was being broadcast live at seven thirty in the evening on the second Friday in September. Diligent work by her young researcher, Sadie, had ensured that the first five rows of the studio audience would be filled with the boisterous, attention-seeking old regulars of Vampires. To further enhance the relaxed, end-of-term atmosphere of the evening, the lone chair normally occupied by the featured guest was being replaced by a squashy, four-seater sofa. Lili would be making her television début, Laszlo de Lazzari was going to relay the story of how Vampires had so dramatically changed hands, and – at Loulou's request – the president of the Foundation for research into sudden infant death syndrome was putting in a brief appearance in order to update the public on the work they were doing, and to remind them how necessary further fund-raising still was.

Cot death. If Nicolette had lived she would be two years old now. Whenever Roz looked at Lili she was reminded of her own beloved lost daughter.

But Lili was bright, beautiful and lively. Roz had to repeatedly remind herself that Nicolette at the same age would be unable to speak, unable to comprehend, maybe even unable to crawl. She was ashamed to admit it, even to Sebastian, but the knowledge of Nicolette's disability had made her death easier to tolerate. And although she had lost one daughter she had been rewarded with another. Because of Natalie, her life had been so drastically altered that even now she still occasionally woke up at night in a panic, thinking that the events of the past few months had not, after all, ever really happened.

That it had was something she felt she scarcely deserved. All she could do now was try and help her friends.

It had been Camilla's idea to hold the after-show party at her home. Sebastian had suggested an hotel and Laszlo had offered Vampires, but Camilla had persuaded them that the house was easily large enough, and with the added advantage that the children could crash out upstairs without interrupting the celebrations. As a special concession she allowed Sebastian to hire a team of caterers. Natalie begged to be allowed to dye her hair pink for the occasion. Rocky, hopelessly overexcited by all the frantic activity in his home, had needed to be forcibly restrained from entering the kitchen and terrifying the caterers out of their wits. When Charlotte ventured into the back garden she discovered Marty and Rocky sitting side by side on the terrace, devouring an entire tray of prawn vol-au-vents between them and making equally heavy inroads into a vat of chocolate mousse.

'My grandmother's coming to the party!' shrieked Natalie, bursting into the bedroom where Camilla, Roz and Loulou were choosing Loulou's outfit for the show. 'She's just phoned and said she'll be here by six.'

Marguerite, meeting Sebastian and Natalie for the first time three weeks earlier, had handled the situation with her usual aplomb. Sebastian, who had dreaded the initial encounter, was soothed by Natalie's confidence.

'Don't worry, let me handle this. I'm getting really quite expert at introducing myself to my relatives.'

And Marguerite, happily, had been charmed.

'If you want to live until six thirty,' remarked Roz drily, 'you won't call her grandmother.'

Natalie landed unrepentantly in the centre of the bed. 'I just caught Zoë kissing Laszlo in the hall,' she announced proudly, running her fingers through her dark hair until it stood spikily upwards away from her face. 'Isn't it great, the way when redheads blush they clash with their hair?'

'Bitch, bitch,' scolded Roz lightly, eyeing with horror the green and blue cotton sweater which ended just below her daughter's young breasts and the scarlet and silver stretch mini skirt which scarcely covered her pelvis. 'I hope you aren't thinking of wearing this little get-up tonight.'

'Nico thinks I look great,' Natalie declared, as if that settled it. She adored Nico.

'Of course he does,' countered Roz. 'He's Italian. And I'm telling you that you look like a hooker. Go and change into something decent.'

'Zoë and Laszlo,' said Camilla with a low whistle when Natalie had flounced out of the room. 'I didn't know about that.'

'This place is like Noah's ark,' grumbled Loulou, balancing on one leg as she struggled into a pair of Roz's black leather Nicole Farhi trousers. 'And I'm the old spinster left on her own. These are too small for me, you skinny old witch. Where's my dressing-gown? I'll wear that.'

'How about my sequinned dress?' suggested Camilla nobly. She had been planning to wear it herself.

'Too flashy for the cameras,' advised Roz. 'And everyone will expect you to sing like Shirley Bassey. Keep it simple and steer clear of stripes.'

'I told you. My dressing-gown.'

Roz raised her eyebrows. 'Now she thinks she's Hugh Hefner. You want something plain and stylish, Lou.'

'I want something strong, like a double gin,' said Loulou, her silver-grey eyes reflecting growing panic. 'This stage-fright is a terrible thing, Roz. Next time your daughter has a brilliant idea just tell her to get knotted, OK?'

By the time Roz, Loulou and Lili were ready to leave for the television studios the party downstairs was already well on its way.

'It's rather like getting married,' said Loulou, trying to joke. 'Just as the fun really starts, the bride and groom have to wave goodbye and shoot off on their honeymoon, poor sods.'

'Happy birthday,' shouted Marty cheerfully, sensing that this was an occasion for presents.

'Don't panic,' Nico told her, kissing Loulou's pale cheek. 'You look terrific. And don't even *think* about all those millions and millions of viewers sitting at home watching you –'

'Flawless,' pronounced Zoë, stepping back to admire her work. 'I have to say this, Cami. When I first saw you in that hospital bed I nearly died. The doctor who sewed up your face deserves a medal. If you ever feel like trying a spot of modelling . . .'

'Don't change the subject,' said Camilla sternly. 'I asked what was going on between you and Laszlo.'

Colour rose afresh in Zoë's cheeks and she gazed helplessly at the powder puff in her hands.

'Loulou and I went over to Vampires the other week. He's taken me out a few times since then. It's early days yet.'

'But so far . . .?'

'So far, so very good indeed,' confessed Zoë with a shy smile. 'In fact, perfect. But what about you?' she added, turning the tables and surveying Camilla with calculated shrewdness. 'You do realize, don't you, that we're all churning with curiosity wondering what's going on between you and Nico.'

Stepping into the shimmering dress of petrol blue sequins, Camilla turned away and lifted her hair from her neck so that Zoë could zip her up.

'Nothing much.'

'Oh, of course not,' said Zoë with heavy sarcasm. With characteristic bluntness she paused halfway up the zip. 'Are you sleeping together?'

'No!'

She shrugged. 'OK, no need to sound so appalled by the idea. He isn't exactly Quasimodo, after all. So what is going on?'

'Nothing,' repeated Camilla with stubbornness and the very faintest trace of pique. Since that last day at the hospital Nico had made no further mention of the future. His habitual teasing continued as it always had, but she was under the distinct impression that it was just that: a habit. He was drawing discreetly away, backing off in such a manner that her own confused feelings would be spared. He was letting her down gently, she had decided, in the hope that she wouldn't realize why.

It was a cold, sad, unhappy sensation and Camilla hated it.

'I thought Roz said he wanted to marry you as soon as his divorce came through,' persisted Zoë, adjusting the combs which held up her own hair and glancing at Camilla's reflection in the mirror.

'Maybe he went off the idea.' Camilla was trying desperately hard now to sound unconcerned. 'We never did seem to get our timing right, after all.'

Her hands, she realized as she reached for her dark blue high-heeled shoes, were shaking.

'Well, perhaps the time has come to synchronize your watches,' declared Zoë. Trained to be observant, she wasn't missing a trick. 'I know these things, darling. You and Nico are so bloody *English* sometimes I could shake the pair of you.'

'He's Italian,' protested Camilla weakly, and received a dark, meaningful stare in return.

'Exactly.'

Downstairs Natalie was teaching Marty to hand-jive, Nico was setting up the video recorder and Sebastian was deep in conversation with Christo and Laura. Charlotte and Toby, together with Zoë's two daughters, were dancing through the kitchen. Rocky, tied to the leg of a settee in the sitting-room, was whining piteously in the hope that someone would set him free.

Just as Camilla finished pouring a fresh round of drinks, the doorbell rang.

'Grandmother!' exclaimed Natalie joyfully, and bolted out into the hall.

'So shy, so retiring,' sighed Zoë, exchanging glances with Camilla.

'Granny, Granny, Granny!' shouted Marty, racing out in hot pursuit of Natalie.

Loulou's nerves had miraculously vanished. To her amazement she was enjoying herself. The rumbustuous crowd from Vampires, complete with darling Tommy in his boxer shorts, were providing just the right touch of informality and their good-natured heckling had put her so much at ease that she couldn't imagine why she'd ever felt nervous in the first place. Even under the sizzling heat from the studio lights she felt calm and unfazed, answering questions easily and contributing lines which had the entire audience in fits of laughter.

'So do you ever miss those days when you were running Vampires?' asked Roz, and Loulou shrugged.

'Sometimes. We had a lot of fun. I miss seeing all the customers.' Inclining her head, she glanced momentarily in the direction of the audience. 'Well, maybe not *these* customers, but some of the others were OK . . .'

Loulou was looking better than ever, thought Mac. In a plain yellow vest, belted at the hips over white leggings tucked into low-heeled yellow boots, she looked so blonde and . . . golden . . . that the pull in his chest was almost unbearable. And she was being so bright and funny, and at the same time compassionate, that his sense of loss was heightened to an intolerable degree. Loulou should have been his, should be his now, and he had blown it.

So engrossed was he in the programme that he didn't hear the front door open and quietly close again. Cecilia, standing in the doorway of the sitting-room, watched him in silence for several seconds. The video recorder beneath the television was taping the same programme he was watching. But even if that didn't give the game away completely, the expression on his face could leave no-one in any doubt.

When a floorboard creaked beneath her feet he twisted round, looking so guilty that Cecilia didn't know whether to laugh or cry. Her modelling skills leaping to the fore, she composed her face into a blank 'catwalk' smile and sat down in the grey leather chair opposite him.

'We could watch something else . . .?' he said dutifully, and Cecilia shook her head.

'It looks interesting. Keep it on.'

'I thought you were staying down in Cornwall tonight.'

'The shoot was cancelled. Half the crew went down with food poisoning.'

'That's nice,' said Mac absently, his attention riveted help-lessly to the screen.

'Mmm,' said Cecilia, taking two bottles of nail varnish from her bag. Russian Red or Pretty Flamingo? Damn, she was going to need an emery board to tidy up that thumbnail, too.

Several minutes later when she looked up and glanced at the TV screen she saw the little coloured girl, Loulou's daughter, romping on the sofa with a distinguished, rather sinister looking man with a black eye patch who was holding her by her scarlet braces.

'That's Lili, isn't it?' she said quietly, and Mac nodded. That was Lili all right. The child he had spent so much time with right up until the moment of her birth.

'She's beautiful,' said Cecilia, and turned her attention back to the second coat of polish. The second coat was always the trickiest.

'You've been married three times,' said Roz, settling back in her chair and ignoring the autocue. The hard part, the brief discussion with the president of the Foundation for research into cot deaths, was over and he and Laszlo had departed the set to tumultuous applause, taking Lili with them. Now she could properly relax. Discussing men was something she and Loulou had done a thousand times. 'What do you think was the worst mistake you ever made?'

'Getting married, obviously,' replied Loulou promptly, winking at the audience. 'I don't seem to be very good at it.'

From the audience, Tommy shouted: 'That's not what I've heard,' and everyone collapsed with laughter. When they finally began to quieten down, Roz said, 'Seriously.'

'Seriously,' echoed Loulou, her silvery eyes betraying genuine sadness, 'I haven't always behaved very well. I'm not talking about infidelity – I have never been unfaithful to *any* of my husbands – but I suppose I tend to act first and think later. Some of my decisions turned out to be embarrassingly bad ones, although at the time they seemed right. I'm too impulsive, I suppose.' Glancing distractedly at her hands, bare of rings, she lowered her voice and added, 'I know I deserve them, but I do have regrets. Real regrets . . .'

'Such as the occasion when you threw your husband's only change of clothes out of a hotel window and into a pond?' suggested Roz gently. Loulou, startled, hesitated for only a moment. A faint smile hovered on her lips, but there was infinite sadness in her voice as she replied quietly, 'That *was* the worst mistake of my life. More than anything else I wish I hadn't done that. Who knows, if only I'd exercised a bit of self-control in those few moments instead of behaving like a spoilt bitch, the rest of my life might have been quite different.'

Mac felt his insides disappear. The blood was pounding in his fingertips and in his ears. He couldn't move.

Roz was winding up now, allowing Loulou to express her faintly libellous opinion of unscrupulous journalists who tricked their way into people's lives, before drawing the interview to a close. Another well-known presenter, laden down with a spectacular bouquet of flowers, appeared on the set to wish Roz luck for the future and to tell her how greatly she would be missed. Even Mac knew that Roz hated his guts, but she accepted the flowers with gracious surprise and kissed the gay presenter's smooth cheek. The cheering audience applauded wildly and Roz thanked everyone for their support. Mac barely heard what she was saying; his mind was buzzing frantically.

How clever Roz had been. How subtly she had introduced the hotel incident.

And how the hell was he going to find the words he knew he now had to say to Cecilia?

There was a tiny clink of glass as Cecilia placed the restoppered bottle of nail polish on the mirror-topped coffee table. Crossing her long legs, she held her outstretched hands before her, surveying the ten perfectly painted pink nails with apparent absorption.

'You'd better go,' she said, her low-pitched voice absolutely expressionless.

Mac turned once more to stare at her, scarcely daring to believe that he had heard her correctly.

'Oh, Mac.' Her slender hands dropped to her lap in a gesture of despair. 'I'm not stupid. Anyone with half an eye can see how it is between you two. It really isn't all that much fun, you know, living with a man who's so very much in love with someone else.'

He shook his head, struggling to assimilate her words. The sense of relief when he finally understood that she was serious was incredible.

'I'm sorry,' he said, meaning it.

'I know. You're a nice man.' Nodding towards the TV screen,

she added, 'She seems very nice too. I hope it works out for you both this time.'

'Thank you. So do I.' Rising to his feet, Mac crossed over to her chair. After a moment's hesitation he bent and kissed her forehead.

'I've been expecting this to happen,' she said unsteadily, and tears glistened in her beautiful topaz eyes. 'But it's still horrible.' Standing up, she managed a tentative smile. 'Give me a hug before you go, Mac? Please? A proper hug.'

Wordlessly he opened his arms and drew her towards him, his lips brushing her smooth dark hair, his hands tenderly stroking her back.

At last Cecilia pulled away, averting her face as she wiped her eyes.

'Go on,' she whispered, 'before I make a complete idiot of myself. I look so ugly when I cry . . .'

'You don't,' Mac assured her. 'You're a beautiful, beautiful woman. And before long you'll find a man who *can* make you happy.'

'Please go,' repeated Cecilia helplessly. 'I'll stay here tonight if that's all right. Tomorrow I'll pack my things. Jacky has a spare room in her flat – I can go and stay there until I find a place of my own.'

Racked with guilt, Mac said, 'Stay here as long as you like. You don't have to leave straight away.'

Cecilia shook her head. 'Oh yes I do,' she said softly. 'And so must you, Mac. Go to her now. *Now*.'

Chapter 59

When Roz and Loulou arrived back at the house the decibel level rocketed. Having watched the programme, everyone knew already that it had been an amazing success, but even Roz admitted that the public response to the show had been staggering.

'Our unloved little old spinster,' she announced proudly, placing her arm around Loulou's shoulders, 'has received thirty-seven proposals of marriage, twenty-four job offers ranging from the downright dubious to the highly prestigious, and the promise of a screen test for the next Bond film.'

'Miss Moneypenny!' shouted Natalie, as Nico gave Loulou a congratulatory kiss.

Sebastian opened the first bottles of champagne and Zoë ran to answer the door as the first of the Vampires' crowd arrived back at the house to join in the celebrations.

Nico found Loulou alone in the kitchen thirty minutes later. Oblivious to the sounds of wild partying around her, she was standing at the sink, clutching an empty wineglass and staring out of the window into the blackness of the garden beyond.

'You're supposed to be celebrating,' Nico reminded her, surprised to see her there.

Fighting the waves of desolation, feeling guilty because he had caught her like this, Loulou shrugged and grinned.

'Just catching my breath. It's been quite an evening.'

'Bullshit. You're hiding.' With a stern look, he refilled her glass and steered her into a chair. 'Now tell me what's wrong.'

Loulou hung her head in shame. Nico had always been able to see right through her.

'I'm lonely,' she said at last. 'I'm thirty-five, Nico. And alone. I hate it.'

Loulou, ever the drama queen, was speaking with uncharacteristic lack of drama now, he realized. These, entirely unembellished, were the bare facts of how she felt.

'It's an after-effect,' he said, as firmly and reassuringly as he knew how. 'I feel like that after a concert. When the adrenalin-high wears off you feel depressed and wonder what you're supposed to do next.' It wasn't strictly true, but he had to make her feel she wasn't alone.

'All those men phoned the TV station tonight,' Loulou continued evenly, 'and offered to marry me. Oh, I know they weren't serious . . . but at least they took the trouble to phone and say it, and they don't even *know* me. What a crazy bloody life. Only the men who don't know me are interested. The ones who do, run a mile.'

'Mac, of course.'

'When I married him I thought it would be perfect,' said Loulou, desolation in her voice. 'And he turned out to be more trouble than the other two put together. I wish I'd never met him.'

'Don't be silly. You got your wires crossed once or twice . . . it happens to us all. But you can't wish that you'd never met him, Lou. Just think of all the good times you had together.'

'That's the trouble,' sighed Loulou, pain flickering in her eyes. 'I can't stop thinking of them. And it hurts like hell. D'you know, I really thought that after Cecilia's birthday he might contact me. But nothing. Then tonight, on the show . . .'

She gestured helplessly. 'I thought: If he's watching now he might realize what I'm saying and forgive me. I had this wild fantasy that he would phone, or turn up there at the studios . . . and he didn't. More nothing. I just feel so *empty* all the time . . .'

Camilla watched quietly as Charlotte, a tray of asparagus rolls balanced precariously on her lap, gazed up at the family portrait above the fireplace. The children had greeted its return, just one week ago, with evident pleasure and to Camilla's relief the sight of it no longer caused her pain.

Perching on the arm of Charlotte's chair, she helped herself to one of the rolls and stroked her daughter's silky hair.

'Are you going to get married again?' said Charlotte, her eyes still fixed on the painting.

'Maybe one day. If I meet someone we all like,' she replied cautiously. 'Why, sweetheart?'

'I think Daddy's going to get married. He's got a girlfriend called Rebecca. The other day I heard them talking about churches.'

How strange, thought Camilla, that the news had absolutely no effect upon her. It was like hearing that a distant friend was remarrying.

Proceeding with care, she said, 'Do you and Toby like her?'

'Oh yeah.' Charlotte shrugged as if the question was irrelevant. 'She wears really tight pink trousers. And she doesn't try and force me to eat onions. She's nice.'

'Well, that's all right then.' Camilla was relieved. For a few seconds they both watched Natalie, attempting to teach Sebastian to dance. Roz was cringing and Rocky howled in protest. Unnoticed by the dark-haired man in boxer shorts and a bow-tie, Lili methodically filled his beer glass with broken crisps and cashew nuts.

'Is Nico your boyfriend?' asked Charlotte abruptly, and Camilla almost choked on the remains of her asparagus roll.

'He's a friend, darling,' she replied, glancing hastily round to check that he wasn't behind her. 'Nico's a good friend, that's all.'

'Oh,' said Charlotte, evidently disappointed. 'Then you aren't going to marry him?'

'Good heavens, no.' Camilla, her tone determinedly cheerful, stood up. Being given the third degree by her daughter was not something she felt able to cope with at the present time. 'Sweetheart, I'd better go and check on the rest of the food. Could you pass that tray around and ask Roz's mother if she'd like another drink?'

'Because if you *were* thinking about it,' persisted Charlotte doggedly, 'Toby and I want you to know that we really do like him. Just in case you were wondering.'

'Oh, thank goodness you're here,' said Poppy, when she opened the front door and saw him standing there on the step, his dark curls plastered to his head and his beige leather jacket darkened by the rain.

Mac hesitated, trying to place her.

'We met – fleetingly – at the Easter Ball in Gloucestershire,' she explained kindly. 'And at Vampires once, too. You're absolutely drenched.'

'My car broke down. I couldna' get a cab. It's raining.' His Scottish accent was enhanced by nerves. 'I suppose she *is* here?'

'In body if not in spirit,' said Poppy briskly, attempting to usher him inside, 'but we're relying on you to change all that.

You aren't going to be beastly to her now, are you?'

'Me?' said Mac, eyebrows arching in astonishment. 'Beastly?'

'Oh, come in. Stop prevaricating. Fancy me being able to say that incredibly complicated word! Must be the champagne . . .' She paused, lost in self-admiration, and Mac blinked the rain out of his eyes.

'I'd rather wait here. Could you find her and tell her –?'

'Right away,' intercepted Poppy happily. 'How gloriously romantic. I'll send her out with an umbrella. Hang on just two secs . . .'

When Loulou appeared, still dressed in the yellow vest and white leggings she had worn on the show, she said shyly, 'We're having a party. Why don't you come in?'

'Not yet.' Mac gazed at her, his hands clenching inside the pockets of his jacket, his stomach muscles tensing at the sight of the girl whom he had never been able to stop loving. 'I don't have anything to celebrate. Yet.'

'Poppy's given me her umbrella. Look, it's got Popeye and Olive Oyl on it.' Babbling out of sheer panic, Loulou struggled to open it and almost took her eye out on one of the spokes as it burst suddenly to life. 'I didn't even realize it was raining . . .'

'Come for a walk,' said Mac, taking it from her before she maimed either of them for life. 'Calm down; stop blathering. I want to talk to you.'

The streets were black and glistening with rain. Puddles reflected the orange glow of the streetlamps and only the occasional swoosh of car tyres broke the silence as they passed by. The plane trees, ragged black outlines against the heavy sky, dripped heavier raindrops on to the stretched dome of Poppy's umbrella. Loulou, wanting to be as wet as Mac, took it back from him and carefully closed it, hooking the handle over her bare arm and lifting her face to the rain.

'We'll always argue,' he said, wondering whether to take her free arm, 'but as long as we both know that it doesn't really matter I think we could be OK.'

'OK?' she said in a low voice, as a man with a rather smart scarlet and white umbrella splashed past them. 'What do you mean, OK?'

'I mean,' he said with a sigh, 'that I don't think we can be happy without each other. I love you, and I can't seem to love anyone else. It's over now between Cecilia and myself.'

They were still walking side by side, not touching and not looking at each other. Finally he stopped and turned, taking Loulou's cold hands in his colder ones. 'What I mean,' he said, speaking each word with desperate care, 'is will you marry me? I love you. I will love Lili. I want the three of us to be –'

'Mac, wait.' Her tone serious now, Loulou forestalled him. 'This is important. How do you *really* feel about Lili?'

He shook his dark head, dismissing her fears. 'I know I was jealous, but I came to terms with that a long time ago. Lou, she might not be mine, but she's a gorgeous little girl. It would be impossible *not* to love her ... after all,' he added, taking her hand and kissing it, 'she's your daughter. And she's every bit as irresistible as you are.'

'Oh Mac, do you really mean that?' sighed Loulou, and this time he nodded, his eyes never leaving her face.

'I do. And I *promise* you that this time we'll make it work. So now, you heartless woman, will you please agree to marry me so that we can at last get out of this bloody rain?'

The Popeye umbrella tilted at a crazy angle as she flung her arms around Mac's neck. 'Yes, yes, YES!'

Chapter 60

Marty didn't need to say a word. Nico took one look at the appalled expression on his face and realized that he had to move fast. Grabbing Marty's small, clammy hand he led him swiftly out of the room and up the stairs.

Glancing round the room, Camilla wondered where Nico was. Charlotte was teaching Zoë the mechanics of belly dancing. Poppy and her husband were deep in conversation with Sebastian and Roz, and Toby had been adopted by a rowdy, rumbustious group from Vampires who were teaching him card tricks. Marguerite was nose to nose with Laszlo de Lazzari and Natalie, in a shady corner of the room, was bewitching a pair of raffish young City brokers who could scarcely drag their eyes from her bare navel.

Camilla prayed that Loulou and Mac weren't outside having another fight.

And where was Marty? Realizing that he was nowhere to be seen she slid quietly out of the noisy, smoky sitting-room and tried the kitchen, but apart from a couple wrapped in an intimate embrace in front of the freezer and a remarkably guilty looking Rocky with mayonnaise round his mouth, the room was empty.

She was only halfway up the staircase when she heard Nico's voice, low and comforting, and for a moment thought that he was with one of the girls from Vampires. The white-hot stab of jealousy she experienced sent shivers down her spine. I have no right to be jealous, she thought, taking a deep breath and pausing near the top of the stairs. And I'm not spying on him, either. I'm looking for Marty, that's all.

The bathroom door was wide open. Having moved silently along the thickly carpeted landing, Camilla watched unnoticed as Marty's small shoulders quivered and he retched once more into the lavatory bowl. Nico, one arm around his waist, murmured encouragement and mopped the boy's sweating forehead with a damp flannel. Camilla's heart went out to Marty as he gasped and sobbed, and clutched at Nico's hand for reassurance.

'There you are. Good boy. All finished now?' said Nico gently, rubbing Marty's back and wiping his tear-stained cheeks with the flannel. Marty nodded and staggered to his feet, holding out his arms for a comforting embrace. Without a moment's hesitation Nico hugged him and Camilla heard Marty say brokenly, 'I love you.'

'And I love you,' said Nico, smiling and rumpling the boy's short, spiky dark hair. 'But I'll love you a lot more when we've cleaned your teeth. Which is your toothbrush?'

'The green one,' said Camilla, stepping out of the shadows and realizing how very, very much she loved Nico. The jolt of jealousy, followed by the incredibly touching scene she had just witnessed, had forced that knowledge back into the forefront of her mind and she didn't know now whether to laugh or cry because no-one understood better than she did how appalling it felt to love someone who no longer returned that love.

Avoiding Nico's eyes, she reached past him for the toothbrush and said, 'It was very kind of you to look after him. Whoever would have thought you'd be so good at dealing with this kind of thing?'

The words came out sounding far more offhand than she had intended, and almost deliberately insulting. Nico threw her an icy look.

'Me of all people,' he said shortly, mocking her. 'Incredible, isn't it?'

Flustered, Camilla turned her attention to Marty who was spitting toothpaste foam into the grey-marbled basin. 'Are you OK now, sweetheart?'

He nodded, pale but proud. 'Sick!'

'He ate about a gallon of strawberries downstairs. He'll be fine now.' Nico, still guarded, watched Camilla's reflection in the mirror. Dammit, why the hell couldn't he say what he wanted to say!

'Well, don't have anything else to eat,' admonished Camilla, smoothing Marty's hair away from his forehead.

He shook his head vigorously, then grinned his wide heart-warming grin. 'I love Nico.'

'Nice to know I'm appreciated,' said Nico lightly when Marty had left. Camilla, desperate to keep him there a little longer, examined her own reflection in the mirror and pretended to fiddle with a strand of hair at her temple. 'I didn't mean to sound sarcastic just now,' she said hesitantly. 'And I am grateful to you for looking after him. Sometimes I say things and they come out wrong.'

Nico leant back against the basin and watched her twirl the strand of hair around her index finger. 'Sometimes I don't say things because I'm not sure whether I'll like the replies,' he said, breathing in the mingled scents of Camilla's perfume and Marty's toothpaste. 'Maybe we should all be more like Marty, just say what we think and to hell with everything else.'

'Maybe we should,' agreed Camilla cautiously, her heart

thumping against her ribs. Gaining in confidence, Nico adjusted his stance so that he was once more addressing her through the mirror. Winking at her, he said, 'Go on then, you first.'

'I – I can't,' she stammered, aching with loneliness. Nico was standing only inches away from her and it might just as well have been miles.

'But you must,' he explained, frowning slightly and moving fractionally closer. 'It's important, you see.'

'Why?' she countered, panicking and afraid that he was playing some awful game with her.

'Oh, bloody hell, Camilla!' Grabbing her arms, Nico shook her. 'It's important because once, years ago now, you deliberately seduced me. And ever since then you've been running away, finding excuses to back off whenever anything remotely interesting threatens to happen.' His green eyes darkened as he glared at her. 'And I'm telling you now that I'm just about bloody sick of it.'

Joy mingled with outrage as she realized what he was saying. He wanted her, he really *did* still want her . . . and he was placing *her* entirely to blame for everything.

'That's not fair!' she gasped, her sequinned dress ricocheting rainbow dots of light as she struggled to wrench her arms free. 'I was married, you were married . . . you got married first! I didn't force you into that –'

'Oh yes, you bloody did. You turned me down flat . . . what the hell was I supposed to do, join a monastery?'

'You were supposed to make me change my mind!' exclaimed Camilla breathlessly, and Nico's dark eyebrows arched in amazement.

'After you'd told me what a disaster I was in bed? Jesus, I spent the next two years proving to every woman I could lay my hands on that I wasn't. Talk about hitting below the belt . . . Tell me the truth now,' he demanded, his fingers gripping her arms even more tightly. 'Was I really so terrible? *Was* I?'

She stopped struggling. Telling Nico that had been the single biggest mistake of her life. Deliberate, destructive . . . it had been an act of revenge, tragically mis-aimed and one which she had never stopped regretting.

'Of course you weren't,' she said in a low voice, her eyes betraying her longing and regret. 'You were perfect. And I *am* sorry.'

'So if I'm that perfect,' said Nico more gently now, 'why do you still turn me down? If I'm so damn perfect, how can you possibly resist me?'

This truth game, thought Camilla with trepidation, was getting scary. Having hidden her true feelings for so very long she didn't know if she could handle all this blatant honesty now.

In the silence that followed she listened to the raucous noise of the party downstairs and wondered if Loulou had returned yet with Mac.

'I'm waiting,' Nico reminded her.

Stiffening her shoulders, she met his gaze. 'You're a rock star. I'm a divorced, widowed mother of two, almost three children and I have scars on my face and body that will never completely disappear. Why should I go to bed with you again just so that you can prove how irresistible you are?'

Exasperated beyond belief, Nico pulled her into his arms and kissed her, hard. He kissed her cheeks, her nose, her chin and her neck, and avoided her mouth entirely.

'Don't make excuses,' he whispered in her ear, before kissing that too. 'You know damn well that I want to marry you.'

Shakily, her entire body yearning for the final kiss he had so shrewdly withheld, Camilla said, 'But you are married. You aren't divorced yet.'

'Yes, I am,' he white-lied. The decree nisi was due to come through in the next three or four days, but Camilla could be so damn stubborn sometimes and she wasn't going to wriggle away now after all this effort ... 'My divorce was finalized yesterday. Caroline's happy with the settlement, I'm just glad it's all over, and poor old Paddy doesn't know quite what's hit him yet. To his amazement he's grown rather fond of her, and that's not his style at all.'

'Oh,' said Camilla in a small voice. If Nico didn't kiss her now she was liable to do something drastic.

'Oh,' he mimicked, teasing her. At last, at *last*, he was in control. 'Well, any more excuses or have they finally run out?'

'You could have *anybody* ...' she said, gesturing despairingly at the door. This was ludicrous; here they were in the bathroom of all unromantic places, discussing marriage.

'That is the most pathetic excuse I've ever heard,' he declared, 'and certainly the last. Camilla, if you don't start agreeing with me this minute I'm walking out of here. You'll never see me again. Is that what you'd prefer?'

In silence she crossed the bathroom, closing and calmly locking the door.

In silence she turned back to face him.

In silence she undid the buttons of his white shirt, sliding it away from his tanned body and dropping it to the floor behind him.

'You aren't seducing me again, are you?' he said, as she started to undo his trousers. 'Because I don't want you to think I'm just an easy lay.'

'Stop complaining,' said Camilla evenly, her mouth only

inches from his. With tantalizing slowness she brushed her lips against his jaw . . . his cheek . . . the very corner of his perfect mouth. Her hand, sliding inside his unbuttoned trousers, found him thrillingly ready for her. Nico was breathing deeply now, trying to force himself not to join in with the seduction.

'Promise me you'll still respect me in the morning,' he murmured, unable to prevent himself reaching out and touching her honey-blond hair. Moments later the combs holding it up joined his shirt on the carpet beside them.

'How amazing,' remarked Nico as her hair brushed against his bare chest, enervating a million nerve endings. 'Here we are sharing an intimate moment together and for once you have all your clothes on.'

Smiling, Camilla unzipped her dress and allowed it to slither to the floor in a glistening heap. Wearing only silk underwear, and sheer dark stockings, she looked so feminine, and so utterly desirable that Nico could barely control himself.

'Well, almost, anyway,' he said huskily, in an effort to divert his mind.

Except that any diversion now was impossible. Neither of them took any notice at all of the timid knocking at the bathroom door.

'I think you're only interested in my body,' said Nico, kicking off his shoes as the footsteps outside receded, and waiting for Camilla to approach him once more. He exhaled slowly as she came towards him and placed her hands upon his hips. Their bodies were so nearly touching now . . . they had both waited so long for this . . .

'I'm extremely interested in your body,' Camilla promised him, trailing her fingers lightly down his thighs. 'You did want me to be honest with you,' she added, as Nico opened his mouth to protest. 'And now I'm going to be. I do want to marry you, more than anything else in the world. I love you. I can't believe you'll ever understand how much I love you. And now I want to make love to you. Do you think you'd mind awfully if I did?'

'Honesty is the best policy,' said Nico, reaching for her and smiling with sheer, delirious relief. 'I think I can cope with that, and if it gets too terrible to bear I suppose I could always just lie back and think of Italy . . .'

Millie's Fling

Jill Mansell

When Millie Brady saves Orla Hart's life she doesn't realise how drastically it will change her own – not least because the boyfriend who is asking her to move in with him at the time promptly storms off in a huff.

Actually, Millie's relieved. She's quite happy to enjoy a restful man-free summer in Cornwall. But best-selling novelist Orla has other ideas. She's determined – for her own reasons – that Millie should meet the man of her dreams.

Dropped wallets, roller-skating gorillagrams, the world's most flirtatious boss and a helicopter in the back garden all conspire to produce a summer neither Millie – nor Orla – will ever forget.

Acclaim for Jill Mansell's novels:

'A jaunty summer read' *Daily Mail*

'An exciting read about love, friendship and sweet revenge – fabulously fun' *Home & Life*

'Slick, sexy, funny stories' *Daily Telegraph*

'Fast, furious and fabulous fun. To read it is to devour it' *Company*

'Riotous' *New Woman*

0 7472 6486 4

headline

Now you can buy any of these other bestselling books by **Jill Mansell** from your bookshop or *direct from her publisher*.

FREE P&P AND UK DELIVERY
(Overseas and Ireland £3.50 per book)

Millie's Fling	£5.99
Sheer Mischief	£5.99
Good At Games	£5.99
Miranda's Big Mistake	£5.99
Head Over Heels	£6.99
Mixed Doubles	£6.99
Perfect Timing	£6.99

TO ORDER SIMPLY CALL THIS NUMBER

01235 400 414

or e-mail <u>orders@bookpoint.co.uk</u>

Prices and availability subject to change without notice.